***The Empty Throne Series***

Book One

# What Lies Beneath

Michael R. Lowe

W & B Publishers
USA

Cover design by Michael R. Lowe

ISBN 9781635543193


I dedicate this book to my wife, who inspired me to pursue my story and build this fantastic world to which the story unfolds.

Thank you to all who take the time to read this book, this series is going to take you on a journey filled with epic fantasy, storytelling, darkness and mystery. Please look out for the sequels to be released:

Blood and Cinder
The Fallen Order
Dawns End

"Not all who wander are lost" – J.R.R. Tolkien

## Table of Contents

Even the gods fear what lies within the abyss, for they are of the light which binds the realm, undone by the darkness from the deepest depths.

When the dead rise from the ashes of helpless despair, how do they come to bear with their unnatural existence? They do not, for they are pawns upon a board, serving powers beyond the realm of their own meaning.

For when the world was created by the celestials above, they poured into it the very essence of their being, only the very qualities that would constitute a perfect world. Yet disparity must be honoured, light and dark, good and evil, life and death, order … and Khaos.

For within the flow time lies a constant battle between the disparities, tipping the hourglass and unearthing the legends that were buried in time, long ago. Hence, is the inevitable endurance of the living and the cycle of the Bloodlines.

As time flows through the never-ending hourglass of fate, the legacy of those long-forgotten stay buried beneath the sand. Kingdoms rise and fall into darkness. Like the proverbial ash from the eternal flame that burns deep within the heart of man and beast alike, to be buried deep beneath earth, blood and cinder.

Perhaps it was all coincidence, or possibly fate. But none the less, events were set in motion that would determine the future of all, and that of nothing.

*Beware the three sins of old,*
*Cast into fire the apparition of darkness and deceit,*
*Right what has been wronged and flourish anew,*
*For that is the cycle of blood and cinder,*
*And the weight for which the disparity is burdened*

# PROLOGUE: THE DARK DREAM

It was not the cold that sent a chill through his body, but that something out there was watching him. Waiting. The night was at its darkest, stretching far across the horizon; a black desolate land filled with death and rot.

For many thousands of years, the thick and murky fog blanketed the barren plains. A malice so dense not even the light from the heavens could seldom relieve the deprived earth–though who would want to see horrors that may lurk deep within.

The atmosphere was peculiar, an eerie presence hung deep within the atmosphere, sapping what little remained of the life force from the land. Even the deep air felt toxic to breathe, bringing swift death to all who would bask in its fumes–that is, if the darkness didn't claim you first.

The winds were harsh and its bite bleak, whistling through the dead branches as they clawed at the man stood shaking beneath them.

"We should not be here!" Jerod urged, his anxious eyes gazing across the bleak surrounding, his ragged breath nervously condensing before him as it drifted off into the black. "This is a place for the dead."

His voice was soft, untouched by the horrors of the realm, still young within its youth.

Neither of his companions turned to his pleas, his tense words fell upon deaf ears. They opted to remain within the shadows.

"We must leave," he protested, "We accomplish our mission, we do not need to venture farther into the unknown."

"Quiet!" snapped a voice from shrouded in the dark. His voice was gruff and hoarse as it crackled from years of inhaling the impure air.

Jerod wavered in his response.

The night was getting darker. A faint silhouette of two men crouched before him flickered in the pale moonlight, absorbed into their surroundings. "Was there more to this journey than meets the eye," he pondered to himself "What were the true intentions of the Legion."

The Lands of Cinder, or the Darklands as they had become known as, was their mission. Though knowing of its true goal was left deep within the shadows.

"If you don't cease your troublesome worries, then I will gut you where you stand," replied the voice in the shadows. "If I don't do it, then this land will."

The wind howled as it shuddered through the nearby trees; the air rippling across the face of the already nervous Jerod. A third figure lay concealed upon the ground; he wanted no part in the petty squabble between his brothers; only to remain stalwart and leave with his life.

Such obscuring darkness would not stay for long–not that any light could bring warmth to such an abyss.

"But my very bones chill in the night air," said Jerod, stamping his feet against the black ground below, "Can we not light a small fire? Or head back to the encampment at least? This cold will be the death of us all."

"How big a bastard are you?" snapped the voice in the dark, "A fire within these parts will be a beacon to anything and everyone out there! And you are a fool to think otherwise."

"But a fire could at least keep the darkness at bay," replied Jerod, "Stop it from eroding away my very soul."

The peering eyes of the figure in the darkness glinted in the moonlight, staring harshly and furiously at the young scout.

"If I say there are to be no fires, then no fires there shall be!" snapped the voice coldly.

Jerod nodded quickly and pathetically, a whipped dog muttering in the darkness, "Besides, accidents can happen out here to even the most skilled of scouts, and who knows what may become of you should your tiresome worries not cease to reach my ears."

The shadowed figure laughed to himself.

Jerod gulped, unsure of a response to give that would rescue him from this unholy nightmare. He asked for no power; he desired no fame. Forced to venture out into certain death is all they had ever granted him since he joined.

"I wonder what they will do to you first," said the voice aggressively, "Deserters don't get the honour of a quick death you see."

He edged closer, drifting slowly as the fragments of moonlight rained down upon him.

"Perhaps they will flay you, piece by piece, all the while keeping you alive just long enough to feel each and every cut," he whispered, a sadistic tone encapsulated his voice as he became more visible to Jerod's eyes, "Or perhaps they shall boil you alive, melt you into oil for the swine."

A white emblem glistened in the moonlight, a sword sprouting jagged wings atop a tower shield–the mark of the legion. A Black dyed gambeson tucked neatly beneath a scuffed chest plate wrapped tightly round the man as he approached.

"Or perhaps they will submit you to the Holum Di and just see how quick they can truly break you." hissed the shadow, "For that has always been my favourite to bear witness."

His face now clear within the light of the moon: jagged and rough, a face so sharp even the very light was cut as it gently caressed his features. His greyed messy hair tucked round the back of his head. He was 15 years his senior, yet his face was old and withered, as pale as the moon above. Such a lack of sunlight would do that to such a man. His breath smelt putrid, passing by his disgusting slither of a tongue as it waved outside his mouth. Warm and foul, it was urging Jerod not to gag on its essence.

Shaken, Jerod stepped back, part in fear, part out of disgust.

"Willem!" exclaimed the third companion, "Leave the poor boy be, he will do his duty just as you and I."

Jerod sighed a sigh of relief. At least he was not alone with this monster that stood before him, Willem turned his face contorted with disgust.

"Hah, he will never be like you and I, Harlon," he responded, "I'll be there, I'll be there when he falls, I'll watch as he breaks like the child he is and runs like the countless others before him."

"Please!" Jerod begged, "We have already done our duty, let us begone from this forsaken place!"

Willems gaze returned, fixed upon the young scout. Jerod looked to his feet. A wave of shame and anger flooded his body, his heart racing as if facing down a wild beast.

"What was that?" Willem groaned; the words could barely escape his mouth through the gritting teeth. "You dare lecture me on what to do! This mission is over when I say it's over. If I hear but one more pitiful plea falls out of that cock hole you call a mouth, then desertion will be the least of your worries round me."

Willem's face grew with anger, his face tightened so much that poor Jerod thought his veins would burst in an explosion of malice and contempt. His hand firmly grasped upon the hilt of his unsheathed blade. Gripped excessively. Sharpened exquisitely. It was clear its blade had not been used in some time, but nevertheless, Willem knew how to handle it very well.

"There is something down there," Exclaimed Harlon, his voice hushed deep in the darkness, "Something moves within the shadows."

The two men froze, the fateful words they hoped to never hear, in but a mere second all seemed but forgotten.

"What do you see?" questioned Willem, "What is it?"

"I'm not sure," replied Harlon, "Just movement at the base of the mound."

Deep within the darkness below them flickered such shadowy apparitions between the trees, vanishing as quickly as they manifested before ceasing to be and returning to their slumber.

"Tell me what you saw," Willem ordered, his full attention upon the prone Harlon entangled within the brush. He crouched down beside him, a beast waiting to pounce.

"Twas too dark, all I could make out was a moving glow between the branches," Harlon responded,

"It could be what we have been searching for," Said Willem, "Maybe that fool Farrul isn't such a waste of a scout after all."

Willem stood up, his hands rubbing against the bristle of his chin. He began pacing the area; the dirt crunching beneath his boots. Jerod could see a spark of fire within Willem's eyes, a dash of recklessness and pride.

"We must go back and report this now!" Jerod exclaimed, "Those were the orders from the high elders!"

Silence, not even a felled tree in the darkness would have heard, only a cold harsh wind responded to his anguish.

"Are either of you listening to me!?" Jerod said bitterly, "We aren't even supposed this far north of the old fort. Guldern was the peak of our mission, none have ventured this far as of..."

Willem merely glared at Jerod, ceasing his pleas, muttering incoherently to himself as he swiftly moved in and out of the darkness, his eyes still fixed to the overgrowth before them.

"Whilst we are away from the bastion my word is the law!" he spoke with a terrifying presence, "I am the judge, the jury … the executioner and if you dare to question my authority once more, I shall personally free your head from your shoulders."

"Y-yes, commander," Jerod mumbled, stepping back like a whipped dog.

"Good," Willem responded, a small smirk stretching his rough face and moulding with the many scars that adorned his face.

"We move out," snapped Willem, "Harlon you take the left flank, I shall take the right."

He glared towards Jerod.

"And you little piss stain, you shall go straight," hissed Willem, "After all, what is a trap without its bait."

Jerod's face instantly dropped as he watched Willem and Harlon disappear into the dense blackness before him. He sighed. His mind could not figure out which was more haunting, the bleak loneliness that stood before him or an eternity under the command of Willem. Although deep down he knew which he would prefer to be a part of.

Jerod stepped down from his position, creeping silently towards the darkened copse. The journey down was a great struggle, with no visibility in the thick black fog. Many scraps of debris littered across the ground left him crafting a chorus of noise during his descent.

He looked up. The pressure had dropped in the air and the cold began to bite once more. The storm was coming.

Far in the distance, a large storm cloud could seldom be seen, ten miles long and a deep purple hue woven within its thick clouds. Though a strange phenomenon in the lands to the south, such a sight was a common occurrence in the hostile land. The great swirling eye at its centre ever so carefully watching and waiting. For its next prey.

A sudden jolt brought him to a stop.

"Damn cloak," he cursed, straining to get it free from the entanglement. The cloak tore, leaving a few ragged fragments caught within the thorns that grasped at it. He sighed to himself before tucking it away in his black satchel.

As he fumbled with his cloak and satchel, it caught his gaze in the corner of his eye. He gulped as he raised his head. A pair of deep glowing eyes staring straight through him, not fifty yards ahead of him lurking quietly in the icy darkness. He froze.

It felt as though his feet were stuck firmly in a bog, yet they laid firmly planted atop the marshy waters. It took a few moments, but he soon found himself free from the constraints of the earth. As he lifted his gaze once more to meet with the eyes, he found himself yet again alone in the darkness. Was it his imagination? His fear that conjured up an apparition? These lands plague the mind and dull the sense he thought to himself.

The uneven terrain proved most difficult to traverse. He began his advance by tripping over a rock by his feet, tumbling into the boggy marsh ahead. It's cold murky waters consumed his hands, prickling them with an icy chill. Through the mixture of soft mud and dense flora, a strange metallic object brushed against his fingers. It was hard and detailed, fastened atop a long chain gently floating within the water.

He grabbed it and pulled back with the muddy sludge coating his forearm and hand like a thick black glove. There it was, glinting amongst the mud. A small pendant suspended upon a silver chain.

"And what do I have here?" he muttered to himself, "A pendant? though these markings are unlike anything I've ever seen before."

A confused look fell upon his face as he scanned the jewellery he pulled from the bog. It was of intricate but ancient design, there were symbols embossed upon its surface that he had never laid eyes upon before. Two flames intertwining below a radiant sun had been exquisitely etched upon its front. It was well worn, with much of the gold having been lost to the weathering of time. Upon its rear was a more crudely but still finely engraved 'F', though its meaning was all but lost upon him.

He had been so lost in its alluring gaze that he had forgotten the reason for his presence. As he snapped himself out of his trance, a light in the depths of the forest caught his eye.

"There you are," he whispered to himself, staring captivatingly through the branches.

The branches grasped at him as if trying to pull him away from what was to come. Or perhaps to hold him down to seal his fate.

It was a struggle to pass through the bramble; sharp thorns pierced his flesh and tore his garb. With perseverance and determination, he pressed forward.

The dead forest was thick with decay and heavy with regret. The path was narrow, overgrown and twisted. He could feel the forest penetrating his mind as roots would to earth, occasionally a single beam of moonlight would break through the thick canopy and bathe showing an unseen beauty to the forest.

Jerod looked back, for but a mere moment in the forest had dulled the passage of time and for now, the trees stood together looming down upon him. Dark and dense with misery and grief dulling the senses, for it is an easy place to get lost, not knowing which way is true. For if one is not too careful and strays from the path ahead, they may truly lose themselves.

Pushing through the sharp and jagged twigs, he finally broke free of the entanglement, hitting the cold hard ground bruised and bloody. It took a few moments for him to gather his senses as he laid there, his face hugging the dirt. It was a strange situation, for the ground was dry with no moisture or foliage within the clearing.

He grunted as he pulled himself to his feet, scanning the surroundings. Still grasped in his hands was the pendant glowing ominously at its surroundings. A strange presence hung in the air, watching… waiting. It felt strange and despite not a soul in sight; he did not feel alone.

A large stone stood tall atop a large mound at the centre of the grove, looming over him with a dark and terrifying presence. Not even the trees beyond the boundary would dare venture within its ominous shadow. The longer he stared at it, the more it resonated within his mind. As though it were trying to speak with him, edging him closer to it.

A faint humming rung through his head as he edged in closed, a faint aura shimmered around him, distorting the air like a shield cloaking the monolith.

Jerod stopped before the shimmering wall. The air danced around him as heat would rise from a fire, though there was no heat and only a cold mirage. He gazed upon its surface, his vision distorted, producing a majestic wave of dancing trees and swirling light dancing.

Many thoughts raced through his mind, blending a mixture of fear and intrigue, "This is not of any illusion I have seen before" he thought to himself.

The winds made their presence known to him, blissfully scratching at his face and cold bitten fingers.

With one hand he covered his eyes, shielding himself from the shimmering force stabbing into him. With the other, he reached forward.

The air felt strange on the other side as his fingers plunged through the boundary, crisp and dry as if time had not touched it for many years.

"How?" Jerod exclaimed, "How does such an occurrence come to be, it is though I have stepped into the Nether realm and forever submitted myself to its fate.",

His eyes squinted in confusion at the sign of such a paranormal sight. As he waved his hand before him the lights floated around, grains of sand he thought as he pushed them one by one. The light brightened even his blacked plate of the legion as it glimmered upon his chest.

Never had he seen anything quite like it, carved into its stony surface were etchings of an ancient and bygone civilisation.

"Intriguing," he murmured to himself, edging closer and closer until his breath bounced off its surface, catching dust and moss in its wake. It was old, older than he thought possible. Dust crumbled beneath his shaking fingers as he washed away its surface, brushing aside the constricting ivy as it tightened its grip.

As if by some divine intervention the wisps of light converged upon one and other taking shape into a transcendent light floating about his vicinity. It crashed to the earth, absorbed into a network of root and veins as they pulsated towards the base of the monolith.

An inscription formed across its surface, manifesting the words of a language long since abandoned by man. It glowed brilliantly mysterious. The lone scout cautiously approached the face of the stone, his mind beckoning him to leave such a dark aura, yet his body chose differently.

"By the Gods, what are you?" he said loudly, "A marker? A tablet? A waypoint?"

His eyes flickered up and down, jumping independently from his curious fingers as they ran between its smooth grooves.

Despite much of the language being forgotten by the minds of mortal man, a few words distinguished themselves from the common tongue.

"Thrawn … Ampti … well, those were the old Vindictarian for the throne and empty," he muttered to himself, "That would explain who your creators were at least."

He whispered to the monolith. A strange feeling shivered over his body, as though monolith responded to his remarks. He shook his head in disapproval,

"What are you doing," he cursed to himself, "It's a damn rock, but a stone in the earth, neither sentient nor living."

Disappointed in himself, he continued, after all, something seemed to wish him to. He felt compelled to.

A rumbling rattled deep within the confines of his mind, pressing and pulling against his head and tongue as if forcing him to speak.

"I don't understand," he said aloud, "Why would old stories be inscribed upon a rock from thousands of years ago? They are a fabrication of the realm, propaganda to keep the masses in check."

"It speaks the truth," hissed a voice from behind his left ear.

Such a fright knocked Jerod from his concentration, freezing him as though a statue. He slowly turned his head, peering over his left shoulder to lay his eyes upon the culprit. However, the same as before, he found himself alone. Quickly he turned, scanning his surroundings only to find he was more alone than before.

He took a step back, "What is happening to me," he thought, "I am talking to nothing".

He pressed his stiff hands to his aching forehead, curling his fingers through his dirt-laden hair. He stepped back further, raising his eyes to meet with the monolith, this unnatural object that taunted him and plagued his head.

"What are you!" he shouted angrily, "Leave me be!"

Twisting and turning as the air rumbled around him, his hands grasped his face, convulsing it,

"What do you want from me?" he shouted, "Show yourself or by the Gods, I will not hesitate to respond!"

With a flash of moonlight, he drew forth his sword.

"Stay away from me!" he pleaded; the rumbling within his head shifted to a sharpened pain, clenching his temple in pain.

"Get out, just get out!" he cried, "Get out of my head, you fell creature."

He dropped to his knees, digging his roughened nails deep into his temple, dropping his sword to the earth with a thud.

"I'm not going to emerge from this," he stuttered, "This land will become my grave, forever to wander its wastes for the rest of time."

His breath quickened as the panic set in.

And then … he fell.

The darkness was deep, a sea of blackness that delved across his gaze. Such was the abyss that surrounding him, an endless void of nothing yet everything for its pull was strong, and nothing could escape from its grasp. His thoughts ended abruptly as the earth struck him back into the realm of the living.

"Fuck!" he cursed, lifting himself up steadily clutching his wound. A sharp splinter of wood had pierced his side, not a mortal wound, but enough to rattle his senses.

As he looked around, all he could see was nothing but an abyssal black. The first strike of the flint sparked a flurry of glowing fragments bouncing around him, a flash of the floor showed a cobbled ground thick with dust. The second strike sprinted ahead, dancing around a crude and crumbling pillar by his side. Finally, a flurry of flames erupted before him, engulfing the torch and flooding the room with its light and warmth alike. With the torch held aloft his vision within the cavern became clear, pillars of natural brimstone rose from the ground creating this enormous cavern. Dark and damp.

"Incredible!" Jerod exclaimed, "Such a wonder has laid hidden beneath these lands for so long, untouched by no one for many years it would seem."

Littered across the walls of the cavern, the roots of the nearby thicket had burst through the dirt only to twist and turn away from the cavern before him.

A lone beam of moonlight shone through the newly formed hole a few meters above Jerod's position, bouncing across the rocky surface before it was consumed beneath the black. An unusual sight caught the corner of his eye as his eyes adjusted to his surroundings.

Aa vast array of stone statues encircled the room, charred, mangled and scorched, their purpose and creators forgotten to time and lost within the rock and earth. There must have been hundreds; all warriors by the looks of it all poised for battle, their very weapons welded and fused to them as though they were a very part of them.

Jerod looked deep into the hollow eyes.

"And what by the Gods are you," he whispered,

The face of the statues were twisted with malice and rage, darkness and death. A faint screeching rung through his ears, blurring his vision. It was almost as though he was being pulled into a deep trance, though he struggled to resist its call.

"Release, release, release," whispered a voice in his head. It hissed with hateful intent.

The sight of the statues converged into the shadows further before him, their lifeless husks fixated upon but a single point.

The lone sarcophagus. Layered so deep beneath the stone and earth, not even the moonlight could reach it. For he could feel, it was brimming with dark energy. Many chains wrapped and bound and strangled every inch with great might. A great pillar stone rested atop the sarcophagus. Its mighty weight bore down upon it. Whatever was inside was not coming out. One thing became most certain, however, for this was no cave; this was a tomb.

Drums, the low thump echoed through his skull as he approached the chained sarcophagus, beating faster and faster alongside his weary heart. The crumbling guardians encircled the stone casket, observing him cautiously as the darkness in their hollow eyes swallowed him.

The sarcophagus was thick with cracks and warped with malice. Whatever lay within the darkness wanted to be free.

"Whatever you did must have been horrific," muttered Jerod, his eyes caressing the stone with great pleasure, he looked back at the encircling corpses before returning his gaze to the coffin, "To be cast into a tomb to which no light can gather and no life may escape, your crimes must have certainly matched with your fate."

"Whoever you were, history did not want to keep your name alive…"

"Or your deeds known…"

"Or for your body leave these grounds again."

A low chain drooped beside him, broken at its centre, floating gently in the air. Coated by a deep rust that roughened the surface. He cautiously reached out, his fingers trembled, though not with excitement or fear. But something different.

It burned with intense pain, scorching the flesh atop his fingers as it blackened his skin. The pain was unbearable. He dropped the torch with a thud and grasped his hand, screaming in agony. A molten glow emanated from the chain burning with a mighty brilliance pulsating down the links, dissipating into the stone-cold sarcophagus.

A longing silence befell the world. Time itself had halted for a mere moment. The cracks burrowing deep into the stone surface of the sarcophagus glowed a deep purple, pulsating slowly and brightly. Quicker and quicker it flashed, tainting the walls with its deep hue. The environment was deafening with the beating of the drums as they pounding against his chest, the screeching and scratching inside his head splitting his mind from deep within. Jerod held his head in pain, trying to block out the pain from within as the ground trembled and the skies cracked. Then yet again, all was silent. Before Jerod could regain his composure, a thunderous clap echoed throughout the tomb, spilling a blinding light into the darkness. The force struck him hard in his chest, propelling him through the air before crashing into the dirt as the room faded into darkness.

He couldn't tell whether it was the burning in the air or the burning sensation that brought his mind back into the present. Many sensations prickled across his singed flesh, keeping the hair upon his arms stood high on end. It seemed like an eternity as he lay there upon the cold hard floor, summoning what little strength he could find to pull himself to his knees, coughing up a pool of blood.

"Fuck! …" he spluttered, struggling to catch his breath.

Shards of his breastplate lay strewn across the floor, the fragments trimmed with a glowing hot edge.

"It burns, it burns so much, get it off, get it off!" he exclaimed, "What the hell was that!"

An intense pain burrowing beneath his chest, scratching and thumping that shocked down his arm, twitching deep within his nerves. He clawed at his charred gambeson, tearing it off piece by piece, burning his fingers black with char and ash.

As the moonlight struck his skin, it displayed a feathered scar across the side of his chest, red and burnt, running down his limp arm. A steady stream of blood trickled down each finger, its warm flow dripped onto the floor. In his dreary state, he squinted across his surroundings as his dizzying head regained its balance.

"W-where are they!" he stammered to himself.

The tomb was as empty as the night sky. The stone guardians had vanished into the darkness as though they were never truly there. That is when he heard it creeping within the darkness, a whisper hissing with great anguish and torment. It bounced around the room echoing from all sides sending him into a nervous spin trying to find its hateful voice. He was sweating profusely, feeling the water trickle down his face as the drips bounced from his skin.

"I can't stay here," he said,

"I must warn the others, the legion, the kingdoms … anyone…" he panicked,

"The first sin has been cast, it trembles in the deep, go now and tell your legions," hissed from within the shadows, "We are coming!"

He froze, a dark aura grasped his body as it tightened around him, pinching deep within. Crystalized droplets condensed around his breath as the very air shifted into a deathly cold.

The grinding of claws circled the room as a faint but heavy breath passed emerged from the darkness, silencing the night in full terror. The way was clear, all he had to do was make his move, grapple at the rock cliff face to the pale light above him. Deep within the darkness, faint and glowing eyes flickered amongst the light, the dark aura surrounding it obfuscated the rest of its figure.

Never had he ran so fast in his entire life. The roots and branches snapping at his heels in their attempt to halt his momentum. The storm above had progressed quickly, raging above him with icy winds and freezing rains. Shadows moved within the woods, breaking the line of sight as they vanished deep into the copse, following, stalking, hunting.

Even the blackest night would not stop the weak and weary scout from plunging into the darkness before him. Darkened figures stood dormant in the shadows, watching closely as he sprinted away. Every glance he took towards them he saw nothing but their dark apparitions scurrying forth.

Far above him branches twisted and cracked from the great storm billowing above, deafening winds that created an almost eerie silence.

A shadowy figure came crashing down before him, narrowly missing crushing him to the floor. It struck with a force that knocked Jerod from his feet, sending him tumbling into the nearby thorns. He clambered around in a panic, thrashing and flailing in all directions. Thorns pierced his skin with ease and precision, pinning his clothing to his body. Despite the deathly appearance, they were remarkably sharp and strong to have broken through his armour.

A thick fog was slowly enveloping the surroundings, swallowing all it touched with a thick and grey appetite.

He pulled himself from the heavy suction of the mud that pulled him down; it was cold and crusty, draining him of his energy. It was then through the corner of Jerod's eye that he saw it, a torn cloak bearing the insignia of the legion.

"Hey!" Jerod shouted, he sprinted over to the lumped figure on the floor, "It's me Jerod, we gotta go, we gotta get out of here,", he spluttered, all the while grabbing at the prone scout.

"Come on," he urged, "There is something out there, I don't know what it is but it's coming for us! Gods, I wished I had never found that tomb."

Silence, not a sound came from him, as he lay there, warm and still cloaked in torn garbs and surrounded by an array of broken branches that he pulled down with him.

"Stop messing with me! Get up!" Jerod screeched, grabbing the tattered cloak and thrusting it back with all his might. He reeled back in horror at the sight that befell him, scorched flesh and burning eyes emanated from the anguished face of the once-living Harlon.

"Harlon, what did this to you!" he screeched, "How can anything cause such horrific mutilation upon the body of a man."

He paused briefly, scanning his surroundings cautiously for any sign of movement.

"What if it's still here, what if it lurks high atop the trees or nestled deep within the bushes," he whispered, "I cannot stay here, I must warn the legion for I fear something has been released upon this realm that brings only death."

The young scout clambered to his feet, his mind racing back and forth, trying to assess what was hunting and stalking him and his entourage. A sudden eeriness crept across his shoulders, a feeling that dawned upon him intensely.

"The statues," he muttered to himself, "It can't be, such an illusion does not exist."

He gazed back down his path, his eyes were teary and terrified.

As he looked back upon the mangled corpse of Harlon, the realisation that such expressions had been painted across the faces of the stone guardians in their slumber.

"It's impossible!" he pleaded, a cold shudder befell his tense soldiers, his body stressing not to look. He forced his gaze behind him, fighting every inch of his being to do so. A flash of lightning erupted amidst the storm and fog, illuminating the area.

"It's gone!" he gasped. The body of the late Harlon had vanished from beneath his nose, a muddy pool of blood and ash lay in its wake.

"Enough of this madness," Jerod Shouted, "Show yourself and cease such primitive stalking!"

His voice echoing into the winds before falling silent upon the forest.

His lamentation soon ended upon the realisation that his fate was still in the balance. Whatever had killed Harlon was still out there, lurking within the shadows. For all he was aware of, its eyes could be watching him closely from beneath the shadow of the darkness.

Pulling himself together, he ran. Faster than he had ever run before. Each branch from the encroaching trees descended on him from above, cutting and lashing at his fear. The adrenaline surging through his veins drowned out the pain and fatigue.

He broke through the darkness, finding himself once more standing within the opening to which he parted from the others. A silhouette loomed in the darkness, stood ahead of him, shadowy and concealed. He froze in his tracks, holding his breath for fear of making a sound. Upon closer inspection, the mark of the legion became emblazoned within the moonlight.

"Willem!" he cried, "Am I glad to see you, we must make haste, something is hunting us through the darkness, it has already felled Harlon and I fear we may be next."

Willem remained silent.

He bolted over to his leader, climbing the small embankment to his perch before collapsing upon his knees. Never had he felt such joy to see his superior, in any other circumstance he would have rather seen a dagger protruding from his back.

"We need to get out of here now!" he shouted.

The silence continued to descend upon the two, only the sound of his ragged breath could be heard. His body was tense with anticipation and anxiety as he awaited but a murmur from his superior. But again, he heard no response.

"Did you hear what I said?" he shouted, "Something is coming for us, if we do not move swiftly then we will never see the light of day again!"

Still nothing. Anger took over him, his thoughts turned towards the sanctimonious attitude of his captain. However, now was not the time for such arrogance, time was of the essence.

"Willem! You bastard say something!" he screamed, "Throw your fucking pride to the side for once in your grandiose life and listen to me!"

Jerod struck his commander's shoulder with anger. Though Willem merely swayed in response, absorbing the blow, silent and hollow.

Confusion set into the young scout, his anger turned to panic he slowly reached out and tapped on Willem, still no response. He cautiously edged forward, strafing carefully around the towering warrior, his eyes glazed with fear, begging that he was wrong.

He stood in front of Willem.

The sound of his beating heart drowned out the voices in his head screaming of the danger. Sweat flowed from his brow to his chin like a river.

The sight was still as gut-wrenching and horrific as the first encounter. The tall and proud Willem stood dead as the trees that surrounded the glade. His mangled, writhing corpse told stories of an otherworldly side to the deadly warrior.

He pulled himself together muttering incoherently, trying to make sense of the situation that before him. A small glint caught the corner of his eye. Embedded into a tree, mere feet from where he stood stuck Willem's sword, the blade blackened and corroded as if burned in the inferno of hell. Willem must have put up a ferocious fight against the shadowed assailant, yet even his skill with a blade was not enough to save himself from death.

Jerod rushed over to the tree, his hands grasped the hilt and after much straining and force, he was able to free it from the tree's embrace. Surely this could be proof enough for the elders, evidence of their encounter beyond the sanctuary. Jerod brushed his hand against the charred sword. It was blunt and coarse, as though left for a hundred years to rot in the wilderness.

Behind him, to the left, to the right, surrounding him, whispers echoed through the trees, watching, waiting for their moment. Though he could not see them, he could feel their eyes delicately caressing him, hungry and savage.

Whatever was out there spoke in a language that he could not understand, nor could he even comprehend its origins. A crackling voice of fire and brimstone, with words filled with anger and spite. They around him, responding and communicating in a feral array of howls and otherworldly hisses.

Such distractions had too long drawn away from his concentration. He could hear the shadows moving, slowly but surely, as they moved in to surround him.

Every step forward the shadows would move in front, behind, side to side, forever shifting and altering his course. He knew they were in command, controlling his direction and guiding his steps.

Time felt convoluted the further he ran. Had it been minutes, hours, days? Nevertheless, he persisted. Not far behind him he could hear the slashing and biting getting closer, then distant. They were taunting him, playing with their prey before closing in on the kill. Such sadism and torment was the way.

Just when all hope seemed to disappear from his mind, a light appeared off the horizon.

"There it is!" he cried, "Oh blessed be my fortune, I am but within close distance to sanctuary, I just hope I can relay my message soon, the legion must know of what I have discovered."

Closer and closer he gained upon the heavenly sight of the legion's fortress, the Last Bastion. Waves of emotion washed over him as he burst into tears of joy and terror. He had done it. He had survived the expedition, though to say successfully would all be down to perspective.

The warmth of the great fortress loomed before him, for it was a grand and mighty spectacle to behold. Carved into the heart of the northern passage and the throat of the mountain stood the great gate. Despite its decrepit and ruined appearance, it was the safest place to be within the Darklands.

He looked back, nothing. Whatever was snapping at his heels had disappeared. It must have retreated, maybe fear of the looming fortress had caused it to abandon its pursuit and slink back into the shadows.

"Hah!" he shouted loudly, "Go back to your foul lair once more, for you are nothing when compared to the might of the legion."

As his attention shifted back to the sanctuary before him, he was met with a dominant force, throwing off of his feet and into the dirt.

"Ugh stupid you are Jerod," he said to himself, "To run into an oak when so close to safety, thank the Gods the creatures have retreated."

He lay there for a short while, his head throbbing whilst his ears rung with a terrible screech. As his gaze shifted back to reality, he came across a site most unsettling, for it was not an oak that lay in his path. An imposing shadow crackled before him in the cold, damp air. He could scarcely breathe through both the wind being blown from him; and that of utter fear.

With a hiss, the shadowed figure moved in closer, twitching and limping in a grotesque form as the ground cracked beneath its feet. Again he heard the words of an unknown language, though he could not understand its meaning, its intent was all but clear. Cramping and numb with cold, he dashed away, clawing at the ground in his desperate attempt to create distance with the threat.

It was too late. A smouldering claw grabbed him by the neck, its touch scorching his skin painfully. It was then he hurtled through the air. Such inhuman strength sent him crashing down upon the ground. Again and again, like a rag-doll in the breeze, lifting him high and slamming him to the ground with tremendous force and ferocity.

Jerod coughed up a great deal of blood as he slumped to the ground. He was no longer alone, surrounded and trapped, every corner of his eye and shadowed figure lurked, lusting for his blood. However, they all stood still, remaining steady and waiting.

"What are you waiting for!" he spluttered, pulling himself up once more to his feet, "You chased me for all those hours only to stare upon me! Come on then, kill me!"

Though still, they waited.

The sun was drawing near, he could feel its warmth bathe upon the back of his neck, warm and soothing. The eyes of such strangely perverse creatures continued to stare at him, almost looking confused as to what he was, or maybe what they used to be. It almost felt as though they were sad, crying tears of purest fire as they dripped from within the cavernous void that was their eyes.

A whisper grew behind him, murmuring and muttering incoherently in a language most dark and fearsome. He instantly recognised it from back within the tomb. Its frightful hiss was no mistake.

"What are you?" he wept, falling to his knees as if to pray, "Why are you doing this?"

It grew closer and closer. The sound of claws grinding at the floor sent shivers down his spine. All became clear, the voices, the tomb, the storm, the monolith, all grew clearer within his mind. He closed his eyes as his heart raced faster and the whisper grew even closer.

He could feel its warm breath stroke his neck; his blood pulsated through his veins as a ghastly claw wrapped around his head. Rough and grotesque as it tightened its grip, burning through to his very soul.

~ *"You told me it was going to be simple, nothing bad would happen"* ~

## Chapter I: Heart of the Storm

The horrified gasp for breath was long; arduous. A dull throb pressed from the inside of his head, promptly making him groan. As he raised his dirt-laden hand to reach up and tenderly caressed his bruised forehead, it felt as though every bone in his body had fractured. He felt neither here nor there, split between past and present as encroaching morning sun-drenched him with its embracing rays.

The young man glanced across his surroundings. Dawn was breaking through the sky, shimmering with a blood-red hue. The crisp, cold air of the night was slowly relinquishing its hold as the faint rays of the sun-warmed against his skin. It was early still, yet the night was dissipating around him.

The reek of death and blood filled his nostrils, even in the fresh morning air it proved to be foul and overbearing. As far as his eyes could see, through the thick smoke and early fog, lay the burning remains of carriage beast and man. Much of the land had become bogged down and filled with a dense marsh. Though some appeared to be shallow, others had become suspiciously deep. It was then the story unfolded, for the stench of death only ever follows those who bathed in its evil deeds.

The site of an ungodly slaughter had stained the ground thick with blood and the charred ashen remains of what had fallen. Cinders laid where carriages and barricades had once stood, littered beneath them the corpses of the victims of such barbarism. Bodies mutilated, strung up and burnt. Whoever orchestrated such savagery was well versed to its song.

The lone survivor pulled his hands close into his chest, trembling with cold and fear, grasping at every ounce of warmth he could muster. It took a few attempts to bring himself to his feet, for the ground was sodden, toppling over marsh and bodies alike. He stumbled against the folly of the dark and treacherous wind, grasping at whatever he could anchor himself down with.

"The day appears to be dawning," he croaked, a gentle voice hoarse with dehydration that left his throat dry and cracked, "It would appear a storm is brewing, the air has dropped and the skies follow with grey winds."

He looked around to find himself truly alone, without company.

"And who is it I speak to," he mumbled, "Yet, more importantly, how did I come to be? How did I get here?"

He whispered softly to the wind, as though it would hear his plight and spring upon him, but alas it did not.

The ground was a difficult terrain, such excess of blood and dew had trampled the earth into a slurry. Many of the surrounding bodies had sunk deep into its red murky clutches. Littering the fields with a stench that could not be resisted, only accepted. A boy no younger than himself lay at his feet, left to rot and wither as though never to have existed.

It was difficult to tell enemy from enemy amongst the carnage, for it was mostly littered with women, children and the elderly. A few armour-clad warriors came into view here and there, immersed by the morning fog. Yet death had already claimed them. He crouched down to better observe the warriors. Two symbols could be made out across the dirt-laden gambesons and plate. On one there lay two winding serpents ascending a broken spear; the other, a phoenix bound in flight, a sword grasped within its talons.

"Is there anyone out there?" croaked the young man. Neither the smoke nor smell of blood helped his throat as it choked him. His voice echoed amongst the dead, bouncing across the water and returning as though someone out there was repeating his words.

The silence in the air drew across his skin, prickling his flesh in a sombre sadness, for not even the dead would speak of what happened so recently.

What remained of the surroundings he could make out to be an encampment of sorts nestled beside a gentle stream. The hulking mass of burnt woods and the singed fabric was all that remained of the tents, carriages and posts.

"Such death and destruction," he muttered, "Who would wish to inflict such horrors?"

Stumbling through the blood-soaked mounds drained what little strength he had. Its stony bottom dug deep into his heel as he trudged through its thick waters. The thicket of spears lay buried deep into the mangled corpses, hoisted high over up in the air as they dripped pebbles of red into the murky ground.

He waded through the area for some hours. Its boundaries showed no ends as the mass graveyard spun far and wide in every direction. By his count, thousands rotted upon the ground.

Daybreak had passed, leading into the midday sun as it burned away the dense fog that surrounded him. Pillars of light burst down through the clouds, unveiling more death in such a beautiful aura of the sun. He drew closer to the fresh stream that cut through the battlefield; he was mightily parched. Most of the blood and dirt washed away as he plunged his hands deep into the icy cold water, gurgling its freshwater frantically. It felt good, pure and cleansing; it was by sheer luck that it remain pure from the hostilities of the marsh. Then a noise reached his ears.

"Psst."

It crept up behind him, startling him rather suddenly.

"Who goes there?" he snapped back, "I thought there be no survivors amongst the dead, show yourself."

At first, the silence was long and drawn out, not even the winds howled in response.

"Over here," hushed a faint voice. It was close by, probably a few feet at most. It was the perfect place to hide from wandering eyes, it would seem.

"I will say it again," he said firmly, "Who goes there?"

"By the cart," replied the voice.

His eyes drew across his surroundings, stopping at the charred and mangled cart not a few feet to his side. A broken blade lay at his feet, rusted and shattered at the hilt. It was better than nothing.

The squelching of the bog made it difficult to remain quiet in his approach–not that stealth was really required. He brandished the broken blade directly before him, grasping it with two hands, all the while trembling with fear.

"Show yourself to me," he ordered aggressively, "And no funny business."

Even though his blade was pitiful and broken, it provided him with a comfort of sorts. It made him feel less naked without it.

"I watched you searching through the area," replied the soft voice, "You are not Rekeshi are you?"

"Rekeshi?" he replied, "What do you speak of?"

"Then surely you must be Farrosian then?" asked the voice, "A dweller from the desert, perhaps?"

A confused looked passed across his face, wrinkling his brow.

"I do not know of such people," he replied, "Show me your face, so I may gauge your threat!"

Though he did not remember the feeling of fear or anxiety, he certainly remembered such emotions now. A tremble in his legs he could not control, it could almost have been mistaken for the cold biting into his flesh had it not been for the vibrance of the sun.

"Please don't attain to violence upon me!" the voice pleaded; a bloodied hand raised itself from behind the smouldering wreckage.

"Stay where you are!" he shouted at the carriage, "Who are you!"; the broken point of his blade forever homed in on the faceless voice.

"Not so loud!" replied the voice, "There may be others out there, searching amongst the dead for survivors."

"And what makes you think that I am not one of them?" he replied, "Why call out for me if you fear those which may also walk upon my footsteps."

There was a long pause, prompting him to halt his push forward and wait for a response.

"Well?" he beckoned,

A bloodied hand grasped on the side of the cart, trembling with fright and weakness as it hoisted up a sight he did not expect.

The voice came from a rather young looking individual, no more than fourteen years of age. He was covered heavily with blood and ash, with several light cuts that ran across his cheek, still fresh and laden with dirt. Despite his bloodied complexion and frightened demeanour, he was a rather handsome in appearance, piercing green eyes and what you only have amounted to a head of thick blonde hair, though laced with blood in its current situation. His skin paler than the whitest white, amplifying the dirt that clung to his cheeks.

"I watched as you paced across the field," the young boy replied, "I have seen many pass through here the past couple of days looting and stripping the corpses clean like vultures, yet you did not, nor did immediately descend upon me when I called for you, why is that?"

He stared back at him cautiously. It wouldn't be amiss if this were a trap of sorts, ready to snap when he delved too deep into the jaws of the beast.

"You say that you have watched others pass through?" he asked, "For how long have you hid within the wreckage? More so, explain to me as to what happened here for such an onslaught?"

The boy's face looked shocked as it looked upon him. Twitching as though reliving the memory to what happened upon this field of blood.

"You mean to say you were not part of the retinue?" asked the boy, "How did you come to find yourself upon these lands?"

"I awoke in the presence of many bodies," he replied, "I have no memory to any events that led to my being here."

The boy edged closer into view. He was rather skinny for his age and definitely not that of a fighter it would seem. He dropped his blade to his side, for despite his worries it was clear there was to be no danger with this boy.

"You must have been in the battle it would seem," said the boy with his mouth agape, "Maybe you suffered a head injury of sorts that has afflicted you with a loss of memory, I have heard of such things occurring many times within my studies."

The throb in his head returned. That could explain a lot of things here. He drew his free hand up to his forehead to suppress the dull pain.

The boy shuffled about to gain a better view of the figure that stood before him.

"My name is Silas," he said, "I was travelling with those you see before you before they set upon us, what name do you go by?"

He thought for a while, trying to gather whatever may still function within his head; whatever memories may emerge and tell him but a fragment of himself.

"My name … is Arturius," he said. It was about all that he could remember of himself. How, how can one lose all of his life and be left with nothing but a name to live by?

"Why are you hiding?" said Arturius, "Why not attempt to flee this area if you have stayed here for so long?"

He edged closer to Silas, curious as to the young boy's survival amidst the carnage.

"When the fighting broke out, I hid here on my mentor's orders, I'm a scholar you see," replied Silas, "so I'm afraid that I am not much use in a fight, or anything at that matter besides books, but something happened that scared me truly."

"What was it?" asked Arturius.

"Darkness," replied Silas, "A darkness to which no light could escape from, a darkness that consumed many and all within its path as it extinguished the flames of all it touched, and it disappeared, a flash of blinding light and when my eyes came to all lay dead, and my leg pierced by splinters of wood."

Intrigued, Arturius moved in closer, captivated by the story unravelling before him. Oblivious to any danger that could leap before him.

"I don't know what did it or how it all came to be," said Silas, "All I know is that it sapped all the light from the brightest of days, left me in a solemn state surrounded by whispers of doubt."

Arturius couldn't help but feel something eerily familiar about such a tale. Shrugging it off, he closed in on the young boy. The ground here was much firmer, allowing his feet to tread upon the surface without sinking into the thick marsh.

"Who were they?" asked Arturius.

"Who was who?" replied Silas,

Arturius peered around him, counting the many bodies that lay cold upon the surface. Some had now since submerged into the swamps; slowing falling into a grave of endless despair.

"Those who lay slain across this land," said Arturius, "You say you travelled with those that lay dead upon this ground, surely that would mean you know them?"

Silas nodded,

"Indeed, I did," he replied, "they were refugees of the old Farrosian kingdom, seeking shelter wherever and with whoever they could find, sadly the Rekeshi are not ones to take prisoners and sought to finish what they had started some many years ago."

Silas grunted in pain as he repositioned himself atop the charred carriage. Blood had flowed through its cracks, settling on the already deep-red floor beneath him.

"You seem confused," said Silas, "You truly have no memory of the times that have passed, do you?"

An uneasy feeling swept through the air. As if something or someone was watching them. Again, it was a presence that felt familiar in a manner he could not place. It prickled his skin and sent shivers seeping swiftly down his spine.

"It feels like I have fallen into a deep hole, only to have emerged missing a part of myself, forever lost within the dense gravity."

Silas winced in a great deal of pain, clutching at his leg and side.

"I know this is a lot to ask of a stranger," he said. A faint breeze blew across the cold front. Looming over the young boy, what remained of the carriage flapped around, spreading its ash and dust around him. "But I am need of your help and will be forever grateful for your assistance."

Silas pulled himself up from the ruins in a solemn struggle, his face straining and contorting as the cart creaked beneath him. The shirt covering his body stained with blood, slashed at the hip in tatters, exposed the soft flesh beneath. He was of a slim build, not much in the way of strength or muscle but clearly something he made up for in intellect.

He crippled over in pain before he could make it to his feet, crashing down into a heap, splintering many of the rotting planks beneath his weight.

"Easy," said Arturius, "What happened to you?"

"Alas, some Rekeshi footmen who attacked us spotted me," replied Silas, "They gave me a parting gift in the form of a swift puncture to my side."

He was badly wounded; his strength being sapped by every waking minute they spoke. Time would be of the essence if he wished to not depart for the afterlife.

"What do you need?" asked Arturius, "How can I assist you? I am afraid I know little in the way apothecary or medicine."

"It's okay," said Silas, "I know what must be done, however, in my current state I find myself unable to attain such resources to complete such an action if you could be so kind as to fetch me a few ingredients I would need to halt such an affliction."

Arturius nodded, dropping his rusty and broken blade for it to fall into the boggy marsh, descending into the depths of its darkness. By the smell of the air it was clear the young boy's wound was festering, a poison had been coated upon the blade that slipped through his flesh. He was growing paler by the hour.

"You should lie still," beckoned Arturius, "Though I know little of medicinal properties, I know that exerting yourself will only allow the poison to quicken in its spread."

With two hands he firmly grasped across the wound, stemming the flow of blood as best he could.

"Ugh … its anticorax poison," said Silas, "Rare within these parts of the realm but extremely common within the lands of the Rekeshi," he groaned.

A deep network of black veins rooted their way across his skin from the deep cut.

"What do you need of me?" replied Arturius.

"I will require leaves of the Elodeas plant," Silas gestured over to the nearby stream, "It's a weed that grows next to water, can't miss it looks like a foxtail."

Arturius nodded, his thick black hair waved across his brow, woven with deep unnatural purple strands. The nearby stream was littered with all manner of flora, waving gently against the water's soft current. Long thick bladed grass, wide floating panels, shimmering white petals. His eyes cast upon the stream shining with the waters a deep blue, scanning every inch of the area.

"There you are!" he whispered, reaching into the icy water, his hand waving gently beneath the surface to the leaves Silas had spoken of. He snapped the stem and ran back over to the injured boy.

"I have what you need," he said, holding his hand out to the young boy, "Wasn't too difficult to find.".

Silas pulled himself up, sitting reclined across an uncomfortable pile of broken planks.

"It requires blending," said Silas, "I am afraid I need a little more from you, you will need to chew it into a paste, however, I must inform you, it contains a rather refined taste."

His eyes met with Arturius, an apologetic plea across his face mixed with desperation.

Arturius looked down upon the leaves, they looked rather enticing, fresh and filled with green. However, the facade soon faded as he stripped the leaves from the stem, funnelling them into his mouth. The taste was utterly vile, a bitter tincture of heat and bitterness. He nearly threw up as the mixed juices trickled down his throat, prickling as it washed back.

All the while Silas had been rummaging through his satchel, removing an assortment of vials and tools, before settling with a dirt-laden cloth.

"This should do the trick," Silas said, passing the cloth across to Arturius, "Spit out the tar onto this.".

The relief was cut short by the spicy aftertaste burning his numb tongue. A mass of ground leaves emerged explosively from his mouth, spitting profusely to get as much out as possible. He passed the concoction back to Silas where he promptly pressed it against the open wound, wincing in pain as he bit his lower lip. Once the pain subsided, Silas let out a sigh of relief as he bound it to his body with the singed cloth that flapped amongst the wreckage.

"You have my eternal thanks," Silas breathed, "There is a camp not too far from this location, it would have been my destination had such an encounter not have occurred, you should come with me, Selwyn will wish to speak with you."

"Who is Selwyn?" Arturius questioned, he recalled in his faint memory a Selwyn, nothing more than the flicker that passed quicker than it appeared.

"He is the leader of my company, has been seeking any refugees and scattered soldiers from the fallen kingdom.

He may very well provide you with answers to your loss of memory," Silas replied.

Arturius thought briefly, for he did not know this boy or the man of which he spoke. Yet he could very well hold but some of the information that he was seeking.

Suddenly the two heard faint voices bellowing off into the distance, vanishing into the fading fog. He quickly concealed himself next to the injured Silas, coating his presence with the mangled remains of wood and cloth. Thankfully, the clouds were blackening. A storm was brewing quickly, perhaps enough to conceal them further.

"I will come," said Arturius, "You will need assistance to the camp as well, such an injury will hinder you greatly on such a journey no matter the distance."

In the distance a retinue of footmen waded amongst the dead, though their words were not yet audible, it was clear there would be hostilities; should they remain at least.

"We need to move," whispered Silas, "My camp is to the east through the forest of Hollowclaw."

He pointed across to the dense forest spread throughout the distant plains, its trees towering across the horizon with its thick canopy.

The shadows of a few men formed off in the distance.

"The only presence you will find amongst the mob of the dead are either those who put them there or those seeking quick plunder," said Silas, "regardless of which is approaching, we are in no position to contend with their wills."

"Can you stand?" asked Arturius. The wound at his hip would most definitely slow down the young boy.

"Possibly," said Silas, He pulled himself to his knees only to yelp in pain, the wound spat out a torrent of blood staining his shirt with further blackened affliction.

A voice faint in distance beckoned sharply, a single lone footman gazed across the field, momentarily locking eyes with the silent Arturius before averting his gaze. A deep breath billowed from his mouth.

"That was close," he said, relinquishing his grasp from Silas's mouth, red and bruised from the intense grip forced upon it, "You are in no condition to move by yourself, here allow me to take your burden at least."

"My apologies," gritted Silas, "This may prove more difficult than I thought."

His hand trembled as it pushed firmly into the wound. Blood seeped between his fingers, a river of red passing slowly towards the earth.

The two locked arms as Silas bore down on the shoulders of Arturius. His frame was much smaller than he first thought, shorter than him by a foot, with barely enough meat on him to feed the vultures circling above.

"We will move from cover to cover," said Arturius, "It would be foolish to attempt such a trek whilst risking conflict with those behind us."

They darted from wreckage to rock, obscuring their path by whatever means lay presented before them. After all, there were plenty of bodies to cover such tracks and provide able hiding should they require it.

Every inch of the ground made was a blistering agony, shards of rock and debris grinding within his wound, wincing upon each step he took. Occasionally Silas would trip as the pain overcame him, pulling Arturius closer to the ground as he strained to keep them level.

"Steady now," Arturius would snap, tightening his grip around the young boy, pinching him with a hint of annoyance, "You'll pull us both down if you aren't careful! If you must bite down upon your collar and quench the pain."

"My apologies," Silas groaned, his face twisted in pain as he would regain his footing, "This wound, it weakens me greatly, I am not sure how much longer I can keep your pace."

Arturius patted him hard between his shoulder blades.

"You can do this," he said, "Just keep your head straight and focus on reaching the forest's boundary."

~ *"Fret not young one, when this is all over, a new dawn shall arise"* ~

## CHAPTER II: ESCAPE FROM THE DARK

Before either of them could react, a whistling arrow grazed past the ear of Arturius. Splinters flew in all directions as it buried itself within the old oak that stood a few feet before them.

"Shit, that was close," sputtered Arturius, "It would appear our friends back there wish to speak to us rather amicably."

"It's the Rekeshi," said Silas, "Whatever you do you must not engage them, they are bloodthirsty and skilled with a blade I fear you won't last in engagement with them, especially absent of a blade yourself."

Frantic shouting in the distance soon revealed their presence. A foreign language echoed through the air. It was sharp and slick. Though he could not ascertain as to the conversation that was at hand, the tone of such a word was aggressive and forceful to show malicious intent.

"He is calling for the others he travels with," said Silas, "They mean to take no prisoner."

"You can understand that!" Arturius said, puzzled and confused.

"That I am, I have studied the many dialects within the realm, though many speak using the common tongue some still choose to abide by the old languages of their forefathers when journeying across the wilderness," Silas replied, "What they speak in is old Rekeshi, a language spoken in the days of old when the kingdoms were locked in much grander warfare some hundreds of years ago."

"Must be useful to know what others speak of behind your back, it would seem," said Arturius.

A second arrow grazed Arturius's ear, faintly cutting his skin as the fletching brushed past. The minor pain flowed through his ear as the blood swelled from the slight cut. It jolted hard into the mud ahead, flexing as it came to a stop. The shaft was a deep black, finely cut white feathers protruded at the tip.

"How accurate are the marksmen of the Rekeshi?" Arturius asked, his head jolted to the side in a slow reaction.

"Very accurate," replied Silas, "It would appear that they are having an off day today."

He further tightened his grip and quickened the pace of the two. Silas frantically breathing through the pain and fatigue. As the two plunged into the deep waters of the stream before them a chilling cold rushed over them chattering their teeth with repetitive taps. Much of the icy waters washed away the blood and dirt stuck thick across the two, lashing and lapping as they pushed their way through.

Arturius could see the fear in Silas's eyes more clearly, tears of bloody streaks running across his face.

"I can't let them take me again," Silas muttered to himself, hiding the pain of his wounds. An effort to escape from his past, maybe? Only true determination and fear could outweigh the pain.

The gap was closing quicker each step they took, too slow was their pace and soon the attackers would be upon them. As Arturius glanced past his shoulder,

"One … Two … Three …" he wheezed, "Three pursuers I can see chasing us down, two press forward armed with blades and bucklers, the third holds back further, the marksmen we have already acquainted ourselves with."

Silas remained fearfully solemn, more focussed on trying to go forward than thinking behind. His breathing was heavy and gargled. The wound may have penetrated deeper than its appearance.

"Do you know how to fight?" Silas groaned quietly, his eyes shifted to meet Arturius, heavy and bloodshot draining of life.

Arturius remained silent.

For he did not know, no memories of conflict or brawls came to him in such a decisive moment.

"Let us press on," he replied, "I do not wish to find out if my skills fall short of theirs."

He avoided making eyes with Silas for some time as the two continued in their escape.

Despite the visions of the midday sun looming high above them, the skies darkened, mixing with a greyness that swept swiftly as rain.

"Strange, the sky is growing darker," said Arturius, "Yet the sun shines brightly above us."

"It could be a storm brewing," replied Silas, "Such is the occurrence upon these lands, for they are cursed with more death than one can fathom."

Footsteps bounded behind them, heavy and unrelenting in their pursuit. More shouting crept up behind him, this time directed upon him. Hurrying forward, Arturius tripped, catching his foot within some rabbit hole or across an old root. The two fell heavily to the ground. Arturius sunk his hands into the marshes ,surprised that they sank deeper than he thought possible. Silas tumbled a few steps in front, luckily landing upon a hard section of the ground. For but a mere moment, the water that settled below him looked like a mirror, reflecting his rugged features back upon him. A faint flicker showed a face behind him, dark and shrouded by shadow.

Before he knew it, the first swing came tumbling down from above, charged and heavy with intent. Arturius swiftly moved from its path, the serrated edge of the blade whistled through the wind as it passed by his ear. The attacker was clumsy, putting all his weight forward with the arrogance of success. He cursed with vicious sounding words before jutting forward into the bog. It left Arturius ample time to assist him in his greeting with the ground accurately kicking the back of his knees, sending him plunging into the depths.

The skies had now thickened with darkness, spread far across the horizon. It would have been a normal sight had it not been for the encircling blue skies in the distance. “Strange,” he thought to himself, “What darkness blots out but a fragment of the sky during the day!”

The pursuers so eagerly warmed from the chase had failed to even notice, so fixated on their prey he could have easily mistaken their ignorance for blindness.

No sooner had evaded the first strike, another came from his second pursuer. The jagged blade descended upon his neckline as he attempted to avert its path in such close quarters. This time, however, the blade met its target.

It would have been far worse had it not been for the uneven surface he stepped back to. Allowing the blade to graze his collarbone, gently gliding across his skin–A minor cut with no significance. He was however greeted with a strike from the pommel as it shuddered through his jaw, burning his face as he fell back towards the ground.

A faint aroma glanced from the blade, burning his nose with every breath he took. Poison, the coward’s killing tool.

An aggressive flurry of swings of blinded accuracy followed. Each shimmering attack edging closer and closer to its mark. Such frustration with each swing ended up glancing off the water’s surface and cutting down tussocks that littered around them.

In a desperate frenzy, Arturius summoned strength he had not known, countering a failed lunge with a heavy stamp into the chest, crumpling the plate and sending the aggressor cascading through the air. The blade dropped to the ground with a thud as his grip loosened, allowing the unarmed Arturius a chance at redemption.

As he looked back behind him, the first footman had pulled himself free of the water’s grasp and regained his footing. The marsh waters had soaked deep into his armour weighing him down hard. A myriad of small waterfalls breezed out the cracks in his armour. He brandished his blade high in a downward strike, easily deflected by the now armed Arturius. Hard and fast came the ensuing attacks, left and right, only to deflect with great ease. It was as if the skill of the blade had naturally emerged from within. A well-timed parry met with another slash, knocking the combatant yet again off his balance.

At a glance in the corner of his eye, he noticed the archer preparing his shot–cowardly to strike whilst your opponent is facing away–releasing the arrow as it hurtled through the air towards him. Grabbing the scruff of his neck, he pulled the imbalanced man into the path of the arrow, striking him deep in the chest. Its force was so strong that the head of the arrow burst out of his back, leaving a trail of red to follow. The point stared at Arturius, lamenting over its failure to meet its true target. The Rekeshi's knees folded beneath him to pray. Arturius watched as the light vanished from his eyes–clean and quick.

Now wasn't the time for victory. With the second footman brandishing a vicious-looking dirk, he screamed a bloody hiss as he jumped forward. But he was ready. With a forceful grunt, he threw the blade at its former master. Whirling through the air as graceful as an eagle, its faint shadow mimicked as it swiftly pursued it from the floor. It plunged into his chest, aided by the crumpled breastplate he had caved, releasing a torrent of blood and sinew. It forced the feet from beneath into a heap upon the floor, letting out a last gasp as he sank into the swamp–two down, one to go.

Arturius let out a long breath, for this fight was still not over.

"Silas, pull yourself from the floor," he shouted, "Now is our time to flee this encounter."

Such fatigue was bearing down upon him. The skin atop his collar had begun to burn; he had hoped that the graze hadn't rung too deep and spared him of such festering affliction.

Silas continued to lie still upon the bog. His faint breath rippled against its waters sent a wave of relief over Arturius.

Then searing pain soon grasped his thoughts, toppling him to the floor. He let out a powerful cry, transitioning into a strenuous scream. It burned plentifully as scorching water would singe upon the skin.

It was the brilliant white fletching's that first caught his attention, floating graciously before him. He followed the shaft with the tips of his fingers, smooth and lacquered in a deep black that ended upon his shoulder.

As he fell back to the ground, he found himself once again peering upon his reflection in the water. And yet again the face shrouded in shadow stared back at him.

"Again you stare back upon me," he gritted with pain, "Silas! You must awaken, I fear there is something else afoot here, and this wound prohibits my capabilities to resist death."

The sound of leather bounding against the dirt sent the shadowed figure fleeing deep with the darkness of the bottomless swamp. Arturius looked up to meet with his aggressor. The archer had since donned a vicious kukri as he closed in. Then it all changed. An aura, thick as tar, bubbled from the ground, covering its surrounds like a molten night's sky. The ground shook as with might, knocking the balance of the pursuing foe; stumbling as he tried to regain his footing. An abyssal black dark as the deepest night swallowed all in its path.

The lone Rekeshi wavered in his chase, no doubt relenting in his pursuit of the two to this familiar presence. His voice grew heavy and frantic, shouting unintelligibly into the darkness.

*It* emerged from deep within the shadows. A being enshrouded by a deep black fog; a cloak that concealed much of its true form. Its face, however, bore through the nightmarish darkness clear as day. A twisted and malformed skull that held no flesh and weaved no sinew. It's eyes a deep darkened haze that flowed from its face, a torrent of unfathomable black mist that dissipated into the air. It loomed down upon its prey. The lone archer cursed, slashing frantically at the creature that had manifested before him. His shiny blade glinted into the shadow, disappearing before emerging blackened. Burnt. Broken.

As though a will of its own, the darkness latched onto his blade, infecting it will its hatred before piercing his arm. Burning and tearing, it ravaged his forearm horrifically, though he could not see well the screams painted a rather vivid picture for him.

Before the Rekeshi could react, the creature unsheathed its monstrous claws, griping about him from the neck, dwarfing his feeble stature with its size.

"Now is my time," said Arturius.

He grasped at the shaft of the bloody arrow, tearing it from his flesh. Screaming quietly as his arm quivered, the trauma sending a spasm surging through his body.

Far in the nearby distance, his eyes met with the nameless creature, now aware of his presence as it howled a deep and thunderous screech. Its ear-piercing shrill creased the leaves upon the trees, violently rippled against the water and bent the very air to its will. Though frightening as it was, its cries appeared to be more of torment and pain.

In the failing light, he scrambled over to Silas, digging his feet in deep with the marshes, though still taking care to step upon more solid ground. Silas still lay unconscious, blood seeping from his hip as it dripped into the deep waters surrounding him, staining as red as the summer wine.

"Come Silas!" he muttered, "I will not leave you to fade in such a place, though I fear we may struggle upon two wounds."

Silas did not respond. Too far had he sunk into obscurity and too much had his body suffered by the poison. It would be up to him to see them survive this day.

It took all his strength to lift the Silas across his shoulders, ignoring the fresh puncture that the arrow had made, hindering at his movements. And so he ran, faster than ever before, or so he assumed.

It was not far to the forest, maybe if he could break the creature's line of sight and slip into the cover of its own darkness. He looked back over his shoulder.

Shimmering through the mirage of darkness, the nameless shadow had turned its attention to its prey. Spewing forth a blackened mist from its gaping jaws, washing past such malevolent bone. It seeped into the mouth, ears and eyes of the flailing Rekeshi, still lashing out with whatever strength remained, but to no avail. It was then his screams turned upon him, deathly and gargling as the mist drew back into the mouth of the creature.

Arturius quickened his pace, forcing his legs into the dank swamp as once more the fear fell upon him.

"This is not good," he muttered to himself, "We are still some distance from the forest and I fear it will soon be upon us having finished what was left of our pursuer."

Though his words strayed away from the deafened ears of Silas, he drew upon the comfort of not feeling alone as he spoke.

The monster slammed the ragged body to the ground, its grip evermore tightened as it loomed over the man. It let out an ear-piercing screech, the likes of which caused Arturius to falter in his path, encumbering him with intense pain. He looked back just as the black mist thickened, an apparition of a man emerging from the body of the Rekeshi devoured promptly by the shadow. The man fell limp, lifeless and cold.

It now turned its gaze upon them as they halted, hungry for more. Soon the menace swept across the land with an eerie presence intent on leaving none to escape from its domain.

Arturius gritted through the pain, moving faster but cautiously along his path. He couldn't risk falling victim to the depths below, for it would prove most fatal to them both. The woods were now with immediate proximity. The smell of elm and birch licked his nose. It was sweet and sharp, invigorating his senses.

The essence of the forest in front, the deep aura of darkness to his rear. Both deathly close to each other. In the intense blackness, he could feel the claws of darkness glancing off of him. Tireless and unrelenting as held no quarter.

As the thick bristle and branches broke before him. He burst through the thicket collapsing to the ground, Silas fell a few paces to his side. The ground was soft, filled by the array of needles and leaves that cushioned his fall. He buried his face into the floor, biting at the dirt as he awaited his fate.

The seconds grew into minutes. He lifted his head, poised and ready, yet nothing happened.

“It’s gone,” he whispered to himself, “Vanished into the darkness perhaps, though I still feel its presence upon me, taste its putrid breath.”

For the forest was empty. Devoid of life, and stark of death around. He looked back through the bristle of the trees, and there it waited.

The creature looming menacingly at the boundaries of the forest, its eyes piercing through as its mouth drew in remnants of the surrounding light. He looked back and forth, confused by the answers that did not come to him.

“You cannot enter the forest can you?” he whispered, standing to his feet, “I can see it in your eyes, not fear or fright, you wish to pounce upon me where I stand yet you can’t.”

The creature remained undeterred, undefeated, unbroken. It just floated before the forest, staring. The black cloak waving in the breeze lapping over its misshapen arms, grotesque and empty. It was of nothing that could be explained upon this realm.

Arturius cautiously approached it, taking measures to ensure he did not stray too far from his sanctuary. Carefully he examined that which he could. It's head, a twisted skull of fangs and horns enshrouded by a thick shadow, a shadow that flowed down and merged with that of its body. Its torso appeared to laden thick with fur blacker than the darkest night. Its arms bore no flesh, no skin, an amalgamation of various bones and branches. No doubt trophies from its prey through the years. But its eyes, its eyes, told a thousand tales.

As Arturius stared deep into its shadowed eyes he felt everything, the pain of countless souls stripped from their flesh, the insatiable bloodlust and the eerie feeling of companionship within the dark.

A voice echoed through his ears, repeating the same words over again, words that seemed ever so familiar.

It slowly crept back, never looking away, gliding effortlessly through the air. It let out a crackling roar before dissipating into nothing. Whatever it was, it had now gone, called back to its master, no doubt to be directed to others who may fall under its shadow.

Arturius fell to his knees, the fatigue and pain had finally caught him.

"What have I woken myself into," he said, falling back into unconsciousness as was cradled by the. Many mysteries ran through his mind as he lay there falling into a deep sleep, yet none were more prominent than the creature he felt so strangely attached to, a link between souls.

Then the world fell silent.

~ *"Are we not to wait for the others?"* ~

## CHAPTER III: KHAOTIC REALITIES

Night had fallen, or so it seemed. A gentle light tangled through the twisting branches of the dense trees above. The ground itself was hard, yet the soft pillows of dead leaves cushioned him across his back. Far from the edge of the forest had they delved, for its air thin with the suffocation of the forest. Far off into the distance, the occasional rustle of wildlife burrowed throughout the foliage, their eyes glinting in the blackness before vanishing.

Arturius creased forward, pulling his weight upright, something which his muscles were most discordant of. It was the crackling fire that drew his attention first. Its flames glowed a brilliant whitened yellow as it licked the air in a caressing dance.

Crouched beside it, Silas sat looked solemnly through the flames. Entranced and depressed as the flames whirled in the reflections of his eyes. A heavy burden was weighing on the young boy's mind, the entire world blocked from existence as he recessed deep into his thoughts.

Beneath Arturius's feet, the twigs crackled and snapped, jolting the young boy from his trance.

"Oh, your awake!" Silas spoke gleefully, "Glad to see you are back with the living, how are you feeling?"

"Surprisingly well," replied Arturius, "Tell me, how long have I been out for? I do not remember arriving in this section of the woods."

Arturius grunt as he perched himself on the opposing side, his eyes squinted as lowered himself to the warm floor, avoiding the burnt debris which the flames had spat out.

"Well, you wouldn't remember such an action, as it was I who moved us here," said Silas, "As for your journey into the beyond, around a half-day or so, though I can't speak for the time before I awoke, you were unconscious before me."

Arturius nodded in acceptance, as though unsure what to make of it all.

"How fares your injury," asked Arturius, "In our hasty retreat it wore down on you heavily, damn nearly got you killed as well",

He nodded to the now re-bandaged hip poking through the tears in his clothing.

"The affliction has been suppressed," he replied, pulling back his shirt, "I'm still not out of the woods yet, however, you bought me a couple of days before it shall return, you must tell me how you escaped from the Rekeshi, it is not a feat easily done in these dark times."

Arturius sighed with relief, a weight had lifted from his shoulders gleeful that his effort did not fall in vain. Though it was rather short-lived, for even his own mind screamed for him to abstain from a mention of the nameless creature.

"That is a relief," said Arturius, "Though there is not much to say of it. I was able to dispatch two of them, however…"

He paused briefly.

"The other must-have fled for fear of being next," he continued,

As he spoke of the encounter he reached for the wound upon his shoulder, for strangely enough it no longer burned, nor did it bleed either. A great confusion swept through his mind, his hand frantically prodding and poking across his seemingly unharmed flesh. Though the wound had vanished.

"Are you okay there?" Silas asked,

Arturius quickly dropped his arm, brushing away the dirt across his hands.

"Ugh, yeah, I am good," Arturius replied, "Must've pulled my arm back in the marshes, just a little tender is all."

Impossible, he thought, no such wound could have healed in such a time. There was something at work that was truly beyond his comprehension.

"Was it all in my head?" he thought to himself, recounting the events that led up to him now, "Impossible, I pulled the arrow myself, I felt its steel brush against my skin". He could not trust his own memories. Either way, they abandoned him long ago.

"What's going on?" Silas said nervously, "You seem to have let your mind run astray."

It took some time for Arturius to respond. In his head, he was pacing back and forth, stitching together each fragment of his memory to unravel the truth. He peered over at Silas, his body tense and his eyes anxious.

"It's nothing," Arturius replied, "My mind is still a mess from earlier."

"Not to worry, my friend, many strange things have since occurred within these last few years," said Silas, "Believe me when I say that waking up in that field was the least of your worries."

Silas laughed a little at his remark before continuing.

"Though keep your mind sharp within these woods," said Silas, "I do not think that the forest in inherently evil, whatever others may say of it, but one thing is most certain, peering eyes watch from a distance and the mind will soon question its own sanity."

"Then why set up camp within such a forest?" asked Arturius, "Surely such a risk is not worth the taking?"

"Exactly why it is a perfect way forward," said Silas, "Many are hesitant to enter such a forest, even more so when night falls upon the sky, it makes for a much safer respite from those which would pursue us so."

"While I understand and agree with your premise, I must also contest to further questions," said Arturius, "For if those which would pursue us on land dare not delve into this forest, then why is it so? What keeps them from entering?"

He offered the question well, for it may make way for a better understanding of why the nameless shadow did not enter.

"These woods are old. Ancient, I dare say," said Silas, "So old in fact that the annals of history begin during an age when these trees predate even the very first that walked these lands."

A faint shudder swayed through the trees, swatting away at the flames that flickered before them.

"There is something that lives deep within the heart of the forest," Silas whispered, "It walks between the trees, bringing with it a tenseness in the air, it wasn't until a few years ago, seven to be exact that people disappeared, and the rumour of the whisper that wanders re-emerged once more."

Arturius leaned in.

"What is it?" he asked, "What walks through the trees?"

"No one knows," said Silas, "No one has seen it but those which are dead, and no one wishes to be the one to find such unknown forces when they walk along the shadowed path."

"I do not wish to meet this entity of which you speak of," said Arturius, "Though if no one has seen or met with such a thing then how did the rumours come to be?"

Silas leant forward, pricked his fingers together as he rested upon his thighs.

"Well, if the whisper does not get you, then the Fayories will surely do what they must," Silas whispered,

"Fayories?" said Arturius confused, "As in the magical sprites of the forest? Now that is something that I can remember, though they are gentle in nature, not that which would drag you to your death and doom."

"Aye, those are fairies that you speak of," replied Silas, "Whilst you are correct, a Fayorie however, is a dark creature of the forest, sprite by day, ghoulish apparition by nightfall, not something I wish to discover anytime soon."

"And what will stop such a fate for us?" questioned Arturius.

Silas pointed to the incandescent flames billowing before them.

"Fire my friend, fire," he replied, "It will keep both the whisper and Fayories at bay, and they will only consume you should you stray from the path."

"You comfort me with your confidence it would seem," said Arturius, "Where you will go I shall follow, I do not wish to discover that which you speak of in the depths, though would a fire not draw our presence to those that may embrace such horrors and delve in after us?"

The burning fire was bright. Reaching far out into the darkness of the forest. In such a confined and looming setting, it was a risk to such stealth. Still, Arturius felt slightly unnerved by its presence. It was as though the very flames were attempting to swat him away from such a place.

"Believe me when I say this to you, I would rather face a hundred Rekeshi blood thirsters wearing nothing but my undergarments and armed with a broken stick than relinquish that which holds such darkness at bay."

"So, the fire stays then?" he choked.

"Yes, the fire stays," Silas bluntly replied. For that which lurks within the dark, Silas's demeanour changed from that of a frightened child to a leader who could inspire hope. A mighty gift.

It made his body quiver, his hair stood on its end, and his skin prickled just to think of such horror. Despite all that he was lost to him from his time long before, the fear that comes from the empty darkness truly terrified him.

A cold wind rustled the trees above them, the very forest itself came to life in the presence of the two by the fire.

The aura of the forest bore harshly around them, its pressure exerting upon them as if the forest itself was closing in around them. The flames had since diminished, a mere fraction of the size they once were. Silas stoked the fire. The flames enveloped the fuel, growing in size.

"Is there anything more that I should know in such a place," asked Arturius, "Any treasures I should seek of?"

"There are some," Silas replied,

He found his gaze peering out into the beyond, as frivolous as it was a part of him wished to see but a glance of the mysteries that stayed hidden from view.

"There are rumours of an artefact of a dominant power that lies in the unchartered parts of this forest," said Silas,

"Unchartered?" said Arturius gasping, "how big is such a place?"

Silas nodded in acceptance, twisting around to his side.

"That way three hundred miles," he said pointing northwards,

"That way four hundred miles," he said pointing south,

"That way six hundred miles," he said pointing east, "and that way 10 miles," he said gesturing to the entrance from which they burst through,

"Incredible," replied Arturius, "A size that truly makes you feel as insignificant as an ant in the storm."

"It is said that it is guarded by the spirits of all those who lost themselves within the forest, those who strayed from the path, those who succumbed to the darkness within," Silas whispered, "And that such darkness has taken hold of them, that only light can keep them at bay."

He gestured towards the burning fire, its powerful light brilliantly illuminating the small clearing they sat within. A shield against the darkness that lurked.

After the encounter from earlier, Arturius knew deep down that such supernatural phenomena were more than possible. Many eyes followed his every movement as he looked deep into the trees that surrounded him.

"Something appears to weigh on your mind still," said Silas, "Are you sure there is nothing that you can discuss to ease your distress?"

Arturius shook his head, though in truth much was whirling like a storm, battering the recesses of his mind.

"Nay, there is not," Arturius replied, "It's just been a long day, the first thing I remember since waking is death, death and darkness it would seem."

Silas remained silent, though a glimmer of doubt glinted across his face. He shrugged it off as a lost cause. Though the forest floor was dry and coated with a blanket of needles and leaves alike, there was a faint trickle of water that echoed in the distance.

"So what heading must we take to find ourselves upon your camp?" asked Arturius, "With such mirrored trees and darkened pathways, how can you be so sure ours is the correct way?"

Silas smiled,

"You should have a little faith, my friend," he quipped, "The leader of my camp, a great man. He left me with such a message that would lead me through the darkness, to follow a path only shown to those of sharpened mind and unwavering wills."

"You speak of him so well," said Arturius, "He must be a great man, I cannot wait to finally great him, so what is this message he left you?"

Arturius leaned in, eager to listen to this so-called 'faith'.

*"When the false path lies in turn, follow the breath of the forest to unveil the shadowed path. Only then shall the ardent be shown the light"*

Arturius stared down at the proud Silas, his face brimming with disappointment.

"That's it?" he said, dismayed and depressed, "That explains nothing to us, though if it is all that we are left with then I suppose it is all we can do, for I do not wish for another encounter with …"

Arturius quickly held his tongue, too close had he come to speaking of that which he had held back.

"Encounter with what?" Silas asked fervently,

"With the Rekeshi that chased us down," replied Arturius quickly, "I do not wish to see if more were present in the marshes."

The young boy scowled gently. In no way was he hiding the suspicions he had raised within himself.

"Likewise," he replied coldly, "We should move."

He passed him a makeshift torch, crude but efficient as it billowed to life amongst the life of the fire.

The forest was thick, its path narrow and twisting through the cramped emptiness. Trees that stood towering above them, so monstrous that the very roots had sprung forth from the ground, carving many arches into an eerie tunnel from which their path was set.

Even as their eyes adjusted to the dense dark, they could still see only a little way to either side. By now they were much deeper into the forest, whatever light had been before having been shunned by the encroached branches that loomed above. The trees themselves tightly packed and heavily constricting faltered their movement upon the uneven surface.

Every breath they took in was stale and stuffy. The very air had become foul from its years of isolated ruin, untouched by anything of the living. It was not long before the air had thinned out and the dizziness set it.

Occasionally Arturius swore he could see someone watching them from afar, an apparition that followed them donning his own face. It would smile upon him menacingly before falling back into the shadows, whispering gently as it did so. It was an eerie sight, perhaps a soul long lost to the forest. He shook it off "Must be the forest plaguing my mind?" he thought to himself "It can make you feel things, hear things … see things".

They had to keep going; they had no other option. The affliction was taking hold of Silas once more, first; it began as a limp and then developed into much worse. From time to time he would stumble into the darkness, only for Arturius promptly return him back into place.

"Easy now," said Arturius, "Keep your feet steady, for when you delve into the darkness I may not have the strength to pull you back again."

There was no doubt in his mind that the affliction of the forest was weighing heavily upon him. Forward felt backwards, backward felt forward. After a while even the trees were beginning to watch them with glowing eyes of darkness, though not enough however to illuminate their way.

"How much farther is it?" Arturius gasped, "I do not know how long we have been travelling for, though it feels like we have not stopped for days and my body is tiring once more."

They had in fact only been travelling for a couple of hours. Yet the forest infected them with a dangerous haze of the mind. Seconds felt like hours, hours felt like days. No wonder so many never returned.

"I am unsure," Silas stammered; his breath was growing weak as his life abandoned him. "The path is still remaining true, whatever fear or doubt may plague our minds we must press on".

His words were twisting, contorting into a language of their own as his tongue failed him.

"Are you feeling okay Silas?" asked Arturius, "I fear your mind is altering your speech, or your wounds are weakening your spirit please hold on, I will not have you fall within these dark trees embrace."

Before long, the path had grown into a fork, to the left twisting in darkness, to the right malformed into black. Silas paused, his head flicked between the two, left, right, left, right. The flames erupting from his torch licked the dry bark of the trees, brushing against the leaves that did not sway. For some powerful force, an entity of the force disliked the clumsiness of the young boy in his attempt to set the forest ablaze. Accident or not.

The pitch-darkness that enveloped them was too thick to see before them, all they could see were the eyes of the forest staring back at them. Gleaming like red, green and blue diamonds in the sky. Disappearing and reappearing in a mere moment across the thick black canvass.

Some time had passed, the young boy had yet to make a decision.

"Why do you wait?" Arturius whispered, no reply emerged from Silas, "What is the matter with you?".

He reached out, grasping him by the shoulder. He was shaking. Cold and twitchy as his head continued to jump between the paths.

"The affliction is becoming too much for your body to bear," Arturius beckoned, "If we falter any longer then I fear you will not emerge from this darkness as a being of life."

He pinched at his shoulder to garner a response, yet the boy remained silent. His body was tense and strong, Arturius struggled to grapple control of it as he fought back. It was as if it was no longer the young boy was within his own body. Tightening his grip, Arturius spun Silas about, rustling amongst the leaves. A few branches snapped, echoing deeper into the forest. The forest responded in kind with a torrent of growls and groans, bouncing between its trees, laughing uncontrollably at the two entrapped within its lair.

The dying flames on Arturius's torch lit dimly enough to caress Silas's face, claws of shadow wrapped through the creases caught in its embrace. Never could he have imagined the twitching, vacant expression that consumed the young boy. His eyes gave no rest, for they were white with fury, sending the young boy into an uncontrollable spasm. Silas's gaze broken straight through him, evermore focused on the claustrophobic forest gradually shrinking around them.

The shaking did nothing. If he shook the poor boy anymore, he could well kill him, his delicate body already weakened as the poison ventured deeper within him. It was a swift strike to the cheek that brought him about. Dazed and confused, his breath gasped as though submerged beneath the water.

"W-what happened?" he cried, the dim light concealing his panicked state enough for him to gather himself.

"Your mind left you for a moment there," replied Arturius, "My apologies for such a violent awakening, but I feared that should you not come about then our hopes of continuing would have dwindled along with our light."

A red mark formed across Silas's face, stinging and bruised. Arturius felt a hint of guilt at the pain he inflicted, but none so more as if he had allowed the Silas to die on his watch.

"Ugh, my head feels split and drained," said Silas,

He paused as scanned his surroundings, locking onto to each feature he could see before turning to Arturius.

"Where are we?" he said weakly, "Who are you?"

"The affliction has reached your mind it seems," replied Arturius, his own head being weighed down by the intense aura within, "A mixture of the forest air and lingering poison within your blood is accelerating your deterioration, it is as though the forest itself is stealing away your breath."

Then he realized, maybe the riddle itself held some merit to their survival.

"Quick," he barked, "Do you remember the passages from the message you spoke of?"

Silas looked confused, he strained as his mind backtracked, looking upon the stranger that demanding words from him. At first, it looked as though he might pass out as his face burned a deep red, holding his breath into asphyxiation.

"Steady, steady," said Arturius, "Take your time, though do so with haste."

Silas nodded; it was clear the surrounding air was slowly disorientating him. Erasing his mind. Preparing him for the vast eternity to roam the forest, another spirit lost. He recited the words passed on to him with great difficulty as his mind slowly fractured.

Though it was not the whole passage that Arturius cared for, merely a simple phrase.

"Breath of the forest," Arturius whispered, "The key was before us the entire time."

Silas stared blankly back at him, rubbing his tender eyes as he swayed from side to side.

"This is it!" Arturius shouted, grabbing Silas, thrusting him over to the fork "The false path that lies before us, one will lead us to safety, the other I shall guess not so much"

"What do you mean?" replied Silas, nearly tripping over the tangled roots beneath his feet.

"I will show you," said Arturius, excitement burst from his voice,

He thrusted his flaming torch forward, held aloft as its brilliant light gleamed down from above. The flames flickered no differently than before. Drifting gently with the mellow breeze above.

"There!" he whispered, "Do you see it?"

The flames flowed along with the winds, moving silently towards the darkness of the shadowed path. Yet they did not flow from side to side, only arched slightly to the left.

"It would appear that the flame has chosen to dance for us," muttered Silas, jumbling deep within his head.

Thirst and hunger were beginning to set in. It had seemed like an age had passed since they began their trek through the darkness. There was no use in trying to hunt. The darkness proved too thick to catch whatever may lurk within, for even that may not have been edible.

Water was running scarce too. The sounds of flowing water echoed through the leaves, though they dare not drink from the forest. For it would most likely poison the body along with the forest's very air. Silas had told him stories of the streams that ran through. A network of veins, the lifeblood of the trees. Its waters would run crystal clear, shimmering in the moon as a river of diamonds. Its enticing waters would quench the thirst of the strongest whom may enter, yet it would only lead to their immediate demise.

The path was growing more arduous and difficult to overcome. Its path constantly shifting. Its tunnels blacker than the night and littered with thick webs that proved difficult to tear through.

The high paths ran up the giant roots, puncturing the earth, leaving large chasms below. One slip and you would find the abyss to swallow you whole.

"How long has it been?" asked Arturius, his head was throbbed harder than before, "Surely we must be nearing sanctuary."

All Silas could muster was a series of incoherent babbles and mutters, his mouth drooling from the illness that spread.

Both were tired and weary. They had been travelling for three days now, surviving only by the dwindled rations that lay festering at the back of Silas's satchel. An assortment of fruits and berries would pass them along the path occasionally, ripe for the picking, there sweet scent enticing and deadly. Despite the temptations, they held firm. Fighting back the wolves that growled within their stomachs, keeping to the strict rules passed down to Silas.

*"Do not eat or drink from the fruits of the forest...Resist the temptation...fight for control"*

A vague warning, yet deathly in its consequences.

Just as the last shimmer of hope was swallowed from view, a glimmer of light fell through the darkness. With every step forward, the light moved more distant as if toying with their desperation.

"There!" urged Arturius, "In the distance, do you see?",

His disdain towards the forest was already at its peak. He could feel the beast from within trying to burst free as his frustration was overcoming him.

"Now is not such time to see what is not there," babbled Silas, his words slowly made less sense as time passed.

"Fear not Silas, hope lies ahead," said Arturius, "I can see your body is failing, and your feet stumble beneath you, allow me to assist once more."

It took all his strength to grapple at the limp boy, hoisting him high across his back. The lack of food or water had dwindled his strength greatly, and even the weight of such a small frame felt more than he could handle.

They pushed far and fast, no longer caring for branches they broke, why should they, they all seemed the same. Constricting them within a prison of wood.

The light grew strong, brighter with each step they took. Arturius could feel its warmth bathe him from afar, so long had the damp cold of the forest bitten at him that such a distance heat melt him from within. Their walk turned into a jog, their jog into a sprint, and before long they were almost fighting between themselves to the front of the pack.

Horned walls closed in with branches of sharpened stakes, needles that punctured them all over. The branches drew at Arturius's face, its nails cutting deep into his face. The faster they ran, the harder it became.

In a flash of light, warmth and air, they broke through the great wall of vines and branches. Crashing down atop the dry ground together, they fumbled beneath each other in an attempt to poise themselves before the encampment. Yet it was empty. The fire was still hot to the touch as the flames roared high. The cascades of shadows filled the walls of trees that lined its edges, jagged and terrifying as they loomed above.

"Where is everyone?" asked Arturius, trying to pick up whatever sign of life he could find. Only the crackle of the logs burning could be heard within the confines of the camp. He turned to Silas, only to find himself alone. "What is going on," he thought to himself. A dizzying feeling swept across him as the floor arched its way towards him. Striking him hard to his face and chest.

*~ "And sacrifice all the glory to the others? No, we shall press on" ~*

## CHAPTER IV: HARSH ENCOUNTERS

The first thing he could feel was the tight grasp of the ropes burning against his skin. He awoke to find his head hunched over his chest, his back pressed firmly against a thick and tall oak. As he sat there in the dense darkness, he pondered over the events that led him once more into a situation he could not fathom.

There was a faint aroma that hung in the air, the sickly-sweet smell of tree sap dripping slowly throughout the glade; the dry smell of pine and elm mixing into the air. Upon the edges of his prison, the decay of the forest's trees devoured the fresh air with a putrid aura. As a gentle breeze flowed past his nose, he caught the scent of sweat and blood, definitely men of at least middle age; they must be lurking somewhere further off it's the forest.

The hard-cold ground passing sharply through his clothes, scratching with a deep tingling sensation. Judging by the indentation beneath him, others must have been held captive in his place many times before.

It all felt like a deep sleep. The surreal sensations that whisked through his body made his eyes twitch and legs jitter with excitement. His eyes were blurry, only just able to make out the darkened figures that stood before him. He counted three in total. The rest could have been well concealed or just merely invisible to his failing vision. They did not appear to move, locked in place as they studied him.

Bursts of adrenaline surged through his body. Excited and energetic, the very opposite to how he felt during the perilous journey.

"Try anything and ill slit your throat!" said one voice. The voice was distorted and deep. Arturius shook his head vigorously. It sounded unnatural. He nervously tried to squint through the blurry view, much to no avail.

"I don't think he heard you," replied another voice. This one was much higher than the previous. The voice seemed to echo through each ear as if spoken from all around. Overwhelmed, Arturius panicked, sweating profusely as he tried to wriggle free.

"Ah, the wonders of the wyrmflower extract," laughed the first voice, "No doubt your feeling woozy and disorientated right now, I'll give you a little advice, don't fight it for it will burrow deep within your veins quicker."

"Don't forget about the hallucinations," said the second voice, "I added that myself, adds a little kick to the entire experience."

The constantly falling sensation sent shivers through his stomach. The room was spinning faster and faster as time grew on. It was never ending. Every movement, every motion he made to settle his balance was only made worse, drifting him in and out of consciousness.

He awoke again coughing and spluttering, his lungs filled with a frigid chill of water leaving his clothes drenched and stuck upon him.

"We can do this all day if need be," said the deep voice, "I suggest you talk now, who are you? What business do you have delving into the darkness of the forest? Of whom do you owe allegiance to? Answer me or you shall face much worse than a little cold water!"

He looked up to the sky; it was dark. Though not a darkness of the night, but that of the absence of light for the forest would allow nothing to escape from its deep embrace. There were no fires lit around him, possibly instilling more fear of what may lurk within the darkness edging ever closer to him. Only the faint shadows of his captors could be seen, passing around him swiftly and silently.

Arturius was recalling the events of the past, the heaviness of the air was dwindling him upon his body; a growing darkness that was proving difficult to shake.

"Silas!" whispered Arturius worriedly, he looked around in the darkness past the concealed trio that stood before, "Please you must help, I came here with another, stabbed by a blade of poison, an affliction was slowly seeping through his blood and draining him of life, please you must have seen him!"

He frantically searched the area, though it was to no avail. Bound and blackened made it impossible. The interrogators remained silent, only the mutterings between them reached his ears, though it was less than audible.

"Please, I beg of you," Arturius pleaded, "Too much has he suffered as of late, please I will tell you all I know, just please don't allow him to pass."

Despite his delirious state, he held firm. He cared not for his own wellbeing, but that of a stranger, a boy he had only just met.

"You speak of your hostage, don't you?" replied the wispy voice, "Rather strange for a Rekeshi to take such care of his spoils. Tell me, was it your plan to use him to get to us? Or was it just to get a kick out of watching him slowly fade from this realm?"

"Indeed, it is," said the deep voice, intrigue floated from his mouth, Arturius could just about make out his silhouette. Tall, muscular. The rest of his features still obscured from his sight. The second was much smaller, leaner. He was hunched slightly, his right arm contorted and. The third figure he could not see, yet he knew he was there. He could sense it, smell his odour as he lurked back from the others.

A glint of steel flashed within the darkness, sending streams of light flickering across the floor. He could hear it scraping against leather, sharpening more and more until it disappeared from view.

"So, here's what's gonna happen," said the deep voice, "Now I myself am not one to dabble in the affairs of torture, I find it rather primitive, my friend here, well he relishes in it, brings him great joy."

An undertone of anger coursed through his voice.

He continued, "now if you choose to resist my questioning, I may very well leave for a short while, maybe enjoy a good slice of ham, and leave you with him for a while."

Amidst the dim darkness, he could see the silhouette move to his left. Cold steel pressed against his middle finger as it parted from his clenching fist, sharp as the cold that surrounded him. A faint chuckle could be heard, the shadow smacking his lips in joy as he pried the finger away from his clenched fist.

"I'm gonna ask again, who are you," the deep voice beckoned, "Why did you seek us out? Who do you serve?"

The shadow tightened his grip, nearly breaking Arturius's finger.

"My name is Arturius, I…" he was interrupted suddenly,

"What are you doing here?" Growled the deep voice,

"I don't know, but I…" he was silenced again,

"Enough with the games," he beckoned, "How about we show he how serious we are!"

He felt the blade pressing harder against his finger, cutting slightly into the flesh. His finger felt warm and wet, a trickle of blood caressed along its edge before dripping from the tip of his finger.

"Please, just listen…" said Arturius,

"Maybe we should take an eye," interrupted the wispy voice, "That will show him how serious we mean to be!",

Arturius was confused, "They think I'm Rekeshi! They can't be with those that attacked earlier"

"I'm not Rekeshi!" he beckoned; his voice fell onto deaf ears.

"How did you know about us," said the deep voice, anger consuming his words, "Who sent you?",

Arturius could feel his heart pounding within his chest, whilst there was a grip of fear choking at his throat. It was more annoyance that was pushing him on.

"Listen to me!" he shouted.

Though the others merely shouted over him, uncaring of his plight.

"Who do you serve?" barked the deep voice.

"How did you get here?" growled the wispy voice, "Tell us everything you know!"

The intensity of the questions smothered him. He felt as though he were drowning in a torrent of words and spiteful speaking, a cascading barrage of questions, forcefully beckoned. He felt small, tiny, worthless. An insignificant mouse cowering before the two looming predators, helpless and alone.

"I don't know," Arturius screamed. He sighed, slumping down further to the ground "I don't know."

The shadowed aggressor loosened his grip on his trembling fingers. It wasn't fear that brought him to the brink of despair. It was nothing, the nothing that lived deep within his mind. The nothing that failed to know who he was. The nothing that led him to this very moment, unprepared and useless.

"I have no memory to serve me thusly," he shouted; the rage seeped from his mouth as he spat at his interrogators. "When I awoke upon the aftermath of a battle, I knew nothing but the name of which I was given. It was then that I met the young boy, Silas, he was injured, and I agreed to help him reach his encampment."

There was a hushed silence. Not one voice beckoned at him further, listening with great intent to the bound Arturius.

"Where is he?" demanded Arturius, his thoughts still well fixed upon the wellbeing of the young boy, "I came here with him in the dark, if you have done anything to him by my word I will not let you live to see the light of day again!"

Primal aggression emerged quickly with his words; a rage uncontrollable, as though left to fester for a thousand years.

"Though I do not remember who I am, or where I came from, there is one thing I am most certain of," said Arturius menacingly, "I know that my skill with a blade is quite refined, just ask the Rekeshi that lay silently upon the marshes."

Further silence gathered around him, only the hushed whispers between the two that stood before him could reach his ears. The third still silent as ever before. It seemed like an age before they took notice of him again. His arms were tiring more by each passing second. They were pulled back hard, stretching behind him slightly, cutting off the circulation. The tingling in his fingers reminded him of a dream, a dream of darkness and despair before he woke from his slumber. *"Strange, I had no memory of this before, yet it feels as though it was there all along,"* he thought to himself.

The voices that echoed before him interrupted his thoughts once more. This time they sounded different. He could still tell it was the same people as before, but the twisted malformed sounds sounded more, normal.

"Tell us what you know of the company in the dark?" said one voice. He could tell first it was the deeper voice of the two, except this time it sounded lighter, softer.

"Nothing," replied Arturius responded, "I know nothing as I told you thusly, I have no memory to garner my journey since before I awoke upon the marshes."

There were mutterings once more upon the glade, this time however his hearing was not so obscured, though the words did not reach him well, he could make out a few murmurs.

"What if he is lying," said the less wispy voice,

"It matters not what you think," said the deeper voice, "We are to extract whatever information he has in his feeble mind; besides, he knew the way to the camp. Only the company has been told of such a riddle."

They turned back upon him.

"You have one last time to come clean with us," said the deep voice, "After that I cannot promise you to remain unharmed."

The shadowed figure looked down upon his bloodied hand.

"Or any more harmed than before," he whispered softly,

"I already told you!" snapped Arturius in frustration, "I don't know what you are talking about, show some reason to this madness!"

"Maybe he speaks the truth," said the withered voice, "Perhaps he does not remember that which came before him."

"It is a trick well known to the Masked One," said the deep voice, "Stripping people of their memories, their humanity, their very soul, leaving them a husk of themselves, the perfect infiltration some would say."

While the others were speaking, Arturius rustled around trying to break free of his bindings. Though all was to little avail, a quick nudge from the shadow behind him quenched such resistance. He had almost forgotten of the third interrogator as he lurked behind him quietly.

Turning back to him, the others spoke more softly, whether it was the tonic they gave him that was wearing from his body or the realisation he was not of what they spoke.

"I guess you give us no option really," said the deep voice, "We will leave you to it."

He could make out the faint nod from his silhouette, gesturing towards some unknown entity that lay before him.

"What do you mean?" said Arturius, "Please just tell me that Silas is safe, that he has been treated for his wounds!"

Thunderous steps echoed behind him. The searing pain that enveloped the side of his face swiftly interrupted his pleas. A strike of intense hatred came from the shadows, a blunt force that echoed through the forest, sending the trees into a frenzy. He could only sit there as the pain swelled across his face, sweeping him to the side. If it weren't for the binds pinning him to the tree, he would have struck with the cold, dark ground. Before he could regain himself, a flurry of fists landed against his face and temple. Relentless in their pursuit, they gave no quarter or rest, one after another, each making its mark with deadly precision.

Blood filled his mouth, choking him as it washed down his throat. Every gasp of breath was responded with another strike, each with increasing intensity.

"Please! … Stop!" Arturius pleaded, though they did not halt.

The relentless punches felt never ending. Just as he would slip into unconsciousness, the strikes would intensify. At this point the blood must have been streaming from his face, he wasn't sure if it were the warmth of his own blood or the numbness of his face as it throbbed in the dark.

A few curtains of dim light had formed from the canopy above, showering small pockets across the small glade. *"Morning must be at its break,"* he thought to himself, eyes fixed at the glimmer that waved between the leaves. It wasn't enough to show the faces of his captors however, only a few parts were caught in the light, a hand, an arm, a foot. It wasn't until the clenched fist broke through the light, homing in to meet with him, that he could notice the mark atop the arm. A phoenix in flight, sword grasped within its talons shining across the crumbling and torn fabric.

Of course, this wasn't the first time he had seen it. It emblazoned many of the corpses that littered the fields. When the knuckles of the attacker struck his tender jaw, it sent a powerful shock-wave through his head. Many images flickered through his head, each one the symbol shone somewhere in the foreground. Embossed deeply into a shield, fluttering high atop a banner, carved deep into stone. It was powerful enough to send an intense ache through his head, shivers rolling down his spine as he spasmed uncontrollably.

"In Unity lies strength," he uttered, spitting blood from his mouth, weary and broken. He did not know why he said it, or how the words came forth upon his mind, but alas, things were very much about to change.

The attack ceased.

A tense mood filled the glade. Arturius was glad the beating had stopped, unsure as to how much longer he could have endured.

"Go get him!" hushed an unfamiliar voice, "Tell him that it is of urgent matters."

Pain and fatigue had finally gotten the better of him. Or was it the intense sensation that had just burnt through his mind? Regardless, he slumped back against the tree and closed his eyes.

The icy chill of water drenching every inch of him promptly interrupted his sleep. It chilled deep to the bone, cleansing the thick blood that clung to his skin and knocking the breath from his lungs. In a panic he gasped, choking heavily as he spluttered and spat from his aching jaw. The small glade was no longer shrouded in heavy darkness.

Dim lights illuminated the area faintly. The trees were tightly packed as they formed a natural barricade from the rest of the forest. A single lone tree in the centre to which his bindings anchored him to the floor stood tall and strong. Its roots emerged through the earth, grasping at everything in their path.

Five now stood before him, staring with great intent as if seeing a ghost from their past. Two he recognised immediately. The malformed arm buried deep into his chest stood furthest away, scars covering every inch of his exposed skin. His gaunt expression could have mistaken him for a ghoul or ghost by the more superstitious. His hair was rough, almost pale white. Stood next to him was the aggressor, clad in an old worn armour, the same sigil emblazoned across its chest. Faint but recognisable. Neither young nor old, his long black hair had been stretched tightly back and bound at the back of his head.

Two more stood further back within the shadows. His eyes were still blurred, unable to make any discernible features. The fifth, however, was clear as day. He knelt right in front of him. So close that he could feel the heat emanating from his body. He was old, grey-washed hair cut back short. By counting the wrinkles that rippled across his face he could almost tell his age, a few scars were sewn into his flesh hinted towards that of a battle-hardened warrior.

"Speak quick and don't lie to me," he said, his voice old and croaking, dulled by the countless wars he had been a part of, "How did you come to know those words?"

His hand was poised gently across his knee, worn and rough from the hilt of his sword.

"What?" replied Arturius, still aching from the beating he took earlier. The old man sighed heavily, containing such frustration that built within him.

"Quickly, you spoke a phrase to my man earlier, what was it?" he iterated, "What words did you speak of."

Arturius thought hard. His mind was still a tangled web of past and present he was trying to piece together. *"What words?"* he thought to himself. His mind couldn't quite catch the memory that was sprinting at the back of his head.

The words fell from his lips before he could even think of them, as though a voice inside his mind was controlling his actions. It was almost as if he was not as alone as he initially thought.

"In Unity lies strength," he repeated. It was a familiar sound that lay deep in the recesses of his memories. He tried so hard to understand the saying, where did it come from? How did he know it?

"In Duty lies Honour," replied the old man. He stared deeply at Arturius. The longer he stared, the older he appeared to grow, "What name do you go by, son?"

"Arturius, my name is Arturius," he replied, "or so I think to believe, with all that has happened before me as of late, I am truly unsure of that which I already know."

The old man grunted, caressing his cracked hands slowly; he did not break eyes with him as he sat there, still bound.

"Have you ever heard of the fallen kingdom?" he asked. His eyes never blinked, his stare was more than intimidating, it was heavy. That's when he saw it. Deep into the eyes of the old man, he saw not anger or rage, hate or evil. He saw pain. A type of pain that can consume a man filled with regret, a regret he could not yet see. It was as if his mind was whispering to him, a flicker here and secret there.

Arturius looked deeply back into his eyes. In their reflection he saw death and destruction. And the failure of one could not stop it.

"I have no memory of such a place," replied Arturius, "what is it? Could it be where my past lies? Please tell me I need to know of what history I may possess."

It seemed a while before the old man spoke once more, but alas he did so with great pride.

"Those words you spoke, that is the motto of the fallen kingdom, my kingdom," he said, the pain growing stronger behind his face as he fought to contain it, "Farrosia, land of the rising dawn and home to the greatest warriors and people seen since the fall of the north."

Despite all his efforts, he had no memory of such a place could not remember. Only fragments of memories lay active within his mind. A life, long since forgotten, buried deep within such a broken mind. He wanted answers, and now he had a way to get them.

"I want to know who I am," said Arturius, "I need to know who I was, where I am from and what my purpose is."

The old man looked deeply at him, thinking hard about the choice he now had to make, the huddled whispers from the others floating around. He could not hear what words they had to say but knew they were not good.

"You see, I have myself a rather large predicament here," said the old man, standing before him proud and tall "You are an anomaly, for I knew everyone within my kingdom, everyone," he paused, walking amongst his companions gracefully.

"Yet I don't know you," he continued, "You know of the words carved deep into our lineage, yet you do not know our name, you show up in the middle of nowhere and just so happen to stumble upon our encampment, anyone else in my position would pass you off as a spy, perhaps even an assassin waiting to bury your blade deep within my back."

"Please, I just want answers," replied Arturius, "I am no spy or assassin, I only came here at the behest of the boy I saved, Silas asked me to accompany him here.",

He stared deeply into the eyes of the old man, pleading in a language of sight and silence. Pivoting himself against the tree, he drew in closer, edging more and more until the bindings pulled him back. A few more murmurs came from the back of the glade, a single shadow whispering in the ears of the old man, softly. It was a familiar voice that graced his presence, young and refreshed.

"And you can vouch for him?" said the old man, "You tell me he is to be trusted?"

"Yes," replied a voice deep in the darkness, "He saved my life."

"Then be it on your head," said the old man, "And free him from those binds."

*~ "By the Gods, such death and miasma warrants no affliction such as this!" ~*

## CHAPTER V: A VENGEFUL OCCUPATION

The binds dropped to the floor–a swift slice of steel saw to it. His wrists swelled once they released the constriction, a torrent of blood streamed down his face, dripping to the ground as tears of red. One of his captors threw a cloth at his feet, walking away silently in disgust. Arturius dusted it carefully and pressed it to his face, soaking up the rivers of red.

Many had retired through the archway that led away from the glade. Only two remained before him. The old man approached him; he was still cautious, but no longer saw to him as a threat. He stood tall and stout, time had eroded away at his features leaving him old and grey. Much of his armour had been chipped and cracked. Hastily repaired with whatever tacks and trinkets could be scavenged; though it was clear by its upkeep that it was instilled a level of pride that could only emerge from the mind of a stalwart warrior. His tattered cape flowed gently in the breeze, displaying the same sigil as before; a phoenix clutching upon a sword.

"My apologies for your earlier treatment," he said, "With such dark times upon us one can't be too sure as to the true nature of those who stumble upon our encampment. I have dealt with many assassins, vagabonds and brigands who have attempted to claim my head. And all of them I sent swiftly onwards to meet with their Gods."

He looked up and down at the beaten Arturius.

"You're a mess," he quipped, "Seems like my men have done a stellar job of rolling out the welcome party."

Arturius tried gathered his thoughts, the throbbing bruises aside his temples didn't better his thoughts, leaving a painfully dull sensation ringing through his head.

"Who are you?" said Arturius, curious yet intimidated, "After such a warm reception you provided it is the least you can explain to me."

The old man grunted, raising a brow at the demands of the stranger before him.

"I suppose I have no reason to distrust you at the current state of affairs. Very well," said the old man, he straightened his stance lifting his chin up high and proud, "I am Selwyn Alvast, Captain of the Farrosian first legion, second sword of dawn, what you see before you is my company, those who will continue the fight against the eradication of my people."

*"Such pride!"* thought Arturius. It was as if the old man had transformed, such a presence sent a shiver down his spine.

Selwyn glanced back before speaking again.

"I know you have already met young Silas here," he gestured to the small silhouette loitering at the back within the darkness. The young Silas stepped forward. He was pale and weak, sapped of his strength as he hobbled forward. Arturius exhaled, a sigh of relief that echoed around. It placed a small smirk upon Selwyn's face.

"Am I glad to see you," he sighed, the weight of his worries lifted from him, easing away all the tension built up within him, "I feared you dead. Lost back within the darkness of the forest."

Silas chuckled to himself.

"Well, if it weren't for you, there is no doubt in my mind that I would still lay upon that carriage, just more dead," Silas said laughing, "Either that or lying dead in a ditch with a Rekeshi arrow burrowed within my back."

"I feel we both would have found ourselves lay upon those marshes," said Arturius, "If it weren't for you I would have still been wandering amongst the dead. And who know what would have happened to me then."

Arturius thought back to the carriage, the mutilated bodies strewn across the field, many had the same sigil emblazoned upon them.

"When I awoke there were many bodies marked with the same sigil," he said pointing to the phoenix chiselled across Selwyn's breastplate, "That is the sigil of your people is it not?"

It was then the realisation came into full effect. He could sense it deep within Selwyn's eyes, sorrow and pain and regret.

"Hmm, it would seem you're not as useless as we previously thought" replied Selwyn, "A keen eye and an aptitude for detail makes for a mighty skill. Yes, that was the sigil of my people, it represents rising from the ashes of ruin to become a mighty kingdom once more."

"Was?"

Arturius sank deeper into his mind.

"Then that would mean those that I saw upon the marshes, they were Farrosian? They were your kin?" said Arturius, "What happened to them?"

A single tear ran down the side of Selwyn's face, brushing between the roughly cut stubble that adorned his chin. He tried to conceal it behind his toughened exterior, not wanting to show weakness. So quickly had his pride vanished before them.

"They were what remained of the Farrosia, the last of my people to escape from the purge," said Selwyn.

Arturius shifted his feet. He could see Silas, his head hanging as he sobbed quietly.

"What happened?" replied Arturius.

Such genocide had occurred around him, and yet he knew nothing of its execution, its motives or reason.

"I had heard wind of a group of Farrosians holed up within the old keep of Farahorn to the east of the Corpori mountains," said Selwyn, "As was my duty as the second sword of the dawn, I fell upon me as the last of the high command to protect our legacy. I rode out to meet with them post haste, however, I could not have imagined what I was about to face."

He folded his arms tightly, not to intimidate, but more to hide the small tremble in his hands. Arturius's eyes were very observant, for they did not miss a thing–even in this darkness.

"What did you find?" said Arturius eagerly,

"The group turned out to be nearly a thousand strong. Men, women, children," replied Selwyn, "I couldn't believe my eyes, I never thought so many had escaped from the slaughter, I truly felt blessed. There was more than enough to form a substantial force again, rebuild the Farrosian grand army.",

Arturius edged closer, his heart beating faster as the story unravelled.

"They were neither broken nor fearful," Selwyn continued, "The problem was however, that they had sought shelter far too close to the enemy, the Rekeshi border was but a few miles to the Northwest of them. I could risk them to fall into the enemy hands once more, I needed their strength and numbers."

He paused as he raised his hand to his mouth, cupping his chin before continuing.

"And what were your plans?" asked Arturius, "To bring them into the forest?"

Arturius glanced upon his surroundings.

"The trees here seem too tightly packed; you would never manage to get them all within."

"No, goodness no," replied Selwyn, "The plan was never to setup within Hollowclaw. Far to the east lies the old Drangviri fortress of Var t'uth, a crumbing fortress from the old era, though still heavily fortified and positioned highly strategically. It was there that we decided would be best to shelter and rebuild the Farrosian lineage. Then maybe one day we would once again have the strength to reclaim our homeland and thrive once more."

He spoke with grand passion and pride, his spirit lifting at the thought of a restoring his life once more. However, Arturius couldn't help but feel that his duty to his kingdom and will to rebuild would overshadow his true protection of his people.

Again, his face sank as the story continued, an emotional journey of twists and turns.

"We were betrayed!" Selwyn muttered, gritting his teeth as he hid away the pain, "We don't know why or by who, however, only those you see in this forest are what remains of my people, once a kingdom, now a rabble no fewer than ten."

He shuddered to consider what they had endured at the hands of these genocidal maniacs, butchering anyone with ties to the old Farrosian kingdom. It would appear that death was the most generous of gifts that the Rekeshi would serve, otherwise you may end up bound for the dark void of nothing. It was unclear how many had been captured, not that capture would have been an option for them.

"Why such persecution for you and your people?" he asked, "Surely to broker peace with such might would prove more fruitful to a rising power?"

He could feel his heart beating to the drums in his head, getting faster and faster as time grew on.

"It all began 7 years ago," replied Selwyn, "My kingdom was proud. A noble and strong dynasty that shone as a beacon to all. Far and wide a symbol of the peace that we lived in."

Selwyn paced himself–never breaking his gaze with Arturius, a part of him still trying to read his newly acquired 'prisoner'.

"Farrosia was seen as the beacon to the realm. A promise of peace and prosperity so long as the Farrosian line endured. My King, Lord protector of the Farrosian people, the realm and all who shone beneath the white phoenix, Kyrius second of his name sought peace with the Rekeshi, a bitter rivalry that had endured through time."

"The other kingdoms were closely allied to us," Selwyn continued, "We were seen as a beacon of law and order across the realm. Centred at its heart was what allowed our influence to flourish and grow. After all, we had the bloodline of Farrosia at our helm, strong under the monarch Kyrius, second of his name. A line that would endure. Or so I thought."

"What happened?" asked Arturius, "If such a line were strong then did it not endure? Surely such a legacy could not be so easily extinguished?"

The burden of truth weighed a heavy toll upon the old captains heart. Even now the wounds of his losses, though old, still cut as deep as the day they were cast.

"We had brokered peace with all but one kingdom of the realm, Rekesh, for they were a powerful and mighty kingdom. Its warriors as fearless as the night and strong through the old blood of their ancestors."

"The Rekeshi felt that Farrosia's influence had grown too far and wide," interjected Silas, "Through their own paranoia they saw such peace as a cloak of endangerment towards their own people and way of life."

"Indeed they did," said Selwyn, "Many wars broke out between ourselves and the Emperor of the Night. And when the night of the realm was at its darkest, thus began the war of attrition. A brutal and bloody conflict that suffered for some many decades. That was until the distrustful emperor Villius fell in battle, leaving his only heir Gared to ascend as emperor of the Rekeshi."

"I am assuming that wars only grew bloodier from that day?" asked Arturius, "To lose one so close I could only assume would bolster a vengeance within the new emperor that could not quench even the most bloodthirsty of warriors."

Selwyn shook his head.

"On the contrary, the exact opposite occurred. The new emperor had seen first hand the horrors of the war his father had started. In his own wisdom he sought peace and prosperity for all that dwelled this realm. And so ended the long and bloody war." Said Selwyn, "Although in our joyous state, we deigned to see the darkness that was slowly creeping our way."

Though the darkness of the glade concealed much within its vicinity, Arturius could still feel the tension that emanated from the two that stood before him. The young boy, quivered at the mere mention of such a darkness.

"We heard news so suddenly of a new being to walk through the halls of the Black Keep, a being that controlled an ancient evil long believed to be but a mere myth." Said Selwyn, "And in one fell swoop, the throne of the Night was Usurped. However, something then happened that we did not anticipate. For this new monarch, this new imperator, reached out to us. He extended the olive branch of peace, seeking to create new relations with ourselves. Something I wished to have queried much sooner on."

His hand rested upon the pommel of his sword–poking out from beneath his cloak. It was worn down; the gold had faded, leaving only minor fragments that glinted in the light.

"In all my years of service I have fought, bled, and suffered with my enemy. Though what came next cut wounds deeper than any knife that has ever met with my flesh before."

Arturius edged closer, his heart beating faster and harder than ever before. Somehow his mind seem to focus on this usurper, as though in some way his path had once crossed. Selwyn continued to pace about the glade, his eyes occasionally flicked to meet with the young Silas as he stood back listening.

"My king was elated. This alliance of Night and Dawn could finally bring about a peace that would ensure the realm finally becomes a haven to any and all." Muttered

Selwyn, it was clear by his voice that such an ordeal was too good to be true.

Selwyn fumbled with his belt, brandishing a short dagger. Magnificent in craft, embossed with the finest jewels and gold from he could have laid his eyes upon. Its jagged edges looked sharper than the night, cut through streams of light as they shone through it. He held it before him; the jewels sparkling with a magnificent brilliance.

"His gift, was this." he said, "Ironic isn't it, a dagger announced for peace. It was more like an insult to our own intelligence. For even then we did not see what was to come. The lord protector, my equal, an arrogant and foolish man begged and begged my King to accept such an offering. A request he soon accepted."

"I fear that I already know the conclusion to your journey" whispered Arturius, "though I find myself incapable of averting my ears, I must know what happened. Surely one man cannot bring about the fall of a kingdom!"

"He was no man" muttered Silas, "He was a monster. No worse, a monster can still be tamed."

Selwyn nodded.

"Exactly what many of us thought," replied Selwyn, "How could such a man exact such terrifying power upon us, but alas we only discovered what had happened once the dust had settled."

The men stared each other down, one telling the story of his downfall, the other seeking the story of his own.

"I'm guessing the diplomacy failed before it had even begun?" replied Arturius.

"It was a bloodbath," said Selwyn, "Before we knew what was to be it had already happened, during the slaughter I found this dagger protruding from the King's back, embedded so deep it was no wonder it did not cleave him in two."

Selwyn paused, he had stopped pacing and perched himself atop a felled tree, pushing down upon the pommel of his sword–keeping it from catching at the stump.

"At the hands of the Usurper?" asked Arturius.

Selwyn shook his head, looking down at his feet as he gripped his sword tighter.

"Our very own lord protector in his last dishonourable act plunged the dagger into the king he swore his life unto." Hissed Selwyn, "The coward had turned to our enemy."

"It was a dark day for the realm" muttered Silas.

"The darkest and most chaotic sorcery I have ever seen, as if plucked from the Khaos of old itself, burning black and abyssal." Said Selwyn, "It tore through our ranks, burning man, woman and child with no discrimination."

Strangely enough, this was not uncommon to Arturius. The beast that chased them to the forest was brimming with this energy. Could it be that this was a creature of the Masked One?

"Tell me more," beckoned Arturius, "What else unfolded upon that fateful night? Perhaps it shall restore the memories that forsook me."

"Within the fray was Etheldra, the first sword of the dawn, my mentor and close friend," said Selwyn "She mounted a heroic last stand. An attempt to buy us enough time to evacuate as many as we could. By the gods she was strong, even as the blood filled her lungs and choked the life from she continued to fight. The strength of man tenfold as she bested scores of Rekeshi elites. By her side as though her very shadow was the Wolf knight although once the fight was over, both of them had disappeared, never to be seen again."

Behind his eyes, the genuine pain of his past was apparent. He waited for the rest of the story to unfold, but it soon became clear that it was to be difficult retelling.

"How many of you survived the purge?" questioned Arturius.

"It is hard to say," replied Selwyn, "We were scattered across the realm, our home destroyed and nowhere to go, though I focussed on finding survivors it was to no avail."

Arturius gritted his teeth. Too many similarities had fallen before him, answers that he sorely wished for. Though he knew it deep down in his heart to remain silent, he felt compelled to speak.

"There is something I have seen as of late," said Arturius, "Back upon the marshes, a creature of darkest night and blackest day emerged from the swamp, I saw it first hidden within the reflection of the waters, then it became clear that it was not merely an apparition."

The old captains' eyes widened. He had perked up his interest within the matter, and his facial expressions made it all the while clear.

"And why did you not speak of this earlier?" Selwyn queried, his face caught between shock and anger.

"Fear," replied Arturius, "I did not truly know if all was a fabrication of my mind. And besides, I was not given the warmest of welcomes."

Selwyn grunted, nodding gently before speaking.

"Tell me more," he asked calmly, "Why is it that young Silas here was not made privy to such an event?"

"Silas was already unconscious upon the ground," replied Arturius, "Our pursuers saw to that before I hastily sent them on their way, the creature was cloaked in shadow and bore no flesh. With its presence the sky darkened and blotted out all the light, piercing me with a great uneasy feeling."

Arturius fell silent, reminiscing about the encounter once more as vividly as it was the first time. He carried on speaking.

"I watched as it drained the life out of our final pursuer," he said coldly, "I watched as it burnt his very flesh to the bone leaving nothing but cinders and ash to fall from him before it drew out a dark and blackened apparition from his mouth."

Such was the relief that washed over him, despite all his strength he struggled to hold back secrets from even the strangers that stood before him. It was as though a force was refraining him to speak, a behest of his own will. He could see by the expressions that grew across Selwyn and Silas that this was no mere attack, nor was it of a creature common to those parts.

"And this creature, it came for you?" asked Selwyn urgently, "Did it touch you? Did it to anything besides pursue?"

"Nay," replied Arturius, "Though it gave a chase of frightening speed, however, it would not follow us beyond the boundary of the forest, it was strange, as though a force was stopping it from entering, it wasn't soon after that it disappeared, taking with it the darkened skies and blacked floor."

"That is all?" said Selwyn, "Did it make any attempt to communicate?"

"No, it didn't," replied Arturius, "Why would a creature such as that speak to that of which it hunts?"

Selwyn remained quiet, looking back at Silas as they communicated once more with the whites of their eyes.

"You know what it is, don't you?" said Arturius, "What is it? You must tell me; you may have more of the answers to the questions I still hold!"

"How close did you come by it?" asked Selwyn.

"I got close enough," replied Arturius.

"Tell me," said Selwyn, "What happened?"

Arturius composed himself for a moment–it wasn't easy recalling such an ordeal. The mind is a delicate flower–nurtured and it will blossom, plucked and it will wither and die.

"It was strange," said Arturius, "As though all that was beautiful had been sapped from the world leaving only pain and anguish, when I looked deep into its eyes I saw pain, much pain and sorrow, it was almost as though it was looking back upon me scared and frightened, I know it sounds ludicrous, not a moment earlier it would have torn me apart."

He paused briefly. A whisper echoed around the glade, caught in the wind that flowed gently. It muttered the same phrase repeatedly, again and again. A calm and nurturing voice it was.

"The Empty Throne calls," he muttered,

A wave of dread came billowing from the face of Selwyn. He did not no one could turn as white as he did without first visiting the realm of death. He waited for him to respond, yet the silence only continued to deepen. Arturius could see the weakness bearing down on him, grasping him gently before he stumbled to the floor.

"What did you just say?" he asked, "How did you know of such a thing!"

A confused feeling came over Arturius. Had they not heard the winds, the voice that whispered oh so quiet.

"I heard it just now," said Arturius, "It came in the breeze, a voice softer than air, did you not hear it?"

"By the gods, then it's true," replied Selwyn, tormented by some unknown darkness within him.

"What is true?" asked Arturius, "What is the Empty Throne?"

"The Empty Throne has awoken, and with it comes only death, destruction and Khaos."

A chill that had nothing to do with the cold passed through him–freezing him to the core.

"I have heard that before," said Arturius,

"Heard what?" asked Silas. He had been remarkably quiet through the entire ordeal, only now stepping in to ease the pale Selwyn from further aching of the mind.

"Before I awoke, I recall having dreamed a dark and terrible dream, a dream that felt more pain, fear and dread felt as real as it would if awake."

Pain shuddered through his chest, a burning sensation that passed from his chest and down his limp arm.

"Though I cannot remember all that transpired, there is some that my mind has retained," he continued,

"Such as?" beckoned Silas,

"There was a land, shrouded in eternal darkness," said Arturius, "Shadows that crept through the darkness, a great feeling of dread and terror that plagued the mind, and there was mention of this Empty Throne, though in a language all but forgotten it would seem."

The old captain exchanges a glance with him. Much of the colour had returned to him, bearing new life into the age-old man.

"And you have no knowledge of such a thing," asked Selwyn hoarsely, "No memory of a throne, or shadows, or Khaos?"

Arturius shook his head.

"This is the first I have ever come by such a tale," replied Arturius.

"Oh my boy," said Selwyn condescendingly, "You have no idea what you have awoken to, forget fairy tales and stories my lad, for this hear is more real than the ground you stand upon."

Arturius remained silent, perturbed by the words spoken to him.

"Yet, there may still be hope for us yet," said Selwyn, Arturius felt his chest tighten, his fingers trembled slightly as he tried to hide them from view, "Listen and listen carefully, there is much of your path that is shrouded by darkness, I may not know your past but I know of what your future will bring," he looked around making sure that no prying eyes or sharp ears were joining them.

"All will become clear in time, but for me to tell you now will change that which has not yet come to be, as of now I trust you, show me that you are the one I have been waiting for these past seven years!"

Coming closer to grasping the mysteries of his path, he nodded, a decision that could easily bring upon him a downfall into darkness. He decided to put his full trust into a man he had known only a few hours. Yet somehow seemed to have known for a lifetime.

"For now, you must keep this all to yourself," cautioned Selwyn, "As of now, only the three of us are to know about this, do you both understand?"

He looked to Silas, who in turn responded with a gentle nod. His gaze averted to Arturius. A serious glare forced a nod out of him too, unsure whether in agreement or just out of fear.

"Come then, an introduction is to be made,"

From beyond the glade, Arturius could see the light more clearly. It made the trees look gentler. Alive. The three strode from the glade. A twisting tunnel of darkness led towards the light ahead.

"This way," said Selwyn, disappearing into the intensely bright light, followed by Silas. All eyes had since darted towards Arturius, judging his every move as he hobbled into the warmth of the hidden encampment.

*~ "It won't be long now; the path to our goal has finally unveiled" ~*

## CHAPTER VI: OVERTURE OF DARKNESS

It felt to be an eternity of wandering through the darkness. Relief overcame him when he could feel the warm glow of the light smother his skin. Most of Selwyn's retinue had already made themselves comfortable, continuing with their duties as nothing had changed.

As the trio emerged from the darkness, all eyes drew before him. It was expected after all, a stranger with no allegiance would stumble upon such a hidden camp, all the while having survived what many of theirs did not. Some would have called it suspicious, an anomaly of mysterious origins. But not Arturius, he had seen enough in his brief journey to make the impossible possible.

What he did not expect, however, was the mix of emotions that stared before him–one would have assumed hostility all around. A slight nudge spurred his legs forward into the wolfs den. He looked at the blood and dirt that stained his clothes. What kind of impression would he make before them in such a sorry state? One man scoffed in the corner–it was apparent he wanted to be heard.

"You are a fool to trust him, Selwyn," he barked, "It will bring us nothing but ruin and misfortune."

Selwyn looked upon him with great contempt.

"Easy Dovan," Selwyn replied, "Whilst I still draw breath know that my word is the law around here!"

He was a relatively large man, clothed in a darkened mail that yet again bearing the mark of Farrosia, his long dark hair tied back tightly behind his head. His was a darker complexion than his companies counterparts, but no more scarred than the others.

Another spoke up quickly, his ragged breath crunching through the air filled with anger and resentment.

"He speaks the truth Selwyn," he said, his eyes were fixed upon the arrows perched within his hands. The tone of his voice was calm and collected, though a hint of prejudice fluttered through every now and then.

"You welcome this filthy stranger into our camp. Low born, a peasant mucked in the dirt of his kind. Just look at him, not fit to serve the boots he has no doubt licked, how can you be so naive to the situation? … he is most definitely a –."

"Enough Robbard!" snapped Selwyn, it was enough to quell the insubordination flowing through the camp, "You speak as though you are still suckling from the teat of that overbearing woman who made you believe that you are better than the rest of the world. If I say I trust him, then he is trusted, so quench your pettiness and remove that silver spoon so brazenly wedge upon your arse."

A small chuckle tittered from some of the others around the camp. The young man, now known as Robbard, plunged his arrows deep into the ground before storming away from the camp. Tall and stout, a man of more noble upbringing it would seem, judging by the clean-cut, remarkably groomed complexion of his face. Not to mention his disposition towards those of more impure blood. His armour was more finely polished and intact than the others within the vicinity. To have such pride in his appearance even in such dire circumstances only bolstered his mark of nobility. He paused before breaking through the line of trees at the furthest edge, refusing to look back upon the others as he did so.

"So long as the blood in my veins gleam the golden dew of my forefathers, I will never allow the likes of him to be with us," he muttered sarcastically, "Sir."

He was further accompanied by Dovan spitting in anger as he muttered incoherently to himself.

"Does anyone else have anything to add?" questioned Selwyn, his posture firm, only lessened by the sarcastic undertone of his words. Everyone remained silent, only the faint bristling of the trees that followed Dovan and Robbard into the darkness could be heard.

The others in the clearing appeared much more at ease than their counterparts, still hesitant, but not hostile. He was unsure what to do. Such a warm welcome left him rather apprehensive at first, but his aching body and grumbling stomach told him what he needed.

After a not so long moment, a young man came bustling up next to him, brimming with excitement.

"So, you're the one Silas picked up in the marshes?" he asked, "Tell me what happened? How many Rekeshi did you slay? What was it like? the dead, the battle? How fares your sword skills? …"

An unnerving torrent of questions flooded Arturius. One of the others interrupted quickly. The younger man showed similar physical attributes to Dovan, slightly darker skin, albeit without such scars to spoil his young and handsome face. His garbs were tattered and he appeared to wear no armour of sorts, perhaps his age is what held back such a privilege around here.

"Easy Jorik, leave the newcomer be," said another, "You know your brother will beat you into the ground for talking to him."

"Fuck off, Karlan, I am my own man. Dovan doesn't control me!" replied Jorik, his attention shifted to the individual leant against a nearby tree. Scraping at a half-complete block grasped firmly in his hands, chipping away as he flicked the wooden flakes onto the ground. He was bound tightly back a blackened leather, forcing out his slim yet athletic features. Long dark brown hair concealed most of his face, though leaving just enough free for him to concentrate upon his craft.

"Ye little shit, haven't you got duties to be attending to, boots to polish, armour to clean, balls to fondle," said

Karlan with a faint smirk. He pointed his knife toward Selwyn, the old captain was deep in observation over a worn. Jorik glared intensely at him, his younger manners acting defiantly towards such orders. He thrust himself away from the conversation, darting towards Selwyn in a strop.

"Sorry about him, he gets a little excited when fresh blood walks in," said Karlan. He looked up and down the battered Arturius, "Although it looks like you really are the fresh blood in this instance."

He laughed hard, smacking the tender back of Arturius.

"Never the less, it's good to have someone else to talk to amongst this rabble," he continued, "Between you and I the conversations were getting rather stale."

The '*minor*' interrogation still dazed Arturius from earlier. It was such a relief to encounter a less hostile approach by the unfamiliar figure that stood before him.

"Names Karlan, it has dealt me much luck along my travels. Especially with the ladies. You must be the mysterious survivor of the marshes they have all been talking about, tell me, did you get to wet your tongue a bit?" asked Karlan.

Arturius looked confused.

"Wet my tongue?" he replied,

"Aye, wet your tongue, popped a vein? Bashed skulls? Penetrated the rabble?" Karlan said mockingly.

"You mean killed?" said Arturius shamefully.

"Well, well, well, I do so believe you have tasted the bloodlust of our inner beasts" replied Karlan, "Tell me how many?"

"Three…"

"Impressive, will have to keep an eye out for more for you to slay, oh mighty slayer of the Rekesh!" bellowed Karlan.

He was a tall man, towering leagues above his own. Scuffled hair drooped down to his shoulders, split and dry as they waved in the gentle forest breeze. He looked much more different from any of the others. His eyes burst with darkened tones, whilst his face shimmered with a moonlight glisten. His darker attitude to the living sent shivers down Arturius's spine.

"So what name do you bear?"

"The name's Arturius," he replied.

"Good to meet you Arturius," replied Karlan, "Welcome to the resistance, or what remains of it, anyway."

Karlan dropped his woodwork and moved over to the gentle fire, perching himself on one of the felled logs that lay next to it.

"Come," he beckoned, "Join me, I wish to know more of yourself."

He patted on the space beside him with one hand, stoking the flames of the campfire with the other.

Confused and wary, Arturius hesitantly made his way over. The warmth of the fire reddened his skin as it expelled the cold that had burrowed within.

"So, tell me then, how you ended up with a band of low life's such as us?" asked Karlan, "I suspect it was not of your own volition."

He burrowed his teeth into the smallest morsel of meat he had seen–more bone than meat.

"It's hard to say really," replied Arturius, "One moment there was darkness, deep and endless darkness, then I awoke to the stench of death and blood, a field of corpses littered around me."

"So, in the wrong place at the wrong time then it would seem, meat?" laughed Karlan, his loud bellowing voice drew the attention of the others, briefly distracting them from their duties before they continued.

Arturius looked down at the slither of meat dripping between Karlan's fingers. God knows what poor decrepit creature it came from. Though the hunger rises with the deep confines of his belly cared not of its source.

"Please," replied Arturius. Though it was more out of politeness than desperation.

"I like you Arturius," said Karlan, "May I call you Art?"

"Sure, I guess," replied Arturius. He bit down into the charred flesh within his hands. It was dry, tasteless and burnt. It would seem that the residents of this camp cared not for quality and more for the most edible they could acquire.

Confusion couldn't quite explain what he was experiencing right now, from the hostile beating earlier to this rather pleasant encounter. *"Who are these people?"* he thought to himself. *"How long have they hidden within the forest?"* judging by the lack of running water and discomforting smell it was clear that they had resided here for some time. A faint odour hung deeply within the air. A scent of death and decay. Swarms of flies would occasionally land upon the armour of the company, feasting upon the faint stains of blood that smothered the surfaces. It was clear that hygiene was far from the thoughts of the people surrounding him.

"Well *Art*, stick by me and you'll have all that you have ever wanted in life," said Karlan, "After all, we are but the resistance, should we fail it will be pretty easy to sneak into another society and live out our lives again. Earn a few coin, Bed a few harlots. Live the life of royalty eh?"

By now some more hesitant members of the ragtag resistance had eased their worries upon seeing this outsider more humanely. Aside from Karlan there was Selwyn, Jorik and Silas. He had not much of a warm experience with the others.

A rather feeble and twisted thing approached him, scurrying painfully in a contorted limp as each step looked like a struggle. Even Arturius winced in pain as he hobbled towards him.

"Well, you don't look much like a Rekeshi assassin, teehee" he croaked, his voice garbled with the pain of a dying animal–He looked dreadfully dead. Missing most of his right arm, half of his left leg had been replaced with many wooden contraptions and his face looked as though someone had dipped it in a vast array of acid–melted and malformed into a hideous beast. As he limped over to Arturius his nerves twitched and spasmed with a faint glimmer of psychological damage buried deep beneath the surface.

"But if the young master Silas trusts you, then I suppose that can be well enough for me" he continued.

His malformed and twisted body creaked as it sat down beside him. Arturius watched as he reached for some of the gruel simmering atop the campfire, his hand tremored as it stretch out above the burning flames. A gruesomely frightful sight at first as the withered man drew his sleeve back across his mottled skin, then the pity washed over much of the disgust. Arturius felt shamed with himself, he knew not of the history behind such a person yet felt compelled to judge his appearance in abhorrence.

After some time, he had forgotten his stares hadn't ceased, quickly obscuring his view to hide his embarrassment.

"Some would s-say beauty is only f-found on the inside," said the malformation, "Though m-most people would say that I-I'm the exception. Don't w-worry, I've learned to live with the s-stares."

He quickly reached for a small vial of greyish liquid conceal beneath his garments, quenching draining its viscous contents down his gullet as he struggled to swallow it.

"Ah much better" he hushed, "Do forgive me, my body is not what it once was. The concoction helps with the receptors in my brain, long ago they were damaged irreparably. This helps maintain the focus for a while, stops the stammers and twitches."

"Im sorry" replied Arturius, "It was improper of me to-."

The Withered man raised his hand.

"Fret not young-un. It's not the first time my appearance has caused such disconcerting stares. Most pass me off as a vagabond, Undesirable, wretched castaway or worse. But for you Ozark shall be my name."

"Ozark, I'll remember that" replied Arturius, "you have certainly made an impression upon me to say the least."

"I get that a lot" laughed Ozark, "besides looking like this for as long as I have, kind of makes you immune to the stares and judgment. It defines me as much as it pains me."

As the fire grew colder the spark between the grew brighter. They sat there for some hours talking back and forth–about anything and everything. They laughed. They cursed. They bonded. Ozark had filled him in on the rest of the retinue. Of course, there was Selwyn, the undisputed leader he had been here from the very beginning, fighting back with anything and everything he had at his disposal. Even his bare hands at one point, naked and dirty upon the streets of Vastern. Silas, it turned out, was a keen horologist, herbalist and scholar–it would definitely explain his quick knowledge that suppressed his untimely demise.

There were the brothers two; Dovan the elder and Jorik the younger. Their personalities the personification of opposites as it would seem–No doubt because of some troubled past they do not wish to reveal. The others that stormed out along with Dovan was Robbard, a nasty piece of work according to Ozark, yet a masterfully skilled marksman capable of shooting with deadly precision–He could gracefully snipe the flees off the back of a stray dog from a thousand feet away. In other words as deadly as they come. His attitude and mannerisms were built up from years of spoilt riches, being the eldest son to the old nobility of Farrosia, his wealth and title stripped from his grasp before ever tasting its sweet nectar. Finally, there was Burak, a hulking beast of a man with the strength of an ox behind him–he knew it not to be wise to get on his worst side.

The night had gone quickly, leaving the flames of the fire now a simmering pile of ash and cinders.

"There is someone else I should mention to you, however, it would be unwise of you to pursue any conversation with him for now," said Ozark, he slowly but surely turned, his movement was difficult until he could silently gesture to the man sitting in the farthest reaches of the den.

"Over there, mulling in the darkened corner of the forest, you see him?" whispered Ozark.

Arturius carefully peered over his shoulder. Sat deep in the darkness–so easy to have missed him–was a lone figure deep within thought. Blanketed in dense cloud of abyssal nightmare like the very smoke rising from the fire's remains.

"That there is Garton, a humble man once you get to know him, but a damn temper if ever you saw," said Karlan, "Though troubled doesn't even scratch upon the surface of his story."

It didn't take long before Arturius could see that the mist surrounding him, was him. His body was broken and cursed; the many features of his face covered by the mist concealing him from reality. Where his body was missing, a faint aura of burning red shimmered, as if holding him together by some cruel twist of fate.

His chest tightened at the sight of the smoke, suppressing his desire to breathe as he watched it dissipated into nothing. Garton's ghastly gaze met with his own, sending shivers down his spine before he promptly averted his gaze back at the cinders of the campfire.

"What happened to him?" asked Arturius. He thought back to the appearance of the shadow creature encounter from earlier, its essence the same as that of Garton. Could it be he survived an encounter with such a creature? *"No,"* he thought to himself, Selwyn would never have so forcefully requested its sighting to remain in the dark.

"I'm afraid that it is not my story to tell there," replied Ozark, "Best left for another time, or until he finds it within what remains of his heart to find trust within you."

Ozark shuffled his warped body to better relieve his aching comfort,

Never had he believed that such a rag-tag bunch of misfits could find such solitude in one and other company–He knew there and then that he would fit right in.

"No doubt you are curious as to my current appearance," Ozark asked,

He panicked, deep down he had wanted to know what could possibly have left him so malformed, yet his shame overcame his desire to probe. He squirmed slightly, trying to think up an excuse and show restraint to his prying mind.

"I-uh … it's like-," Ozark interrupted him,

"No need to show restraint, everyone is curious when they pass their first glance upon me."

Arturius swallowed, waiting for the story to unfold, unsure how to respond to the frightening ordeal he had gone through.

"You see. Despite all the others here, I am not actually a Farrosian," he paused, a slow but sure smile glimmered across his heavily scarred face, "I am Rekeshi."

Arturius's brow rose significantly, *"Rekeshi!"* he thought to himself, *"The very empire they are in open rebellion against".*

"How did you end on the opposing side?" he questioned; Ozark's face dropped suddenly–it was hard to tell through the thick abnormalities strewn across his face.

"Opposing side you say," he hushed, "For me, there is no opposing side. The day my kingdom fell to that bastard usurper was the day we stopped being ruled by a true Rekeshi."

Ozark's eyes grew dull, the pain of his former way of life expunged from existence as he recounted the fateful days from his past.

"You see unlike the tales and myths that portray us as cruel and vicious snakes, my people were peaceful," said Ozark, proud and triumphant, "Yes there were wars, bloodshed and lives lost, but you name me any other kingdom, empire or state that not partake in the blood of war, staining their hands with the innocent of the realm, even the proud and noble Farrosians have a history of deceit and blood that would shock all to the core."

His words rung truthfully; no kingdom could possibly have survived until this point to not have blood dripping from them.

"What happened?" he asked,

"I was royal advisor to the emperor, Grand Advisor my title within the great empire was anointed to me, a title I held with honour for 19 long years."

He looked deeply into the cinders. Small flickers of flame emerging through the ash licked his face with tepid heat.

"All was well in the empire, until that darkest of days when the Masked One strode through the doors of our great halls, I knew when I first laid eyes on him that the darkness that followed him was that of true evil, an inherent evil that is born when one comes to be, an evil that cannot be expunged."

A shudder went through Arturius, a shudder he could not explain.

"Did he do this to you?" he said, gripping at the wood he sat upon until it splintered.

"He did, but not quite yet," replied Ozark, "For you see he was cunning and manipulative, all the worst of the of *someone* condensed into one being, he didn't have to do anything he knew that with the right push, we would unleash it upon ourselves."

The anger within Ozark's eyes met with the pity of his own.

"I told them," muttered Ozark, "I told them all to cast him out, banish him from the realm, seal him away from the light of day, but what use were my words with the promise of power unimaginable to all, the day my homeland fell was the day they foolishly welcomed him with open arms."

Ozark let out a garbled sigh. The tale was proving too much for the exhausted man to relive.

"When the dust had settled, and the power was truly seized, then he sought to have his way with me, the only one who saw through his tricks, the only one defied his manipulation," Ozark snapped angrily, "They broke whatever bone in my body they could find, setting it improperly as it healed, they poured concoction after concoction upon my skin and watched its melt away my features, they would beat me within an inch of my life only to stop before it was snuffed away from me, he found death to be too easy for me and wanted me to watch through my failures, the world he was about to shape, bend to his will."

He halted, choking on his own breath. Clambering to regain control of his own body.

"What force could he have behind him to contend with the power of your empire?" ask Arturius, "What banner did he fly behind him to declare such wanton destruction."

"That's the irony of it all I suppose, for he was just one man," Ozark chuckled to himself, painfully, "One man brought an empire to its knees, seizing it for his own twisted gains, he poisoned the mind of our emperor feeding him lies, manipulating him into submission, and that was when he struck."

Arturius looked deep into the embers. He could see the story unfold as it was told, black and grey as the breeze brushed aside the ash.

"He unleashed a power that I never have seen before in my life, I had heard rumours, stories of what he commanded, I believed it all to have been legend until then," said Ozark, his eyes turned cold as he relived the horrors of the past. He wanted to ask but couldn't bring the words to say it, merely a stare asked the question–for it showed fear of the answer.

"The Khaos!" he whispered, extinguishing what remained of the lifeless flames before them, "The living embodiment of the fear of the Gods, feeling only malice, cruelty, pain and anguish."

No matter where he looked, the repetition of the Khaos emerged like smoke from a fire forever finding its way back to him.

"What is the Khaos?" he asked, "No matter where I go, or whom I speak to, the word of this Khaos seems to find its way to me, even in my dreams, I hear its name muttered in the darkest reaches of my mind"

Ozark looked at him, stunned with disbelief.

"You've never heard of the Khaos? the entity which even the gods themselves fear," asked Ozark "The legend of the edicts, surely?"

He shook his head, a little disappointed with his inadequate knowledge of the legends foretold.

"Perhaps in my past," replied Arturius, "But that has long since abandoned me, and I fear that it shall remain as such."

"Well, the Khaos isn't a creature, or a weapon, or anything for that matter," said Ozark, "It's an entity, a being that takes no form, but takes from you every, your life, mind, and even your body."

Ozark paused. Slowing down to catch his breath; it would have seemed such excitement hadn't found its way into his life for some time.

"Legend has it that deep in the northern reaches of this continent, stood a tree, not a tree of ash, birch or oak, but a tree born from the seed of some unknown deity," said Ozark, "The elder tree of old, the Eterntree, and beneath its deepened roots of twisted imprisonment lay the Khaos, to be locked in an eternal battle deep within the confines of the earth, keeping it from emerging and consuming everything with blood and cinder."

The excitement continued to overwhelm his fragile state.

"Many thousand years ago, there was another realm that shared the blood-soaked ground upon which we stand today," said Ozark, "Vindictaria, the mightiest of all kingdoms laid claim to the accursed lands north growing rich and powerful with the vast wealth it hid."

"Did they grow too powerful?" he asked, "Unleashing the Khaos as a means to bolster whatever power they could grasp at?"

"On the contrary, they were led by the greatest man that ever-lived Akaramis, a great warrior king, he not only knew how to use a sword but more importantly when to use it," replied Ozark, "The Masked One wields a power he could not comprehend could do, a child with a dangerous toy as he wreaks havoc upon this land."

"He sounds like quite the individual," said Arturius, "I can only imagine what deeds he performed."

He wanted to know more, pushing his tiredness and aches aside for as long as he could.

"His deeds were indeed legendary, and his story great," replied Ozark, and thus he began his long tale of the great warrior-king and his war against the Khaos.

*Akaramis was an immensely powerful and influential knight. Travelling from the far-east he searched for a purpose in his life. Mightily known for his reputation as an ever-merciful and proud knight–something rarely found in the knights from the age of old. He travelled far and wide, fighting in many wars where he tired of the constant death and destruction that would lie in its wake. For even though he was born a soldier, raised a warrior, deep down he had an eternal longing for peace. After many years wandering through the wastes of the world, he found himself upon the fresh land of Xovia. More so, he found himself in the presence of a rather peculiar and unestablished lord far in the north. Surrounded by a vast array of enemies that would not hesitate in exploiting the feeble strength of the lord and his people, it had left him desperate for an answer to his people's survival. And so Akaramis had found his purpose.*

*After answering the call, he set about defending his new home. Scores of enemy soldiers would smash at his gates and hammer at his walls. Yet none found successful in such endeavours. For in times of battle he was the first to swing his sword, be it for himself or for his homeland– though in truth he never cared for his own life, so long as his peoples were safe. In a matter of years and in the blink of an eye, the minor lord had found his new position uncontested. His enemies absent to contend with and brought with it his absolute power. And so he grew, in strength and wealth, exploiting the rich and fertile lands and the while forgetting the brutality he and his people had. And as with all, his hunger for power grew. For it was never enough. And the people knew who their true saviour was. As quick as he gained power, so too did he lose it. They declared Akaramis the true king of the peoples to the north, a nobody far from a land unknown to all, now somebody with a true purpose.*

*The old lord, cast from his seat, experienced a pain he had never felt before, not of sadness or regret, but a thirst for revenge. His plans, however, did not proceed, for even his own men abandoned him. Their respect for the new king was stronger than the loyalty to their lord. Upon hearing of the plans in which the old lord attempted to unleash the Khaos, Akaramis set forth to secure the protection of his new kingdom.*

*They erected a grand tower around the ancient tree that sealed the dark entity from consuming all life. He built the great kingdom of Vindictaria around it, an attempt to appease the darkness that lurked deep beneath it. To ensure that his people would not fear the impending death that brewed beneath its surface, he placed his throne before the tree, its self at the mouth of the prison to ensure that he be the first to plunge himself into the abyss. And stop its evil from consuming his people.*

*Many years passed, and the Khaos laid in its slumber. The kingdom prospered and grew into a might which had never been seen before. Yet the king's mind was still ever focussed on the threat which lurked beneath him. And as predicted, that time did soon come.*

*When the seal broke and cast the world into what seemed to be never-ending darkness, Akaramis knew what needed to be done, for this was the time the king had truly been waiting for. Whilst his power had diminished over the years, leaving him degraded–yet still powerful, he did not waiver. Without hesitation he plunged himself deep into the belly of the Khaos, never to be seen again. For his strength was no match for the force that he encountered.*

*It took the combined strength of the other realms and the heroes of old to push back the Khaos and seal it within its prison once more. The devastation, however, had proven too much for his kingdom, the lands scorched and skies blackened, leaving behind the lands of cinder to which no mortal that has ventured into has ever returned. Some say that you can hear his screams echo in the winds, burning deep within the Khaos, his spirit torn in agony along with the people he sought to protect, waiting for the day he can be released from his eternal anguish.*

"Ever since that day the Khaos laid dormant," interjected a voice from behind, both men turned promptly as Karlan strode towards them, "Waiting for its time to break free from its shackles and lay waste to our lands."

With crossed arms he circled forth, perching himself atop a log opposite Arturius.

"I see this nut job been filling your head with fairy tales and myths," he laughed, prompting a scoff from Ozark watching the passion leave his eyes.

"Cock," muttered Ozark under his breath, just low enough that Karlan failed to hear his curse.

They must have been up all night, conversing like friends, sharing an old past together, laughing and reminiscing. A part of him knew that Ozark was an outcast even amongst his own companions–Out of disgust or prejudice, he would never know.

Dawn was breaking through the leaves, casting its sweet sunlight upon him as he sat there, basking in its radiance. Strange, however, for the light should not have been able to greet him in such a place–a good omen for the future to bring?

He barely felt tired, his pain and fatigue had since been numbed away a jittery feeling tingled down to his fingers making him feel restless and alert. The ever so watchful eyes of Ozark promptly saw this affliction that was taking its hold of him. "Ah," he muttered, "The effects of the wyrmflower extract are still coursing through you, my apologies I do sometimes get carried away with the dosage."

Before he knew it, Ozark ushered him over to a crude, dimly lit table. Mixing and mashing and straining an assortment of herbs and extracts, all the while muttering to himself. "It is a rather unique flower that blooms only in the deepest recessing of the southern swamps, making it rather difficult to acquire, especially if you are to avoid the Wulkren that lurk beneath the marshes," whispered Ozark, "However, it has an exceptionally strong poison rooted deep within its nectar, one drop is enough to kill a fully grown man, with an extract diluted enough you can negate the deathly side effect and replace it with a more, woozy one, making it extremely effective and sought after these days."

A vial filled with a pungent black liquid was presented before him,

"There we go," whispered Ozark, passing the small vial of a clear and rather putrid-smelling liquid, "Be sure to make sure you are comfortable before taking it-"

The wise words of wisdom should have come sooner, for he knocked back the foul liquid, feeling it burning through his nostrils and down his throat–It was out of sheer desperation for the trembling to stop. Within mere seconds his vision had blurred, the lights peeking through the canopy of the trees spun vigorously around him–a whirlwind of white and yellow. As he floated gently to the floor, drifting across a vast sea of empty space. Before crashing to the floor once more.

*~"At what cost, the damage has already been done"~*

# CHAPTER VII: SOLEMN DESIRES

How many times must this happen? Yet again he had rendered himself helpless and vulnerable during such a strange selection – Though some had proven friendly by now. It was comforting to know that he had been carried to a softer surface, rather than left on the cold hard floor as before. However, the bruises on his sides proved that it was a less than amicable result.

Arturius lay there quietly, glancing carefully at the trees above, watching as the leaves flowed peacefully in the gentle breeze. Occasionally he would spot a glimmer of the blue sky – if only for a second. Yet it was enough to remind him that there must still be some beauty left in this world.

When he truly thought about it the test was simple in a brutal way. From the violent beating to the secret meeting, before eventually falling victim to another concoction that battered his head. Any more and he would begin to lose his senses for good – for they had been strained past their breaking point.

At the very least the concoction had some effect, the trembling and full-body ache had since vanished leaving him refreshed, ready to fight another day. He looked around precariously, expecting more of the unexpected to fall atop him. Yet all appeared normal.

Everyone in the camp was continuing with their day-to-day life, as he was but a distant memory from the past. Jorik, Dovan, Robbard, muttering amongst themselves – the occasional eyes glanced over at him before returning promptly. Karlan, Burak engaged in a bitter challenge of strength fighting to a stalemate. The ever so solemn Garton still lurking in the corner meditating in a dream-like trance, his vaporous body more volatile than he previously witnessed – No doubt reliving a memory of his past.

His hands grasped the sides of his makeshift bed, hoisting to his feet, the leaves and twigs crunching beneath his feet as he stood. Ozark shouted him over from across the camp, his words muffled by the trees – as well as his slurred speech.

As he made his way across the camp, his eyes met with the young Jorik, eager to further pursue his acquaintance. The words did not come out of his mouth however – a quick slap at the back of his head, courtesy of Dovan saw to that.

"Ah, there he is, come back to the light I see," bellowed Selwyn, his face brimming with joy – the likes of which he had not yet witnessed.

"How long was I out for?" he grimaced, rubbing the coarse dryness from his eyes, "What was in that drink?"

"A few hours, give or take," replied Ozark, "the concoction was meant to dispel the remainder of the wyrmflower extract, I added a bit of seed of the Aven for a good measure."

A briefly quiet titter formed around his scar encrusted mouth.

"Well, seen as though you have had the opportunity to meet most of us here, I had best get down to the serious stuff," said Selwyn, he gestured in front of him at the opposite end of the map. Still, he could feel the eyes of Dovan and Robbard stabbing daggers into his back – it would take a lot of convincing to ease those two.

"First things first," said Selwyn, a more serious undertone bellowing from his voice, "What do you know of us already?"

A ridiculous question indeed, he had next to no memory of the time beyond those trees, all but what he had already lived through.

"Nothing I'm afraid, Sir," replied Arturius, "The only memories I have are from the moment since I met Silas within the carriage, everything after that has been what has led me to you now."

Selwyn laughed to himself, sparking a slight chuckle from the others gathered around him.

"Sir! Well that is indeed a title that I have seldom heard lately," he placed either hand atop the table to support his weight, "There is really no need for such formalities here, Selwyn will do nicely."

A scoff emerged from behind him. He peeked back to see that bit of disgust roll from Robbard's face, making no attempt to hide the brief insult. "*What a great start,*" he thought to himself, a wave of embarrassment sent a red blush over his face.

"Come now it's no bother at all, around here we are all equal," Selwyn shouted before whisper under his breath "Except for the fact that I'm leader amongst us." Selwyn winked at him quickly as he said so, concealing it from the others.

"As I said before, we are what's left of the Kingdom of Farrosia, continuously pursued by the Rekeshi war machine due to our resistance, and should I hope so, be a threat to them," said Selwyn,

"What do they call you?" he asked, curious as to the many barbaric names that would be bestowed upon them.

"Rebels, heathens, anarchists, terrorists," said Karlan, his voice emerging from the rear of the camp, still locked deep in his trial of strength with Burak.

"You think of it, that's what we are out there, to the world beyond the forest," replied Selwyn, "Regardless however, our mission has always been straight and simple, disrupt the Rekeshi aggressors by whatever means necessary."

"And to bring down the masked one!" interjected Silas,

"Yes and that too," said Selwyn, "I will not allow him to bury us any further into the ground, the masked one has proven he is indeed the greatest threat to not only us but for each of the other kingdoms as well, our aim is to unite the kingdoms under one clear goal-"

"-Hah!" shouted Robbard silencing Selwyn as he spoke, "The other kingdoms are a joke, the Ska'al, those bloodthirsty warmongers flocked to the masked one as soon as he showed his power, they only see strength as a worthy leader."

Such anger towards the other kingdoms was quite apparent – and potentially well warranted.

"The Samopethi, those tree lovers drew back into their dense woods, isolating themselves from the rest of the war whilst we were slaughtered in the droves," Robbard shouted, "Oh, and where were the Verdenese when we need them the most…"

The camp fell silent, each one of its inhabitants grew gravely sombre the more he unravelled their desperation as he pierced sharp looks upon each of them.

"That's right!" he shouted, "They were breaking bread with the enemy as their armies lay sieged to their own people!"

No one responded in kind, it was clear that all were agreeing with the passionate anger Robbard was projecting. Arturius could make out the grief of a past he wished to long forget in his eyes.

"The kingdoms are a joke, a piss stain on this realm, they could all take after the ancient kingdoms of old and bury themselves deep within the dirt where they all belong."

"Steady Robbard, a lot happened back then," said Silas, huddled close to the map he had been examining,

"Really, you're going to defend them?" snapped Robbard, "I used to have a life before all of this, duties, honour, respect, where is it all now? Gone, just like those I love, those I cared for, snuffed out because none came to us in our time of need."

"There is more to it than any of our comprehension," replied Silas, "When the masked one came he brought something with him that none could contest with, the other kingdoms acted out of fear, not self-interest."

Wise words from such a young boy, fate would definitely guide him well in the years to come. The response from Silas only seemed to burn a deeper hatred of the kingdoms with Robbard.

The Silence carried through the faint wind, passing for an age. Had it not been for the bounding figure breaking through the bramble, crashing down atop the well-kept stacks of provisions. The mood shifted suddenly as one by one the others jumped into action drawing an assortment of blades, bows and battle-axes ready to bear down.

"They're here, they're here!" the cloaked figure shouted, rolling atop the floor in a tangled mess.

"Stop!" order Selwyn, his command came not a second too late, the blade of Karlan brushed carefully against the skin drawing a scarlet line across his neck. The cautious leader approached the hooded figure grasping firmly as he tore away his hood. A young man lay upon the floor surrounded by steel in all directions. Selwyn sighed greatly.

"Gods give me strength," snapped Selwyn, jerking the young man to his feet, "How many times Kezin, you were nearly cut down where you stood, there are a lot of anxious people in this camp, you must make your presence known to us before advancing!"

Kezin ignored the surge of anger directed at him, stuttering with a terrifying excitement as he tried to find the strength to speak.

"They're here!" he shouted again, "In the old village of Riftmyer, the Rekeshi!" he gasped.

The poor soul nearly passed out delivering the message lying there as the fatigue and fright overcame him.

"So soon!" responded Selwyn, his gaze now focused on the map he was previously pondering over.

"What purpose would they have sending a company to that backwater village?" asked Dovan, turning to his leader.

"Maybe someone talked, maybe someone ratted us out," said Robbard, his gaze met with Arturius, he could see there was something in his eyes, a piercing deep blue –

deeper than the skies above – that immediately laid the blame upon him.

“What are you saying Robbard?” said Selwyn, his eyes not moving from the assortment of scrolls he had since scattered across the table.

“You know exactly what I’m saying, Sir,” replied Robbard, prompted a brief glare from Selwyn before returning to his more pressing matter at hand, “Ever since ‘*he*’ found his way into our presence, Riftmyer has become overrun with Rekeshi, we nearly lose Silas and to make matters worse it has splintered this group”.

The group remained silent waiting as the clash of wills begun.

“How has your judgement become so clouded-” snapped Robbard, only to be interrupted by Selwyn slamming his fists atop the table – nearly breaking the damn thing in two.

“Enough!” shouted Selwyn, “There are powers at work here far above your understanding, Robbard.”

Such an outburst shook the group to its core, a side of Selwyn had shown far from his usual face – a darker more, terrifying side. Even Robbard, the hot-headed and brash young man looked shaken he could see deep in his eyes that he knew he had overstepped.

“The only one here causing a rift between us all is you!” said Selwyn, his rage had not subsided as he continued to chastise the ever so shrinking Robbard, “You know nothing of what it takes to lead, the sacrifices you must make nor the paths that you must follow!”

Arturius watched on as Selwyn towered above his brash subordinate, with menacing intent.

“You may question my motives, you may question my plans, but you will never again question my loyalty to our mission and to the company, boy!” he spoke softly, yet harshly as he hissed at the shaken Robbard – To perform such a feat whilst enacting no violence is what made him such a terrifying foe.

Selwyn turned to face the rest of the group, all but Garton were watching in awe and silence.

"Does anyone else have anything to add?" Selwyn beckoned, his voice had grown course by the brief encounter making his words stale and sharp. No one said a thing.

Arturius had nearly forgotten about the young man as he lay upon the floor, bruised and tired – His attention had been somewhat warranted to shift. Kezin gasped for breath, unable to finish his message before the harsh encounter.

"That's not all, Sir," he croaked, Selwyn turned on point, digging his heels as he spun about to face Kezin, "The doors to Nordellar have been opened!"

Selwyn went pale, a ghost from his past maybe or the news he had been dreading to hear the most. The others around him muttering amongst themselves in confusion. It took a while before anyone spoke and even then, it seemed forced and unsure.

"So the rumours are true then," said Robbard, "The masked one seeks the lost crowns of the ancient kingdoms."

The words fell up the ears of Arturius leaving him embraced with more confusion, yet familiar in the flicker of older memories that were beginning to resurface – not substantial but enough to garner intrigue.

"It would certainly appear as such," replied Selwyn, his hands buried in one and other, "I had feared such a mission would come to be by the enemy, though I had hoped that it hadn't surfaced so soon."

"It would explain the increased numbers of Rekeshi roaming the hills," said Dovan, eager to get in on the conversation, "Perhaps they are looking to secure the border around us, potentially drive away any resistance before it meets them."

"But why attack Riftmyer?" asked Silas, more concerned for the well-being of the villagers, "They are a poor village with no strategic value, nor do they possess the numbers of weapons to contest with even a small reconnaissance party."

"They have been offering us supplies over the past few months," said Dovan, "Perhaps someone let slip they were aiding us? Or perhaps they are gathering up more from the outlying villages, I've heard rumours of the Rekeshi taking away the many villagers from all over the realm, none to ever be seen again, some twisted experiment perhaps?"

"Perhaps," replied Selwyn, "Something we must definitely keep close to the ground, any rumours, any whispers I need to know."

Kezin spoke up once again. He was still laid upon the floor in agony – running for six days and nights would do that to any man.

"They knew of the aid that was offered to us," said Kezin, still gasping for breath, "I was able to sneak away before they noticed my presence, I fear what may have become of them."

Selwyn nodded promptly, he knew deep down he needed to act, he could see it glimmer within his eyes, whispering all that was going on inside his head as it unravelled.

"It would appear that time is of the essence with us," said Selwyn, "Our priority will be the old ruins of Nordellar, thankfully Riftmyer lies along the road, as such we shall resupply and support the civilians by whatever means we can offer."

"What of the nobody you have graciously welcomed in?" said Robbard, "You can't be serious to allow him to journey with us."

"I am deadly serious," replied Selwyn, "He goes where we go, and you will come to accept such a decision whether you agree with it or not."

Robbard scoffed, quickly exiting from the area. Selwyn took it for dejected acquiescence.

"Pack up anything that's not one with the earth, once we are gone, we are gone," said Selwyn, an undertone of worry hidden deep within his voice, "We shall move out within the hour."

Without any more left to say the group sprang into action, in a wild organised frenzy as they equipped and supplied themselves for the prospect of a skirmish. They were able to clean up what remained of the camp with frightful speed, picking whatever meat was left upon the bone as the Arglefish would in the rivers.

Arturius was left standing in the middle of an ever so shrinking encampment, not sure as to how he should continue.

“Can you ride?” asked Selwyn,

“Yes,” Arturius replied, “I do believe so.”

“Good, there is a blackened saddle over in the corner, a bridle lies not too far behind it,” he gestured to the neatly placed saddle atop a makeshift shelf towards the exit, “They are yours to use during this journey.”

It was exquisitely crafted, a deep blackened leather that gleamed against the flickering torches by the trees, the gold embroidery had since faded away leaving empty grooves running across its surface. The sigil of Farrosia had been burnt into the leather to forever remind the rider who they fought for – It was well worn yet still perfectly useable.

“You can take ‘Dusk’ she is a feisty mare; however, her stamina is unmatched,” said Selwyn, “Hopefully you will fare better than her former master.”

A glimpse of sadness twitched across his face before he promptly brushed it aside.

“You have got to be fucking with me,” snapped Dovan, “You are going to give him Yohn’s horse, he has barely begun to rot in the ground and you are already to soil his memory thusly.”

Selwyn gave him an aggressive look, a look that tested his patience with him.

“Give him a blade as well,” ordered Selwyn, his eyes locked on Dovan in anger. As such Dovan returned his gaze in kind, clicking his teeth in dismay. He pulled an old blade tucked away within his pack throwing it at Arturius feet before angrily turning away. The blade was old, blunt and rusty. He grasped it with one-handed noting its poor craft and terrible balance, it could not cut through butter even if he tried.

"What the hell am I supposed to do with this," he shouted, "It's rather heavy at the pommel and light upon the blade."

He waved it aggressively above his head, shaking it aggressive end. Dovan looked back, a slight smirk stitched across his rather pretentious face.

"Whatever you damn well you want," he replied, "Turn it on your own neck for all I care."

He promptly turned his back on him and walked off into the shadows.

By now the company was ready to move out, the former base of operations had been stripped bare, nothing more than a few scraps left for the forest, perhaps as an offering to appease the spirits – though more like a token of thanks for refraining from consuming them all.

The journey out of the forest was nothing like he had previously encountered. Selwyn marched them carefully through the darkness – precision was key. It wasn't long before they finally broke free from the darkness, the intense light of the sun burned the back of his eyes, it took some time before his eyes readjusted to the pleasantness of day. The lush fields of green were a comforting sight indeed, time was rather convoluted within the trees of Hollowclaw forest, what seemed like a mere two days had in fact been eight.

A strange sensation grasped him once again, a strangely familiar feeling he felt once before, as though a presence had finally been able to meet back with him once more. The deep denseness of the forest shrouded many things it would seem.

A hidden path along with the edge of the forest led them to a small alcove, a small hiding spot to keep the horses – the dense woods were no place for such magnificent creatures. He spent some time loitering between the group as they fitted the horses with a vast array of saddles and bridles, taking time to comfort their old companions with a brief reunion.

Far into the darkest corner stood lonesome from the rest of the harem was the black mare Selwyn had spoken of. The horse seemed quite apprehensive at first to the approaching stranger – no doubt still lamenting over the loss of its master.

"Easy, Easy," said Arturius, "I am not here to hurt you."

The horse was growing restless and impatient, rearing before him as he approached. At a passing glance, he could see Robbard and Dovan watching him closely, almost smirking in glee as the horse grew aggressive at his attempts to calm her.

"Easy, I'm not here to hurt you," he reiterated, slowly approaching her step by step. The two were not too dissimilar, alone and unwanted.

"If you will allow it, I would be most appreciative if you would let me ride upon you," he whispered, "I promise you, I'm neither heavy nor am I a threat."

He whispered gently to the great creature, hushing and soothing as calm as a river flowing gracefully along.

It appeared to be successful, the horse began to calm, huffing and snorting instead – almost as if in deep conversation with him.

"There we go, easy," he said, stretching out his hand, her skin shuddered as he carefully approached – still nervous, still cautious. He could feel his own heart thumping inside his chest, nervously trying to hide his emotions.

Soft, she felt so soft, her mane flowed graciously down her neck as his fingers brushed through it like the wind through the trees. They both looked deep into each other's eyes, he saw himself reflected deep into her hazel eyes – A young man, dirty and bruised.

"It's going to take four weeks to reach Nordellar, as long as the weather holds, a week to reach Riftmyer as long as the roads remain undisturbed," bellowed Selwyn, he was mounted atop a hulking stud of a horse, its muscles were as thick as the trees that sprouted around them, a deep black coat with the occasional smear of white.

"Will we be stopping along the journey," queried Burak, his deep voice matched his appearance – intimidation must come naturally to him, "four weeks will put a lot of undue stress upon all of us, not to mention the fatigue upon the horses, they will require rest just as much as us if not more."

"If required," replied Selwyn, "We will journey through the night, that way we can slip past any sentries that may be patrolling the surrounding borders, should save us much time and hold the element of surprise for us. The quicker we can reach the ruins the less of a force there should be to guard it."

He clenched his fist and with it pounded his chest above the heart – a salute to his brave men. They all returned in kind. Though the apprehensive Robbard took some stares from the leader in order to respond.

"Garton you take the rear with Arturius," shouted Selwyn, "Show him the ropes and fill him in on anything you think will benefit us, and keep your eyes open for any straggling scouts, don't want them sprinting ahead whilst their head still remains firmly upon their shoulders."

As usual, Garton remained solemnly silent, a quick nod was all that he would respond with.

With the light of day, Arturius could finally get a closer look at his new companion, the dark had enshrouded his appearance more effectively than he previously thought. What in all the realm could keep his body in such a condition, neither death nor living, decayed or broken. As he gazed closer, inspecting the husk that rode aside him it was clear to be a curse of the sort. Broken and fractured skin covered his body, rather stony in appearance with crevices that deepened, burrowing into his being. It looked as if an explosion – frozen in time – had erupted from deep within him, expunging a miasma of darkness and mist alike. He couldn't help but stare. Again he saw the faint aura that shimmered red and blue holding his shattered pieces together; perhaps it was what remained of his soul, clinging on to whatever still remained.

"I do not believe we have been introduced," said Arturius, his attempts to be polite proving fruitless to the sombre Garton, "My name is Arturius as you have probably already been made aware of."

Garton remained silent; the hoofs of his horse clicked atop the stones beneath them. His eyes gazing away from him off into the horizon.

"How long have you known Selwyn?" he asked, "Or the rest of them for that matter?"

Still Silence.

"That sigil upon your arm, I have not seen that before, is it from one of the other kingdoms?" trying to elicit a response in any way he could draw only a deeper silence.

"It's no use Art, you won't find him talk much between any of us," said Karlan, peering back from his saddle, "just have comfort in knowing that when we are all dead on the floor, he will still be watching us, silent as ever, the lucky bastard."

He let out a loud laugh, prompted a deadly glare from Garton before his mind wandered away.

"*Curious,*" he thought to himself, "*a curse that prolongs life at the cost of what appears to be a rather painful, nay torturous condition.*"

"So you are immortal?" he asked, an innocent tone to such a personal question, "some might say that be a gift of divine proportions, I for one disagree entirely."

At last, he was able to elicit a response from the cold soldier, a flicker from his darkened eyes as they looked upon his from the corner of his vision.

"I may not have my memories or a life beyond what I have experienced thusly, but I do know that immortality is not a 'divine' gift, it's a curse, and a rather nasty one at that, forcing you to watch as those you care for turn in to dust unable to stop them from succumbing to time, a curse to give you tremendous power over your life only to snatch away the life from those you love."

A strange feeling came over him, a sadness he thought should not affect him. It only proved to him that he had indeed lost someone very dear to him, how horrific it is to be punished in such methods of uncanny terror.

"You talk too much," muttered Garton, his voice was distorted and broken, much like his fragile body, it sounded much like rock crushing against one and other in a rather painful way. He smiled to himself, had he broken through the cold demeanour of the tortured being beside him.

"Maybe you're right," he replied, "But it's better to talk to the living than the dead."

It prompted a gentle smirk from Garton. They glanced at each other briefly before averting their gaze to the path ahead.

The day grew into night and night grew into the day, the sun would rise in the east, a burning ball of intense light and heat. He would watch it pass slowly across the sky before setting down upon the western reaches of the land, cold as death – Its darkness only blocked by the torches ahead.

Every so often Arturius would prod and poke at the broken man, testing the limit of his patience – Something he did not want to exceed.

"At some point, you're going to have to tell me about yourself," he remarked, "I am beginning to run out of material to tell you from my life."

A thin smile stretched from cheek to cheek, amused by his own wit.

"I told you Art, you're wasting your time," said Karlan, "You'd be more successful bedding a Ska'al than conversing with the deep dark mist-ery."

This clearly struck a nerve with Garton, the cracks across his face rumbled slightly increasing the intensity of the aura that surrounded him.

"And have you ever bedded a Ska'al Karlan," Burak asked sarcastically, he thought briefly "Humph, who would've thought that your sister was adopted," he quipped,

"Fuck you," replied Karlan, striking the hulking mass hard in the arm as he laughed a deep hysterical laugh. Arturius could clearly see the bonds between them all – more of a dysfunctional family than a fighting force. The scuffle attracted the attention of the head patriarch, Selwyn snapped his fingers, hard and loud. It was enough to garner the attention of the two squabbling men, promptly silencing them. He leaned forward, almost laying atop Dusk's gentle head.

"So Burak, how is it you became a part of this company?" he whispered. The large man gracefully swivelled atop his saddle, facing him dead in the eye.

"Well you see I wasn't as fortunate as the rest of them here, not born into nobility unlike some amongst us" Burak spoke softly but loud enough for his words to reach the ears of Robbard you promptly exhaled in response.

"I worked as a stable hand for the royal household," said Burak, Arturius raised his brow, "Ironic eh? I was bigger than most the horses you see, made me quite adept at wrestling them away should they grow a bit anxious."

He gestured to his steed, an enormous stallion well-defined muscles bulging from its skin, its ragged brown fur brushed neatly demonstrated his attention to detail with his profession.

"This beauty here, the only one that could fight me to a stalemate, he may not be a looker, but by the Gods, his strength is a beauty."

"Beauty certainly lies in strength," replied Arturius,

"I hear Silas brought you back with him, devoid of memory, a stubborn fuck who's pretty hard to kill by the sound of it," Burak grinned,

Arturius returned a smile, "Yeah, the earliest memory I have is such a meeting, though occasionally I get fragments that seem to slip through."

Burak smiled a deep smile, “Hopefully you can remember some of your old fighting habits, a good challenge is hard to come by these days.”

“Maybe someday,” he laughed back, “You’ve still not told me how you came to be a part of this?”

“Of course,” he replied, “I can get side-tracked quite easily, during the great purge of Dawnstar I was able to take out the Rekeshi force tasked with seizing the royal horses, wasn’t much of a challenge until that hulking monstrosity showed up.”

He could hear the rage burning within Garton as his body crackled and glowed.

“Easy Garton, remember your meditation, focus on the calm,” said Burak, before long the rage had subsided as Garton closed his eyes breathing gently – not that he needs to breath.

“Bit of a sore subject there for Garton, had it not been for him I would have been dead in the dirt,” said Burak,

“Or like him,” replied Karlan, gesturing towards the concentrating Garton as he rode, deep in thought.

“Such a monster should not walk amongst the realm of the living,” said Burak, “I tell you; he is not of the living at all, twisted by some dark force that should be locked away for good.”

“What was the monster?” asked Arturius, “Such a creature must have been ferocious indeed by the sounds of it.”

Burak exhaled long and hard. It took some strength for him to speak once again.

“Monster, yes, a creature no,” he muttered, “For that monster was a man, a hulking beast of darkness that goes by the name of Vortuse, a puppet to the puppeteer himself.”

“I am guessing the puppeteer to be this Masked One you all speak so highly of,” replied Arturius, “I would very much like to learn some more of this mysterious individual.”

“I do hope that such a day truly never comes,” said Burak, “I have seen his magic first hand, destroying every last fragment of a person, splitting them in two as he fractures their mind and takes their thoughts, it is almost as though he is looking for something buried deep within the minds of those he slays, a strange hobby if ever I saw one."

Arturius shuddered, the very stories he keeps hearing of such a dark and twisted man never sits well with him. A twisted evil that would become a complete opposite to his own personality and feelings.

"What happened to you both then," asked Arturius, "During the purge that is?"

Burak looked towards Garton, receiving a quick nod in response from the quiet demon.

"That bastard Vortuse," hissed Burak, "he stumbled upon myself and Garton as we slew the last of the Rekeshi force sent to seize the horses, damned nearly killed me had it not been for Garton forcing me out of the blazing barn, the monster cleaved and hew flesh from across Garton's body, leaving him to burn alive in the very fires they fought within."

Though he tried to conceal it, he couldn't escape the confusion that echoed across his face.

"Sounds like a truly horrific ordeal!" said Arturius, "Though how did he become what he is today? Did Vortuse or the Masked One apply such a curse?"

He was eager to know how such a curse came into effect.

"It stabbed me through the heart," replied Garton, his voice calm yet filled with rage, "I lay there dying as rage consumed what remained of my body, then I woke up."

It stunned even Burak, not many had been spoken to of his ordeal, let alone from the broken mouth of the cursed.

"But how? What magic could possibly exist to cause such an effect," asked Arturius, his whole body leaning in closer for a response. Garton sighed; it was a past he wished never happened but knew he could never escape.

"I woke up, after everyone I knew had been slaughtered before my eyes, I stood there peering over my own corpse watching as the fires around burnt it to ash," whispered Garton, the pain of his past causing his body to glow red with the cinders that first began to claim him.

"My vessel broken and burnt now lay there before me as my world began to crumble, I began the drift away," muttered Garton, "Then that bitch used her magic to keep me from passing on."

In a swift motion, he pulled back his burnt garb, revealing a mark embedded deeply into his hide. Symbols of an old and dark time that burned deeper than the flesh.

"This keeps me from passing on and returning to the ashen grave to where I belong."

Seeing his expression, removed the intrigue from his face, replacing it with horror and deep compassion.

"Is it painful?" he asked,

"Always."

A voice bellowed from the front of the company.

"We will rest here for tonight" said Selwyn, "Burak, see to it that the horses are tethered and rested. Dovan, I'm sure you can procure some game from the surrounding hills and woods. Karlan, get a fire going, nothing too big though, don't want everything around us alerted to our presence."

"Really?" blurted Karlan, "I'm to get stuck with fucking stick duty!"

Selwyn turn him a scowl. Glaring deep and hard at him until he sauntered off into the darkness.

"Everyone else, you know what you need to do"

The others promptly began unloading the supplies from the horses, they had already endured much along the uneven road carrying their masters and equipment. In the corner of Arturius's eye, Ozark once again uncorked the tonic from beneath his garb, knocking it back down his throat to put at bay the harsh realities of such torturous experiences.

"Arturius," beckoned Selwyn, "Come, show me what skill lies beneath one who bested three Rekeshi bloodlurkers."

Before he could react a wooden practice sword came crashing before his feet. Arturius gripped it tightly, its coarse surface pierced his hands with splinters to let him know he was truly alive. As he looked up he was met with the terrifying sight of Selwyn lunging towards him. The old captain moved with astonishing speed and stamina. Arturius reacted fast, swiping his wooden sword horizontally in an effort to catch his attackers neck off guard. Though the reality of the situation became apparent far too late.

With swift reactions and agility, Selwyn swept past the astonished Arturius avoided his clumsy strike and speedily striking him upon the nape of his neck. He toppled to floor with a rising tide of dizziness erupting within his head. The fight appeared to be over before it had truly begun.

"Hmmm, I expected better," said Selwyn disappointed, "Perhaps you will prove me wrong when the need arises."

And with that the old captain turned his back, marching off as he left Arturius to lie upon the cold hard ground.

"Easy there," said Ozark, "You did well young-un."

"How so?" asked Arturius, "I was felled in seconds, to say it was an embarrassment is an understatement of the century!"

Arturius lumbered his aching body off the floor, his head throbbed from the strike to his rear. It felt nothing like any pain he had felt before, its strike was true and accurate. Not a forceful or strong strike, but skilfully placed to manipulate the energies of the body. Masterful and exquisite.

"Nah my boy," said Ozark, "You didn't lose your head for one, and you learned the simplest and most important lesson of all."

"And that is?"

"That you must learn from your mistakes," smiled Ozark, "Mistakes are meant to occur, for without them, you can never know success."

Arturius looked back towards Selwyn, his shadow had since vanished from the camp, but his presence forever made an everlasting mark.

"Come, let us rest" said Silas. The young boy had watched all that unfolded from the side lines, "I dislike these little games he play with the others."

The night came and went quicker that the morning dew. Their journey continued before the break of dawn. The air was crisp and fresh, something that would soon turn as they closed in on the village of Riftmyer.

The smoke rising far into the distance brought the any and all conversation into sudden silence. An image that would forever become engrained upon the minds of those who were to bear witness. Be them weak or strong, all would find themselves at the mercy of the horrors that filled the realm. And the Khaos it left in its wake.

*~ "We must keep pushing on; do not let the others death be in vain" ~*

## CHAPTER VIII: OLD TRICKS

Smoke and ash blanketed the ground as softly as mist would upon the water, flung into the air as the hooves of their horsed scraped along the hard earth beneath. It was an eerie feeling that hung in the air, the sadness of many tortured souls penetrated deeply into Arturius–making him extremely uncomfortable. What remained of this village looked more like the aftermath of a great catastrophe, the ground so scorched from intense fires that it cracked deep into the earth.

Judging by the charred remains it was some days ago when the destruction had occurred, still warm, still smoking.

"Company on me!" ordered Selwyn, prompting the others to converge around him orderly and swift, "Stay alert, the fires are still rather fresh, there could be insurgents lay in wait."

He dismounted his tremendous steed gracefully slamming his feet into the ground releasing a soft assortment of ash and dirt floating into the air. The others followed suit. He grasped a handful of the warm ash that littered the floor, watching as it tumbled through his fingers to be taken away by the gentle breeze.

"It's ash," muttered Silas, "Most likely from what remains of the hovels."

"Or what remains of the residents," whispered Garton coldly,

"Lovely thoughts there, Garton," mocked Karlan.

Silas looked back in disgust, quickly dropping the ash within his grasp and heaving at the thought of what may coat his finger.

"I don't know what happened here, but by the Gods, we will find out," bellowed Selwyn, "We need spread out and cover more ground, Dovan, Jorik, you cover the chapel and its surroundings."

Gesturing towards the dilapidated structure across the courtyard,

"Robbard, Karlan, Burak, you check the town hall. If there are any survivors, they would most likely seek refuge there."

He pointed down the road to the charred building, its corner partially collapsed from the flames.

"Garton, Arturius, you two cover the road that runs through."

His voice was quick as he snapped his orders. No doubt time would be of the essence here.

While the rest of the company spread out, darting into all directions, Garton flicked his head forward, gesturing to Arturius to move along. There was a single structure untouched by fire, blackened by the intense flames that had licked them.

The ground crunched hard beneath their feet as they slowly and cautiously meandered through the smoke. Every step he took Arturius clutched harder at his dulled blade–Not that it was much use to him right now–He looked over to see the broken man striding through the smoke, the pain of the ash and charred remains were opening old wounds to which he had suffered from previously.

"Garton, you okay?" asked Arturius.

The burnt man grunted in response, clearly not in the mood to talk right now–and who would blame him.

"What happened here?" he asked, "The flames have scorched the very earth itself, even the very stonework has melted into nothing."

He found his eyes gazing across the smog-filled landscape, the wind occasionally blowing it clear before more would quickly replace it.

"Nothing good," muttered Garton, the fear of the ash and flames still present in his eyes.

"Hey, look at me," Arturius whispered, Garton begrudgingly turned to face him, a hint of annoyance fell upon his face, "All is good my friend, whatever happened, it's in the past, don't let it consume you-." he coughed as smoke rushed into his lungs,

"No matter what happens, I will be here beside you, you may not have had the pleasure to get to know me as of late, but I believe in one thing more than anything,"

It caught the attention of Garton. Without turning, he could feel the gaze of his vision bending to the corner of his eyes.

"Actions will speak for me," said Arturius, "I will prove to you I am worthy of your company."

Garton gave a small smirk to Arturius, the anxiety slowly diminishing–observant through his physique no longer burning with anxiety.

"You got heart kid I'll give you that," replied Garton, "Shame you will most likely die before I see more of it."

He quickly removed himself from the conversation, returning to his quiet and solemn state once more.

An uneasy feeling crept up on Arturius as waded through the deep ash, crunching beneath his boot. The ever so soft surface made a noise most uncommon to his ear.

"Hang tight," he said, holding his hand up to Garton, who immediately stopped to observe him.

He crouched down low, a few inches from the surface. Uneven and unnerving. Beneath the faint aroma of burnt oak, charred stone and scorched earth lay the foundation of blood and bone. Grasping the finger of his glove with his teeth, he tugged tightly, freeing his hand from the leathery grip.

It was still warm as he dug into the ground, deep and dry, brushing aside swathes of ash until his fingers glanced off a strange surface. Staring back at him was what remained of the villagers.

Never had he expected to see the scorched skull of a former resident peering back at him as he unearthed the poor soul.

"I think I've found the villagers," he muttered, "Poor souls didn't even stand a chance."

With his naked hand, he grasped at the cinders, watching as they cascaded either side of his shrivelling fingers. The further he dug, the more he wished he hadn't. Scores of the charred remains of the many that once called this desolate ruin home, lay deep beneath his feet. Devoid of flesh and life. Scattered across the mass grave. Men, women and children from all walks of life, butchered in their homes.

Beneath all the death lay remnants of a crimson flag singed around its edges. Adorned in the centre, the ghastly sight on the coiled snakes intertwining around a long spear embroidered with the finest cloth in the realm. The old cobblestones lay untouched, clean and dry underneath its folder grasp. Garton stood still–and silent as usual–his eyes fixed upon the charred remains of a small child, clutching the larger bones of a woman–though burnt the crude jewellery around her neck gave him his answers.

"And they say I have no soul," whispered Garton, "It's one thing to cut down your enemy and spill his blood across the earth, but this."

He paused, his voice cracking from what remained of his broken heart, "This is barbaric! unforgivable"

They counted at least thirty–of all ages–hollowed-out remains of the village's inhabitants left to rot in the streets as all that they ever knew turned to ash among them.

By now Selwyn had heard the commotion between the two. Upon joining with them, his face contorted into a truly horrific sight, his eyes grew heavy as he waded amongst the dead. Though he appeared headstrong and proud, it was evident that the burden of guilt was bearing down upon the righteous leader. He knew that the village knew the risks of conversing with such outlaws and what fate would become of them should they be discovered. Yet deep down he knew only he could shoulder the blame.

"What do we do now?" asked Ozark, hobbling over to Selwyn as his eyes refused to break away from the mass grave before him. Dovan and Jorik appeared through the smoke, coming to a near stop as they passed over the remains.

"The bastards," shouted Jorik, "How dare they slaughter such innocent folk, by the Gods I will slay every last one of them."

His young mind struggling to come to terms with the image burning deep into his head.

"Quiet child," snapped Dovan, "You wouldn't be able to slay the mutton upon a banquet table. Keep your mouth shut and head down! Was this the work of that bastard!?", pointing at Arturius.

The shock soon disappeared when he realised it was the tattered flag Dovan had gestured towards.

"The Rekeshi scum will pay for this," hissed Jorik, kicking a burnt-out log, splintering it into a thousand pieces as they scattered atop the ash–screaming in anger to dull the pain.

"Quiet child!" snapped Dovan again, "Can you not see that the adults here are talking!"

"There's a live one over here," shouted Burak, his voice echoed from amongst the ruins, "Careful not to let escape! They are a slippery one!"

The sound of footsteps crunching across the floor circled them. Their eyes aimlessly trying to follow the sound.

"The damned peasant is fast!" shouted Robbard, shrouded in the smoke, "I can barely see before me, somebody stop it!"

The tapping of footsteps bounding beneath the cobbled stonework grew closer and closer. Darting from side to side in the distance. Faster and louder.

"This damned ash is too thick! It blinds me!" shouted Burak, "They are heading south towards the town centre."

"Nay you lumbering imbecile," replied Robbard, "They head east, try to cut them off."

A frenzied panic began to set in, left, right, centre no one knew to where this mysterious entity would follow.

Arturius drew his blunted blade. Poised and rearing his dug his heels firmly into the ash.

Faster, faster, faster. The footsteps grew louder, heading straight towards them, falling in quick rhythm like the hounding drums of war. A silhouette illuminated against the smoke before breaking through the intangible wall. The shadow struck him in the gut, knocking him back a few steps and propelling the ash covered figure backwards, crashing to the ground.

"A girl?" said Arturius. Lowering his guard. He dropped his shoulders and lessened his stance

"It's a girl, hold your guard!"

"Say what?" shouted Robbard, his voice approaching from behind the young girl. She looked a mess; torn rags clothed her body–dirty and partially burnt to black–she couldn't have been old six years to the day. She was heavily malnourished, a mere mixture of skin and bones if at that–the poor soul mustn't have eaten in days.

The sound of Robbard's bellowing voice sent her into a scurry, fleeing as quickly as she emerged. The others tried to catch her, but her nimble frame eluded their pitiful efforts.

"Well done, Robbard you lumbering halfwit, you scared her away," snapped Dovan,

Robbard quickly emerged from the smoke, covered thick in ash, giving him the appearance of a stone statue.

"Fuck off, big-nosed twat," replied Robbard rather eloquently, "She was probably scared by that filthy face you wear. Besides I'd like to see catch her with such feminine hands then. You are more fit to wash my garbs than contend with the likes of me."

promptly saluting his comrade with a rather vulgar gesture.

"Enough!" snapped Selwyn.

"Great work you lot," mocked Ozark, "In your love to demean one and other you have allowed the terrifying creature to escape!"

"Don't you worry your pretty little head off cripple," replied Robbard, "I catch the little runt!"

"No one is catching anybody," said Selwyn, "She is frightened, she is starved and neither of you idiots is helping the situation shouting so aggressively."

"Well, we need to get her somehow," said Burak.

A cloak of ash flowed from his shoulders, washing away in the tepid breeze.

"She might be the only person in this godforsaken realm who has a shred of thought as to what happened here."

"What the fuck happened to you two," bellowed Dovan, nearly crying with laughter at the sight of the two ash-laden warriors, "You allowed a little girl to get the better of you, damned if I must for the Rekeshi will quiver in their boots."

Each of them stared daggers at Dovan as they slapped the ash and dirt from their armour, falling from them, grey waterfalls of soot and smoke.

"The damned building fell upon us, didn't it," snapped Robbard, "Had to practically lift it off us before we saw the girl running off into the haze."

Such a response only intensified the laughter bellowing from Dovan, who promptly received a fist full of ash to the face, choking and laughing more as he brushed it away.

Selwyn sighed. He was in command of a group of children too focussed on pricking and prodding each other for a fight than seeing the job done.

"Garton, do me a service and get the girl," Selwyn sighed.

Garton gave a quick nod, stomping through the dirt in the survivor's direction.

"Wait!" shouted Silas, "With all due respect Sir, Garton may not be the best idea to go hunting down a little girl."

The broken warrior let out an annoyed expression as he stared down the young boy.

"If I may, I think she needs a more friendly, less intimidating face to approach her," said Silas, he looked over to Garton, "No offence, but Garton sends shivers of fear into even the most stalwart of men, allow me to go after her, I am young and most probably a lot further from those that caused such destruction than the rest of you."

Despite the annoyance in his eyes, he agreed with the comment. His appearance is the talk of nightmares for little boys and girls.

"Fine," said Selwyn, the care of the matter had since drained from him, "But you're not going alone, Arturius follow him after the girl whilst I sort out these fools."

"Seriously!" snapped Robbard, "You're going to let Silas go with -."

"Oh Fuck off Robbard you inbred twit," interrupted Burak, dropping a brief wink to Arturius as he passed him.

He nodded to Silas and followed him into the unknown, visibility was very harsh he could barely see his hand wave before his face–let alone breathe the surrounding air.

"Stay close Silas. I don't know if there is anything else hiding out here," said Arturius, his voice fell short of him due to the denseness of the floating ash, "Now is most certainly not the time I wish to discover more mysteries that may lurk within this darkness."

~ *"And what of the outriders? they should be here by now!"* ~

# Chapter IX: Fangs Of The Serpent

The shadow of Silas was faint in front of him, despite only being a couple of steps ahead. Every step the two took forward only resulted in the ashen mist growing ever darker.

"Nah, it looks like any threat is long gone now," replied Silas, "Whatever came through here has long gone. Taken away the spoils of an easy slaughter, still I will feel most comfortable with your presence beside me."

Despite the encroaching darkness and lack of visibility, the two remained close, always within arm's length of one and other. Walking through the smoke and close quarters of the ruins felt claustrophobic, even the air was scarce, which only further fuelled whatever panic would emerge from the two as they delved deeper into the unknown.

"How the hell are we supposed to find her in all this," whispered Silas, waving his hands in the air trying to dissipate the thick smoke, "I can't even see my hand before my own face, it's impossible."

"Quiet!" hushed Arturius, "There in the air, do you hear it?"

A faint whisper echoed through the air to him, quiet but clear. Whatever it said was unintelligible, but still better than the silence they were following previously.

"What are you talking about?" whispered Silas, "I hear nothing but the crackling of that which burns around us, everything else is silent."

It was so clear to Arturius, as clear as day itself, why was it absent from the ears of the young boy that accompanied him. It called to him gently, a quiet hum that pulled him further into the void of ash and smoke.

"This way," he whispered, darting to the left through an old stone cobbled archway.

"Hang fast," replied Silas, trying to keep up with him, "You move too quickly, I fear that I will lose my way within this maze of smoke."

But Arturius didn't wait. Much like a hound on the trail of blood, he sniffed out the whispers coming from the distance. He followed the sounds, turning when they grew quieter, following breadcrumbs left behind for them along the track.

"Can you just wait a minute," asked Silas, even when he demanded he was polite as ever, "How do you know you follow the right path, we could be running in circles, just wait, please!"

"This way," Arturius called once more, "No time to speak."

Truth be told, he had no idea where he was going. An echo through the air aided him through the thicket of charred wood and blackened stone, whispering relentlessly. Just as the whisper grew into a deafening hush, so too did it fade into the winds. Flowing freely to the outskirts of the town.

It wasn't until they reached the dilapidated house on the edge of its borders did the whisper truly cease to be. It was a crooked and falling to the ground, though not because of the blazing inferno that had passed through. What remained of the door had been left ajar and the surrounding ash disturbed by movement.

"In there," said Arturius, staring deeply into the dark house, "Deep within the house."

"What's in there?" replied Silas.

"The voices," he whispered, his body slowly edged forward, uncontrolled with a mind of its own, "The voices through the ash, they chanted a sweet murmur gently as we navigated the smoke, they called to me and disappeared into that house."

"What did they say?" asked Silas, clearly unnerved by the revelation of such abnormalities, "It is not normal to hear such things amongst those who lie dead."

Arturius did not respond, instead, he elected to continue in his pursuit.

Before long he had descended into the darkness, leaving a worried Silas to trail behind him. Beyond the darkened doorway, dim lights reflected off the ash as they flowed through the holes upon the roof. A thick blanket covered the floor as snow would in the cold. Every step they took the floorboards creaked a chorus of twists and groans, rejecting their very presence and letting all that lurked within aware of the new guests.

Fresh footprints trailed across the floor, zig-zagging in a panicked pattern as they darted from room to room. They were small. It was definitely hers. The indent deeper at the toes suggested she was sprinting hard and fast–what would you expect at the sight of the company. However, as Arturius followed keenly through the house, the indents grew shorter. The distance between the paces came closer. And then they stopped.

Upon closer inspection of his surroundings, it was apparent that this was a family home, impoverished but still homely. What made for beds were neatly wrapped away in the corner of the first room, a mere bed of straw and cloth. Crude chairs sat neatly around the table, the food still sat atop, uneaten and rotting. The attack must have happened suddenly for everything in their lives to have halted so abruptly.

"Even the poor can't escape the injustice in this world," Arturius turned about, Silas stood there pondering over the conditions that were laid out before him. The scraps of food that had been left in the slaughter were not enough to feed a small child, let alone a starving family.

"The elite and powerful sit in their stone fortresses, exploiting the position of those deemed beneath them, the lowly peasants of the realm," mulled Silas, "They feast more in one banquet than these would have seen in a whole year, why is there so much disparity in the world, so much disorder."

A lonely tear rolled down his cheek, absorbed into a paste by the ash stuck upon his cheek.

"There is something I wish to speak with you of Arturius," said Silas, "Something I was advised against by Selwyn, I have kept this secret for all my life yet around you I feel especially at ease, as though I have garnered a deep trust for you all my life."

Silas looked him dead in the eyes, a secret of the most dangerous kind.

"I–," Silas was unexpectedly halted,

The floorboards wailed and echoed through the desolate house, a noise shuffling in the corner. It quickly drew the attention of both of them. A ragged carpet that lay across the floor with its corner upturned caught the eye of Arturius. Creeping quietly, he approached, taking great care to step quietly through the room.

It was clear by the dust that had been brushed aside, leaving the rough floorboard clearly visible.

"There!" exclaimed Arturius quietly, "Something lies beneath this."

As he ran his fingers across the carpet until he felt a solid bump around its centre.

"Come, Help me with this."

The two of them gripped at opposite corners of the rug, throwing it to the back of the room. A sparkling cascade of ash and dust spread through the air before gently descending back into its slumber. Beneath it lay a wrought iron handle. The faint outline of a door crept along its edges.

"It's a war shelter," said Silas, "Crude but still useable."

"A what?" replied Arturius.

"A war shelter, many in the dark times, used it to hide within in the event of a pillaging party. The ones I have seen are much more elaborate, but they all serve the same function."

Again the sound of feet shuffling beneath the floor met with their ears, scurrying around as a mouse caught trekking through the darkness. The two locked eyes across from each other, Arturius crossed his arms across his chest before gesturing at the trapdoor. Silas responded with a quick nod, darting his gaze back towards the door, burying his feet into the floor ready to pounce. With a trembling hand, Arturius reached for the handle, grasping firmly against the cold iron, its rough surface cutting deep into his hands.

Before either of them knew it, the door had flung open, nearly ripping its hinges from the floor. There lay frightened child, curled up within the darkness, grasping at the dirty locks of hair concealing her face. The surprise of hands clasping around her body would've been enough to induce the terror into anyone as Silas sprung forth, stopping her from sprinting off into the smoke once more. She screeched a deafening squeal as she writhed around in his arms, struggling and straining before digging her teeth into Silas's forearm.

"Argh!" Silas cursed, "She bit me!"

Such searing pain lessened his grip on her enough to allow her to flee as he clenched the deep bite marks that were oozing red. She sprinted hard and fast, darting over and under every obstacle in her path.

"Wait!" shouted Arturius, "We aren't here to hurt you!"

He leapt aggressively across the furniture in pursuit. She was quick for a young girl, especially one who had braved the desolation for so long. After tumbling over and under everything in his way, he could finally grasp the back of her tattered clothes, pulling her back to him with a quick tug. She did not take it well, lashing out as she tried to prise herself from his arms. Tightening his grip gently but firm as he tried to quell her rage-induced panic.

"Shhhh, it's okay, it's okay," he whispered calmingly, "We aren't here to hurt you, we're here to help. Calm yourself."

Her struggles faded as he repeatedly spoke to her gently and softly. Easing her from her panicked state. Eventually, she lay still, silent but still breathing heavily under her condition.

Her condition was very poor, succumbing to hunger and the elements, wasting away into a sickly shape.

"You okay over there?" asked Arturius, still grasping the little girl in his arms, Silas nodded.

"It's not too bad, stings a little, but I'll be fine," he replied, "Nothing a tonic and bandage won't fix."

Both directed their attention to the child, trembling in his arms as she stared solemnly into the distance. The poor soul must have seen horrors her young mind could never have comprehended.

"What's your name?" asked Arturius, cradling her in his arms as she gently pressed herself to his chest–strange for one to feel such warmth in a stranger. She remained silent, not quite ready to converse in her apparent captors.

"It's okay you don't need to talk right now, but know you are safe," he said, lifting her up whilst holding her tight, "We had best head back, by the looks of it this house may fall any minute, don't worry, however, I won't let anyone hurt you."

He glanced over to Silas, still clamping down on the bite wound across his arm.

"We should head back to the others," said Arturius. The girl struggled a little, unwilling to go to the monsters that had previously chased her within her mind.

"Easy, it's okay, they are good people, I promise," he said reassuringly.

The smoke had since begun to dissipate, slowly unveiling more of the carnage that had been unleashed upon the village and its inhabitants. Scorch marks darker than the deepest blackness painted vivid shapes across the walls.

Such intensity was the inferno that even that which should not melt had laid in a hardened molten pool upon the surface of the floor.

~ *"I see the tracks, though no presence of life appears to be near"* ~

## CHAPTER X: OMINOUS SHADOWS

With visibility vastly improved it was not long before the trio had regrouped with the rest of the company, many of the structures had since collapsed upon themselves, unable to stand with the devastation around. It revealed only more of a disgusting sight to the horrors which these people had suffered, slain in their very homes. A disgusting number of corpses mangled and burnt now lay across the street. The others had been hard at work, carefully rounding them up to prepare them for the burial they deserve–rather than be left out to rot.

Selwyn sighed with relief upon seeing the two emerging from the thinning smoke. How long had it been since their departure, he thought, staring at the company as they worked away? Robbard and Dovan appeared disappointed by the emergence of Arturius, no doubt hoping for an accident to swiftly bring about his untimely departure from the group.

"There you both are," he bellowed, a smile emerged from his rough face now strewn thick with ash, "You worried us for a while then, a long time has kept you from us, I sent Burak and Karlan to search for you both."

Behind them emerged a scoff from Dovan and Robbard–not that it came as a shock to him either way.

"And what do we have here?" said Selwyn, approaching the young girl as she tightened her grip around Arturius.

"Found her hiding in one of the houses outback," said Silas, "She's pretty shaken up Sir, no doubt the attack has mangled her mind."

"I would expect nothing less," replied Selwyn, "To have witnessed such horrors, and no less survived through them would traumatise such a gentle mind."

The old leader cradled his hand.

"I'm Selwyn, my lady," he spoke softly, "And what is your name?"

Such a soothing tone took Arturius by surprise, a soft blend of peaceful tones and a strong protective gruff. The little girl remained calmly silent, looking up into the eyes of Arturius. He could see the genuine fear in her eyes, not the fear of man, but that of a child who has lost everything.

He laid her down gently. Her bare feet disappeared into the thick ash upon the floor, grasping high around her ankles.

"It's okay," said Arturius, "You can trust him, he will not hurt you."

Suddenly a gentle smile grew across her face–The innocence of a child is the purest of all emotions to behold.

"Phie," she whispered, "My name is Phie."

Not once did she avert her eyes, focussing carefully upon the greyed man that stood before her.

"Phie, a beautiful name for a beautiful girl it would seem," Selwyn smiled, "And do you live here Phie?"

She nodded, shuffling her feet in an anxious dance.

"I see, do you live here with anyone else Phie, your mother, father?"

She nodded again. An undertone of hesitation filled his voice. He knew deep down the answer to the question he was about to ask.

"Where are they now?" he asked. She looked directly up into his eyes. Her dirt-laden face showed no expression as it lay emotionless from the horrors she had witnessed.

She shrugged.

A slight momentary relief. It was more than possible that they could have escaped, ran to get help–but why leave her to an unknown fate.

"You have done so well to make it this far Phie, what happened here? How did you survive?" questioned Selwyn, guilty at making the child relive the horrors of her past–though a necessary evil.

"They came, they came in the night," she said, a bland, monotonous tone shrivelled with the broken innocence, "They started taking people from their homes, mother wanted to play a game with me, she told me to hide under the floor in the scary space and that she would come to find me later."

To hear such words come from one so pure, dug deep into the hearts of everyone around. Even Garton–with a will of iron–fell sway to the emotions that brewed.

"I waited for a long time," she continued, "Nobody came and it got scary in the dark."

"And what happened next?" asked Selwyn calmly,

"I left to search for mother," replied Phie, "Sometimes I hide too well and she can't find me."

Selwyn held his breath, nodding for the little girl to continue.

"When I opened the door, there was a lot of smoke," she continued, "I thought maybe mummy had forgotten about dinner again, she can be silly like that sometimes."

"Did you see what happened?" asked Selwyn rather impatiently, "Did you find your mother?"

"No," replied Phie gently, "I went outside and everything was burning, I could hear some screams that frightened me a little, I went off to find mummy and daddy to make sure they were okay."

"And what did you see?" whispered Selwyn.

"There were some big bad men, with the faces of nasty monsters screaming at everyone, hitting them hard with metal sticks until they stopped moving,"

Arturius swallowed hard. It was truly difficult to hear such words come from someone so young.

"I saw the village chief talking to the biggest one," said Phie, "I couldn't hear what he was saying, but he was crying a lot, I heard him keep saying they are not here."

"Where is he now?" asked Selwyn.

"He's over there," replied Phie. She pointed across the wastes of cinders and ash. Suspended high above to the houses, lashed with blackened chains, was the burnt and mangled corpse of a lone individual. His ankles had chained him above an open fire pit, slowly burnt to a crisp. A few metal spikes had pierced various points across his body, no doubt to maximise the effect of pain upon his body before death.

Hope was looking rather dim for the possibility of any more survivors. Selwyn gulped as a trickle of sweat fell from his brow, swallowed up by the dirt beneath his feet.

"Did you see anyone else, was anyone taken away or let free?" asked Selwyn, the nervousness in his breath become more apparent with every second that passed, were you able to locate your parents?",

"I saw daddy being pushed around on the floor," replied Phie, "Though I think he was tired from everything, he was lay on the floor as they moved him with the others that were also tired."

Arturius peered over his shoulder. A stomach of iron or callous minds was holding back the tears from everyone else in the company.

"They kept asking questions to everyone over and over again," she whispered, "But everyone started getting too tired."

The group looked on as the young girl, tormented by the acts she had witnessed described, in horrific detail the inhumane slaughter that has befallen the village. The village chief had appeared to be the first victim of such a crime. Between the rest of the inhabitants, they drew a form of lottery, stripping mother from daughter, father from son. Though in truth, there was nothing lucky about either outcome. It sounded as though those who knew nothing were of no use to the aggressors, put to death in ways more horrific than anyone could have foreseen.

“What happened to those who talked Phie?” interrupted Robbard, prompting a piercing glare from Selwyn, who immediately reprimanded him for interrupting. Phie merely shrugged, exhausted from such a vivid retelling of her encounter.

“You have done well little one,” said Selwyn, “Rest, know you are safe now.”

“How?” asked Silas, “How can one enforce such brutality to those unable to fight back”,

Many of the others remained silent, disgusted by the acts of terror enacted on those they once called friend and ally.

“Because there is such evil in this world, an evil that needs to be stamped out at the root,” said Ozark. He had spent some time gathering whatever rags and cloth he could lay his withered hands upon. Hoping at the very least to provide the dead with some dignity upon this realm.

“Nay,” Arturius whispered, “There is no good and evil rooted within this realm.”

He spoke hushed yet within close earshot to the others.

“What do you mean?” asked Silas, “Of course there is good and evil, how can this not be proof enough for you.”

“There is only action and consequence,” replied Arturius, “Good and evil is defined by the victors, or at least those who survive the upcoming storm.”

“Spoken like a true scholar,” replied Ozark, impressed with the philosophy that emerged from his mind, “In another day and age I could’ve made a fine politician out of you.”

The company carefully laid the many souls to rest, digging graves deep into the earth so they may remain undisturbed in their slumber. It was difficult. Digging so many graves in one day amounted to nothing more than psychological torture for the weaker-minded of the company,

Arturius watched as each body they buried wore down on them.

They had lost much time in the pursuit of the greater good, seventy-three graves–unmarked and crude–had been erected in the lush fields that encircled the ruins. As time had passed, the debilitating smoke had all but vanished, allowing the light of day to shine once more upon the fallen, unveiling the true extent of the horrors.

"Will you be going after the others?" asked Phie, curious was her mind, for even amidst the unhallowed scenes that had unfurled before her, a glimmer of hope remained.

"What others?" said Arturius, confused.

"The others they took away,", replied Phie, "They put them in a cart and took them away."

A glimmer of hope shone through upon, pounding deep within his chest. Arturius contained himself, trying to remain calm and collected as he spoke.

"Of course we will," he replied, "Maybe you can help me a little then?".

Phie nodded.

"Do you know which way they took them and how many?" asked Arturius.

She nodded again.

"They took two carts," she replied, "Mummy was on one of them."

She pointed to the eastern path the led from the village,

"They took the bigger ones that way,". She continued. She turned about and pointed to the western path that led from the village.

"Thank you Phie," smiled Arturius, "Don't you worry we will get them back."

It was clear by the tracks stamped into the ground that they had been corralled into tightly packed herds. The footprints were of all shapes and sizes, large and small, long and short. Scuff marks in the dirt would only prove these poor souls had been chained by the ankles, forced to walk in humiliating columns as they were hustled into the back of the carts Phie witnessed.

"Any more luck with the girl," said Selwyn, "I couldn't help but notice her speaking to you some more."

He approached swiftly to his side; his skin whiter than usual. His eyes growing heavier with despair.

"Yes," he replied, though he was not yet willing to depart the new information, "But first I want some answers from you,"

His question appeared to come as a shock to Selwyn, never had another demanded answers from him before. The shock on his face faded as he realised the truth could not be kept from him any longer.

"You want to know about the settlers here," he replied, "Very well."

He gestured for Arturius to sit beside him.

"Yes, it is true, the good people that lived here supported us in our efforts, supplying us with what food and resources they could spare, an act I can promise you made me more grateful by the day,"

Arturius looked upon him with eager eyes.

"You knew that the very act was defiance against the Masked One, yet you allowed them to continue, why?" asked Arturius, "surely you knew such assistance would send them to their deaths if caught!"

"I was desperate," replied Selwyn, "You have no idea what it's like to have so many look to you in their time of need, or watch as your own men starve, or when those you care about are dying and you don't have the means to ease their suffering before you judge me on the outcome of my actions today just remember that everything I did I did for my people."

He looked at his surroundings, the destruction that lay before him a stark reminder of what comes with war.

"This is why a balance must be restored to the realm," said Selwyn, "The whole nature of the Soulus is delicately balanced, just a slight tip of the scale can have drastic consequences, and what happened that day seven years ago kicked the scales over completely, those who helped us in whatever way they could know what needed to be done to save the realm and restore balance."

The old captain gazed across the destruction, still guilt-stricken by the weight of risk he had thrust upon those he so wished to protect.

"Why must so many die in the name of one monsters' goal for total power." hissed Selwyn.

"Perhaps he is not seeking power untold," replied Arturius, "We have no way of knowing what is hiding in the darkest recess of one's mind, we can only assume that there is a clear disparity between us and them, though sometimes that is not truly the case."

Arturius stood up, walking a few steps ahead before turning to face Selwyn. His face hung with sadness, fighting with his own inner demons for control of his emotions.

"They didn't die in vain, my honourable captain," said Arturius, "They believed in you when hope seemed all but gone, they gave their blood so you may have a chance at restoring the old as new,"

Selwyn looked him in the eyes, the blood of the innocent stained his hands indefinitely. Yet Arturius did not care about past mistakes, for they lay far in the past, a place that could not be changed.

"Don't despair Sir," he continued, "You gave them something more powerful than anything found in existence."

Selwyn looked upon him with doubtful eyes.

"And what would that be?" he muttered,

"Hope."

Such words sparked a long-lost emotion within the captain. A rush of warmth brought life to his skin once more. He smirked to himself, before bursting into a full fit of laughter.

"You truly are a remarkable one I tell you," said Selwyn, his voice brimming with excitement, "It would honour me for you join this company, a fully fledged companion and see that such inspiring words of wisdom continue to forever bolster strength within me anew."

He promptly stood to his feet, crunching hard against cold ground as his blade glinted against the sun full of splendour.

"Kneel!" he ordered

By now the rest of the company had emerged around him, observing the anointment of a new member, a luxury they had seldom seen in the past years.

Arturius quickly obliged. Dropping upon one knee and crossing his arm across it tenderly, bowing his head as would the penitent man. He thrusted the tip of the sword atop his left shoulder, resting in gently and with exquisite precision, yet gently cutting into his flesh.

"Do you agree to stay true to the values of this company in protecting the innocent, stamping out the evil that has taken control of this realm and helping those who need it most?"

"I do," he replied,

"Do you promise to give your life, in the pursuit of good, order and light?"

"I do," he replied,

"Do you swear to restore balance to the realm and continue to do so until your last dying breath?"

"I swear," he replied,

"Then rise, rise forth into our company and join the ranks of our order, so that one day we may see the great phoenix fly once more into the dawn."

As he rose high from the ashes, he felt almost reborn. The hot cinders reminded him of the pain in the realm, the pain he would fight to cease.

"In unity lies strength," proclaimed Selwyn,

"In duty lies honour," replied Arturius. The words that had been buried deep within the recesses of his mind now brought forth clarity, a newfound purpose within him.

While many of the others were jovial at the anointment of a new companion, some were not. Still,

Robbard refused to accept him as one of their own, going far as to snuff his advance and wander off into the ash.

"It brings me much joy to have you on board with us," said Ozark, he stretched out his withered arm, an honour that Arturius returned clasping his forearm with gratitude, "I expect great things to come for us now, I saw two ravens flying up high earlier, it is a sign."

"Here we go again," bellowed Karlan, "The old fool and his superstitions again, watch out for black cats and rabbits' feet."

A swift backhand from Burak knocked the wind from him, staggering back against the charred remains of an unknown structure crashing into it with a mighty crash–He truly had great strength beyond anyone else around.

"Give him a break, Karlan, and you don't have any faith, superstition, something to believe in?" barked Burak. Despite his gentle disposition, he was intimidating when angered.

"The only superstition I believe in is myself," said Karlan, brushing the soot off his clothes, a smog of blackened dust erupting from him with every strike, "And whatever the mobs of dead may leave for me to plunder."

As Karlan's feet crunched beneath the desolate earth, his hands-supple as they were-plucked trinkets from the bones of the poor souls.

"You know what, for poor beggars and destitute vagabonds they sure had some fine tastes" sneered Karlan, "Such jewels may fetch a fine price in the slums of the realm. But this, this stays with me."

Beneath the charred remains and soft ash, Karlan bequeathed upon himself a blade of exquisite craft. Adorned with fine jewels and carved gold of a feminine physique. *"How could such deprived villagers afford such luxuries?"* Arturius thought to himself, although luxuries in these parts were scarcely seen in the form of gold and jewels.

"I've always wanted a special lady within my life."

Karlan promptly sheathed the blade, casting aside his old rusted dagger for the new blade.

"Leave it be!" snarled Dovan, "Have you no respect for the dead! Leave them in peace. Along with what little they had in this godforsaken life."

Karlan shook his head.

"And leave it all for the Reavers to plunder! I think not," replied Karlan, "Besides, I always feel more comfortable with a woman strapped between my thighs."

The others though visibly discomforted by the remarks deign to speak out.

"Superstitions," scoffed Karlan, "Such vilified beliefs will get you no further in life than those that now litter the earth beneath your feet."

"Ignore him Arturius, believe what you want to believe," said Silas, "He doesn't understand what it means to have faith in something other than yourself. For the record, however, two ravens foretells great prosper in the days to come."

"And one raven?" asked Arturius.

"Means death shall arrive swiftly," replied Silas, "Often in the form an augur of shadow and darkness."

"Or that there will be many corpses for them to feast upon later that day" laughed Karlan, undeterred by the darkness of which they spoke. The others merely scoffed about his attitude, neglecting to allow him the audience to which he was seeking.

The many diverse and strange superstitions spread far across the realm to which they inhabit, each one more obscure to the last, offering tales of good fortune or omens of an ill death.

"Arturius, to which heading were the prisoners directed," asked Selwyn, "I'll be damned if I allow another one of those poor souls to be lost into the darkness of the snakes' lair."

He stood tall and proud, grasping the pommel of his sword. A changed man.

"Phie spoke of some villagers being taken away in carts, and by the tracks they left it would appear they were all bound in chains," said Arturius, "They took the largest and strongest of them westward and the others on an easterly heading."

Arturius gestured over to the tracks he previously uncovered.

"It can't be a coincidence!" muttered Selwyn, as he gazed off into the horizon,

"What do you mean?" Arturius replied, "What is a coincidence?"

Selwyn remained silent a little longer, continuing to stare off towards the east. He was muttering incoherently beneath his breath.

"Sir?" said Arturius

Selwyn promptly snapped out of his estranged focus, straightening himself up as he fumbled with his voice.

"Sorry, I lost my mind in thought," Selwyn said, "And you're sure she saw them head in that direction?"

Arturius thought for a moment.

"Without a doubt," he replied, "She is a remarkable young girl, to remember so much through such horrific acts."

Selwyn knelt beside the tracks in the dirt. He peeled off his gloves, stuffing them into his pockets. Gently running his fingers over the many footprints beneath him as he darted from one to another, briskly rubbing a sample of dirt between his fingertips.

"And you believe she spoke truthfully?" Selwyn asked, "that her words have not been manipulated through trauma or forces unseen?".

"Absolutely Sir," replied Arturius, "May I ask what relevance this bears upon the situation?"

Selwyn crept across the floor, a predator scanning the ground for the tracks of its prey. Before anyone could interrupt him, he came to a sudden halted, brushing his hand across the floor, examining the residue across his hand intently. He tasted it.

"It's just as I thought," he said, bring himself upright, "There is a salty taste within the soil, minor but potent enough."

"And this can help us how?" asked Robbard sarcastically.

The Captain turned to his company, the setting sun beaming behind him darkening his figure as the winds blew briskly around him, creasing his cape as it flowed behind him.

"The salt in the soil is unique to the caverns of the Vale of Eryne," replied Selwyn, "The waters that run through those lands come from the dark sea, depositing deep within its earth."

"So, in other words you mean to say–," said Ozark,

"- Yes, Ozark," interrupted Selwyn, "It means we are headed for the Akavirian homeland, but more importantly this means they have made passage through the Dwelvar gates."

"But those gates have remained sealed for thousands of years!" exclaimed Dovan, "Locking the land into an eternal servitude of nothingness, no one has ventured within since the way was shut."

Selwyn nodded, acknowledging the worry from the younger warrior.

"The gates will open upon one condition and one condition only," said Selwyn, "And such an event can only mean one thing, the ancient city of Nordellar has awoken from its ruin."

"Then the prophecy is true," Said Dovan, who had been silent since witnessing the massacre, "The Empty Throne has summoned the call, the crowns of old echo in the deep for their convergence."

"So, it would seem," whispered Selwyn

"Then we need to act fast, Sir," bellowed Robbard, "More will come to attempt to make passage into Nordellar, the technology and arsenal that must lie beneath its shadow will allow one to command near-absolute power of the realm."

Arturius stared upon him with astonishment. His attitude until now had been much more hostile towards himself and Selwyn's decisions. Now they seemed but a mere whisper in the past,

"What are your orders!? Sir," bellowed Robbard,

Such respect was followed by the others nestled around them.

"Kezin!" Shouted Selwyn,

The young man jumped from the shadows. A peculiar individual, so silent and obscured, Arturius had forgotten that he was even there. As he emerged from within the shadows, the light bounced off his dulled and blackened hair as it draped across his face. He was a sickly thin figure, not a fighter within the group, though his skill set lay more within the methods of sabotage, espionage and, sometimes, assassination. After all, who would suspect such a small and shrivelled looking man to commit such deeds. Karlan spoke rather highly of him, commenting that should you require a way in or out of a castle, the darkest secrets of your enemies or even an accident to befall an entire city, then he was your man.

"You called Sir," whispered Kezin. His voice was ever so soft and supple, quieter than the whispers he would indeed pluck from the mouths of his marks.

"Go to our allies, tell them of what we have discovered." said Selwyn, "Tell them the void calls for that which is lost, the whisper has been found and the heir of the dawn moves with the shadows, tell them the time has come to make our move."

"As you command," whispered Kezin, a gentle smirk emerged upon his darkened face before he quickly disappeared back into the shadows, not even disturbing the ash that lay beneath his feet.

It was a strange feeling that overcame Arturius upon Kezin's disappearance, for when he slunk into the darkness it was almost as though a whisper that had been murmuring within his head was snuffed out for good.

"Our time has come men," bellowed Selwyn, "Today is our day, the day when we pursue those that have plunged this realm into this wicked darkness, today is the day we will begin the true fight, for no more shall we lurk within the shadows, today we fight, we fight for those we have lost and those who are oppressed, I ask you all of one thing and one thing only, will you follow me once more and reclaim what was stolen from us?"

An uproar of chanting and salutes prompted Selwyn's speech. In the corner of his eye even little Phie raised her arms above her head in applause; though perhaps she was too innocent to understand the nature of such words.

"Gather whatever you can carry," continued Selwyn, "We move out within the hour."

Arturius approached the young Phie, sitting patiently atop the broken stone wall that encircled the village, gently swaying to and fro with the wind.

"You have been most brave to survive out here as long as you have," said Arturius, "Do you have anyone to go to, any family that can look after you."

She shook her head, all the while retaining her innocent smile.

"No," she replied, "There is only mummy and daddy, everybody else left long ago."

"It's not safe for you to stay here," said Arturius, "Perhaps Selwyn will allow you to come with us, at least you will be safe."

Phie continued to look at him, her smile never fading as she continued to sway.

"It's okay master Arturius," she replied, "Daddy will wake up soon, he will look after me and then you can go get mummy for me and we can be together again, she won't be hard to find she wears a pretty necklace I made for her, it has beads and charms that daddy helped me to make for her."

It was unbearable. The thought of such delicate innocence being abused by the horrors that scorched her mind sent shivers through Arturius. Her mind was broken beyond what any man let alone a child should ever experience. To leave her here in such a harsh wilderness would amount to nothing more than a death sentence for the youngling. Even if by some chance her mother still lived, it would be nearly a fortnight before the two could be reunited once more.

"But Phie, they could be gone a long time, it's not safe for you to remain here," he said, crouching down beside her as he gently brushed the hair from her face.

"It's okay, daddy will wake up soon, he won't leave me," she muttered, "He is just tired."

Through all the heartache and pain, he could see that her mind had truly fragmented, her innocence crushed into dust. Arturius could only watch as her spirit deteriorated. A lone tear rolled down her expressionless face, soaked up by the dirt that clung to her face.

"Okay Phie," whispered Arturius, croaking his voice as he forced the words from his mouth, his throat and heart burned as he forced it out.

He turned away to go re-join with the others, only to feel a gentle tug at his belt. As he turned Phie had stood at his side grasping at his leathers with an enormous smile across her face.

"Thank you, sir," she said, "You are a very nice man, much nicer than the men that came before, especially the big scary one."

A wave of uneasiness flowed through his chest, crunching at his emotions and quickening the pace of his breath.

"This scary one. Did he say anything or do anything different to the others?" he asked,

Phie nodded quickly, not letting go of Arturius's belt as she thought hard.

"He was big, bigger than you and daddy," she whispered, "He was the one who hit people that fought back, I heard them talking to him a lot, calling out his name whenever someone wouldn't talk."

"What did they call him little one?" asked Arturius hesitantly,

"They called him Vortuse, I think," she replied,

He turned pale "This is not good," he thought to himself, "There were a lot of scores to settle with this monster. Such an encounter could cause the others to act rashly and without persecution or thoughts of a sound mind."

"Thank you Phie, you're a beautiful little girl, here take this," he handed her his ration pack, made up for each of the companions along for the journey, "It's some food and supplies, take them and go to your house, don't come out for anyone else."

From far across the ruins he could hear Selwyn shouted forth.

"Let's move out everyone, we won't stop now until we reach the Dwelvar gates, the journey will be long and arduous so I don't want to hear any of your complaints along the way," such a booming voice echoed across the plains sending a murder of crows scared into flight.

And with that they departed, moving swiftly away from the ruins of Riftmyer, wiped off the face in a mere night. As the group rode on, Arturius looked back upon the charred remains of Riftmyer. Stood at the corner of a burnt house was the young girl waving to them, a dirty cloth in hand. When she finished sending them on she gently covered the body of a lone man sat up against to wood, finding comfort in his stiff embrace as she cuddled close.

Arturius looked back at the others, each one guilt-stricken with grief, the type of grief that comes with failure and responsibility. Despite Selwyn's attitude, his confidence and a positive new outlook, it was clear that deep down a heavy burden weighed upon him. Every step his horse took, clicking against the ground was like a clock counting down to the conflicts ahead–And they would indeed find that on the journey they had set out on.

"Sir," Arturius whispered, galloping up to the captain at the front, swiftly and with grace, "I must speak with you in private, it concerns matters you must hear of."

The old captain looked at him. Nodded and strode off ahead with his new knight.

"What seems to trouble you, my young recruit?" Selwyn asked, resting his hand atop the horn of his saddle, caressing it nervously.

"Phie told me of a man that took part in the village's slaughter," said Arturius, "Though in her words he wasn't a man but a big scary monster."

Selwyn darted his eyes over to him. A glimmer of fear and worry exploded from deep within him.

"It can't be!" he replied with great regret.

"I am afraid so Sir," said Arturius, "I fear Vortuse may be present at Nordellar, and with such a history with the others, it may prove rather difficult to control such deeply rooted emotions."

"Shit!" he exclaimed, "This isn't good at all, does anyone else know of this information?"

Arturius shook his head. The air had grown cold, biting at his body and prickling his skin all over. Though it was not the temperature that sent the shivers down his spine.

"Good, let's keep it that way for now," replied Selwyn, "Such news may prove too much for them to handle at this moment right now. We need everyone to be level-headed for the fight to come."

The journey was long and tiring; they did not rest, rarely slept, all of them focused on one thing and one thing only, reaching the fabled Dwelvar gates. A sight of which he had been told would be nothing that he could ever have imagined.

*~ "I can finally see the way, a light gleaming within the darkness" ~*

## CHAPTER XI: LIGHT IN THE DARKNESS

After what seemed like an age, the company finally reached its destination during the late hours of twilight. The air hung low with a thin humid mist, coating the land with a dense blanket that stretched far and wide.

The sun had not yet coated the land with its warming light, leaving only the dense blackness of the dark to greet them so coldly. A chill in the air bitterly wore down the company, no fires had been lit–they couldn't alert anyone to their presence.

Arturius rubbed his hands aggressively, trying to conjure up whatever warmth he could muster, *"By the gods it's cold"* he thought, his teeth chattered so loud he had to clamp his mouth shut.

"We wait here until sunrise," whispered Selwyn. The skies had broken with vast rays of red and orange, the sun was emerging slowly, streaming down warmth and light alike. A sudden breeze blew crisp, fresh air into their way. A new day had begun.

Around them the light painted their surroundings with brilliant colours, a vibrant land lost to nature. Arturius felt the trickle of the morning dew fell upon his face, dripping from the trees he stood beneath, cold yet refreshing.

"Keep your eyes alert," said Dovan, scanning the words afar as if waiting patiently for something to emerge.

"What for?" asked Silas, sitting down beneath a great ash tree.

"Wolves, bears, anything that preys on the flesh of man," replied Dovan, fixated on his surroundings, "There are many creatures of a great mystery that lurk within the darkest depths of the forests that surround us, and they will not hesitate to make their mark."

Far in the distance, a great shadow loomed across the expansive forests. The occasional howl and murmur of its inhabitants worried the more nervous of the company. Who only knows what dark and decrepit creatures lurked deep within its embrace?

"At least wolves would put up a better fight than the Rekeshi bitches ahead," Robbard said, "Maybe I will get to let loose a few arrows their way, should they venture to close."

Robbard sat up against a tree, slowly grinding a whetstone hard against tips of his arrows–as if they weren't already sharp enough.

A sudden silence descended upon the company. The sound of a crackling fire and booming thunder travelled with the wind. It sent the horses into a shrill panic, taking the combined strength of the company to restrain and calm them. They all looked amongst themselves uneasily. No one dared to speak.

"What the hell was that?" beckoned Arturius, unaware of the fear in the eyes of those around him, "It sounded as though the very sky has split, releasing the force of the heaven down upon us."

"Black thunder!" muttered Ozark, tensely gripping the reins of his horse.

Selwyn exhaled worriedly, "This complicates things greatly."

"What's black thunder?" questioned Arturius.

He looked to the others, yet they were too distracted with the thoughts running through their minds.

"It's the Rekeshi master weapon," said Selwyn, "It's an essence known only to the high Warlocks of Vastern, a powerful creation that produces fire and thunder, reducing anything before it into nothing."

Arturius sat down upon the soft grass, pondering on this destructive force he had just witnessed with his ears.

"It was once believed to be lost to the ages, its recipe supposedly lost in the great tragedy of the towering inferno," croaked Ozark, "It was remade during the rise of the Masked One, more terrible and more powerful than ever, it burns with a heat so intense the very earth melts into ichorous earth, unextinguishable by water, sand and smothering alike, the last it was seen was seven years ago when they unleashed its full might upon the Farrosian capital of Dawnstar."

"A dark day that lay a blight across the Farrosian lands, forever tainting its beauty with blood," muttered Burak, "Scores of Farrosians lost into the night, not even their bodies were left by the raging inferno as it consumed flesh and stone."

Selwyn who had remained eerily quiet until this point finally chimed in.

"It was the primary reason for many of the other kingdoms near-immediate surrender," said Selwyn coldly, "Such death was let loose in the realm, a power that could go uncontested and would strike fear into the hearts of everyone at a mere whisper of its name."

Ozark smiled; a bright idea came to fruition within the corners of his brilliant mind.

"If black thunder is truly upon us, then they must have brought considerable stores with them to their encampment," said Ozark, "As is the way of the Rekeshi alchemists, never do they want to head out of Vastern with too little in their stores."

Selwyn looked at him, puzzled.

"And this helps us how?" replied Selwyn, shrugging at the frail man, "Thank you for such an input Ozark, but I think we all gathered for ourselves that there will be plenty more of the destructive compound to overcome."

Ozark sighed unenthusiastically.

"You misunderstand," he replied, "If we were to procure some samples from this cache, or even the lot if the opportunity arises, then we could have ourselves a sample of their greatest weapon, reverse engineer it, alchemize the produce and fire it back upon them in a blazing inferno."

"No!" replied Selwyn stern and sudden, "I will not allow this company that was founded upon the ideals of honour and the sanctity of life, such a weapon will only plunge us down a path we dare not follow, that damned concoction brings only death and a hunger for power, something I will not have whilst I still breath."

Arturius watched as Ozark's face shifted from the gleeful opportunity to the disappointing decision. The others muttered amongst themselves for some time, dividing them all and producing a rift to the potential of such might.

"But Sir, if we could just–," said Dovan, only to be interrupted from across the formation by Burak,

"You can't seriously think any of us could control such destruction, Dovan," hissed Burak, "Or do you forget of the ashes that fell upon our home when they first unleashed it upon us."

"I am merely suggesting-," replied Dovan,

"Well, don't!" snapped Burak, "I didn't survive the purge of the dawn only to see us all become that which we despise the most."

By now many of the others had turned their attention to the conversation at hand, sparking an argument between brothers and kin.

"Whilst it was a tragedy to lose so many of our own that fateful day Burak, imagine the blow we could deal setting up a few caches around the Rekeshi capital," said Robbard, "could you imagine the look beneath the Masked One's attire when he sees his kingdom go up in flames."

The bellowing voice of Selwyn crushed the malcontent spreading through the ranks.

"Enough!" he shouted, "My word is final, all I shall allow is the opportunity to destroy such a weapon, but only if the opportunity should arise!"

He stared directly into each one's eyes.

"Are we understood?"

A chorus of understanding and disappointment sounded within their voices. Yet all stayed loyal to his wishes.

As they all moved across the woodlands, more and more did the crackle of the black thunder shudder through the trees, bending their frames to its terrifying will. Every step closer they took ruptures and tremors swayed their movements and hindered their approach. Its intensity was so great that Arturius could seldom believe it when he was informed that they were still some miles from its epicentre.

The woodland provided the perfect vantage to their reconnaissance. If only the Rekeshi had the thought to post a few sentries within the thickets around their camp, it made such infiltration all the easier. With only one useable path that led to the main road from the Rekeshi encampment, it made defending their position a rather simple task. Though the encampment at the foot of the great mountain was vast and well supplied. And this was also heavily guarded.

Selwyn sent Robbard and Dovan ahead of the company. Both were accomplished with the way of the bow, excellent hunters and well disciplined; their keen eyes could catch a squirrel darting within a dense forest in the dark of night, their reaction could fell such a creature even easier. Selwyn boasted of their prowess for some time, complimenting them on such vigour and stealth. For they had made a name of themselves amongst the ranks of the Rekeshi legions, 'The piercing winds', for the last thing you will hear is the deathly whistle of the wind, and before you know, death will have claimed you.

"They've been gone some time now," mutter Karlan, nervously pacing a few steps before the opening, "It was to be a quick mission, in and out. Why do they falter?"

"They know what they are doing," replied Selwyn. He stared closely down the path before them, "Give them time, they will see it through."

"What if they've been captured?" asked Karlan.

Selwyn responded, cold and emotionless.

"They won't," replied Selwyn,

"What if they've been killed?" hushed Karlan.

"They haven't," snapped Selwyn, "Now stay your tongue, I do not wish to hear of its blabbering any longer, it insults my thoughts."

Such a nervous trembling was taking hold of Selwyn, it was clear that he too was worried about the outcome of such a mission.

The night was growing around them, amplifying the many sounds of deep. One by one they chirped and chant, mocking them as they sat enshrouded in such a deep blackness of the trees. Whatever lay in within its dense reaches was hungry for the flesh of man, something that would surely become available soon.

They had agreed to be back before nightfall, allowing for ample time in which to prepare for such proceedings in the coming morning.

"I cannot bear this any longer," hissed Karlan, "I am going to look for them."

"You shall do nothing of the sort," snapped Selwyn, "You are neither silent nor adept enough to make your way through these woods as they would, you shall wait for their return."

"Skaveth!" beckoned Karlan, "What use is waiting if they are not to return!"

"Insult me all you like, Karlan," glared Selwyn, "For it will only bring you pain quicker and more furiously."

The intense stare through the darkness ceased the vocal assault of the disquiet Karlan. He continued to stare as the beaten warrior slunk back into the shadows.

"Whilst I admire your admiration of our hunters Selwyn," whispered Ozark, "I too am ill at ease with our current situation, they have been absent for some time, I know you wish not to think of such an outcome; however, we must prepare for it none the less."

Ozark looked upon Selwyn for some comfort and ease from his worry. Yet only the back of his head spoke silently toward him.

"They will be fine," said Selwyn, his voice becoming more agitated with the malcontent of the others.

"But Sir, we need to face the facts," pleaded Burak, "If by some chance, Gods forbid they have been captured or killed, then the Rekeshi, even in their incompetent state, will surely send patrols to search the area, it may be only a matter of time before they stumble upon our here refuge."

Selwyn remained silent. His only focus was to the pathway ahead, the ever-shrinking and dimming pathway, despite the rising sun seemed to only darken as the hours ticked on. This only suffered more as the group grew only more restless.

With each passing minute they grew more and more apprehensive of the surroundings–In such dense woodland, it would be far too easy to lose sight of any predator within.

"I'm going to search for them," snapped Burak, brandishing an enormous battle-axe that lay resting against a nearby tree, "Who's coming with me?"

Before anyone could react, Selwyn slammed his fist against the tree to which he leant upon, splitting its bark violently.

"You shall do nothing of the sort!" barked Selwyn as he turned to Burak, "Or I shall have your head as a traitor and insubordinate swine."

Both men stood toe to toe against each other, glaring deeply upon one another. Such ferocity even surprised the hulking beast that was Burak, causing him to concede such anguish and to slump into the shadows with Karlan.

"If I say they will be back, then they will be back," hissed Selwyn, "If anyone else has an issue with that, then I will be happy to remind them again."

The group remained silent.

"Well, that was intense," laughed Karlan, promptly receiving the burning eyes from both participants.

Arturius shuffled over to Silas and Ozark, both sat inconspicuously amongst the shadows. Both had been muttering between themselves. Quietly, away from the ears of the others.

"How are you both doing over here," he asked. The two stopped muttering immediately.

"Could be better," laugh Ozark, gesturing across his body. A humorous attempt at brushing off his disfigurement.

"Good to hear," chuckled Arturius, "Silas?"

"Nervous, I suppose," he stuttered, "It's not every day you get to be one that enters a kingdom sealed away for a thousand years, who knows what lies beneath shrouded in mystery."

His body shuddered. A lot can change in a thousand years, who knows what secrets may lay in wait within this legendary place.

Before long, the night had grown to its darkest reach, blanketing the land with a thick obscuring blackness. It was during this time that the surrounding woods had fully awoken. The lack of visibility amplified every sound that emerged from the dark, heightening the senses. The darkness had an unusual edge this night, tipping further into the unknown than before. It left them feeling as though the very night itself were closely watching. Waiting.

Arturius shrugged it off. They had travelled harshly the past five days, travelling farther and farther on the tracks of the Rekeshi aggressors. The mind can be easily swayed when tiredness follows closely in its tracks. Yet he couldn't help but notice this uneasy chill in the air. Something was different. Something was worse.

A stiff wind had been blowing across the land, unrelenting and unforgiving. The trees rustled along with the many others that lurked beyond the visible barrier that lay before him.

Ever since he had first felt the intense tremors produced by the black thunder, he knew something had changed. All-day, he had felt as if something had awoken, from deep within its lengthy slumber. Watching him.

Arturius elected not to share his thoughts with the group, after all, they already had much cause for concern with the absence of Dovan and Robbard–both still yet to return from their reconnaissance. The only light around was the faint flick of the will-o-wisps dancing deep in the darkness.

"A cold chill echoes through the night, and so too does death follow, upon its white horse of dancing darkness, pale and cold as the night that follows," muttered Karlan,

"Didn't know you for much, the poet Karlan," Selwyn replied sarcastically, "Perhaps I shall have you conduct the sonnet of my life; glory behold in life as he shall in death, has a nice ring to it I think."

The others shared a quiet laugh.

"Would you look at that," smirked Ozark, "what happened to the *'I'm my own superstition'* eh."

Karlan blocked them both from his thoughts. It was the first time Arturius had witnessed a serious tone come unearthed from the usually laid-back trickster. The laughs promptly ceased as they returned to the reality they were stuck in. Still watching, still waiting. For anything.

The silence continued to grasp at their throats, no one dared to speak. No one knew what wise words they could conjure to quench the anxious thirst of them as they sat so solemnly depressed in the dark cold. He could feel it all too well as he sat there, waiting as the icy night chill clawed at his face.

It was the breaking of branches, the rustling of leaves that broke the tension–only to replace it anew. The others crept into position, Silas and Ozark to the rear of them all, away from any potential threat. Arturius gripped the pommel of his blade, it swung heavily to the left. Thanks to the kind effort of Ozark it had now been sharpened to deadly effect, now death would be all too real, should it find its mark.

He listened carefully to the forest; the tightening of Leather grasping at the axe of Burak, its razor-sharp crescent edge hung from the thick wrought iron that clasped to the pole; the shuffling of Karlan, crouching low as he drew his daggers before his face. Though he could not see him, the glint of metal could be traced low within the air, sparkling against the dim moon.

"Eyes front," whispered Selwyn, "If we can allow them to pass before we strike, make it quick, make it efficient."

The rustling grew louder. Each of them homed in on the brush before them, ready to strike.

It was a great relief when the two hunters burst through the treeline, panting and wheezing.

"It's about fucking time," beckoned Burak, slamming his axe into a nearby tree. Its heavy swing nearly cleaved the tree in two, "Damned nearly gave me a heart attack you fucks."

"You had us all worried," said Selwyn, a breath of relief shimmered from his mouth, a sigh releasing his tension, "What kept you so?"

"The camp is a little more well-defended that previously thought," said Dovan breathlessly, "Many weapons, many guards."

He must have sprinted back faster than the winds themselves, winded and fatigued with countless twigs emblazoned across his attire.

"Not to mention countless slaves they have in their employment," interjected Robbard, "Working them to the death it would seem."

*"Slaves?"* Arturius thought to himself *"What man thinks him above another to project such brutality",* even though no plan had yet been formed, he knew deep down that he would not let a single one of those chains remain unbroken.

"Tell me what you saw and leave no stone unturned," said Selwyn

It was well known through the eyes of Robbard, no detail could go undiscovered, no stone left unturned. Even Arturius had nothing but admiration for his skill. A keen eye and a sharp mind can find even the most obscure secret within the darkest corners. After all, such were the options of a noble in the times long since diminished. On the other side, Dovan was no more a nobleman than the horse he rode upon. Impoverished and orphaned, he grew to survive the harsh world that he was thrust into, raising his younger brother on the dangerous streets through thick and thin. Such circumstances left him highly adept at stealth and all kinds of thievery, from picking the pocket of unsuspecting marks, to the more dangerous act of poaching upon a lord's holdings.

"The camp is no more than a mile beyond these woods," said Dovan, "They have set up a well-fortified position at the foot of the mountain, pressed up against the gates, it was treacherous but none the less I got close, not much cover to go by. Robbard damn nearly got rumbled."

"Shut it," snapped Robbard embarrassed,

Dovan merely responded with a vulgar gesture, ruggedly waving before him.

"How close?" asked Selwyn, ignoring the pettiness between the two hunters.

"Close," replied Robbard, "Close enough to see what you required."

"I'll be the judge of that," said Selwyn, unsure as to the value the intel should hold, "What numbers are we talking?"

"Fifteen or twenty, it was difficult to tell," replied Dovan, "They were on constant patrol."

"Well, which is it," snapped Selwyn, "I won't make the mistake of going into the fray lacking adequate intel again!"

"Twenty," replied Dovan hastily,

"Weapons?" asked Selwyn,

"Mostly blades, four bows at a glance, a nasty-looking scorpion positioned centrally will surely prove challenging." said Robbard, "unsure of the adroitness of the personnel. Hopefully, they are all conscripts with little experience."

"Cavalry?" asked Selwyn,

"None of the sort," replied Robbard, "Camp is too packed for any manoeuvrability."

"Any chance of avoiding altogether?" questioned Selwyn.

"Unlikely," replied Dovan, "They have established quite the perimeter, all routes pass through the camp to reach the gates, not to mention the vast line of sight that scorpion may possess."

"Any civilians I need to made aware of?" queried Selwyn, "I want no casualties of the innocent, even if they are of the blood of the enemy."

"Not that I could see," replied Dovan, "There may be scholars and engineers present for such an excavation, however, that and the countless slaves brought from all corners of the realm."

Arturius's heart sank. Perhaps Phie's mother would be present within the mix, after all, the captured villagers were sent in this direction. He decided he would keep a keen eye open for such a woman.

Selwyn grumbled to himself, deep in thought as he processed the intel presented before him.

"If we assault them before dawn arises we can catch them off guard," said Robbard, "At my estimate, they will suffer only a quarter civilian loses, at most."

Selwyn shook his head in disappointment.

"We cannot afford them to further demonise us to the masses," said Selwyn with a serious manner, "They have already painted vast propaganda against us as these bloodthirsty barbarians out for carnage and blood."

For once Robbard was in accordance with him, merely nodding in silence.

"Did you make a note of their positions? Any patrol patterns we could use?" asked Selwyn.

"A few," replied Dovan, "Though most concealed their faces beneath their visors, it made it even more difficult to discern them as they moved. Some mannerisms I could pick up on some, but not many."

The captain looked up to his eager men-at-arms. The late-night frost biting them harshly, the wind flowing through their drapes.

"Remove your cloaks," he ordered, gesturing to each of the company, "If we are forced into close quarters, they'll only become a hindrance and leave the horses untethered, they are smart and will find us later on."

Dovan and Robbard promptly removed the cloaks pinned to their shoulders, allowing them to cascade gently to the floor. The others shortly followed suit. Over the next few moments followed Robbard and Dovan detailing every movement and position of the patrols ahead. The timings, the weapons, no detail was left concealed.

"Silas, Ozark," Selwyn called the two over to the front,

"Sir," replied Ozark,

"You both shall remain at the rear, concealed along the tree line," Selwyn looked at the two seriously, "Under no account are either of you to advance or engage until the way is clear, understood."

Ozark nodded in agreement. Silas did not.

"And why should I sit this one out whilst the rest of you risk your lives!?" argued Silas, "Am I not a member of this company? Have I not sworn the same vows as every other person that stands before you!"

Selwyn stood up quickly and aggressively.

"Draw your sword, master Silas," he ordered

Silas looked confused, unsure as to his intentions.

"What?" Silas replied, "I don't see how this –."

Selwyn moved closer, interrupting the young boy before he could finish his sentence, stopping just a few inches from his face.

"Draw your sword," he reiterated, his voice more serious than before.

The young Silas shakingly grasped at his hilt, carefully drawing his sword from its sheath, trembling as he did so. Even Arturius could see the struggle that was overcoming him as he tried to hold his sword aloft, though it wasn't heavy the poor boys' strength couldn't support it.

Selwyn approached effortlessly and slowly. A swift backhand to the blade knocked it clean from the weak grip of Silas, sending the sword tumbling into the dirt, muddying its clean blade. Then with the palm of his opposite hand, quickly striking Silas in the chest, knocking him to the floor hard and fast.

"If that were a real duel, you'd be dead," Selwyn said calmly, burning about walking back to the others, "And that is why you stay at the rear."

Never before had Arturius seen such piercing eyes emanate from the young boy, spitting daggers at Selwyn. He grasped his dominant hand tightly, the shock of the sword swatted away from his clutches left a tingling sensation of pain running across his fingers. The young boy sat up atop the uneven ground. Arturius promptly offered him his hand, pulling him from the frosty floor. His grip was tight, he could feel the tension building within him.

"Easy Silas," whispered Arturius, "He only means to protect you."

"Protect me from what!" hissed Silas, "I am nothing more than a joke to these people, they can have their glory and honour, I merely wished to do what is right."

Before he could say any more, the young boy brushed himself down, storming off to the rear of the group. Ozark quickly followed him. The rest remained silent.

"We will split into four groups," ordered Selwyn. Under the dim light of the moon he had drawn a crude layout of the encampment.

"Group one, will consist of myself, and Garton," he ran his finger around the side of the map, drawing a thick line amongst the damp dirt, “We shall take the left flank, from what has been gathered this would seem to be the most heavily defended, from there we shall draw the attention of the rest of the camp, I expect they will come rather quickly to defend it so the rest of my plan must be tackled with great haste.”

“Group two, Burak, and Karlan,” he promptly ran his finger across the opposite side of the map, “You shall take the left flank, after hearing signal you will encounter rather weak resistance. It is imperative that you take them out quick and converge with myself and Garton, a double envelop of sorts.”

“Robbard, Dovan, I want you to reach whatever vantage point you can find, the higher the better,” he pointed at several points across the map, “Keep them from flanking us and funnel them through the main courtyard, pick off any stranglers that try to escape also, but more importantly hinder any use of that scorpion, if they use it, it’ll tear us apart.”

“Jorik, Arturius, I want you to move into the centre,” he drew a line straight from the edge of the map to the centre, “Move only once we have lured them to either flank and only then that way your path will be all but clear, you will seize the opportunity to destroy that scorpion, I hear the wooden palisades are rather easy to set aflame.”

Everyone agreed in accordance. The strategy was key, they would have to use the element of surprise to thin the numbers as quick as possible or face possibly overwhelming odds.

As the group disbanded, darting off in opposite directions a hand grasped at Arturius’s arm.

“If you do anything to harm my brother, then I will ensure the path of my arrows shall meet with your head” hushed Dovan.

Arturius promptly brushed aside his hand. Swatting at the hard-boiled leather bracer that complimented his bow.

"Don't you worry about me of Jorik, I'll see to it that he remains unharmed," replied Arturius, "Though if you threaten me again then I can assure that you will come to regret it."

Without waiting for a reply Arturius turned and walked to catch up with Jorik. He felt confused, it was almost as though another being was trying to emerge itself from deep within him.

*~ "Don't stop, even the most foolhardy can fall deep into the abyss" ~*

## CHAPTER XII: DAMNING ECHOES

Dawn would be soon upon them. The groups had since split off into the night, positioned within treeline waiting for the signal. Arturius lay beneath the bramble, Jorik crouched by his side. The morning frost had grown sharper in the coming hours, its icy chill caused their muscles to spasm uncontrollably. He looked back to his companion laying a few feet to his rear.

"You still there, Jorik?" he whispered. He rubbed his hands ferociously, only sparking slight warmth within.

"Yeah, I'm here," Jorik replied,

"You nervous?" he asked,

"A little, you?" Jorik said, his heart beating so loud that Arturius was surprised it hadn't alerted the patrols.

"Somewhat," he lied. In truth, he was struggling to hold himself together. His only experience in this matter–as far as he could remember–was his brief skirmish some few days ago, though it could be said that his victory has more swayed by luck than skill.

"Best we can do is stick close, it will be far more difficult to take us together than alone," he said to the trembling Jorik, "Have you felt the stench of combat before?"

Jorik shook his head. He didn't think the younger brother of such a protective sibling would've been exposed to such horrors.

"Nay," replied Jorik, "Dovan would leave me at the camp whenever they would raid the caravans, left me to sharpen swords and buff armour, be the good little brother I am."

Arturius peered back.

"Try not to think too much about it," he said, "I will not lie to you, it isn't easy, just ignore the smell, and if you can try to know when mercy should be given."

"The smell?" asked Jorik nervously,

"Aye," replied Arturius, "The smell of blood and fear is a nasty odour as far as I can remember, most will bask with it, poor souls probably have no choice but to fight under the serpents' flag."

"And how did you feel?" asked Jorik

"About what?" replied Arturius.

"How did you feel the first time you took a life?" whispered Jorik.

"I'm not sure to be honest, though back upon the marshes I honestly felt nothing, for if I had fallen so too would Silas have succumbed to the lifeless void, perhaps in an old life I was quite the killer,", he whispered, "You see there is a ripple effect for every action we choose, some may end good, others not so, but the point is we can never know until they are done, and once done we can't go back and change them."

Jorik looked upon him with great confusion; it was clear he wasn't the most intellectual of the others. But he had heart.

"I don't quite understand?" replied Jorik, "What are you saying?"

Arturius crawled backwards a few paces, carefully picking his way through the brush. Quietly.

"What I'm saying is when you throw your rock into the water, don't focus on the splash, it's the waves that follow which you should focus upon because depending on where you throw the stone, will determine where the ripples will go."

It took a few moments before the Jorik realised the effect of his words.

"Thank you," he muttered, "I think I understand your words, I think."

"Don't mention it," said Arturius, a smile glanced across his face.

The winds picked up, rustling the trees violently before them. A storm was brewing in the distance.

"The wind is growing restless, " whispered Arturius, "This may work to our advantage, its noise could drown out our approach."

"Not for Dovan and Robbard," said Jorik, "Such winds would only hinder their effort to cover us from afar, where one advantage comes so too does another be taken away."

He spoke the truth; a bow is a mighty tool in the hands of an experienced archer. And none came more experienced than Robbard. Though the winds and weather would always be a hindrance, even to the most elite of marksmen.

"I see," replied Arturius. He didn't want to get hit by a stray arrow amidst the skirmish after all. No doubt Robbard would tell a different tale, should the worse happen, "I had best pray and hope that their aim is true today more than it has ever been, for all our sakes really."

"Worry not, they won't miss," Jorik said reassuringly, his bountiful confidence easing the worry in the back of his mind.

"Good to know," he replied, "I'll hold you to that."

"The trees and bush are closely packed up ahead, it would be wise to adjust your belt," said Jorik, "Don't want your blade getting tangled amongst the foliage."

Arturius looked down to his scabbard, the worn leather hilt poking from its mouth beside his hip. It wasn't secured well, flapping about in the breeze–a fish out of water.

"Indeed," he replied, shuffling around trying to grab the sheath. It didn't help his laying upon the ground, no matter which angle he turned to he would pin something else to the floor restricting its movement.

After much adjusting and fastening, he could finally secure the blade more appropriately. Stretched horizontally across his lower back allowed him quick access in close quarters whilst also avoiding it melding with the environment.

"There, much better," he whispered, "Thanks for the advice."

He averted his attention before him. The light was rising in the east. It splintered through the branches above him, dousing the many forms of lichen and leaves he lay upon.

"We push forward, move into position," said Jorik. His voice gave off an eager impression, though he knew from before that it was far from the case.

"Lead on," replied Arturius, "Stay low and if you spot movement ahead drop silently, I will follow should you require me to do so."

Arturius followed, weaving swiftly through the vast thicket, ensuring they took each step with the utmost care. Silence after all was their ally.

Jorik found their vantage point under a low hanging Elm. Its weeping vines proved most effective at concealing them from view, all the while providing them with an excellent field of vision.

"Here," Jorik whispered, gently brushing aside a few vines, "The entrance to the camp lies ahead, we can lie in wait behind this willow until the time to attack comes."

The main path into the camp was wide. Enough to bear two horse-drawn carts side by side. At the far end they had erected a small fortification, crude and wooden, though effective at stopping an assault; or at least slowing it down. The flicker of a few braziers mounted atop–no doubt a warning signal ready in waiting.

Arturius counted three, an archer atop the palisade, eagle-eyed as his attention sprawled across the dirt path. Two men-at-arms stood on either side of the gate. All were clad in a heavy blackened plate, golden marking spun into the Rekeshi sigil atop the metal, worn and dulled. Beyond the gatehouse, he could see the tower-mounted scorpion looming in the distance. That was their target.

Selwyn had informed no one of the signal to converge, only that they could not miss it even if they tried.

“So, what’s the plan?” whispered Jorik, moving aside as Arturius took the lead, “how do you plan on breaking through that first defence.”

He peered through the vines, calculating his options as the scenery unravelled before him.

“We won’t make it ten paces if that archer spots us,” replied Arturius, “The thicket gets too dense for us up ahead so our only option will be a frontal assault.”

“Maybe we could rely on Selwyn’s signal here,” said Jorik

“How so?”

“If this signal will be hard to miss, then surely those guards will also spot it,” said Jorik, “Perhaps we can use the confusion to gain much need distance on the palisade.”

He peered back towards the end of the path. The sky was unobstructed and camp tightly packed.

“Interesting,” he said, “We will truly rely on speed and stealth, mind you, if it distracts them then we will have to act fast, I count about thirty paces between us and them, how fare your legs?”

“They have seen better days,” said Jorik, “But aye, I can make that. Besides what other choice do we have, the entire plan rests on a simultaneous assault. Should we or any of the others fail in their task, it will most likely lead to an all-out rout of our own company, or worse.”

Before they could revise their thoughts, a thunderous clap shocked through the skies, splitting the heavens in an almighty display of pomp and ceremony. The ground shuddered beneath them, waving the weeping vines in a chorus of constricting strangulations.

“Holy shit!” cried Jorik, “What in the Gods name was that?”

"I have no idea," replied Arturius, "Though it came from the western edges of the camp, Selwyn and Garton took that side, it must be the signal."

Arturius was still slightly dazed. The shock wave sent a high ringing through his head, muffling the words that fell from Jorik's mouth. Who only knows what the others closer to the blast were feeling right now; if they were alive, that is.

"What do we do?" Jorik cried,

The poor guy was clasping upon his ears, though not in pain that is physical, but a pain which only leaves scars invisible to the naked eye. There was definitely some troubled past trying to seep its way out.

Arturius looked towards the camp, much to his surprise the guards had left their post. They had absconded from their position and left the gate unmanned and undefended. Now was their opportunity.

"On me!" he shouted, "Follow me and I will keep you alive to fight another day."

Arturius pushed his way forward, breaking through the dense overgrowth. He grasped at the collar of Jorik, yanking him into action as the two bolted down the sludge ridden pathway.

A light rain had fallen through the night, softening the earth, revealing a vast network of roots and rock beneath the mud. Waiting patiently for the careless footing of an unaware traveller, ready to ensnare its victims accordingly. The deep mud quickly proved a hindrance to them both, dragging them beneath its deep surface, every step draining their limited stamina as they pushed on.

"What the fuck is that?" shouted Arturius.

Far off to the left flank, a cloud of gargantuan proportions erupting to the sky lay a dark shadow across the land, "How the fuck did he create such a monster of a signal? Though he wasn't wrong, couldn't miss the likes of that."

"You don't say," Jorik shouted back, "We don't have long, the guards are sure enough to return to their posts, there is no way they would be stupid enough to leave completely."

"You ready?" beckoned Arturius.

Jorik looked down at his blade, his trembling hands echoed across the sword.

"I think so," he replied, "I just hope Dovan is okay, He is all I have left in this world."

"It is like you said, his skill and determination will see him through. Now come, we haven't a moment to lose!"

Even though he his demeanour and composure were calm and collected, he knew deep down that that his nerves teetered on the edge of a knife. One wrong move and he could well end up facing death or worse.

As they approached the palisade, the first of the border guards emerged behind the gate. The detail in his armour became more apparent, an intricate series of waves and trims adorned every inch of the metal plate. Arturius's blade descended upon his shoulder, splitting through his torso as it severed the flesh from bone. Blood caressed the edges of his sword, unleashing a warm red river of death. Its crimson shade soaked into the mud bound beneath his feet, forming a thick crimson paste. A single tear fell from the corner of Arturius's eye, a re-emerging emotion that told him *'this never gets any easier'*.

Before the body fell to the ground, the second footman had appeared from around the corner. The sound of his dying companion alerted him into action. Though it was not enough time to act.

When he charged the struggling Arturius, a faster obstacle met him. Sprinting through the air, Jorik buried his blade deep into the guard's abdomen, so forceful the whole sword damn nearly cut its way through the torso in its entirety. Arturius watched as the point of his blade poked through the gaps in his armour, sending thin waves of blood trickling through its grooves.

The deep sable cloak turned darker as it soaked up the blood. The poor soul had lost his footing, running so hard he toppled over with his mark, pinning him hard into the mud. Jorik watch in horror as the life quickly drained from his opponent, shocked as to the act he had just committed.

They had made it into the gate, but the mission had only just begun.

"Are you okay Jorik?" shouted Arturius, "Talk to me! Listen to my voice."

The young man lay silent, his body remained tense as he stared into the vacant eyes of the warm body that made his deathly bed.

"Jorik I need you to stay with me! If we stay here we are doomed to a fate similar to those that lie at our feet."

Arturius grasped him by the arm, throwing him off the corpse with tremendous might.

"Snap out of it Jorik," he snarled, shaking him viscously back and forth, "You must snap out of it now!."

Jorik did not move. He continued to peer down at his handy work, the warm flesh his canvas, the fiery blood his ink.

"Come on!" snapped Arturius. He struck the dazed brother hard upon his cheek, knocking his sense back upon him.

"Uh-What happened?" asked Jorik, "Where am I?"

"Your mind has cracked under the pressure," replied Arturius, "We are assaulting the camp before the Dwelvar gates. Just know that I am forever grateful for you saving my life and that you did what must be done."

Arturius chose to relinquish such truths and comfort the young boy. For deep down he did not know if the act was necessary, or whether they truly belonged within this fight.

Jorik looked upon his hands, bloody and trembling.

"What now?" he whimpered,

Arturius looked him over with worry.

"We keep moving, though it pains me to ask this of you. You must set this feeling aside and focus," Arturius bellowed, "I shall do everything in my power to keep you safe. I made a promise, and I intend to keep it."

Jorik nodded.

The commotion below was enough to draw the attention of the marksmen, drawing his aim from a powerful war bow, tense and deadly. Arturius threw the stricken Jorik to the floor, shielding him from view. He waited as the faint whistle of the arrow came barrelling towards them, only to hear a faint thud and hiss above them. The Rekeshi marksmen grimaced in pain before his face dropped. Along with the rest of his body.

High atop the overlook in the distance, Robbard and Dovan rained death from above. Their arrows whistled through the air, curving magnificently within the strong winds. Dovan met eyes with Arturius from afar, nodding in thanks. Arturius promptly returned his gratitude.

"On your feet, Jorik," shouted Arturius, "Today is not the day we are going to die."

The trembling warrior found solace in the words of his companion; His hands were sticky with the blood thickening atop them. Through the fear gripping him, he reluctantly obeyed.

"Well, at least there is no doubt about it. That must have been the signal," shouted Arturius, "Come, we must hurry."

The camp was rather vast. He counted tents forty by length and thirty by width, evenly positioned from east to west. Mixed amongst them, the remains of mess halls, barracks and quartermasters all lay empty and abandoned as what remained of the garrison threw themselves upon the newly anointed assailants.

They progressed through the carnage, passing several corpses strewn across the place. Arrows buried deep within the gaps in their plate. Such accuracy was unfounded, they truly lived up to their names. Three downed … four … five. The body count was quickly increasing as they swept through the camp. The scorpion lay in wait at the centre of the camp, unmanned but still threatening as they were caught beneath its shadow. "Such a monstrosity," he thought to himself, its limbs spiked and bladed. At the very front, a grotesque face loomed over, its mouth agape, ready to spew forth death from within. Its eyes following them as they ran, hissing menacingly at them as its tongue wrapped around the exit of the mechanism. It was designed to strike fear and intimidation into the hearts of its victims–not that others needed any more reason to fear such death.

Again, two more camp guards emerged from the vast whitewashed tents that sprawled the area. This time, however, they spoke in the common tongue. Spitting and cursing at the two as they dashed in.

Their swords were exquisitely crafted, castle-forged steel that shimmered in the sun. Jewels adorning the hilt, sparkling brightly as the light glanced from its finely cut surface.

It was clear these were no ordinary foot soldiers. Their armour heavier and lashed together perfectly with hard leather. Atop each shoulder sat sharpened pauldrons–excellent for tearing flesh with tackling.

"Die scum!" one of them cursed, it was rather unoriginal given the situation they found themselves in.

"The demons are here," yelled the other.

At least in this encounter, they would be more evenly matched. The first sprung towards him, his sword leapt high into the air as it trailed down towards him. Arturius blocked it quickly, ringing the steel together, shuddering into his grip.

Before he could react, his face met with fist crunching against his nose. The warm trickle of blood met with his lips. It was a sweet taste as his tongue received the warm elixir.

"Fuck!" he exclaimed, recoiling back a few steps

However, now was no time to squander. He looked over to see Jorik had locked blades with his opponent, each locked in a grapple of strength, pushing harder on the other as they battled for control.

"I'm gonna make you bleed, you svark!" hissed the guard.

Blow after blow pounded against his blocks. Each time chipping away at the edge of his blade, all the while leaving his aggressors sharp and deadly. By the gods, he was quick. His movements were swift and precise as they blurred together. This dance of swords had strung out long enough. He needed to act quick and fast if he were to remain warm.

Arturius caught a downward strike with his beaten cross guard, wedging the razor longsword within its crack. At that moment he lunged forward, tackling with all his weight. If he could just throw him off his feet, he could take the advantage.

His hands were trembling. The mix of adrenaline and fatigue sent his heart into a frenzy. The guard faltered. Arrogantly unaware of the manoeuvre, he was taken aback, plummeting through the air as he crashed on to the barrels and crates to their side. Arturius quickly followed.

Before he could continue the assault, his opponent let out a silent cry. Opening his mouth to curse only spluttered blood. A protruding stake, sheared from the smashed barrel, had punctured his side, slipping between the plate beneath the arm. It was a sure kill.

Without hesitation, he jumped to his feet. His face was bloodied where the guard had spat up his life. Behind him Jorik was losing the fight. He had already received a gash across the face seeping red to his collar. His felled opponent's longsword called to him. Clasping it, he ran towards his ally, poised with his arms far back.

"Get down!" he shouted.

Jorik, upon seeing the order, dropped into the mud, surprising the unaware guard. He never even saw the swing. Only the ground turning as his head departed his body, erupting in a fountain of blackened tar from the stump it once rested upon.

When Jorik found the courage to peer through his fingers, he saw Arturius stood panting before him. Baptised by blood.

"Where to now!" shouted Arturius,

Screams and steel rang across the air. A chorus of whistling arrows would occasionally fall beside them, as leaves would glide across the fall. He had no idea whose arrows they were, but it mattered not.

"There!" shouted Jorik.

He pointed towards the base of the tower. High upon its perch the scorpion lay in wait.

"The scorpion is unguarded; we should make our move."

As they reached the base of the tower Arturius noted the many bodies that lay strewn about its base. Death had already claimed these, but by whose hands they would never know.

The ladder was narrow and crude, plunging splinters deep into their hands as they climbed up.

"We should be able to see much clearer at its peak" shouted Jorik, "Keep your eyes out for the others. And don't get struck by a stray arrow or you'll take me down with you."

Arturius chuckled to himself.

"Glad to see your sense of humour has returned to you."

"With everything happening around us I must distract myself," replied Jorik, "If not then I may lose myself once more."

The ramparts above gave an excellent field of vision. Spanning far across the camp. They could see everything and all.

One … two … three, Arturius began counting the fallen within his sight. Nine … ten … eleven.

Something felt off. A strange uncertainty hung within his breath. Twenty-two … twenty-three. It had become clear; they had vastly underestimated the numbers they had gone against. A few ants fighting against a tremendous storm.

Arturius saw movement at the far end of the camp. The others had fought their way through and had now merged into a single fighting force, swiftly finishing what remained of the opposition. The gates loomed in the distance, casting its immense shadow upon them all. Before he could call to them, his eyes caught a glimpse of a big problem.

The intel had betrayed them. A vast host sprinted forth from the gates, concealed within the ruins, waiting to pounce unexpectedly. The hunters now became the hunted. Arturius flicked his eyes between each of the men emerging from the darkness. He counted at least fifty, fresh and eager.

"We got a big problem," he muttered, "A big fucking problem!"

"Retreat! At once, Selwyn, retreat!" shouted Jorik, "Reinforcements are converging, run!"

Though all effort was to no avail, his voice diminished into a muffle before it reached their allies' ears.

"Shit! It's no use, they're too far to hear us," shouted Arturius, leaning over the edge in uncertainty.

"What do we do?" cried Jorik, "They will be slaughtered!"

Then it was clear. It had been all along. Arturius looked back upon the scorpion, as time felt all but still around him.

"Do you know how to operate this? He asked, laying his hand gently across its broad limbs, "I have never seen such complex mechanisms."

Jorik pondered for a moment. Running his eyes along the various contraptions and configurations, he was able to piece together such functions. He grappled with the hand cranks to the side, struggling as the iron ground against the rust wedged beneath. As he twisted, the cogs beneath them whirred away, sending the platform into an about spin.

Its design was heavily complex, along with something etched within its gilded edges. Various words and nomenclature, no doubt tales of such evil deeds from its past. Laid out at their feet was an assortment of crates and cartridges, as Arturius peeled away at the top of the packs, unveiling a pack of tightly packed and vicious looks barbed bolts.

"Here!" shouted Jorik, pointing up at an empty slot atop the machine, "The cartridges must clasp within the scorpion here, help me load it."

The cartridges were heaving and dense, so much death had been packed into such a small confinement.

The screaming below intensified. Selwyn and the others had since spotted the hoard converging on their location.

"The fools!" Arturius muttered, "They do not have the strength to face such overwhelming numbers, why do they not retreat!"

The cartridge clicked in place, locked down amongst the wooden death machine.

"Ego and pride are what it is," replied Jorik, "Not to mention should they fall back now then we will lose the advantage of holding this war machine, a disastrous result should the enemy reclaim it."

"Hurry and help me guide this thing," snapped Arturius, "We must hurry or soon they will not remain of the living anymore."

Jorik cranked the beast, erupting into a roar of great terror as he did so. For something of such terrifying potential, it moved incredibly slowly. Every crank upon its handle made them even more anxious as the host moved in upon their company.

A large crank sprouted from its side, linking a large pulley to the drawing mechanism.

"I'll crank this," he said, grasping the handle with all his strength, "I believe this will activate its firing mechanism."

Death moved closer and closer to the others. All they could do was watch as the omen of death spread its wings to consume them.

The Rekeshi poured through the outer gates, funnelling into a column as they squeezed through the narrow passage.

Arturius mounted the end atop his shoulder. It was surprisingly light and nimble to move, as he looked down its sights, locking the ensuing force into focus.

"What now," he shouted,

"We unleash hell," hissed Jorik, pulling the crank swiftly with all his weight.

Life sprung to the machine. Spewing a torrent of hailing and whispering needles across the sky. One after another, propelling in rapid succession, narrowly missing the heads of the others ahead. They fell to the ground as the pine needles of the fall would, albeit with more deathly consequences.

The bolts tore through the ranks of the attacking force, piercing with such unrelenting force that many of the rounds swiftly met their rest within the rear ranks. Although they couldn't hear the screams from those afar, they could tell by the actions of their movement the true terror they had unleashed.

Before long, the crank released empty clicks. The cartridge was spent; it was hard to believe that so many bolts had been packed within it.

"It is done," muttered Jorik, still tightly gripping the crank, unable to release his grasp.

Arturius looked upon Jorik. There was a tense expression growing over him, a feeling of regret.

"You okay there, Jorik?" asked Arturius.

"I feel shame," replied Jorik, "Shame and regret, and I don't know why, what about you?"

"I am not too sure," said Arturius, "I feel something that I cannot quite fathom, regret? Shame? Disappointment? I know that we did what needed to be done, but a part of me doubts whether it was truly the right choice."

Jorik remained silent, struggling to comprehend the level of death he had been a part of.

"We should regroup," said Arturius.

It wasn't the sight that made him nauseous. It was the thick smell of death, ripe with blood as it flowed through the camp. A river of red. It was a sense of shame that hung above Arturius's head. He had seen the effects of war, witnessed its brutal ravages and heartless acts. Yet never had he foreseen his future as a perpetrator.

"You good?" asked Jorik. The young man was shaking, trembling where he stood.

"I'm not sure," Arturius replied, "I thought saving the others and seeing them alive would help with such regret, yet it did not."

"Well, if it weren't for you two, it would be us lying in the mud," said Selwyn cleansing his blade of the crimson tarnish, "War is war, after all, it never changes, never gets easier."

"Your words do speak the truth," replied Arturius, "However, to see such reckless disfigurement unleashed by my hands makes me sick to the stomach."

Arturius could only stare, he couldn't help but humanise those that lay at his feet. The bodies that coated the ground in scarlet, now abandoned shells to be left to rot in the open. Many were no longer recognisable, pierced, shredded and hewn into piles of bloodied rags and flesh. The sight made him sick to the stomach.

"You have my eternal thanks, Arturius," said Selwyn, "Both you and Jorik have paved the way for us to continue our mission. Come, see the fruits of your labour."

Before them stood the great Dwelvar gates, a sight truly incomprehensible by the words spoken to him earlier. Arturius stretched his gaze, looking across the vast expanse of rock and stone that grew into the heavens before him. Its walls towered even the tallest trees around, scaling the jagged cliff face of a great mountain that loomed over him. How he had not noticed such a wonder was beyond him. It was as though the mountain itself did not want to be found.

As he drew closer, the intricacies of the carving became more apparent, holding true to the skill of the Akaviri artisans. The many faces of the wall watched him closely, tracking his every movement as the distance lessened. Strangely enough, the gates themselves were rather small. Not much taller than Arturius himself, raised high into the wall itself, leaving a rather gloomy tunnel in its wake.

"We've got a live one here," shouted Robbard, tossing a lone Rekeshi foot soldier into the mud before the others, "Found him lurking in the cracks and crevices of the mountain, say the word Sir and ill end his miserable existence."

He was young. Must have only been a couple years his junior. As he scrambled through the mud, he received a torrent of abusive and punishing blows that further sent him cascading into the dirt.

"Just end him now," shouted Dovan, "Along with the rest of his kin."

He finished with a swift boot into the gut, crippling him over with pain.

"Nah, I say draw it out, let him suffer like the dog he is" replied Robbard, slamming the pommel of his sword between his should blades. Crunching hard as the contact rippled across his bones, "let him watch as we slowly draw him piece by piece."

"We could send him back as a warning," hissed Dovan, "See how far long it will take him to walk back to the black keep with no eyes."

It was as if the two were competing to show the most inventive brutality to commit. Arturius stomach churned. His sickness grew at the action of the other two. How could they become so malicious after such slaughter? When he joined the company, it was to enforce peace and prosperity within the kingdoms. And right now, he was witnessed that which he despised.

"Do you think this amusing!" snapped Arturius, "Do you think this noble! Do you think this honourable! they may be the monsters of this realm, the murderers and savages who only bring death in their wake… Yes, I see monsters here, but it is not he."

A sudden silence befell the group.

The others looked upon him with disdainful eyes, though they deigned to respond.

"And who are you to judge onto us," snapped Robbard, "Was it not you that just laid waste to score of them, plucking each life at the prick of a pin until they all lay lifeless upon the floor, nay it is you who are such a profound monster."

Before Robbard could approach, his path was obstructed by Garton. His presence nearly forgotten amid the carnage.

"Don't even try it," he muttered, staring down upon the former lord.

He turned his gaze back to Arturius, giving a nod to continue. Arturius nodded in return.

"Stay true to the values of this company," Arturius said, looking across the faces of each of the others before him, "If these be the values we are to uphold, then I want no part in this."

He paused to breathe, momentarily losing himself to such a budding rage. Strange, however, for he did not know he could feel such an emotion.

"Yes Robbard, you are right," he continued, "I am a monster, a monster that in the short time since awakening has already laid waste to many and all, there is no doubt in my mind that I have stalked these lands and delved deep within the darkness, but at least I know when to show mercy upon someone, mercy to do the right thing and not bloody my hands further than necessary!"

He thrust his blade deep into the dirt, cracking the earth as he did so. Selwyn grimaced, he knew deep down he was right, yet this didn't absolve the feelings he had within– the rage of his loss and pain of his past.

"He's right," muttered Selwyn, drawing the blood from his blade before sheathing it.

"You've got to be kidding me Sir," snapped Robbard, "After all we have suffered at the hands of the enemy, all that we have lost, now is the time you choose to show leniency!"

"I choose to show mercy," barked Selwyn, his voice sharp with anger, "For this man is unarmed and broken, I can see the fight has all but left him."

"Sir, see reason here," said Dovan, "Should we allow him to live, he will surely report back to the others. We will find ourselves surrounded by many more than we have encountered today and they would trap us with no hope to survive."

Selwyn squeezed his chin. On the one hand, he held the values of his company, the other the lives of his men. Before anyone could interrupt his thoughts, he smiled passionately.

"Oh, he won't be warning anyone of our success," he said, kneeling down to beaten soldier, "Why should we waste such impeccable insight into the plans of our enemy."

He took the silence of the others for acquiescence, turning away as he laid his eyes upon the prize he had been waiting for. Into the darkness. Into the halls of desolation and with-it take in the shadow of Akavars lamentation.

*~"It's just us now, will we wander forever in this darkness"~*

# Chapter XIII: Halls of Desolation

It was dark, darker than the abyss it would appear. Every step they took descended deeper into the black chasm, further from the gentle light growing smaller and dimmer. They travelled two abreast, Selwyn and Ozark leading from the front. Arturius and the prisoner followed shortly behind them.

The fire showed them the way, the faint flicker of light was nearly consumed in the heavy darkness. Yet it was enough to show them onwards. Though Arturius felt that the darkness of the light was not the darkness they should be concerned of.

The intricacies of the wall carving were outstanding, each one unique from the last as it told the story of the Akaviri, their victories, their triumphs, and even their regrets.

“It would be best to save your rations people,” said Selwyn, despite his best efforts his voice echoed down into the darkness before silencing instantly, “From what I have gathered it will be three days journey to the to the great city, provided we don’t run into any mishaps along the way.”

There was a strong smell that hung in the air, untouched for thousands of years as it enveloped the company with a strange dark aura. It was also hot.

“By the gods, it stinks,” cried Dovan, clambering for his mouth as he squeezed it shut, “What the hell is that.”

“What do you expect fuckwit, this air is stale, has been for a thousand years,” snapped Robbard, his attitude towards his early defeat still emanated from his voice, “Not to mention the years of corpse rot that could not escape.”

"This smells like no corpse rot I've ever come across," replied Dovan, "It's almost like it has festered and merged with the fire that dwells below, brimstone and sulphur."

When he truly thought about it, if the halls had been sealed for a thousand years, then what became of its inhabitants. More importantly, however, why did they seal the gates.

"We shouldn't falter in our journey," said Ozark, "The Rekeshi excavation force has been this way."

He crouched to the floor, illuminated by the lingering flames as he grasped a small canteen. It was small, emerald green glass shimmered in the light. The Rekeshi sigil proved thusly.

"How far ahead do you reckon they are," asked Silas, "I don't like the thought of bumping upon their rear-guard within this darkness."

"I don't know," replied Ozark, "Why don't we ask our guest here."

The prisoner seemed uncooperative at first. However, a swift punch to the gut soon changed his mind.

"They entered the gates around a day, day and a half ago," he spluttered,

"How many?" demanded Selwyn. He did not turn to face his suspect, instead focussing on the darkness looming before him.

"I don't know twenty, thirty maybe ..." he replied, coughing up small spots of blood as he spoke,

"I want specifics," replied Selwyn coldly, this time turning to face him, fragments of his face glowed faintly behind the flames. A scowl that made even the darkness shudder.

"I don't know," he pleaded, "You think they would tell me of their plans, I'm nobody to them, not that you would care, you the butchers of Tevahn."

"Silence!" Selwyn snapped, grabbing him by his collar, "You would know more of such an evil than any kingdom that has ever risen and fallen, your empire was raised upon the blood and tears of those it buried to make its foundations."

By now, the whole column had halted, nervously waiting in the ancient darkness.

"You can't lecture me on the morality of kingdoms and empires," replied the prisoner, "You who leave death and destruction in your wake as you fight against another, you're no more than the monster than the stories of demons in the dark."

In a fit of rage, Selwyn threw him to the ground. With his arms bound, he struck the floor. Selwyn turned away from the group.

"Carry on," he shouted, "And get him out of my sight!"

Robbard and Dovan took great pleasure in forcing the prisoner to the rear of the group, obscured by the darkness where they could continue their torment.

"Ass!" whispered Arturius, thankfully out of earshot– he didn't want to give Robbard more of a reason to loath him.

"What was that?" asked Silas, his ears pricked to the mutterings Arturius whispered.

"Uh, nothing," he replied, "I was just wondering what is so important about this place? How has it laid empty for so long?"

"Well, that will be because of the twin dooms you see," replied Silas.

Arturius stared blankly at him. This prompted the young boy to look back at him with true discomfort, watching as his brow wrinkled in disbelief upon realising that he had no memory of the legend.

"Wait, you mean to say you've never heard of the twin dooms?" said Silas shocked at the revelation, "The story of fire and water, the collapse of two dynasties that were to endure until the end of time."

He shook his head. Of course, he had no idea what the dooms were. Until recently, he had never even heard of the ancient kingdom or the halls they were about to plunder.

"It all happened so very long ago, thousands of years as it would have it," said Silas brimming with excitement, "For it was at the same time as the first outbreak of the Khaos of old, in an age when the light and dark were all that ruled the realm."

*Legend says that long ago there existed two powerful kingdoms. That of the subterranean Akaviri, dwellers beneath the earth, blessed with technological and engineering marvels. And that of the Drangviri, great dragon riders and beast tamers high within the great twin peaks of Mt Sundargaard. Both kingdoms sat high atop the realm, for none would reign supreme above them, only dwell beneath their immense might.*

*Though no one knew how the conflict started–no doubt twisted and altered through the ages–both kingdoms were locked together amidst a perpetual war. Their rivalry had endured for many thousands of years melded with hatred and prejudice towards one another. For neither of the races knew the boundaries of mortal existence. They were known as Immorthals, blessed with near-limitless life sharing the blood of their ancestors, making them more alike than either would admit to.*

*Many hundreds of years since the war began, there came to be a prince of Akavar and a princess of Drangmar, and though their kingdoms were at war, they ushered in forbidden love. And as the hate between their two kingdoms grew greater, their love for one and other never ceased, growing more powerful with every waking day. It was after years of hiding their love, that they eventually grew tired of the raging war to which they saw no end. And so began the plot to escape such torment, to flee their kingdoms and start anew. But as with all good things, something would come between. And something did indeed come between the two star-crossed lovers.*

*Whether it be through betrayal or sheer coincidence, the truth of their love escaped, making its way to the delicate ears of both kingdoms' mighty monarchs. They had sealed their fate before they even had the chance to escape such misery. In the hours of twilight, they were seized from the bed in which they laid–a mere day before they were to escape such a life. It was agreed by the two opposing kingdoms, that their love was to be kept a secret from the realm, for the shame of it would cost the two kingdoms family much honour. However, because of the laws of kinship, they could not execute one of their own kin. It was decided that the Prince of Akavar be taken by the Drangviri, and the Princess of Drangmar be taken by the Akaviri. To be executed along with their treason.*

*The Prince was chained by his feet and cast into the waves beneath Kabadeth, the grand capital of the Drangviri. His body lost to the sea, and his heart lost to the woman he loved. Heartbroken and grief-stricken, the Princess cursed the two kingdoms to suffer as she did, to fall beneath the earth in blood and cinders. As they cast her into the molten fires beneath inner sanctum of Nordellar her screams trembled through the kingdoms, a sign of what was to inevitably come.*

*With great fear and ferocity the very earth trembled and split, an echo of her rage carved great fissures in the ground, spewing forth the hatred of scorn. And so too did the flames of her wrath spew forth into the realm. The Drangviri, who sat high atop the mountain in their ancient city, fell deep into the raging sea below, thrashed by the waves and washed away from existence. The Akaviri also suffered a fate all the more devastating. Watching as the ground cracked and molten anguish spouted from the earth consuming ancient kingdom amongst fire and brimstone. Their ancient seat, the heart of their kingdom, sank into the molten earth, where it was buried along with the technology they had created. The two powerful and mighty kingdoms, as they had once been, were no more.*

*It is said to this very day the two lovers long to return to each other, the tremors of the earth are the Princess scorned calling out for her Prince. And the waves clawing at the earth, the Prince eagerly trying to reach her. Forever separated by those that came between them. After all, when it comes to power, nothing is more powerful than the love between those forbidden to do so.*

It was some hours before they finally reached the threshold; a large stone archway signifying the true descent into the ancient realm. Cracked and waning under the pressure of the mountain, yet still, it held firm. Defiant of the colossal giant that bore down from above.

"Be on your guard from now on," said Selwyn, flickering through an old tome nearly crumbling as much as the surrounding mountain, "Beyond this arch we are in territories unknown, aside from the Rekeshi that dug through before us, there will be other mysteries ready to claim our lives."

An uneasy feeling washed over Arturius as he passed beneath the decrepit arch, as if something were watching and waiting for his arrival. Just as the last of the company passed through its entrance, a familiar horror met them. The ground shook with terror, splitting beneath their feet as the shock wave struck them with the very air they breathed.

"It's the princess, she disproves of our entry," shouted Silas, "Come we must pull back, or face the wrath of her bringing down this mountain."

"Nay, that is no spirit," shouted Selwyn, "Its Black Thunder again, though beneath the very earth!"

"Are those fools mad," shouted Burak, struggling to remain on his feet, "They will bring this mountain down upon them and us."

In a split of fate, the archway could no longer withstand such terrible pressure, sending a torrent of rock and earth cascading down upon them. The whole cavern was shaking, spewing an age of dust into the air as it choked all caught within its mist. Arturius could feel his surrounding close in around him, choking the life from his body as the crushing weight struck his back.

"Oh, no you don't!" shouted Dovan, grasping him by his arm, nearly pulling it from its place as he hoisted him to safety.

"Keep moving," shouted Selwyn, his voice muffled by the rocks smashing against the ground. The disorientation clouded his senses, neither up was down, or down was up. The only sense he could rely on was his hearing–although even that could betray him occasionally. Before long, the shaking had subsided, easing to a halt as the last of the stones clicked into place.

"Is everyone okay, is anyone hurt?" called Selwyn, "Speak!"

One by one, each of the company called out in response. It was truly a miracle no one was crushed in the carnage that had ensued.

Arturius looked back at the entrance. Its structure had crumbled, allowing the earth to reclaim its lost territory, sealing them within the halls, no doubt in an attempt to make it their tomb.

"You saved me from death, Dovan," said Arturius, "You have my eternal thanks."

Dovan smirk upon him but changed his demeanour quickly when Robbard looked back upon them, scoffing down at him.

"It was nothing, but a debt fulfilled," replied Dovan, "You kept my brother safe up top, now we shall speak no more of this."

Arturius looked back upon the threshold.

"We have a problem everyone," called Arturius, running his hand across the newly laid rubble before him, "The way out is shut."

"Shit!" beckoned Burak. He slammed his axe hard into the stone, splitting chunks of rocks from its surface. The Hall, in turn rumbled with anger, before returning to its slumber when the brute withdrew from his attack.

"Hold fast," shouted Selwyn desperately, "This rubble is stopping the rest of the mountain coming down on our heads."

"So, we are trapped here then?" yelled Robbard, acting much like a child who is refused their way, "Well that is fan-fucking-tastic isn't it! May as well have let the rock slide do its job whilst we had the chance."

"Not quite," replied Ozark, "When the Akaviri tunnelled out these mountains thousands of years ago, they would have dug many other shafts in the event of a cave-in, there is no doubt in my mind some of these should still remain here today."

"Oh, great. So not only are we trapped here with the damn devils of the west," spluttered Robbard, "but we are also going to have to trudge through a city that expands the interior of a mountain, housing whatever darkness has endured for a thousand years all the while looking for an escape that may or may not be there, did I miss anything?"

"No," replied Karlan sarcastically, "You hit the nail right on the head there."

The others brushed off Robbard's pessimism, no doubt tired of the relating whining they had suffered all these years.

"Look, let's focus on the mission at hand," said Selwyn, "The lost crown is our priority. Once we claim it we are gone, no more tombs of darkness after that."

"That's all well and good Sir, but we have one slight issue with that task," said Karlan, "This city is the largest ever built, vastly greater than Dawnstar, Vastern and all the other great cities of the realm combined."

"Not to mention it consists of many levels," added Robbard,

"Oh, did you hear that Sir," simmered Karlan, "There are multiple levels it would seem, I sure hope that little book of yours gives us a brief insight as to where we should start!"

Selwyn grunted in response, flicking open the pages of his crumbling notepad once more in a choleric fashion.

"From what I have been able to piece together, there is a vault buried deep within the earthen confines of the inner sanctum," said Selwyn in annoyance, "My guesses are that anything of great value or importance be laid within such an impenetrable defence, hence it is why we shall look for the crown there."

He snapped the book shut, waiting for the forceful echo to dissipate down the tunnel.

"Does that satisfy you?" he said disdainfully,

"Yessir," replied Karlan with gritted teeth, "You have my gratitude."

A groan emitted from the front of the company, winded and painful. Arturius turned in time to see Dovan struck to the floor as the Rekeshi prisoner took off into the darkness, utilising the chaos from the collapse to escape.

"After him," shouted Selwyn, "We can't let him warn the others."

Arturius was the first to plunge deep into the fray, as its darkness felt most cumbersome upon his being. His thoughts were not necessarily with catching the prisoner, but more with protecting him. There was no doubt in his mind that he would suffer greatly at the hands of Robbard and Dovan should he fail to reach him first.

It felt more of a labyrinth than halls, twisting and turning within the darkness. Unsure to what may lurk behind each corner, gambling with his own life as he sprinted into the unknown. It was intensely suffocating. The light from his torch glowed only just enough to unveil the obscuring darkness for but a brief moment.

Left, then right, then right, then left. He could easily become lost in such a maze, for there was no guiding light and revealing pathway to assist him in returning to the others. Even the very sounds that echoed through the corridors were not to be trusted. He followed the faint footsteps of his mark just a few paces before him. Until they stopped.

The sudden silence felt unnatural, as though the very sounds had been plucked from the air, devoured by the darkness so deep and pestilent. Every step he took from there onward he took with caution. He held his torch up high, its warmth reflected from the tight corridors. Biting down upon his tongue, he tried to silence the chatter of his teeth, stepping further and further into the beyond.

Traps, he hadn't either thought about traps. If there were any buried beneath the ground, or hidden between the walls, it was only by sheer luck that he had set none off.

"I'm thinking too much about this," he whispered, strafing against the walls as he peered around the edge, "Empty, not a soul in sight, only the whispers of that which does not want to be found."

After what seemed like hours, he finally caught track of something. Here, however, the darkness was not so thick. Crack within the walls and ceiling billowed down an unnatural light seeped through. He snuffed out his torch, burying deep into the earth that was emerging from behind the open wounds of the corridor.

The breathing was getting closer, faint, but closer. As he peered from behind the corner, he expected anything. Perhaps he was even hoping to find more darkness, for at the time it seemed so inviting.

As the curtain of darkness lifted from view, a rather unusual sight fell before him. The prisoner–still bound–kneeling before the dead. Men and women, their clothes torn into rags, lay across the floor, bloody slashes painted across them leading to a river of blood that descended into the black. He couldn't comprehend what he had stumbled upon.

It was most peculiar. For the Rekeshi prisoner did not show joy or delight from the corpses of the enslaved. It was sadness that washed over his face, a genuine sadness that could not be masked. The others soon caught up, quickly emerging from the darkness.

"There you are!" bellowed Selwyn, "you should be more careful delving off into the unknown. There is no telling what may lurk between these walls."

Selwyn looked upon him with elation. All of which soon faded upon further examination of his surroundings.

"By the Gods," muttered Dovan, "Again I find myself gazing upon acts truly barbaric, and to think I thought of the darkness as a plague within these halls, now I wish for it return so I may avert my eyes."

Silas turned away, unable to stomach the sight before him. The knowledge of those that lay cold upon the floor overwhelmed his poor young mind. A faint wind blew over them, as if the souls of the damned were calling to tell their story. Arturius struggled for words, choking back on the emotions he tried so desperately to suppress.

Robbard spoke no words, his anger welling up as he rushed forward, grasping the prisoner, slamming him hard into the stone floor.

"You fucking bastard," he yelled, "You make me sick; your people make me sick.",

No one opposed him, merely watching in silence, allowing him to serve the anger they so wished not to show.

Arturius turned away, unable to speak, groping for words that would not come. There was no use, after all, none would listen to him this time. They all wanted revenge. That's when the glint caught the corner of his eye. Nestled deep into the chest of a woman lay cold upon the floor, a necklace of crude design.

*"She wears a pretty necklace I made for her, it has beads and charms that daddy helped me to make for her."*

The words of the young Phie echoed through his mind as he dropped to his knees, lamenting at the broken promise he gave her.

"I'm sorry, Phie," he whispered, "I was too late, I hope you can forgive me."

He leant down and closed the vacant eyes of the woman as she remains still. She was as beautiful as Phie would boast, such beauty snuffed from the world, forced to partake in a task that neither she nor the others had a say in. He reached down and removed the crude necklace, carefully wrapping it around his neck.

"Something isn't right," he whispered, "Why kill your workers and slaves before reaching the city."

He surveyed the surroundings more closely. True to his belief, the slaves had been cut down by Rekeshi blades. The cuts were clean and true, swift death came to each and every one of them. Yet, there was no sign of struggle amongst the dead, all except for the one corpse that laid most out of place. For this one was no slave.

The single body of a Rekeshi soldier lay amongst the dead, made out to fool any passer-by of a revolt orchestrating by belligerent slaves. This was far from the truth.

His mind had run its course long enough, calculating the possibilities that had unfolded before them. The bound prisoner lay upon the floor bloody and bruised, receiving the onslaught of rage from Robbard's strikes.

"Stop!" Arturius yelled, a fear filled his gut, something more sinister was at work here, something that none here could comprehend. His words echoed into nothing, as though they were never there.

"I won't have you escaping this now," shouted Robbard, unsheathing a dirk concealed in his boot, "I am going to make this feel worse than you could possibly fathom."

As he raised it high above his head, his arm was stopped by the grasp of Garton, the only one to hear Arturius's plight.

"What the fuck are you doing Garton, unhand me," demanded Robbard, "He is one of the enemies, one who left you to be cursed as you are."

Garton looked upon him with open disapproval. What remained of his face showed only disappointment, anguished between the cracks.

"Enough," he muttered, turning his gaze over to Arturius.

"Enough what," Robbard snapped, "He is no different to any of them, it was probably him who drew first blood back at Riftmyer, it was probably he who slew Yohn a few moons ago."

"That's a lie," shouted the prisoner,

"Shut it," hissed Robbard, managing to throw in another kick before being tossed to the side by Garton, fluttering through the air. Such an outburst from Garton shocked the others. This differed from his usual solemn nature.

"Calm yourself, little lord," replied Garton calmly, "Let him speak."

Robbard was unwilling to listen, storming off into the darkness beyond, Selwyn gave a quick nod to Dovan, prompting him to give chase.

"Don't you all see, you are turning your backs on one and other, splintering this group," said Arturius, "It's what they want, why come after us when they can simply allow us to dissolve from within."

He walked up to the deceased down the corridor, promptly kneeling beside the fallen Rekeshi soldier.

"Everything about this reeks of foul play," said Arturius forcefully, "This one wasn't slain by the prisoners around, the wounds inflicted upon him match with the others, this Rekeshi soldier was slain by his own kin."

The prisoner bowed his head, a trickle of tears fell down his face unseen by all except for Arturius. Ozark closed in, further examining the slaughter before them. Gently lifting, revealing and concealing each one that lay cold and lifeless.

"He's right, all slain by the same blade, I should know I've seen it before," said Ozark, lifting his sleeve to reveal a scar of the same pattern, "It was the Deathguards work here, this was made to look like a failed uprising."

The atmosphere felt cold, a chill by the non-existent winds. An uneasy cold, the likes of which only comes when the dead are disturbed where they rest.

"We have wasted too much time here," interjected Selwyn, "As much as a tragedy and crime that these poor souls have endured, nothing can be done for them now."

After all, they had gone through, to leave them in the cold dark halls of desolation–where the sun would never again shine upon them–seemed crueller than the acts they witnessed in their last moments.

Such a cruel and despicable world. Had it not been for the innocence of Silas, closing their terrified eyes, it would've had destroyed all hope for the world he had come to know.

"What about Robbard and Dovan, we can't leave them in the dark," said Burak, gesturing back into the void, "We should send someone to find them, or at the very least wait for their return."

"Fret not Burak, they will find their way to us, Dovan's tracking skills are unmatched even in the darkest of surroundings," replied Selwyn, "Garton, Arturius, you will keep guard of the prisoner, if he pulls that stunt again, kill him.",

He spoke coldly and without remorse.

"A darkness is spreading within him," whispered Garton, "Keep true to yourself Arturius, there is something darker and more sinister at work here, I fear that a time may come when we must even fight the darkness within ourselves."

In truth, ever since they entered this accursed tomb, the pieces of Selwyn's humanity had dwindled and withered. Spreading darkness within him. Darkness that if not expunged would surely consume him. And it was festering amongst the group; strangely, however, it did not affect Arturius or Garton–possibly because Garton himself had no humanity left to afflict.

He had hoped by now that they had reached the end of such delirious walls. There was no use in sulking over it however, according to Silas, more was yet to come. It was said that the journey to Nordellar would take them two more days at least. However, no soul has ever made the journey until now, leading all to expect a different outcome.

They were all growing weary, the veiled darkness eroded away their spirits leaving them hollowed and tired. There was no time to stop or rest. They must continue until they reach its centre. Or forfeit the crown to the aggressors burrowing deep within.

"We cannot continue like this forever," whispered Arturius, "Exhaustion will have set in before we intercept the enemy, we must rest and be of sound mind if we are to successfully halt the expeditionary force's progress."

"Why not take matters into your own hands," muttered the prisoner, "And leave this place before more are lost within its shadows."

Arturius face grew concerned, his very tone was defeated. Nothing like the monsters he had come to hear of within the Rekeshi ranks. This one was different.

"That soldier back there, you knew him, didn't you," he whispered, "I could see it in your eyes at the very least."

Instantly the prisoner grew tense. The mere thought of this seemingly inconspicuous individual had clearly struck a nerve.

"What makes you think as such," replied the prisoner, "He was nothing to me, another sack of meat for the grinder of the war effort."

"You may be able to fool yourself with that attitude," replied Arturius, "but I see straight through the facade. Now tell me, who was he?"

The prisoner shrugged.

"Still, what makes you think I care of another fallen corpse amongst the war that has raged across every inch of this realm," snapped the prisoner,

"Because one would stop and kneel in dismay at the sight of a fallen warrior, not a soldier anyway," said Arturius, "A soldier grows accustomed to the stench of death, and in the pursuit of duty holds back that which afflicts him, not to mention the tears you felled for him, those were tears of anguish."

He looked him in the eyes, black from the surroundings.

"And what would you know of my anguish," hissed the prisoner, "My life is mine and mine alone and I will allow no one else to judge upon it, so say your worst besides, I have seen the way the others talk to you, you are no more of an outcast than I am."

Arturius pondered the question carefully, unsure as to the intentions of the prisoner. Perhaps he wished to further the divide between them.

"I came into this realm with no memory of my old life," replied Arturius, "I have been chased, beaten, stalked, lost and found, with nothing but a name to my being, I have no idea as to my purpose or where I belong, yet with them, I seem found."

The path had become narrower, squeezing the two together into each other's presence.

"Had I not found Silas when I did, I may very well be wander lost still, they took me in knowing I had no value to them nor any skill, to me those are people you should live your life for, a true family to look out for you as you would them."

The prisoner had grown uncomfortable, something was weighing down on him greatly. And by the Gods, he was going to uncover it.

"So, who was he?" asked Arturius.

"Who?" replied the prisoner, trying hard not to divulge.

"The soldier back there, I know you knew him," he whispered, "You may not have spoken as such, but not everyone requires a tongue to talk."

The prisoner sighed, tired of hiding the facade, knowing full well his death could peak from beyond the darkness.

"He was my brother," he replied, choking back the tears of anguish as he fought for control.

"I'm sorry," muttered Arturius, "Though I know not of loss, I can't help but gather the feeling that I have witnessed it previously within my past life."

"I have known plenty of loss," the prisoner replied, "Mother was taken by the affliction when I was a boy, my sister a year later, all I had left in this world was my brother, now he can be at peace with them too."

"And what of your father?" asked Arturius.

"He disappeared from my life some years ago," said the prisoner, "Vanished into thin air, never to be seen again."

"What will you do now?" asked Arturius, "Where will you go?"

The prisoner laughed to himself, brandishing his wrists–tightly bound and bleeding raw. His shadowed face slightly obscured still showed the dismay upon his face.

"Doesn't look like I'll be going anywhere anytime soon will I," said the prisoner sarcastically, "That is if your leader doesn't take my head soon, either way, looks as though my life has come to the end of its road, either this mountain shall become my tomb or I shall be strung up for the unforgivable act of capture."

He could feel it in his voice, there was no hiding it, fear. There was a fear of what comes next for the shackled man. As he stared at him, he could see a glimmer in his eye, a truth of his own disposition.

"Why do you fight for him?" said Arturius. The air was getting hotter, making every breath a struggle, "The Masked One, that is."

"I don't, he is no emperor of mine," the prisoner spat on the floor in disgust, "If I had the power to do so I would have slit that bastard's throat long ago."

His heart stopped in his chest. Could it be that they were fighting an enemy despised by his own people? It was becoming much clearer to him.

"It's the reason my brother lies dead, there are many of my people who are subjugated, forced into a life of perpetual war and domination," the prisoner hissed, "And what for? Some lost crowns! Some power that hasn't been seen for thousands of years; it may very well not exist, you know."

A voice snapped ahead of them from within the darkness. The warped voice of Selwyn had grown darker the further they journeyed.

"Quiet Rekeshi bastard," sneered the old captain,

"I have a name!" snapped the prisoner, "I am not one of his disciples! I bleed just as much as the rest of you and have lost just as much too!"

His words fell silent, echoing through the halls before being silenced by the dark.

"And what do you go by?" queried Arturius.

"My name is Eskiel," replied the prisoner, "Esmir was my brother back there, he was a commander within the Rekeshi 9th Division."

"A commander!?" gasped Arturius, "Why silence such an influential figure? Surely his death would anger countless others?"

Eskiel shook his head. Flicking back the black strands of hair that cloaked his face.

"I told him not to challenge the authority of the upper society," replied Eskiel, welling up as he forced himself to reveal all, "He would constantly challenge the state of affairs back home, making many enemies from anyone that benefitted from the horrific acts performed upon our own citizens."

"It would seem his enemies found their opportunity," said Arturius, "And at the cost of so many others it would seem, what reason did they have to act now?"

Eskiel looked him in the eyes, staring straight through him with turmoil. He still hadn't decided the true nature of their prisoner, only that he had a different heart to the other Rekeshi he had faced.

"He advocated for the abolishment of the class system, to resist the expansion of the imperator and his fanatical goals," whispered Eskiel, forever watching over his shoulder, "He wanted change, and there are some deep in the shadows of the capital who also advocated for such actions."

"So they had him killed through fear of their undoing?" asked Arturius, "Sounds to me like the pinnacle of what will essentially topple a regime."

"No, they had him killed because he was lowering the class of the elite within our society, you see at the very top there are the Valoy, the highest within our society reserved for the rich and powerful, beneath them are the Vahn, respectable within society, many are highly skilled and desired, yet they lack the power and the vast wealth."

The air was getting hotter, almost burning as he listened on.

"Then you have the Graunt, the lowest class reserved for the manual labour, the ones confined to the lower districts and slums, they are frequently looked down upon being only kept in the kingdom because of the blood that runs through them," Eskiel continued, "Finally you have the Slovags, you have already met them, slaves of the powerful, the high class require thousands to serve them, many don't survive the first week of 'service'."

"That's despicable, how can anyone allow it!" gasped Arturius.

Eskiel returned his gaze to his feet, kicking the stones on the ground further along the hallway as he let out a strenuous sigh.

"Is my brother proof enough for you?" he replied, "They snuff the flame out before it becomes ablaze of revolution."

The halls began to level, no longer an aching slope that burned the back of his calves. As the ceiling descended, the flames of their torches licked its surface, elegantly producing a pale green flame that sparkled brilliantly. Ozark drew his finger across the damp ceiling, licking the residue gently.

"Phosphorus," he muttered, "The rocks must be lined with it."

He further examined the surroundings, muttering incoherently as he moved from wall to wall.

"This isn't good," he choked.

"What is it?" asked Selwyn.

"Hold your torch down, don't let it touch any of the surfaces," he pleaded, "The moisture on the walls is keeping it contained for now."

They all lowered their torches, some going as far to snuff them out altogether. Only a single flame glowed the way forward–far at the front of the group.

Before long they saw a light glowing deep at the end of the hallway, its incandescent glow drawing them forth like moths to a flame. The closer they came, the warmer the air grew. Arturius looked over to the others. They were all sweating profusely as the warm liquid flowed down their cheeks, swallowed by the fabric that clothed them.

"By the gods, what is with this heat?" choked Silas, struggling to breathe in the searing heat, "I feel as though we are roasting upon an open fire, to be the main course for the belly of the mountain."

"Don't be ridiculous, little man," sneered Karlan, "There isn't enough meat upon your bones to feed a hungry mouse."

"We must be close to the city," beckoned Selwyn, raising his voice over the distinct crackling that emanated before them, "Stay alert, who knows what lies ahead."

He promptly unsheathed his blade, scraping the edge along the closing walls as it shimmered in the light. The others followed suit.

It wouldn't be too long before they faced the fires of destruction and the shadows that lay in wait. Waiting for a thousand years to finally emerge from its slumber.

~ *"I will not give in, not until my blade bathes in its blood"* ~

## CHAPTER XIV: AKAVARS LAMENTATION

The raging inferno bellowed below them. A swirling whirlpool of molten magma spat furiously at the new inhabitants, threatening their presence. Or perhaps warning them to flee whilst they still can.

"So, the stories are true, consumed amongst fire and brimstone," uttered Silas, "And so the legend unravels."

"Indeed they are my boy, indeed they are," replied Ozark, "Did I not tell you that buried deep within legends lie some truths to be discovered."

The ancient kingdom was truly a sight to behold. A vast network of tunnels and walkways linked the many ramparts along the edges of the cavern. Though calling it a cavern was a vast understatement, stretching far beyond the eyes of the company that stood before them–as if another world deep within the heart of the mountain.

Waterfalls of magma streamed down from the sides of the rocky outcrops, pooling below into the vortex of heat and death. Much of the kingdom's structures remained intact, vast archways and towers continued to dominate the sky. Though the cataclysm that subjected its inhabitants to the horrors of that which lies deep beneath the earth had not given up on its pursuit.

Such craft and skill had not been seen for some time in the realm, structures that would twist and turn about the interior of this hollowed-out giant. To remain standing for so long whilst under such stress can only add to the testament of such technological prowess.

"Steady were you go lads, these walkways have seen better days," bellowed Karlan, parts of the decayed walkway crumbled beneath his feet, nearly sending him plunging into the fires below.

"Someone grab him!" bellowed Ozark,

Burak tenderly but quickly grasped at the struggling Karlan as he struggling to find a footing.

"How has nothing melted away in all these years?" asked Arturius, he ran his hand across the cavern wall. "ouch! It's intensely hot to the touch."

"Careful there, Arturius," called Ozark, "You don't want to be messing with the mineral deposits down here"

He poured some water from his canteen across the walls, crackling with excitement as the glow burst from behind the rocks, sending shrapnel plunging into the depths below.

"Arkanium!" he whispered, "Of course! They built their kingdom atop its deposits, bolstering their immense strength with the only source within this entire realm",

They watched as light glows across the walls, pulsating with the life of the mountain. The vast network of veins sprawled across its surroundings.

"What the fuck is Arkanium?" yelled Burak, "Never heard of anything by that name before."

"I wouldn't expect you to know nothing of the sort my dear boy," bickered Ozark, "You should pick up a book from time to time, you may learn something new."

Burak scoffed at the low insult, neglecting to respond.

"But what is it?" asked Arturius.

"Arkanium was the lifeblood of the Akaviri, they built their cities, crafted their weapons, powered their forges with the miracle ore," replied Ozark, his voice brimming with excitement as he babbled on, "They truly were masters at their craft you see, they discovered a means of breaking deep into the element, unlocking its vast potential within."

He turned back to the veins of the mineral embedded before him, this time however it was cold to touch. As if it had consumed the very heat that had once imprisoned it.

"And what potential did they discover?" asked Arturius, "Apparently it was not enough to save them from extinction."

"The greater they rise, the harder they doth fall," replied Ozark, "And by the Gods, they rose, with such potential within their hands they accomplished more than you could have ever imagined."

"Tell me," replied Arturius.

Ozark looked upon him with glee, much to the bemusement of the others.

"With the right amount of manipulation, they discovered the applications of Arkanium to be endless, imagine being able to toss a rock into a pile of stick to produce fire, or worse at a castle to see it engulf with flames," said Ozark,

"A truly terrifying power by the sounds of it," replied Arturius, "I imagine they conquered many throughout their history?"

Ozark shook his head.

"Then it may surprise you to hear that they did not go about subjugating and conquering," said Ozark, "They were a hub of mass knowledge and science, all kingdoms were welcome within their city, we'll all except for the Drangviri of course, no matter what attempts others made to bolster peace between the two, it would never be an option."

"Then why did no one come to claim the vast deposits following their fall?" asked Arturius, "Surely someone would have thought to seize the opportunity and advance remarkably into the ages?",

Ozark shook his head.

"No, my dear boy," replied Ozark, "You see they were a vast a hub of knowledge, dispersing many recipes and blueprints that shaped the other kingdoms as we know it, however something they kept purely to themselves."

"Interesting," said Arturius, "So what could they achieve with such a mysterious mineral?"

Ozark paused to catch his breath; the heat of the caverns exhausted him quicker than usual.

"Oh my, what could they not do with it is a more appropriate question, its glow that could produce light more intense than a hundred torches, refining it to the point of near indestructibility, that my lad is the true power that these people held," continued Ozark, "what they accomplished was nothing more than incredible."

"Such eloquence," replied Arturius, "I can truly see why this fascinates you as such."

A not-so-subtle cough broke the flow of the conversation quickly,

"If you two are quite finished with fondling each other," beckoned Selwyn, his face growing thicker with weariness.

"Apologies Sir, you know how it is," replied Ozark, turning his back to Arkanium as he returned to his leader, "But if I may have a chance to appropriate some, should the situation arise," he smiled thinly towards Selwyn.

"So be it," sighed Selwyn,

Ozark caressed his withered hands excitedly. No doubt he will find the situation to acquire such knowledge from within. Although something was being hidden by him, the nervous tremble in his hand was faint, yet noticeable.

Amidst the waves of fire and crackling flames, the faint sound of footsteps emerged from the darkness behind them. The already weary Selwyn nervously grasped for his blade, squeezing the hilt as though the neck of his enemies.

"Aren't you lot a sight for sore eyes," beckoned Dovan as he emerged from the shadows, Robbard followed in suite, skulking at the back refusing any eye contact, "Sorry we took so long, it's rather difficult to track in the empty darkness, you could have made it a little easier for me."

Selwyn looked upon them with great frustration. It was apparent that his goals were clouding his morality, a poison upon his mind, that which cannot be satiated until it has truly taken over him.

"We move out now, I'm splitting us into two teams, Garton, Robbard, Burak, Dovan, Karlan you come with me, we will pursue the devils into the heart of this mountain and snatch the crown from their grasp," he hissed with malicious intent before looking to the others, "The rest of you, find us a way out."

The worst of it was the dehumanising treatment of the others. It was as if they were no longer important, a stain upon his boot of which he wished to wipe away.

"What about the prisoner, sir? Or the slaves they took from Riftmyer at that?" asked Jorik, "Surely there must be more working down within this tomb for them?"

"Do whatever you want with him, throw him in the fires for all I care," snapped Selwyn, "There is only one thing that I yearn for at this moment … and it will be mine! As such, all focus will be towards the vault and the vault only!"

The comments sent an uneasy feeling through the group, the noble and caring Selwyn, being reduced to a careless unappreciative husk of his former self. Everyone stood silent for a moment, the heat from the fires sinking its fangs deep into the flesh of all who stood before it. Then without a word, their leader simply turned away, walking off without a glance. It had been left to them to ensure that Nordellar would not become their tomb.

And thus, there was nothing that could be done. His orders had been demanded, leaving them all no choice but to comply.

"Well now, what do we do?" beckoned Jorik, ensuring that he no longer remained in earshot of the more favoured companions, "He expects us to wander these halls, with our cocks in hand, hoping to find us a way out?"

"I guess we search then," replied Arturius. All eyes had become affixed to him as the others looked upon him, their new de facto leader for the mission. It was evident that too long had the group relied upon the teachings of Selwyn in order to progress.

"Which way?" asked Jorik, "I'd rather not spend any minute longer near this heat."

"Well, you might as well get used to it boy," said Ozark, "I imagine most of the city has been consumed by flames, if not worse."

"Well then, I think it only fitting that you be our guide Ozark," said Arturius, "After all, you know the history of these ruins best, where do you suggest we begin to look?"

Ozark stood within a world of his own, oblivious to the attention the question had brought upon him. His eyes remained affixed to the passage the recovery team had abandoned them through.

"What is happening to him?" he whispered to himself.

"Ozark?" said Arturius, edging closer and closer to him, "You okay?"

"Uh, sorry, was in a world of my own there, what was that you said?" he responded, quickly snapping out of his despairing trance

"Are you okay?" Arturius reaffirmed, placing his hand upon his shoulder. His leather armour was hot from the fires emerging below, "I see there is a great worry filling your mind."

Ozark sighed.

"It's the mountain," Ozark whispered, "It's poisoning his mind in ways I cannot comprehend, every hour we spend within its depths seems to cast him further away from the light, I see him fragment and dissolve into the darkness … I fear for him."

"We all do Ozark, I can see it too," replied Arturius.

"His goal is clouding his judgement and humanity," interjected Silas, "I fear he is losing his way, treading down a darkened path to which he may never return."

"That may be, but there is nothing we can do about as of now, let's abide by his order and search for an exit," said

Arturius, "The sooner we can leave this forsaken ruin, the better."

"Lead on then," said Silas gleefully

Many pathways lead through intertwined ramparts and corridors, each one darker than the last. A part of him was still in awe at the sheer scale of what stood before him, looming far into the blackness above.

"The air smells cleaner this way," shouted Jorik as he pointed into the darkest of the tunnels that stretched out before them. It was perfectly chiselled; the smooth floor was only ruined by the rubble from various cracks and crevices that peered from above.

"I guess we follow your nose then," laughed Arturius, ushering the group forward, "Besides, cleaner air can't do us any more harm than there already is, can there?"

Despite the intense heat that glowed at their backs, the air was beginning to cool rapidly. The young Silas smiled softly, wiping from his brow the glistening sweat that was seeping into the floor.

"Thank the gods, I was beginning to lose my mind in that heat," he said, splashing a few drops from his canteen to the back of his neck, "I felt like roasted mutton ready to be devoured."

"Steady on!" cried Jorik, "Easy with the water you got there."

"What?" said Silas, confused, "Why?",

"You really should ration your drink," Jorik said, "Should the worse come, we may need as much as we can get, who knows when we may next replenish our already dwindling supplies."

"Hah, same old Jorik eh," laughed Ozark, "You're not living on the streets no more, ease up a bit."

Thrusting a spare canister into his face as he winked the young man down.

"We have plenty of rations to do us by."

The group advanced further through the tunnels, leaving a rather sizeable gap between each of them as they hurried through.

Etched upon the surface of the stone lay deepened marked hewn from the earth, all in the shape of claws from a beast that barely fit through such corridors, it concerned Arturius greatly. He could not keep his eyes from them, so transfixed upon them was he that he failed to respond to the questions posed by Eskiel.

"Something has your eye," he whispered, nudging the occupied Arturius with his tightly bound wrists.

"What?" Arturius muttered, quietly and confused.

Eskiel tutted to himself, letting out a quiet chuckle as did so.

"I was saying that something has caught your eye," he reiterated, "Care to ease your worries upon me?"

Arturius kept peering back at the scratches. The trailing led him to believe whatever had drawn them had travelled back from where they came from, slightly easing his tensed stomach.

"Or not, I suppose, after all, I am just your lowly prisoner here," he said with a distinct smirk.

"Apologies," he replied, "Just a few concerns of mine."

He looked down at the ropes binding Eskiel. His flesh had been rubbed raw, trickled out spots of blood that soaked into the bindings.

"Come here," Arturius demanded, grasping firmly at the wrists. The blade cut through the rope with eavesdropping it to the floor in clean tatters. Eskiel looked to his confused yet joyful.

"What are you doing?" he asked,

"You pose no threat to me or this group, plus I've been bound as you have before, and believe me, it doesn't end well."

The young Rekeshi cocked his head to the left.

"But how do you know I wasn't lying, or trying to escape to warn my peers," Eskiel asked, "I could very well be an assassin or infiltrator, why trust me now?"

"I don't," Arturius responded with a grin, "Guess I'm just going to take a leap of faith upon it."

For a brief moment, the two stood side by side, not as enemies, but as allies. The others had moved further down the tunnel, nearly cloaked in the shadows ahead.

"We should get moving," said Arturius, "Don't want to get left behind down here."

The network of twisting tunnels and malformed corridors proved most troublesome, tricking even the sharpest among them as the darkness dulled their senses. Arturius continuously followed the deep claw marks buried deep into the walls. Its presence made him feel most uneasy. It wasn't long before he found himself face to face with a rather familiar sight. Though not a sight from his memories, but that of a fragmented dream from long ago.

"Can you feel it?" muttered Arturius, "Listen to the shadows, they call from within the abyss."

"I hear nothing," replied Silas,

"Only the breeze," said Jorik.

The group approached carefully, making sure not to disturb the ash.

The bones of a last heroic vanguard preserved beneath the still warm cinders lay across the hall. Watching, waiting to punish those who may dare to enter their sacred kingdom.

"How curious," spoke Ozark, carefully examining the figures so as not to destroy their form.

"Who do you think they were, or more importantly how old do you think they are?" asked Silas, it was clear to Arturius that the young boy was nervous, shuffling from side to side, refusing to step atop the ash that rested beneath the warriors of old.

"It won't swallow you," said Arturius, calling for the young boy to approach,

"It's an ill omen to disturb the bones of the past," he whispered,

"The dead won't come for you fool," snapped Jorik, evermore the cynical as he squirmed his way through the ash searching for whatever trinkets he may lay his hands upon.

"That may be Jorik, but at least show the dead the courtesy of peace," said Ozark, "You never know if they may watch you as you defile them."

They were delicate … very delicate. Even the faintest tremor would send them cascading into a frenzy. Forever gone from the realm of the living.

The door before them was thick and heavy–no doubt an amazing contraption lay behind its imposing strength. Jorik banged hard as he tried to break through, though it was fruitful in all attempts. Not even the slightest scratch appeared upon its surface as his blade rung violently off of it.

"Stop Jorik," shouted Ozark, "You will break your blade before you even scuff the surface."

Jorik grunted in anger, throwing his blade to the floor as a child. In doing so he disturbed the ground beneath his feet, sending a ripple across the floor culminating in several of the disposed hissing before succumbing to the soft ash below.

"For fucks sake Jorik, now look what you did," snapped Silas, his face contorting in anger at the rude disturbance of the dead, "To disturb the dead is to summon their spirits!"

"So what, the dead are dead, have been for a thousand years now," shouted Jorik angrily, grabbing his blade. The ash coating its surface fell from its edge, a mirage of past and future floating in the breeze.

"Strange," whispered Arturius, observing as the ash floated into the cracks between the doors, "There is a draft behind this door."

"What if that's way out," beckoned Jorik, "We need to get through."

Before Arturius could respond, he resumed smashing at the door with every ounce of strength. He could muster "Bloody fool!" he thought to himself.

Every ring of steel on stone echoed through the halls, its high-pitched noise disturbing the dead that rested within, sending wailing echoes in response. But Arturius had other, more pressing concerns at hand. The last battalion faced outwards, away from the doors, as if in their last stand they were protecting whatever lay beyond its sealed state. He pushed the fear to the back of his throat, swallowing hard to keep it from re-emerging. Whatever they were protecting it from clearly was a monstrous threat to all. The deep gashes surrounding the walls told him all he needed to fear about it.

The ashen warriors lay in formation, a phalanx of twisted spears protruded from the ground even still protecting their treasure after death claimed them. He tapped the jagged spearhead gently, pricking his finger against the cold metal.

"Ouch!" he gasped. Even after a thousand years it had still kept its lethality, sending a faint trickle of blood down his finger. The ash around his feet swallowed desperately every drop that laid upon it, sinking deep into its embrace.

"Careful there!" muttered Ozark, "That's Arkanium steel you are dealing with there, viciously sharp, immensely strong, unbelievably sturdy, any weapons you find down here today will feel as though they were only created yesterday, if I were you I'd snap up whatever you could get your hands on."

Arturius nodded, grasping his bloody finger as he stemmed the flow. It was impressive. Such mastery of their craft was the stuff of legends.

"Sadly however with the last of their race succumbing to the dooms that ravaged the kingdom, no one will ever be able to accomplish such feats again," said Ozark, "it's a true sadness to see such recipes and techniques lost to time",

"Perhaps it's for the better," replied Arturius, "Such technology in the hands of the enemy, now that is a future I dare not think of."

Arturius straightened himself, staring over the many charred bones that poised before him.

"If the last of the Akaviri died in the twin dooms," he whispered, "Then how did these perish? It's clear that fire consumed them, however, something about them feels off. Why protect this door if you knew your race were about to perish."

The group stopped in their tracks, pondering the possibility of an alternate history to that which they had come to know.

"But more importantly, what claimed their lives, and what required them to sacrifice it so willingly," he continued.

Arturius paced forward, his footprints sinking deep into the ground as he carefully waded his way in between the ashen warriors. It was like snow crunching beneath the feet, only devoid of the bitter cold bite that would usually follow. There was one warrior in particular that stood among the others, positioned at the rear, enclosed by the formation.

"And what makes you so special," he muttered to himself, kneeling nervously before the empty husk.

Black hollow sockets replaced what would have been its eyes, sharing its anguish with a gaping jaw–screaming with terror. He gently dusted the plate, removing much of the ash that had cemented itself upon it. It was well preserved, exquisite in appearance and adorned with many precious stones. In the centre was embossed a sigil, a crown gleaming atop a mountain before a rising sun.

"The mark of the royal family," whispered Ozark, crouching to his rear, "That is the sigil of the Akaviri royal bloodline, undisputed sovereign of the mountain."

"What is he doing out here then?" Arturius questioned, peering back at the gold and black armour. Its myriad of markings spoke a tongue unknown to him.

"No my dear boy, this one is not of royal blood, see here," Ozark ran his finger across the metal, "This was one of their chosen, a group of champions sworn to uphold the duty of protecting the monarchy no matter the cost, each of the chosen anointed into service was adorned with a unique sword and armour detailing them for the glory of Akavar, it would seem this chosen was Ornyx, the night hunter his deeds were legendary by the looks of it."

"So whatever he was doing here was of great importance to the royals, it would seem," replied Arturius.

"It would seem that way, though what is a mystery to me," said Ozark, "No doubt his secret lies behind that door."

Jorik still relented in his struggle, his attempt to smash through had failed, resulting in his efforts to shift with prying it open with his dulled blade. It was as if by some unknown force the blade was propelled from the door, sending it flying through the air as it narrowly avoided the two knelt a few paces away. It struck the ashen husk of the chosen, shattering it into a thousand pieces as its fragile composition dissolved before them. The ash choked them hard, lining their throats with a dryness no water could quench.

"You damned fool," spluttered Ozark, gasping for whatever air he could find, "You damn nearly killed us there."

"It's useless," Jorik moaned, "It must be thicker than an aged oak."

Arturius plunged his hand into the cold ash. It was surprisingly light, offering no resistance to his naked hand as it swept through the mounds. He felt the cold of steel brush against his fingertips, grasping it firmly as he unearthed the dulled blade.

"Here," said Arturius, passing the sword over to Jorik, "Try not to take my head off next time."

Jorik snatched the blade from him bitterly. As soon as he released his grip, something distracted him in the corner of his vision. Something glinted in the faint light amongst the sullen floor. Within the neck of the now-empty armour plate, a cord of aged old leather snaked its way out.

"And what do we have here then?" Arturius muttered to himself,

The cord was coarse and dry. As he lifted it from the inside of the armour, he felt a gentle tug pulling it back towards its former master. Faint puffs of ash emerged from its cracks, blowing grey mist across his hands and stealing the moisture from his skin. An oddly shaped stone swung from his fingers, left and right, hypnotising his mind overs its precise edges.

"I think I've found something," he shouted, his eyes refusing to escape from its pull.

"What is it? What have you found?" interrogated Ozark, lunging towards him with desire flooding his face.

Arturius caressed the block within his hands, gently running his fingers across its irregular surface–the attention to detail was unbelievable.

"I'm not sure," replied Arturius, "A totem of sorts perhaps?",

"Let me see," said Ozark, thrusting his hand his way, "Hmm, how peculiar."

"Any idea what we are looking at?" asked Arturius.

"Could be several things," Ozark answered, "A locket, charm, weapon, I'm honestly as unsure as you."

Jorik leaned in close. The two had almost forgotten of his presence, so deep within their own thoughts.

"Looks like a key to me," he quietly muttered,

"Now come here, if this was a key, I would sure as hell be the first to know about it," snapped Ozark, he didn't try to hide his arrogance as he berated the young man, "Besides what key do you know of that has no edge or shape to turn with, I mean really."

"Fine, do as you wish," replied Jorik calmly, "Still doesn't take from the fact that it's a key."

The misshapen scholar scoffed at his remarks, turning back to the object with great intrigue.

"And what has all so suddenly made you the expert on this matter boy," said Ozark sarcastically, drawing a thin smile across his disfigured cheeks.

"Because I've found the keyhole," replied Jorik, stretching a refuted smile across his face.

Both turned quickly to see Jorik gesturing towards a crack deep within the door, its crusted shape that of the stone block they had been passing between one and other. Ozark swallowed his pride, clenching the block in his hands until a trail of blood coated its surface.

"Don't be cocky, boy," Ozark snapped, examining the slot within the door.

True to his word, the crack did conceal a keyhole. Not your average mechanism however, this was more complex and invisible to the naked eye than anything anyone had seen before. The key fit perfectly within its grasp, crunching against its surface until it rested deep within its bosom.

The doors to the room clicked open, and Arturius was the first to promptly grind them open, alert to whatever may lurk behind.

Ozark, on the other hand, took no notice of his steady approach, storming forth with whatever strength he could muster, slamming the doors open. Arturius was unsure of what they may find, grasped the hilt of his sword, ready to use it if the situation arose.

"Well, what do we have here," said Ozark, his voice bellowing from beyond the archway, filled with awe and intrigue.

"What is it?" groaned Jorik, his annoyance with Ozark was growing more with each passing second, "tell me what you see!"

A hand emerged from the doorway, withered and frail as it grasped Arturius's tense arm, yanking him through its threshold with force.

The room was small yet large. A strange feeling overcame him as he glanced about its contents. He ran his hand through his hair, brushing the ash trapped within his face.

"It looks like some sort of armoury," said Arturius,

A myriad of blades, armour and unknown devices adorned the walls, tables and vast array of racks lining the walls. It was nothing like he had ever seen before–or at least could remember. The room had been sealed off from the outside for a thousand years, untouched by time or ash. It was immaculate, such a shame that their presence was deteriorating the preservation of its contents.

"No, my friend," replied Ozark with a gleeful smile, "this is not an armoury, this is a workshop."

"A workshop?" said Silas, the young boy gently examined its contents, worried he would damage the treasures within.

"Yes my friend, see how the blades are still unfinished, not quite ready for battle just yet, I can't believe it has been here all along," laughed Ozark, tears of joy filling his eyes at the sight of such mysteries finally uncovered, "It is here they developed their greatest achievements, science, craftsmanship, engineering, it's all here!"

The poor man struggled to contain himself, his excitement billowed out from every corner of his body. Arturius was worried that his heart couldn't take the elated emotions of the fragile man. Then all the excitement vanished, only to be replaced by shock and fear. Beneath the deep murky darkness sat a shadowed figure, staring deeply at each and every one of them, their face obscured by shadow.

"Show yourself!" shouted Jorik, poking his wrecked blade viciously towards seemingly slumbering man. Yet the figure did nothing. Arturius drew his blade, grasping it firmly with both hands as he steadily approached the concealed individual. It wasn't until his shadowed loomed over that it became apparent this was no threat, a gentle poke with his blade sent the threats arms falling limp to its sides.

"It's okay," shouted Arturius, "I think it's an Akaviri inhabitant, though not so much alive."

As he looked closer, unveiling the shadowed cloak that rested over the corpse, his stomach twisted and cramped.

"What in the ..." he muttered to himself.

The body was in immaculate condition, its skin, bones and clothing were untouched by time–as they had only just passed from the living, "How can this be?"

Ozark sighed through his nose, taking in every scrap of information he could discover. Before they could uncover its mystery, the answer fell straight into their hands–more like it dissolved. The once immaculate body fell into ruin, its skin peeled and floated away whilst the rest collapsed upon itself into a decayed husk of dust.

"That there answers it my friend," said Ozark, reeling back at the rather unfortunate sight, "This room must have been sealed perfectly, preserving the body and everything within it in time, although it would seem time did not agree to our disturbance of its rather balanced ecosystem."

"You mean to tell me," stuttered Arturius,

"Yes indeed," interrupted Ozark, "This room has been untouched since the twin dooms."

"Incredible!" whispered Silas, moving inch by inch, closer to the bones within the room, "But I thought you said there was a draft Arturius?"

"That I did," replied Arturius, "though if this room were truly preserved then there couldn't be such a draft, perhaps this mountain is toying with my mind as well."

"It looks as though he was holding something," said Jorik, pointing to the corpse.

Grasped tightly in its scrawny withered hands lay a book, tightly bound and encrusted with worn gold leaf. Silas grabbed the book causing the corpse to jolt up towards him sending the young boy into a screaming panic as he swatted at the body pinning him to the ground.

"I got you, I got you," shouted Arturius, peeling back the wrinkled body as it snapped at him, before finally succumbing to the elements dissolving into a heap of bone dust atop the floor.

He flicked his eyes over at the panting boy, fear welling up in his eyes as he struggled to contain his terror. Running his hand over his shoulder, he could feel the young boy trembling, all the while clutching at his prize from the ordeal.

"Hey, you're all good. It must have been the wind throwing it around," he lied, there was no doubt about it, what made it move was nothing natural at all.

Silas nodded, straightening his posture as he regained himself.

"I managed to get this at least," he stuttered, "Seems to be a journal of some kind."

"No doubt it was written by our friend back there," Arturius replied with a smile, "can you open it?"

"I think so," he ran his fingers over the spine of the book, then the top. A small click came from the lock at its side, resulting in the book's cover falling open atop Silas's lap. Arturius looked around. The other two were still rummaging through whatever they could lay their hands upon; Ozark waded through many scrolls and scriptures, Jorik through whatever gleamed like gold.

"Come here," said Arturius, lifting Silas to his feet, propping him against the nearby stone table. As the two relinquished their weight atop the table, it dropped suddenly. Not by much, however, only an inch. A series of mechanisms and cogs whirred beneath them, sending gentle vibration up through the souls of their feet.

"What did you two do?" snapped Ozark, dropping his scriptures in a panic to the ever more increasing noise.

A hidden compartment emerged from the centre of the table, releasing all manner of dust and particulates into the air as it hissed ferociously. Arturius swung around covering his face from the scraps propelling towards him, tensing every muscle to keep himself from toppling.

When the dust had finally settled, a frame had emerged from deep within the stonework. Atop it lay a most peculiar of artefacts.

"It looks like, an arm," said Jorik, "Though different, its encased in metal,"

"I've never seen anything of the sort," Silas called, clutching the book against his chest, "What is it, Ozark?"

Arturius halted, turning to face the silent Ozark. "What is going on?" he thought to himself. He was only scratching the surface of the myriad of mysteries buried deep within the mountain.

"I wonder where it came from?" he asked, running his hand across the course surface. As he brushed his fingers along its frame, he felt various indentations running through its face. Words formed before him.

"There's something written along its surface," he shouted,

"What does it say?" replied Jorik.

"I don't know, it's of a language I do not know, Ozark, maybe you will have better luck deciphering, "

Ozark quickly approached, rubbing away much of the dirt to reveal many more words engraved into it. He began muttering incoherently to himself, flicking between the engravings and his notes.

"Only the worthy shall be chosen, to show a sacrifice bound by blood, only then shall the path be unveiled, to the resting place of Akavar, and the crown of the mountain that waits atop pillar and stone"

The group stood in silence.

"Is that supposed to mean something?" questioned Silas,

"In all honesty, I'm not entirely sure," replied Ozark, straining his brow as he pondered long and hard for the unfathomable answer.

It was quite a remarkable piece to be laid out before them all, the intricacy and detail carved into each joint, plate and joist was truly the work of a master artisan.

Though it laid dormant, Arturius could feel a masterful surge of potential brimming within it, almost as if it were calling out to him. It wasn't adorned with the finest jewels or most valuable metals. There was no gold embossed upon it, or flare within its design. It was simple, yet truly impossible.

"This is beyond me," said Ozark, stepping back from the pedestal, "It would appear it was made for an esoteric purpose, for I have never heard of such an artefact within my studies."

It was truly inexplicable.

Silas let out a long breath, calming his nerves. The crumpling paper beneath his fingers brought Arturius back into the fold of the ancient text's contents.

"Shall we," he gestured towards the book,

Silas simply nodded, opening the book as he began accounting from its pages.

"It appears to be some historical annals," Silas mentioned whilst reading through the pages.

"What does it say? How can you read it?" asked Arturius.

"This appears to be noted in the common tongue, occasional Akavirian words do come up, but I can read it," said Silas

"There is mention of splendid success within the Arkanium properties, a successful integration between organic and mineral."

He flickered through more pages, watching as they drifted peacefully across the book.

"The great expansion, the settling within the mountain, it goes on and on," said Silas.

"Look towards the end," said Ozark, "Maybe there is mention of the dooms and crown towards the end."

Silas grasped a handful of pages, throwing them from right to left, nearly tearing the delicate pages from the book as he did so.

"Careful with that, it's a relic of old," snapped Ozark

"My apologies," replied Silas, making sure to take extra care as he proceeded. "The war with the Drangviri, the creation of the grand army, a darkness stirring far in the north."

"That must be the Khaos," said Jorik, "Darkness in the north, it has to be!"

"It goes on, '*Kirin Tar*' the Gods of old, strange though, there are no names of the Gods transcribed here."

"Interesting," said Ozark, "What names does it mention?"

Silas scanned through the pages, flicking back and forth with a confused look across his face.

"I'm not entirely sure, it notes the '*false Gods*' of the other kingdoms, and the '*true elder Gods of old*' it mentions the names here '*Im, Rok and Sul*'," replied Silas,

"Strange indeed," muttered Ozark, "There are no gods within the kingdoms that bear those names that I have heard of."

"Only if you look in the right places," whispered Eskiel to Arturius.

"Gods?" asked Arturius, his mind drew a blank unable to grasp the concept or the knowledge.

"Within the realm, there are many deities worshipped, each kingdom differs in the variety they worship, although most adhere to the same select few; The Goddess of Serenity, Nearyu, God of Death, Skorvath, God of Light, Solayre, Goddess of Darkness, Lumbra, God of Vengeance, Vorsuk, Goddess of Order, Edikta, Goddess of the Sands, Elkan, Goddess of Fortune, Karthan and the Goddess of the Hunt, Averrela,"

"And which do you worship? If any," responded Arturius,

"None really, I'm more of a realist you see," laughed Ozark

A forceful cough bellowed behind the two, "May I continue?" asked Silas Sarcastically.

"Please," Apologised Arturius.

Silas set aside a few pages that fell from the spine, much to the annoyance of Ozark.

"It talks of the twin dooms, '*a mountain of fire spewing forth death and destruction across my domain, I still hear the screams of my people every day as they sink deep beneath the earth to a fate unknown*' It must have been written by the last monarch before the fall, the writing is elegant and well written," said Silas,

"Indeed," said Ozark, "Such mastery of calligraphy was reserved for the highest class within their kingdoms."

"Could it be him," asked Arturius, pointing down towards the remains of the body they pried the book from.

"If it is, then we could be in the presence of the last ruler of the Akavirian dynasty," replied Ozark, his eyes widened to the prospect of being within proximity to such a mysterious bloodline.

Silas interrupted them again, this time with a heavier voice, "Some of the last pages have been written more hastily," he said. The ink was splotched and rushed across each page.

"You mean after the kingdom sank into the fire?" asked Ozark.

"Yes," Silas bluntly replied

"So, the kingdom didn't truly fall after the doom it would seem, at least not in its entirety," said Ozark, his face shocked by the newfound revelation, "Incredible!"

"I can't make out everything that's written, some is too damaged to make it legible '*A shadow moves within the halls, its lurks between the space between earth and stone*' the next line reads '*I found Ornyx, trapped beyond the Bathosphere a company of the finest made a pathway to reach the inner sanctum*' the next few lines are smudged, I cannot make out the writings '*It took them. Three of the men disappeared into the darkness, their screams still haunt my sleep*'," Silas turned to the next page.

"'*It has blocked the way out, carving deep wounds into the mountain, we had no choice but to flee further into the inner chambers*' the next few lines detail the same as before, speaking of a shadow lurking in the darkness, disappearing and appearing as they journey through Nordellar"

"What could possibly incite such terror?" asked Jorik, a faint nervousness emerged from his voice, the first time Arturius had seen it since the assault from above.

"I don't know, I has made no mention of its appearance only '*Shadowed*' and '*Darkness*' describe whatever it is,"

"There's more '*We made it to the vestibule of Arkania, I have sealed the prototype deep within the stone table, its power cannot fall into the wrong hands, I have entrusted the Crown of the Mountain to the chosen Ornyx, they have sealed me within this room to protect me though I know deep down that this will become my tomb'* he appears to have stayed within this room for some time, there are notes that mention words written within the old tongue, *'Eltrari, Divini, Ampti and Thrawn*'."

"The Empty Throne," whispered Ozark, "Even the Akaviri knew of its legend and power, is there anymore mention of it?"

"Only a short section here '*When the Khaos emerges so too shall the essence of the crowns call out once more, seeking out the convergence before unveiling the shadowed path untoward the Empty Thrown, there the worthy shall be tested as the Watcher judges the worth*' any idea on what the riddle speaks of," said Silas,

"Not a clue," replied Ozark, "Is there any further mention of the shadow?"

Silas continues reading.

"Here is something '*I heard from Ornyx today, he spoke to me through the doors, told me how they trapped the beast within the grand vault deep below the inner sanctum descending it into the depths of the mountain, its eternal prison, none of their weapons could pierce its hide, they lost three more to the shadow, Ranor, Alder and Dalton, they could not recover their bodies leaving them within the vault along with the darkness, they deserve much better, Ornyx told me he cannot open the doors for the key has been lost, though I believe it to be a lie to keep me safe within this tomb*' a few pages appear to be missing, however, the writing appears to end here '*I am trapped, I cannot escape, the ground rumbles, the gate has sealed, my end grows near, the fire has come, come to cleanse us of our sins, it has come*' it ends at those last words," said Silas, pausing to take in the words in silent thought,

"It has come," muttered Arturius, "What has come?"

The group stayed silent. A sudden dread and truth fell upon the group as they stood within the vestibule.

"The end, it would seem," replied Ozark.

Arturius looked back out of the doors at the husks of the former warriors of the chosen, the last deeds for their kingdom enacting a final stand to defend their leader. They stood proud and defiant until the very end.

Before any more could be said a great disturbance filled the room, a great noise came from deep within the depths of the mountain, tremble the many ornaments that lay across the stone table. They all sprang forward, their eyes fixated upon the door shrouded in darkness.

"That doesn't sound good," said Jorik nervously.

"Indeed," replied Ozark, "It would seem our Rekeshi friends have found the vault, that could be there attempt to crack it, damn brutes."

"The vault, you say?" asked Arturius, "Is that not the vault mention within the book?"

Silas peeled back a few pages, skimming through before finding the passage he was searching for.

"Yes, it's written here, they '*trapped the beast within the grand vault*' you don't mean to think-."

"They mustn't open the vault!" shouted Arturius as he sprinted forth beneath the archway, laying the last of the Akaviri royal guards to rest within ash and bone.

"The inner sanctum?" shouted Ozark, "That's where the others are heading, we must make haste, "

"Where to?" shouted Jorik.

"The inner sanctum, as Silas said, if that was the vestibule, then the inner sanctum should be through the north-western passage. We will follow the path set by the others."

Heavy feet flung down the hallway as the group sprinted towards the others, praying with every last bit of faith they could muster. The passages were not lit by any delicate light this time, rendering them nearly blind within the deep darkness. Relying only on the sound of each other steps to lead the way. Weaving left and right, then right and left, again and again until they reached the rivers of fire from before.

"This way," shouted Ozark, disappearing into the darkness of the northern passage, his voice guiding them all before they overtook his limp strides. For a man so devoid of structure and limb, he was rather nimble when the time called for it.

"We must hurry," shouted Arturius. The sound of thunderous claps hit them with full force, knocking them to the floor.

"They are bloody relentless are they not," shouted Jorik, "They will bring down the whole damn mountain if they persist."

"Do as I say and push on," snapped Arturius, his fiery voice spurring them to continue, "If we fail now, the others will surely fall."

As the steps descended into the deep darkness, they looked for any sign of the others; but they could see nothing, only a faint glimmer of light deep at the bottom, warm and brilliant. As they burst through the open passage, that's when they saw everything. At least thirty Rekeshi elite guard were spread across the giant hall of the inner sanctum. Vast pillars lined the halls, ascending high into the ceiling where it battled against the sheer weight of the mountain. Perched at the base, was the others, slowly weaving their way closer and closer to the opposite end of the hall. It was a long way to them; their size was but mere ants as the distance loomed before them.

"What do we do now?" beckoned Silas, "The distance is too great to reach them silently."

Arturius gazed across the vast distance they were to tackle.

"We run," he said coldly, "Warn them in whatever way possible, the enemies before us will be nothing if we must face whatever they locked away a thousand years ago."

They ran hard and fast, ignoring each other as they drifted apart. It mattered not who faltered behind at this point, only that they reach them in time. And stop them from releasing the shadow of the mountain.

"Stop!" shouted Arturius, alerting the many Rekeshi soldiers to their presence.

Yet it was too late. The doors to the vaults were in the hands of the enemy. And within it he felt a strong darkness, waiting to be released, hungry for blood.

*~ "Just tell me straight; we're not going to make it from here aren't we?" ~*

## CHAPTER XV: SHADOWS IN THE DARK

The tall pillars loomed around them, the gentle giants being all that was between the strength of the mountain atop of them. Many deep and jagged gashes were painted across their crumbling surfaces. The dead had remained at their posts to the very bitter end, laying before them as mangled skeletons still grasping their blades.

"Kill them all!" screamed a voice within the distance.

Arturius looked up to find himself face to face with the entire Rekeshi elite guard. Each bore the garbs of the elite retinue, a gold-hemmed black plate, adorned with the sigil of the masked one, it's peering eyes staring closely at him as he stood there, engulfed within the flames of the Khaos.

"What the fuck are you doing!" hissed Selwyn, anger and frustration billowing from his face. Arturius wasn't entirely sure who to be more fearful of, "You have given away our advantage, you damned fool!"

"You must not allow them to open the vault," Arturius snapped, "If those doors open then a foul plague shall be unleashed upon us all. A blight that has made this accursed mountain its domain!"

"The command of this company does not fall upon you, Arturius!" shouted Selwyn, "This is my company and my glory, and by the Gods themselves I shall not have you steal it from me!"

The mountain had truly consumed what was left of his mind. Twisted and purged of all that was left of his humanity, now whittled down to the very embodiment of what he despised the most.

"And what did you think I was trying to do here, I will be the one to open that vault, not them!"

"I want all of their heads you hear me every last one!" screamed the voice yet again, unsheathing a rather vicious looking sword as he thrust it towards them all, "this mountain falls under the dominion of the Masked One, bringer of Fire and Cinder, Imperator of the Grand Rekeshi Empire! You shall not sully its hallowed grounds with the stain upon your boots."

"Bringer of Fire?" muttered Arturius.

Before his thought could continue upon its paths his gaze was taken over by a sight that truly terrified him. Stood beside the Rekeshi captain, a towering monstrosity nearly two score his own, threatening and loom above everyone as his eyes refused to vacate the vaults doors. Such armour that lay upon his flesh was intricate and ordained, yet sinisterly stained. Giving thought to all the foul deeds to which its cold surface had witnessed. A single dagger lay embedded within the shoulder of the beast. Though it seemed not to disturb it of its feral thoughts.

"Vortuse!" he muttered to himself,

He truly was a beast among men, his arms thicker and broader than his very torso, fully concealed behind a grotesque helm that sneered at all before him. Strangely however, the seams and slits upon the helms visor had been packed tightly with a strange resin of sorts, blocking any chance of vision for its wearer. A dark thought crept upon Arturius in that moment. Was it to stop Vortuse from seeing out? Or stopping others from seeing in?

"Now, now is your chance my companions," roused Selwyn, "Slay every last one of the Rekeshi scum, I want their blood to coat the floors of Nordellar. I want their screams to fill these halls. We shall be the ones to bring the fire down upon them. And I shall claim that which is mine from the heart of this mountain!"

As though smoke rising from the fire the others swiftly emerged from behind the looming pillars. Breaking forth from their concealment as they rushed forward. A myriad of axe, sword and bow dominated the air as both forces descended upon each other with hateful intent.

It only took one swing from his hefty axe to fell the two warriors that stood before Burak. Arturius watched as their blood bathed his armour, embracing his physique as the two lifeless bodies collapsed into heaps upon the floor. The true strength of the horse tamer came to light, cleaving through armour flesh and bone as effortlessly as he would fell a tree in the forest.

To his right Garton had engaged with several of his foe. His dark demeanour striking an intense fear within the eyes of the supposed elite guards.

"Demon!" one of them cried.

Though no prayers would save him from the fate to be endured. It was as though the very mist he emanated was but a loose extension of his being. Melding into a grotesque shape as he clashed steel with the first of the soldiers. For a former stable hand his was astonishingly adept with a blade, as he carved his way through the ranks of the enemies before him.

"Garton!" shouted Arturius, catching the broken man's attention amid the carnage and bloodshed. Before he could react, a trail of blood flickered behind him, painting a nearby column with a blackened residue. The force and ferocity of the slash clove a section from his figure. Strangely, his face contorted in pain and anguish, for how could such a man feel when already beyond the realm of life? Arturius watched in horror as he collapsed upon his knees, jolting upon the impact of the floor, spraying a mist of intangible haze about his person. The others except for Eskiel remained oblivious to the horror.

Before the breath could depart from his mouth, the thick black haze engulfed the attacker's sword, wrapping its dark embrace across the shimmering blade as it lunged for his quivering hand. As the life drained from the solemnly hollow eyes of Garton, so too did the life of his aggressor, violently severe from his being. Retching, writhing and spluttering as he fought against the miasma of putrid black as it crept its way into his mouth, eyes and nose.

His companions could only watch on as the life drained from his eyes, jolting at every joint that lay bare. And then he stopped.

"Ugh, that was rather unpleasant" snapped the living corpse,

In a brisk moment of rage Arturius lunged forward, a dance of vengeance pulsating from his eyes as he leered towards his foe. However, swift revenge would not come to the light. A quivering hand grappled his forearm, abruptly halting his advance. Only then did he come to stare upon a pair of most familiar and torturous eyes.

"Garton?!" muttered Arturius, "But how?!"

The possessive Garton cracked and creased his neck, visibly uncomfortable with his newfound mortal shell.

"This one has many dark desires," croaked Garton as he caressed his neck, "A dark man indeed, this will prove most troublesome."

Arturius stared a gasp, his mind raced as it tried to piece together the events that had just unfolded.

"But how?!" he exclaimed once more, "I saw you die; I saw the blade pierce your hide and your essence leak into the dirt."

His thoughts were abruptly interrupted as the stench of blood and death returned to Arturius's senses. Gartons eyes creased, and he thrust Arturius to the side, narrowly avoiding the razor edge of the blade that followed in suit. In the reflection of its jagged blade lay many more victims to the skirmish, strewn and hacked across the cold hard floor. Already the halls of desolation had claimed more victims beneath its mighty embrace. It wasn't soon after that warmth and faint aroma of blood caressed the side of Arturius's face, cascading down to his chin as the Rekeshi toppled from his stance, his throat clasped tightly by the crimson grip of his hands.

"Skill with a blade, indeed he had some," muttered Garton, "What message were you trying to relay to us?"

Arturius jolted back into reality once more, his gaze reaching over to the retinue as they began prying the door from its seams.

"You must not let them open the vault!" Arturius cursed, "The door must not be opened, for darkness itself shall be unleashed upon us!"

Garton looked across to the vault, his eyes shimmering with anger and fear, though it was most apparent that it was not from the malevolence that lurked deep within the darkness.

Before he could react, he saw the state of Garton's newfound shell condition glow vibrantly red, cracking and flaring as his form disintegrated.

"Vortuse! You bastard!" he bellowed; his voice drummed loudly across the battlefield, shaking everyone to their core, "Remember me!"

The monstrous warrior remained stalwart and unfazed by the piercing anger.

"I have come to claim your head!"

Vortuse glared over him, unphased and unbroken, instead showing more concern with the opening of the vault to his side than the threats to his front.

"Wait! Garton!" shouted Burak. He tried to stop his companion, but the three combatants before him pinned him down as more poured into his skirmish. Flashes of steel ran across the room, shimmering across the surface of the stone walls. And it wasn't long before the fight reached Arturius and the others.

Jorik was the first to enter the fray. Flashbacks of his encounter upon the surface overwhelmed his head, sending him trembling to his knees. Arturius jutted forward, swiftly intercepting the blade before it came down on his head. He deflected it with the flat of his sword, taking extra care not to chip away at the well-honed edge of his blade. He moved it with such elegance and tender motion, finally a blade made worthy of his unnerving skill, well balanced and light.

The room was amidst certain chaos, Garton had sprung forward, gliding intensely across the room as he lunged for his mortal foe. The cowardly captain still lumbered behind the great beastly warrior before him, taunting and chanting amidst the fray.

"The Masked One grants us power beyond that which has ever existed, we shall melt every throne, we shall raze every stronghold. And through the truest tranquillity shall we find the path to our Khaos!"

*"He never knows when to shut up does he?"* he thought to himself.

Arturius locked blades with his opponent, staring deep into his eyes. Such fury washed over the Rekeshi's emotions, hungry for blood, something Arturius deigned to oblige. Blood splattered across his brow, seeping down to his lips–warm and sweet–a single blade poked from his collarbone as he winced in great pain. Dropping to the floor quickly and suddenly.

"This is not good," said Arturius, "They will surely break the seal before we reach them."

"Get Silas out of here!" shouted Selwyn, pulling his blood-stained blade from the body that folded before him.

"No," shouted Silas, "I want to fight, I want to help."

"I'll hear no more of it, Burak, take him away, I cannot risk losing the key to all of this," snapped Selwyn,

"On it!" replied Burak, swinging his axe high and hard, sending two of his opponents to meet their makers, albeit without their heads. The other combatant thrusted forward, filled with rage at the death of his comrades. A simple manoeuvre, Burak, stepped to the side as the blade glanced past him, drawing the blade of his axe back in a fluid motion, before burying it deep within his stomach. The bloodied soldier let out a loud groan, dropping his sword to the floor as it clanged against the hard surface.

“Come Karlan! We need to get him out of here,” Burak shouted,

They grasped the young boy, each to a shoulder as they hoisted him up, running back up the shaft the group had emerged from.

The rings and clatter reverberated across the hall as sword clashed upon sword, a few arrows whistled through the air pinning death to several of the Rekeshi elite–followed by the rush of hoarse cries. Many lay dead upon the floor, yet it wasn’t enough as countless more took the place of the fallen. Amid the clamour of battle, a deep growl met with Arturius’ ear, dark and grizzly, commanding death throughout the room. That’s when the lock disengaged, and his heart sank deeper.

With a quick movement, several of the Rekeshi at the far end of the room dug their hands deep into the cracks of the vault door, pulling eagerly as the hinges screeched deathly warnings.

“No!” cried Arturius, dashing towards the captain and his men with haste, “Do not open that door!”

But alas, it was too late.

A sinister grizzly snarl crept from the darkness within the vault. Obscured by the deep dark abyss that flowed from its embrace. It was the wailing screech that drew the attention of everyone within the halls. Though it was not from that which lurked in the shadows. A blood curdling crunch silenced the horrific screams. All of a sudden a single Rekeshi guard was snatched between the cracks, his body contorted and convulsed as it was drawn through the crack in the door. Leaving but an explosion of blood within its wake. For but a succinct moment, the room fell silent.

Suddenly the door burst open–damn nearly ripping it from its hinges–striking two of the elite guards that stood unfortunately close to its proximity. Sending them cascading through the air before striking the nearby columns with such force that they wavered in their duty.

“What the fuck is that?” said Dovan, “A demon?”

"Something terrible," gasped Arturius, watching as large smoking claws emerged from the base of the vault. Deep dark eyes glinted from within the darkness.

"Something dark and deadly, it has waited here since the fall of the city. Waited to be released upon the realm once more." Arturius paused. His eyes fixated upon the emerging shadow before him.

"Now is not the time to loiter," he cried, emptying his lungs with every ounce of spirit he could muster, "Let us go now! Before it turns its gaze upon our flesh!"

The others stood frozen in place as the shadow emerged from its lair, a hulking mass of darkness and decay digging its razor claws deep into the stone beneath it. It was grotesque in its appearance, quivering its thick black hide that smoked vigorously like the smouldering flames of darkness.

Its decayed face dropped flesh upon the floor, black drops that bubbled and vaporised into a wisp of smoke as they smother the stone surface. Its ghastly figure could strike terror into the heart of even the most fearsome warrior. As it moved its bones crackled with malice, resembling more like spines than bones through its thick skin. The captain of the Rekeshi fled in terror, ordering the hulking monstrosity to defend his worthless life no matter the cost. He cared little for what remained of his own me, either throwing them into the fold or having his beastly puppet cut them down – should they have had the audacity to stand in his way.

"Slay it, slay it now," he shouted, all the while fleeing past the company whose heads he demanded not a few moments earlier, "Do your duty and protect the will of the empire! Your deeds shall be sung within the great halls of Asphorox!"

"Now!" shouted Arturius to Selwyn, "What are you waiting for, now is our chance to flee!"

The withered Selwyn looked him deep within his eyes, a sickness of the mind turning his head back to the vault as he shouted hoarsely.

"Forward, kill the beast, death to the Rekeshi, I want the treasures within that vault," he ordered. The others stood confused and worried, yet loyal as ever plunged forward along with their captain.

"Fools the lot of them," shouted Arturius to Ozark, "Take Jorik and find the others, I'll get Selwyn and Dovan out of here."

He turned to Eskiel, who stood trembling alongside him.

"Now's your chance to prove what side you fight for," he said, kicking a blade up with his feet as he threw it over to him. Eskiel glanced at the blade, his reflection shimmering back at him before he turned back to Arturius nodding in response.

Side by side they both dashed forward, despite the peril that roared before them, howling at its prey. There were around twenty Rekeshi remaining, half quaking in their boots; the other half commanding the assault.

The beast pounced forward with significant force. Trailing behind it was a long-spiked whip of a tail, barbed and viscous as it swung about its being. Its viscous tendril moved about with a mind of its own, as though a separate entity to the beast itself. It darted gracefully and swiftly, deflecting of the very air itself as it homed in upon the unsuspecting Rekeshi. The hunt was on. The front of the creature would distract the prey. Afterall when faced with such snarling fangs you wouldn't think to watch out for the tail.

It came crashing down upon three of the distracted warriors, slicing two of them with deep gashes across their chest while the other was cloven in two. Spraying a curtain of deep red blood across the floor. Its scent only drove the beast into a further blood craze.

Selwyn leapt forward, striking the beast in its hind legs with all his might; yet the sword thudded a deep crack against its thick skin. Whatever coated the beasts deep black hide was not of the light. For striking it rocked his hand to the core, sending a splinters of pain echoing throughout his skin and bones. Such pain caused him to drop his blade with great pain as it clanged against the floor. The blade was broken.

As the beast spun, snarling and snapping at all around him, it launched Selwyn across the ground, skidding to a halt few feet away. Six more Rekeshi fell to the beast as it tore through their ranks, biting and clawing and stomping upon them all, leaving nothing more than a river of blood flowing down the middle of the hall.

"Selwyn!" cried Arturius, "I am here to help!"

A firm hand gripped Arturius upon his shoulder. As he turned ready to strike down he was met face to face with Dovan.

"No Arturius," he said, "I will retrieve our captain, you make sure my brother gets out of here!"

"Allow me to help!" replied Arturius.

Dovan shook his head.

"You have already helped more than could asked," whispered Dovan. He spoke hushed and quietly, perhaps not to draw attention to his acceptance of the newcomer.

"Keep him safe, keep him alive," said Dovan.

A faint smile crept across his face as he relinquished his grip and drew backwards towards Selwyn.

Dovan closed in beside his captain. His swift and agile feet cascaded relentlessly across the cobbled floor. In a fell swoop he grappled at the hungered Selwyn as he clawed his way towards the open vault.

"Sir, we must go, our fight will be lost if we stay," Dovan pleaded, "Your blade is broken and we can do no damage to such a creature!"

"No!" shouted Selwyn, "Not when the crown is so close within my grasp."

Dovan pinned his mentor to the ground, tightly gripping at his torso in a desperate attempt to pull him away from such a lure.

"Don't fight me Sir!" pleaded Dovan, "We must go, it's not worth losing your life over!"

"Of course it is!" hissed Selwyn.

The old captain broke free of his underling's grasp, running headstrong and unarmed towards the vault. His arms outstretched to receive the bounty from the shadows dark embrace. The others gave chase.

"Someone grab him, we need to get out of here, NOW!" shouted Arturius, jerking back to avoid a rabid slash from one of the guards. His eyes bore deep black pigments, foam billowed from his mouth in an uncontrolled rage. He looked down to his chest. An open wound created by the beasts tail festered and bubbled, spitting out black droplets that fizzed violently upon the ground. He lunged and swung in such a violent and unpredictable manner, as though a puppet upon a string. Before the feral guard could carve his being, Eskiel delivered a swift slashed across the open wound. Silencing the aggression once more.

"Stay clear of its tail," shouted Eskiel, "It is coated with some sort of toxin, a small drop and you may not be able to see friend from foe."

Arturius watched on as four more Rekeshi fell to the beast's violent flurry of slashes and stings. Bearing its fangs down upon one of the unlucky few, shredding torso from legs as the upper body struck him with full force. The warm black blood sprayed over him as he scrambled away from the half-man that lay atop him.

His head felt dizzy as his eyes lost their focus and ringing thundered through his ears. The world appeared as a blur; a wandering motion blotted out by the darkness. Even the carnage

Suddenly the beast let out an ungodly screech, piercing the ears of all that stood before it. Some Rekeshi wailed upon the floor as blood poured from the cracks within their ears. Garton stood to its rear. A jagged blade protruding from its hind leg released a torrent of oozing black liquid, coating the ground as it smoked violently. The beast's eyes grew a frightful rage of red, swinging its tail aloft, releasing a rain of razor spines into the air. Two more Rekeshi dropped to the floor as the barbed daggers that fell from the sky pinned them to the ground in deathly silence. So too did Selwyn, struck in the upper left back screaming in pain. He fell suddenly, reaching out for the vault before him.

"Selwyn!" screamed Dovan, reaching out for his commander.

He too promptly fell behind him.

Jorik watched in horror as his brother fell before him, pierced by too many barbs of the beast to count. Overcome with anger and fear, he screamed in anguish. It took two of them to hold him back as he desperately fought to reclaim his brother.

"Stop Jorik!" cried Arturius, struggling to fight with his pain, "He's gone, there's nothing you can do."

"Everyone fall back!" screamed Ozark, dragging the crying Jorik towards the tunnel, Robbard and Garton promptly followed.

By now the entire Rekeshi force was in full rout, fleeing with whatever remained of their retinue.

"Come Eskiel, swords are no more use here," Arturius shouted fiercely, grasping at his shoulder, "If you stay here you die."

The Beast howled in turmoil, the gash in its hind leg sealed at the behest of devouring three more of the Rekeshi footmen. A fate that would become worse than death.

"This is not good," he shouted, "What magic could keep such an abhorrent alive, it must have slumbered within its imprisonment for thousands of years."

"One that delves deep beneath the earth," shouted back Eskiel, staring back at him with a fearful gaze, "It appears to draw the life from the living to replenish its own failing body."

Even as they fled, obstacles came unto them as the Rekeshi elite threw themselves upon them in chaotic combat. What madness would send them to fight against a foe when death loams over them within its malevolent shadow? A thought that truly terrified Arturius. For fear of failing their grand imperator, their lord and master, the Masked One was more potent than the river of blood that trailed in the wake of the Dark creature.

"You damned fools," snapped Arturius, "Do you want to die."

"They fear what will happen to them should they fail in their orders!" shouted Eskiel. He frantically clashed swords with another of the Rekeshi, deflecting and parrying as the weight of the steel rung through the air.

"You will die traitor!" hissed his opponent, "For nothing escapes the gaze of our lord saviour! I shall honour his with screams of your death!"

His opponent outmatched him in both speed and skill. Forever on the defensive Arturius relieved him of such turmoil with a slash upon the warriors heel.

"Come Eskiel, come and live to fight another day" said Arturius.

They ran for what seemed to be hours. Ascending through the darkness as the sound of tearing flesh and bloody screams echoed behind them.

All was calm for a while. They tucked and turned down the vast network of tunnels, tracing their steps as much as they could remember.

"Shit, shit, shit," panicked Eskiel, "I can't take this anymore!"

"Calm yourself!" snapped Arturius. He peered back into the darkness behind him. All was quiet, too quiet.

"Looks like we've bought ourselves some time, let us not waste such a blessing," said Arturius,

"And that thing, it was huge," said Eskiel, "I've never seen anything like it, not in any kingdom or beyond!"

"Nor have I," replied Arturius, "It's impossible to believe that it survived down here for so long, its life must be eternal, though it would appear that its body does suffer from decay much as our own."

The silence was uneasy, Arturius gritted his teeth, waiting for any sign of the others. All the while praying that the beast does not resurface itself. Every shadow they passed; every darkened corner they ran through watched them with eager eyes. Only to be dispelled by the gentle flicker of light that would occasionally find its way through the gloom.

They stumbled through the dark. Every rock that brushed against their feet felt like another threat looming upon them.

"There!" shouted Eskiel, "Up ahead I see the light."

Far away into the darkness, the silhouettes of the others running into the red glow eased their minds, *"Gods I hope it is the others*" Arturius thought to himself.

Slowly but surely they ascended the small staircase, reeling in as the heat from the fires of doom washed over them. The sight of the others fleeing in the distance brought a safe warmth to his heart, the flowing magma illuminating the way vibrantly as the heat exhausted them.

"Keep moving!" shouted Arturius as his voice carried over to the others.

A rumble behind them sent rocks and stone flying across the room. A bloodied body cascaded through the air plunging down screaming into the whirlpool of fire. Another wailed for help as his body split open by the shadow that emerged through the destruction, his blood dripping from its jagged teeth before sizzling atop the hot surface.

Before they knew it, the creature's gaze shifted to them, fleeing before it. A whistling hum soon averted its gaze, glancing off the monster's fiery eye, sending wisps of dark smoke waving into the hot air. Robbard nodded to Arturius as he lowered his bow, buying them a few seconds of well-warranted time. The arrow had merely phased it for little more than a couple of seconds as it returned to its bloody pursuit.

Up ahead Robbard waited for them, releasing several more arrows, whistling between their heads. Each one glanced off the pursuing beast, its feet pounding upon the cracking ground as the drums of war beckoned for them.

"Hurry!" shouted Robbard, waving for them with his outstretched arm, "Ozark says to go to the Arkanium, they mean to bar the door shut!"

The rest of the Rekeshi guards had been utterly obliterated, their blood staining the body of the beast. Its taste sending it into a frenzy.

They peered down the darkened corridor, no sign of the others in the distance *"They must mean to seal ourselves behind the stone door, it has resisted this creature before it would seem"* he thought. Its strong stone doors could provide an effective barricade against the beast–so long as they could withstand its might.

"Hurry," said Robbard, "We must catch up with the others if –."

His voice came to an abrupt stop. A trickle of blood fell from the corner of his lips, dripping from his chin. Before Arturius could bring his voice to bear, Robbard fell back into the open void, unable to bring sound to his breath as he was flung down into the chasm of fire.

"Robbard!" shouted Arturius. He tried to reach out and grab the knight, but alas he fell.

"Come Arturius!" said Eskiel, "Or you shall share the same fate!"

Shadowed claws grasped around the corner, cracking and crumbling the walls as they dug in deep.

The two made for the others, Eskiel practically dragging Arturius away for fear he would try to take on the beast himself. It was a strange feeling brimming inside him, for despite his harsh critiques and aggressive demeanour, he was still a member of this company.

Not too far behind them, the cracking and crumbling of the corridor walls could be heard loudly as the creature pressed its way forward. Its sheer size was too great for the architecture within, crumbling the ancient walls as it dragged its grizzly hide behind it.

"We must hurry!" shouted Arturius, "If we do not reach them soon, I fear we will be trapped with this accursed beast forever."

"I don't know how long I can keep this going for," panted Eskiel, losing his breath and stamina alike, "my legs burn and breath is shot, I feel as though I will fall any moment."

"I will not leave you my friend," replied Arturius, "I have stared enough into the eyes of death today, and to him, I say no more."

There was a glimmer of light up ahead, someone standing on guard by the heavily fortified Arkania. It was Garton, shouting to the others beyond the doorway.

"I see them ahead," Garton croaked, "start sealing it now!"

The sound of stone grinding upon its hinges tore through the air, a countdown until they would be trapped in the searing darkness that bounded behind them. Arturius glanced back, turning his stomach painfully.

"Eskiel, hurry!" he shouted, as he quickened his pace. He had neglected to keep a check on his companion, the latter of which was dwindling far behind him.

"Shit!" he cursed to himself, closing in evermore on the sanctuary ahead, "If we do not hurry the door shall become sealed!"

"Go on without me!" Eskiel screamed, accepting his imminent fate, "I am only dragging you down, go!"

Arturius bit his tongue hard, the taste of blood welling up within his cheeks.

"I shall not leave you behind!" cried Arturius, "so shut your damn mouth and keep running."

Then he saw it, half-buried in the ash from earlier. The chosen's spear. Mangled yet still sharper than any weapon they had with them. His boots ground hard against the floor; the layer of ash allowed him to glide freely upon its surface swiftly. With his left foot, he hooked the spear, launching it up towards his brow. Catching it with the palm of his right hand, clenching a fist around its coarse surface.

Before he could think, he launched the spear hard and fast, whistling through the air. All the while he remembered the pain the creature felt, the screeching and deathly howl when Robbard's arrow kissed the eyes within its skull. That was what he had aimed for.

Narrowly avoiding Eskiel's head, whipping past him as the beast bore its fangs, preparing to consume. The blow penetrated hard and deep, spewing an abhorrent miasma of dark matter from the socket. Screeching and suffering it fell crashing into the floor, its limp legs mangling beneath its heavy frame as it skidded across the floor.

It wasn't long before the dust soon settled, unveiling the motionless creature crammed in between the narrow walls, a few feet short of the thick stone doors. Eskiel lay at its head, trembling before it as he stared down into the chasm of death behind the razor teeth still coated in blood and sinew.

"You okay there?" asked Arturius, stretching out a hand as he hoisted him to his feet, "Damn, nearly thought I'd be pulling you from its jaws piece by piece."

"Am I dead?" he stuttered, "Have I passed over to the other side?"

Arturius laughed hard and long.

"Far from it my friend," he looked up and down Eskiel, checking for any injuries, "Looks as though you are unscathed my friend."

Lucky for him it was just his armour and garbs that were slashed and torn.

"I owe you my life," mumbled Eskiel, "I'd be suffering a fate worse than death were it not for you to live an eternity within the belly of such a creature would be a nightmare!"

"Don't mention it," Arturius replied, patting him on the shoulder as he approached the creature.

"Ghastly looking thing isn't it," said Arturius, kneeling down closer.

Its stench was truly foul. A thousand years of decay and slumber would do that to such a thing. Most of its flesh had since fallen off over time, displaying only the coarse putrid bones that cracked underneath. What was left of its hide he could not tell from fur, skin or darkness, it smoked with a faint intensity that burnt at his nostrils. Such an entity was a defilement of the purity of the realm, darkness that clings to life–a parasite of the shadows.

"Strange," said Arturius, gazing deep into the wound he had inflicted upon its face.

"What is it?" asked Eskiel, pacing backwards, "I wouldn't get too close to it, that blood has a bite to it."

Arturius ran his finger down the pole of the twisted spear, feeling its cold yet surprisingly smooth touch.

"Strange that the company so many years ago was unable to harm the beast," he replied, "Yet with a spear mangled by fire, the deed has been done."

"Maybe that's it," said Eskiel, "Maybe fire can undo darkness."

A voice bellowed behind them, averting their gaze to Jorik stood peering from the archway.

"Arturius!" he shouted, "Have you seen Silas?"

At that moment, he grasped the polearm.

A burning sensation flooded his left arm. Screeches and howls flooded the mountain once more as the creature raised him up high, clasped tightly within its jaws. He screamed a deathly cry, swatting at the beast's grizzled face as it shook him violently. Every inch he moved, the weight of the shadowed jaws bore down heavier, slicing deep into his flesh.

"It's still alive!" shouted Eskiel, calling for the others to come to their aid.

It was warm and sour, burning quickly through his muscles. A swift snap pierced his body as he fell hard to the floor.

Dazed and confused he thrashed around trying to scramble free from its presence, only it proved more difficult a task to accomplish.

Eskiel grabbed him, dragging him free from his struggling crawl.

"Hurry!" he shouted, jerking Arturius forward as they made for the Arkania. It was at that moment Arturius wished he hadn't looked, wished he hadn't glanced at the stump where his arm used to be. It dripped hot with a reddish-black liquid, spraying from the shredded gashed below the shoulder. It took some time for the realisation to set in before he cursed with a violent wail.

"Get him through the door!" shouted Ozark.

The others were aggressively pushing on the door, grinding it slowly as they closed the gap.

It was cold… very cold, the feeling of life draining from his wound as he lay atop the hard-cold table. The room was falling faint around him as his vision blurred, using what little strength he could muster he turned. Garton and Jorik were frantically pressing their shoulders against the door. It was ajar with the creature's fangs and claws ensnared within the recesses. Eskiel rushed throughout the room, wedging whatever pikes, axes and spears into the cracks, though it all proved fruitful as one by one they snapped and splintered across the room.

All were oblivious to the blood draining for his side, pooling upon the table, a bloody mirror of sorts. Their voices were muffled and hushed. Although it was the creeping death that enshrouded his senses, the reality was far louder and much more chaotic.

"Keep pushing!" shouted Jorik, "Push harder than ever before, we can't let it get in!"

"We need strong barricades!" called Garton, "Try moving the stone monuments!"

"They're too heavy and bolted to the floor!" screamed Eskiel in return, "What of the pikes and halberds?",

"It be no use, they will splinter and snap like the spears before!" replied Garton,

"It's breaking through, what more is there we can do?" called Ozark, "Garton pierce its hide as you did before!"

For the first time, he had finally witnessed the vulnerable side to the undying man, tired and drained as he bore down with the last reserves of his energy.

"I don't have the power left for such a thing!" he replied, "I am spent, already I have reached my limit of death for today!"

Darkness crept in from the corners of his eyes, lingering as they cut off his connection to the realm. The warmth of his blood soothed his worries, gently stroking away the pain as he began to fall under. Trickled between the cracks in the stone table as they fell into the oblivion of the void. Whirring a small flicker of life into the Akavirian arm that lay next to him.

With their ultimate efforts exhausted, the beast overwhelmed their defences, breaking through the doors gnashing and biting. Garton phased into an incorporeal form, the door swatting his mist across the room. Jorik bore a more painful awakening. The force of the beast pressing upon the doors propelled him across the room, knocking the control from his body as he lay there unconscious.

Like a wolf on the prowl, it smelt blood. Clawing its way towards the sweet aroma of rusted iron and tainted ash. It ambled towards him, remarkably forbearing in the presence of its mark. Then came the blinding flash.

A brilliant purple beam bore down within the confines of the room, sparking great pain in the eyes of those who stared into its alluring shine. Such intensity from the light burned a myriad of waves and markings deep into the floor, a series of ancient symbols. It was then from deep within the light, a burning shadow walked from within, its footsteps made no sound, its face gave no smile. Emerging as a beacon of power never before seen.

Slash after slash bore deep into the creature's hide as it brandished its ethereal blade high above its ghostly figure. A purple hue descended upon its body, as though cloaked by the very darkness it purged. The blade greeted every cut with a smouldering burn, cinders that cauterised the wound, stopping it from promptly healing. Arturius's gaze faltered, the darkness consuming his life as his vision fell from his conscious mind.

*"Fear not young warrior, in your time of need I shall be by your side. In your time of question I shall answer. In your time of death I shall live"*

The voice was gentle, soothing as a mother would talk unto her child. Yet as alacritous as the wraith appeared before them, so too did it vanish. Its faceless gaze looking back unto Arturius before it beamed itself into his chest, vanishing from the room. A grotesque burning emanated from the flesh of the shadow creature; the darkness billowed out from within its earthy body as it slumped to the floor, sending a wave of ash floating in all directions. This time the beast was no more.

Arturius's mind dreamed of lush fields of green and rivers of purest crystal, a memory possibly, but there was no way of knowing. Only a deepened darkness fell upon his field of vision, blotting out the sun and trees and grass. And a gaze of a most sinister order, the large looming eyes, angry in their vision, tied down upon the mask of a smiling demon. It watched him intently as his mind fell from his body, turning away into the void of the abyss.

*~ "Stay true my friend, keep your allies close but your enemies closer, it may just save your life" ~*

## CHAPTER XVI: AWAKENING

Despite facing death in the eyes, he found himself awakening to the smell of burning flesh and smouldering bone. He shivered thusly. Every inch of his body ached and throbbed, burning with every minor movement he made. Arturius groaned as he pulled himself free of the makeshift bed he found himself to be lay upon. Cracking and creasing, he could still feel the affliction of the shadow coursing through his veins, yet it seemed to be held at bay for now.

"He's awake!" shouted Eskiel, sitting uncomfortably by his side, "Easy, easy you should be resting, Ozark says you will be fine but there is still much of the venom coursing through you, you must rest",

Arturius braced his hand against his temple, stroking its tender embrace.

"What happened?" groaned Arturius, "Is everyone okay? Is anyone else hurt?"

"Much my friend, but you shouldn't be moving right now," said Eskiel, "orders from Ozark."

As he tried to push himself upright, the click of metal reached his ears, as he pressed his hand atop the surface of the bed. A strange sensation rushed over him, a cold feeling to an ever-changing scope.

He looked down to gaze upon the arm which no longer lay by his side to note a more frightening sight. Embedded deep within the flesh and bone of his left shoulder, a metallic appendage now protruded. He ran his fingers across its smooth surface. It was cold.

"What the hell is this?" cursed Arturius, reeling in from the shock as he scrambled across the floor, "Get it off me, get it off!"

Every motion he demanded the arm swiftly and silently moved as commanded.

"Steady!" shouted Eskiel, pinning him to the floor, "You're in shock, it's understandable, it's not every day do you fall asleep with one arm and awaken with two."

The commotion attracted the attention of the others as one by one they poured into the room.

"Hold him down!" shouted Ozark, "He may reopen his wounds if he is not careful."

The power of his new arm was truly terrifying, it took the combined strength of all the others to hold him down. Even as it scrapped and smashed against the floor it did not break, it did not scuff and it did not fail.

"You are going to be fine," hushed Ozark gently, "Tis but a scratch upon the surface of your flesh."

"A scratch!" snapped Arturius, "Half my arms bloody gone! What's going on?"

"All shall be answered in good time my friend," replied Ozark, "but for now you must remain calm, otherwise I cannot heal your wounds."

It took some time before the panic subsided and his mind accepted the reality that lay before him. As his breath diminished, he found himself in a state of calm he had never before felt, easing away all his worries.

"Remarkable," said Ozark in awe, "It is truly a magnificent creation, to mould so effectively upon the physique of organic matter. Whatever this is, it is nothing of which this realm has ever seen before."

"What is it?" asked Arturius, "It feels so fluid, so lifelike, whatever thoughts I give to it, whatever I command it does so without hesitation."

"A prosthetic of sorts it would appear," replied Ozark, "Though much more advanced, whilst there are prosthetics used significantly within the other kingdoms, they pale in comparison, albeit more primitive to such a design we see here."

"I feel strange," said Arturius, "I should feel frightened, pained, even disturbed, yet I feel calm and collected. Have you given me a tonic like that which you used before?"

"I have done nothing of the sort," replied Ozark, "It would appear that arm has sway over your emotions. It's almost as if it's an entity of its own, helping to ease such negative feelings before they consume you."

Such elegance was the arm, it moved no different to that of his lost limb–fluid and without resistance.

Notched deep upon its surface were an assortment of murals depicted what could only be the ascension of the Akaviri since the dawn. Between the gaps and slots upon the plating, he could peer through into its mechanical constructs–though none of it truly made any sense to him. Silently whirring cogs, springs and all manner of couplings drove each of the spindles, actuators and hinges. How on earth such a contraption was powered was beyond his frail mind, though a part of him was thankful he knew not of the supernatural that had brought it to be.

"What does it feel like?" asked Ozark, eager with the knowledge he could unravel from its use, "can you feel through it? Does it tire you in its use? Tell me I must know."

The desperation in his voice was clearer than the glass mosaics that lined the room.

"It feels remarkably… strange," replied Arturius, flexing it about his person as he grew accustomed to its feel, "I feel not any surface I lay my hand upon, yet my mind seems to tell me I do."

"Incredible, it must have linked itself up with the motor system of your brain, spreading out its information with incredible detail," said Ozark in amazement, "How in all the realms is it that they succeeded in merging metal with man? Mind with matter?"

Before they could say any more, Garton emerged from beyond the hallway. A feeling of deep dismay sent his body into a weary-looking state.

"Did you find them?" asked Jorik eagerly,

"No, there is no sign of them," replied Garton, "I searched the armoury, the second and third halls, I made my way down the winding staircase up to the remains of the astral tower, I looked everywhere that wasn't filled with fire or buried by the earth, all was as silent as a crypt."

"Keep checking Garton, they have to be here somewhere," replied Ozark,

Garton nodded to Ozark, turning around and disappearing in the doorway he previously emerged from. A worried look fell upon the others.

"How?" muttered Ozark, "How could we lose sight of four of our own, it's bad enough that two had fallen within great halls, but this, this is the work of something else."

Arturius gathered his thoughts, clearing his throat from the dense dryness that had settled.

"Who is missing?" he asked with worry in his voice,

"Silas, Burak, Karlan," Ozark replied, "Robbard was with us during the escape but vanished soon after reaching the Arkania."

Arturius looked towards Eskiel. It was clear he hadn't yet told them of his demise, maybe it was out of shame. Though most likely it was out of fear, without Arturius to defend his actions they could have easily turned on the young Rekeshi demanding blood for blood.

"He fell," whispered Arturius, lowering his eyes to the floor, shame welling over his mind at failing to save him, "He fell into the fires below, dragged down by the beast itself before my very eyes, there was nothing we could do."

Ozark fell back towards the wall, leaning heavily against its rough embrace.

"Selwyn, Dovan, Robbard," Ozark whispered, "Today was a dark day. To lose so many of our own and with nothing to show for it, they died in vain along with those who fell throughout this great war of wars."

Eskiel took Arturius's arm and helped him to his feet, wobbling as his weak knees struggled to bear his weight.

"I feared that you had been lost to us," said Eskiel, "Never had I been so delighted to see you breathe once more, it would have been shameful of me to not show my gratitude for earlier."

"Well said," muttered Ozark, "I believe you owe him more than just your gratitude however."

"Indeed," replied Eskiel, "I owe you my life, as it shall now be for yours to command."

"It was nothing," said Arturius, wincing as Eskiel set him down beside the makeshift camp. The crackle of the flames brought back the pain of his bones splintering in his arm once more.

"You truly are an anomaly within my eyes young sir," said Ozark, "I can only say I did not expect to see you walking around again after a wound such as that, tell me are you sure you are not of the divinity, or perhaps even an Akaviri!"

Ozark laughed to himself briefly, before pondering the veritable miracle of such a fast recovery.

He looked down towards his arm, pondering the thoughts as to how he came into possession of such a contraption.

"So who do I have to thank for replacing my broken limb," said Arturius, "Or for saving my life in that matter, Ozark? Only who could have the advanced expertise to even conjure up such a feat, should it be you I am to thank?"

Ozark looked upon him with confusion before the realisation that his passing into his dreams came before the incident.

"What is it?" he asked worriedly.

Ozark quickly cleared his throat, setting down his parchment and ink to his side.

"I'm afraid that's a question even I do not have the full answer to," replied Ozark, "It was not I who fixed you thusly, for yes I assisted in the expunging of the affliction that grew within you, but I dare say such a combination was not of my doing."

"I don't understand," muttered Arturius, "If none of you saved me from my passing … then-."

He paused promptly, following his eyes as they looked to his Akavirian arm.

"Yes indeed," replied Ozark, "I don't know how or why, but during the whole confrontation with the beast, your blood seemed to have sparked some life into this here metal arm, next thing I know there was a blinding flash and it was resting peacefully atop your wound, cauterised and all."

This opened upon a barrage of further questions in the weary warriors' eyes.

"So, I wasn't dreaming any of that then?" bellowed Arturius, "I saw a flash of brightest starlight as my vision faded, and then-."

He stopped suddenly. Perhaps this wasn't the best of times to mention voices emerging within one's own head.

"You most certainly were not," replied Ozark, "How fares your pain and fatigue?"

"Well, my body aches and skin burns," said Arturius, "though I feel as though I plunged deep into the fires below, and came out fiery with death, it was as though someone else was pulling me gracefully away from the light, refusing to allow me to pass, as though there was a job yet unfinished."

Ozark looked deep into his eyes.

"You know, you remind me of someone from a very long time ago," said Ozark crumpling his brow as he strained to think, he paused for a while before continuing "Someone who lived before my time or anyone here for that matter, although the name and history truly eludes me this very moment."

Ozark laughed briefly.

"Although one thing is certain from all this,"

"And what's that?" replied Arturius worryingly.

"There is much more to you than meets the eye master Arturius," Ozark whispered, "Perhaps it is sealed within your forgotten memories, or even lost for good, and I do so wish to crack open the shell of your mind and see what mysteries may come pouring out."

Arturius thought hard. There was more he was learning about himself every day, was it so wrong to think there may be more secret lurking within him.

"But what happened after the intense light?" he asked again, "I have no memory of encounter aside from the vast emptiness I fell into. What followed in the aftermath?"

"I'm afraid my eyes aren't what they used to be you see, the light blinded my vision intensely, it wasn't until a few minutes when it came back to me that I saw the aftermath, the beast lay dead at my feet, a stench of burnt rotting flesh found its way to my nose, and the arm, the arm lay upon your being, clutching graciously upon its new host,"

Eskiel had remained rather quiet through it all, looking down at his feet, holding back a feeling that was trying to burst forth.

"I saw what happened," Said Eskiel quietly, "I don't think I can ever unsee what I saw, sent chills through me it did."

Arturius and Ozark turned to him in unison.

"What did you see?" asked Arturius eagerly, "What happened to me?"

Eskiel stood up, walked over the walls of deepest stone, and gazed upon the murals before him. They were intricately carved and well preserved. It appeared to show three pillars of light cascading from the heavens atop what appeared to be a map of sorts, surrounded by a vast ocean.

"When I heard you talking about the Gods and Goddesses of the realm, it sparked up an old memory of mine from my younger days," Eskiel spoke softly, "Im, Rok and Sul, the elder gods who shaped this world, their worship dwindled over time because of the promises that the younger God's would offer, though they were all filled with lies and deceit."

He stepped closer to the mural, running his fingers to the top of the markings. There, stood above all, shining in incandescent light were three entities, though they took no form it was clear what power they possessed. He pointed to the first.

"When there was nothing, Rok emerged, his glorious power drafted forth great masses of land as far as the eye could see, mountains that reached the heavens and crevices that reached far beyond the depths, falling into a deep slumber beneath the very earth he had crafted."

They followed his finger move over to the second entity at the opposite end.

"When there was something, Im emerged, and with him, he brought forth time, for with time the great mountains would wither into dirt, sand and dust, and the realm now had earth, desert and decay, he too fell in a deep slumber, beneath the very desert that spans the length of the Varib."

Finally, his attention shifted to the third entity, floating in between the others, larger and more radiant.

"Finally, when there was something and nothing, Sul brought forth everything, her gentle touch breathed life into the realm, rivers ran anew, grass and trees grew from the mud and life, and life itself emerged from even the darkest recess of the ground, though unlike the others she chose not to sleep, instead she watches over us all gleaming from the heavens as a beacon of light in even the darkest of times."

Eskiel turned once more, staring deep upon Arturius as he sat there awed and humble.

"You possess the affinity of Sul, a power transposed from the tears that fell towards the land she raised, the tears that soaked deep into the ichorous earth erecting conduits of power. And a damned powerful one at that," said Eskiel softly, "I don't know how or where, but you have touched this power, tapping deep into the power of the elder gods, a blessing of the great one herself!"

"I've never heard of such a thing," said Ozark, "No tome or scroll I have laid my eyes upon ever gave mention of these Elder Gods."

"It's understandable," replied Eskiel, "The study of such mysteries was deemed as heresy, any who made pilgrimage or worshipped the ancient idols simply disappeared. Besides, could you imagine an army that sent tremors through the ground as they moved, conjured great firestorms to decimate cities and kingdoms. Perhaps such knowledge would be left hidden beneath the surface of the realm."

"But by whom?" said Ozark shockingly, "Who holds such power over the kingdoms to instigate such a thing? This land is vast and its inhabitants abundant, surely rumours would surface and whispers unravel."

"They call themselves the cult of Xevihar," hushed Eskiel. He looked worried, as though someone was watching, waiting for him to divulge his doom.

"Xevihar?" questioned Arturius,

"I know no more of it than the name itself," replied Eskiel, "No one who has gone looking for them has ever returned, it was by mere coincidence I learned of their name. A hastily written name upon the ancient scrolls within the Grand Archives."

"You have entered the Archives" Exclaimed Ozark.

"That I have, though it was back during a time when I was but a mere footmen within the ranks" replied Eskiel.

"A footman? Within the Grand Archives? How?"

"My brother was able to pull rank easily within the puppet states," said Eskiel, "Otherwise I would not be here to discuss such matters."

"Remind me when we are free of this accursed mountain to pick your brain of the archives. To enter the Grand archive of Verden is a true privilege in this age."

Eskiel nodded in compliance.

"And this cult of Xevihar, do you know where they originate from?" asked Ozark, "Which of the kingdoms holds their allegiance?"

The sweat on Eskiel's brow shone off the glow of the fire. His nervous disposition was to be expected in the current circumstances.

"Again, it is only the name to which I am privy to," replied Eskiel, "I believe they are deeply rooted within all the kingdoms, pulling the strings from deep within the darkness, perhaps even the masked one himself is controlled by such people. An underground organisation of immense influence and power."

Arturius could see the conversation surrounding this mysterious cult was turning in circles. Eskiel was trembling before him. The mere thought of such a mysterious organisation sent fear through his soul. He was most definitely hiding something from them.

"Tell me more of this affinity you speak of," interrupted Arturius, "What does it do? How does it work?"

Eskiel reclused to the far reaches of his mind, pondering the thoughts and knowledge he had gathered over the years.

"Well, as I said before, it is a gift from the Elder Goddess Sul, the wisest, oldest and most powerful being of the Elder Gods or Kirin Tar as the Vindictarians called them," said Eskiel, "Her power was transposed into fragments of earthen tears. They fell to the earth as she wept upon seeing her creations cause such death and destruction. When one comes into contact with one of the tears they become a conduit of her power. They are blessed with remarkable abilities, longevity and health."

"And these powers you speak of, have you ever seen one before?" asked Arturius.

Eskiel shook his head.

"I have not" replied Eskiel, "All I know is that the powers come in many shapes and sizes, all dependent upon the heart of its host. I read legends of heroes capable of toppling mountains, splitting the seas, even delving deep into the nexus and empower themselves with the souls of the long departed."

"I too have heard such tales" said Ozark, "Although at the time I merely took them to be twisted tales of fantastical adventures. Never had I realised that such legends were in fact reality."

"Arturius, do you have any memory at all of such an event. Anything that may point you towards how you acquired such a gift?"

"I'm afraid not. Or possibly so," replied Arturius, "Much has happened in the past few moons that I never believed to be possible. I do not know what path I took with my previous life, or if that path followed the light or dark. The last thing I remember is waking up upon the moors, surrounding by the death and savagery."

Eskiel thought hard and deep.

"It was rumoured that those blessed with the Affinity of Sul underwent … dramatic changes."

"Such as?" asked Ozark.

Eskiel rummaged around in his pockets, tearing a scrap of parchment crumpled deep within. The two watched as his hands scribbled about, drawing a myriad of lines across the sheet.

"Do you have any memory of this symbol at all?" Eskiel said, brandishing the paper close to his face.

Arturius looked in closely, following every bit of detail with his weary eyes. A symbol of two flames, intertwining below a radiant sun–simple but clear. He thought long and hard, thinking back to every moment that he had encountered so far. Then it clicked.

"Yes," he replied, unsure of himself, "Before I woke I had, I dreamt of such symbols."

"Go on," urged Eskiel,

"Though the dream was strange, it felt rather familiar, as though it wasn't a dream but a memory from long ago," said Arturius, "In the dream, however, I saw that symbol, along with a darkness that I dare not look upon.",

"Dreams are the creation of encounters from your past," interrupted Ozark, "Your mind requires sustenance to create such vivid hallucinations you see, so at some point in your past that symbol was presented before you"

Eskiel held his hand atop his head, exhaling loudly as a stunned face befell him.

"It all adds up then," Eskiel blurted, "The amnesia, confusion, power, the dream, it all makes sense."

"How so?" replied Arturius.

Eskiel tossed the paper into the flames, watching as it crumbled and burned. Its ashes floating off into the distant darkness.

"When one touches the conduit and is granted the affinity, they undergo quite a volatile change," said Eskiel, "Such a distressing act sends the body into meltdown, a complete shock reignites the system as it changes your soul, the trauma is believed to be so great so intense, that the recipient believes themselves to be approaching death! Almost splitting them into two!"

He couldn't quite believe it himself. To attain such power and have no memory of its existence was a truly mind-shattering thought.

"However, there is a catch to such power," continued Eskiel in a hushed manner, "For such a feat goes against the balance of nature, and as such your very shadow is torn from your being, plunged into darkness whilst you continue toward the light."

Arturius looked upon the floor. A part of him wished to deny the rumour and speculation, the other part wanted to know more. Beside him lay the withered shape of a man, albeit disfigured and disjointed. Again there was a shadow for Eskiel, perfectly mimicking his actions in an eerie way. Yet he remained empty. Not a flicker of darkness spewed forth from his feet, not an ounce of shadow.

"By the Gods, Arturius!" shouted Ozark, "How have we never noticed!"

"My shadow," whispered Arturius, "It eludes me, yet I never once thought it be gone, I never even noticed!",

"What is this catch you speak of?" asked Ozark.

"Well, to keep nature within the confines of its precarious equilibrium, the wrong must be righted," said Eskiel "As such your shadow will forever pursue you until your last dying day, watching and waiting for you so that it may enact its vengeance upon being discarded… an act that will kill you, should it occur."

"So somewhere out there, my shadow hunts me down?" said Arturius, "And what form shall it take? To think that a part of me harbours such hatred and malice that it would see me dead!"

"Im afraid so," replied Eskiel, "I don't think I can be of much help either, for all known chronicles of and writings of users succumbing to the shadows of fate comment only on the aftermath. Nothing of the cause."

"No scribe has ever documented such an event?" exclaimed Ozark.

"No, nothing," replied Eskiel, "The last known sighting of such an event were some seventy years ago. A mysterious traveller within the eastern agora of Scarib succumbed to a most violent end. No suspect, no sighting, only a man as cold as the night with eyes of smouldering ash and veins of blackened ivy."

"Sounds unforgiving," muttered Ozark.

"Unforgiving, terrifying, destructive." said Eskiel, "But such powers came with such risk. It is said that some were able to move mountains, cross the seas without a vessel, summon the elements and even remove oneself from their own body."

He stared back upon the mural, namely towards the golden sun that shone high above all else. The mother to his power, and the being behind his lost life.

"To attain such power would indeed render the user a powerful and mighty individual," said Ozark, "Though a terrifying presence to be met if it were on the opposing side of the war and quite frankly a terror to forever be watching over your shoulder. It must be a truly outstanding gift"

"Gift," snarked Arturius coldly.

The two looked at him in deafening silence. Confused as to the sudden change in mood by the miracle that remained in their presence.

"What are you talking about?" said Eskiel, "This is a power that others can only ever dream of, this a power that could tip the tide of the war and topple the Masked One's regime."

He stood up and sauntered over to the many weapons and artefacts lines across the walls, each one crafted with a purpose, a history that told the tale of their life.

"It cost me my life," he replied softly,

"I think you're confused." said Eskiel, "It saved your life, it saved all our lives, without it we would all be in the belly of that beast,"

Ozark placed a hand up the ecstatic shoulder of Eskiel, shaking his head gently as if to tell him not to continue.

"My friend, some people see these gifts in very different lights," muttered Ozark, "Of course to us it is an incredible power, saved our lives and can assist our cause."

He looked over towards Arturius who remained ever silent, staring off into the distance of the room–not much of a sight to behold at this moment.

"But for some it is a curse, to be denied knowledge of your existence, your purpose and life, to be cast out into the abyss and left to find your own way out," said Ozark, "It can send people mad for the truth, and down a path to which they may never return."

A murmur crept from beyond the doorway, attracting the attention of the four poised anxiously within the Arkania.

As it crept closer and closer, louder and louder, the more uneasy they felt as they waited for whatever lurked beyond.

"Who goes there?" shouted Jorik.

Only silence called back to them, whispers that breathed heavily, cursing and calling from out of the darkness.

"Show yourself!"

As the bloodied hand emerged, it slid precariously across the stone, Jorik could wait no more. He lunged forward precariously, showing no sign of thought or regard for his own life. Before the others could stop him, he came crashing back into reality, flying hard back into the corner he came from, striking hard against the stone floor, letting all the air whistle from his lungs.

"Have you learned nothing, you great fool," spluttered a voice from beyond the door.

The light washed over the bloodied figure as they limped into the room, a hand grasping at their side, quenching the flow of blood from falling to the floor.

"Burak!" shouted Ozark, rushing forward to meet with the bloodied warrior, "Oh am I glad to see you, you ugly bastard."

It was then Arturius saw the whites of his eyes spread across his vision, his knees wobbled as they weakened sending him falling to the floor face down. Had it not been for the quick manoeuvring of Arturius and Eskiel, he would've found me with a bloody nose–courtesy of the stone floor.

"By the Gods Burak, what happened to you?" said Ozark, pressing his hands atop his chest and side, stemming the flow of blood. Burak coughed up a river of red blood, splattering over his face. It was warm and thick.

"Traitor!" said Burak, coughing up even more blood than before.

Every breath he took was weakened his body as he faded from the world.

"Burak! Wait! stay with me," shouted Ozark, slapping his face to rouse the wounded giant.

Arturius grabbed his body, twisted him aggressively to his side and striking his back. He coughed up a vast concoction of bile and blood, spurring his breathing once more as the light flickered back into his eyes.

"Fuck me!" he spluttered, "Could you be a bit gentler next time."

He laughed quietly, causing the others to join in. All seemed well as the worries and woes vanished for a moment. Then the laughter turned into a deathlier cough, releasing more blood onto the floor, pooling as a viscous red matter before them.

"What happened?" asked Ozark, "What do you mean *'traitor'*?"

His breath grew weak. The sound of blood gurgling beyond the passage of his throat told them all they needed to know. Arturius leant him against the wall, a large pool of blood was left in his wake running down the room before escaping through the cracks within the walls.

"He betrayed us!" Burak coughed, "Did a number on me as well."

He tried to sit up but was obstructed by the others forcing him to rest.

"Damn it Burak!" scolded Ozark, "Stay still, I can't help you if you keep moving."

Burak tried to speak, but the weakening voice only allowed for fragments of his words to reach their ears.

"He ….. Silas," was all he could muster. They all watched as the life left his eyes and his body fell limp upon the ground. Ozark screamed with all the anger he could muster, striking the wall with all his strength, damn near breaking his hand in the process. Jorik grabbed him from behind, restraining his anger quickly so he could do no further harm to himself.

"Calm yourself Ozark, stay calm," he whispered into his ear, "Burak wouldn't want this now, would he!"

It took some time before he could finally console the withered man, carefully releasing his grasp nervously.

"My apologies," said Ozark, "I lost myself then … it won't happen again."

Jorik grasped the back of his neck, pulling him in closer until they were butting heads.

"Don't you ever apologise for showing emotion," he snapped, "We have lost many today and hiding the pain will not help us on our path."

"He's right," interjected Arturius, "Be angry, be hurt, let it all out, scream to the heavens if you must, just don't suffer in silence."

Ozark composed himself, nodding to both of them as he stared over the body of Burak.

"He was like a son to me," choked Ozark, "I taught him most of what he knew, and now he's gone, drifting into the great beyond with others."

"Then we shall honour his memory," said Arturius, "We shall not let his death be in vain",

He knelt down and closed the eyes of his fallen friend. The least he could do. As he ran his hand down the back of his neck continuing down his back, he felt a sharp metallic sting.

"What's this?" he said to himself, "Sharp and cold with a metallic ring."

With all his strength, he rolled the hulking mass of muscle and bone to his side. Bedded deeply within his back was a dagger, exquisite and bloodied.

"Is that a dagger?" asked Eskiel, "To stab someone in the back is such a dishonour, silencing one who cannot fight back is a cowardly deed",

"I think so," replied Arturius, grasping it tightly as he freed it from the flesh and bone it was buried beneath. He rolled it steadily across the palm of his hand. It was expertly balanced and incredibly sharp.

"This blade, I can't help but feel that it is familiar to me," said Arturius.

Jorik stared upon its bloodied blade, following its edge until he stopped at the ornate hilt and the encrusted jewels that emblazoned its surface.

"No!" he cried quietly, "It can't be!"

"What is it?" snapped Ozark, "Speak boy!"

Jorik fell to his knees, cradling his face as he shook from side to side. His incoherent mutters were drowned by the insistent demands of Ozark for answers.

Arturius pinched upon its intensely honed edge, taking care not to sully his hands with the blood of the late Burak. The hilt was exquisitely crafted, a fine feminine figure lusciously entwined with the lacquered wood that made up the handle. Her face gazed back at his own, a supple and smooth woman moulded into a rather promiscuous position-an eloquent gift of the more vulgar minded folk. Then it struck him.

"This blade, I recognise its hilt!" said Arturius, "I am a fool to have not seen it earlier!"

"W-w-well then, s-spit it out!" coughed Ozark.

The withered man fumbled about his garments, plucking all manner of paraphernalia from his pockets until he found his elixir.

"Back during our investigation in Riftmyer I saw this blade. A blade born from death and ash, found beneath the gaze of two ravens."

Arturius paused, staring back down at the blade that had felled the giant that he had come to see as his friend.

"I watched as this blade passed from the dead to the living, and now it has brought about death once more."

"Enough of these riddles!" snapped Ozark, "Tell me what you know!"

It was clear by the tremors in his hands that Ozark was struggling to contain his agitation. Not even his relaxing elixir could quench the rage that was brimming from within.

"The blade," he replied solemnly, "I know who it belongs to."

*~ "Can you feel it? Something stirs beyond my vision, hungry and wanting" ~*

## CHAPTER XVII: WOEFUL ACQUIESCENCE

"That damned bastard, how could he!" shouted Ozark, "he was one of us and he cast us aside like common swine."

"It can't be true," said Jorik, falling to his knees, "There must be some other reason."

"Use your eyes boy," shouted Ozark, "The dagger, the dead, Silas is gone, everything points to him."

Garton interrupted them, emerging from the doorway, cloaked in shadow as something lay flung over his shoulder.

"Garton!" shouted Arturius, "How fared your search?"

It was a crude deflection. His desperation to avert a riot between Jorik and Ozark was essential during this dark time. Garton said nothing, only sliding into the room, carefully placing the mass onto a nearby bed.

"Selwyn!" cried Jorik, rushing over to his side.

"Found him where he lay," said Garton, "He's still breathing, but just barely."

Arturius knelt beside him. He lay upon the cold floor, content and at ease in the makeshift bed, as if he were resting. Yet his life was slowing draining from him.

He watched as Ozark peeled back the bloodied garbs from his front. Many wounds had pierced his torso, running around to his back; his sword still grasped within his hand; broken to the hilt; his dagger fell from his belt as he was turned, the dagger of peace was broken upon its hilt. Many scars covered his body, from his previous battles in the name of his people. Each one a reminder of the times death should have claimed him.

Selwyn opened his eyes, pained and dying he forced the words from his mouth, much to the protest of Ozark.

"I pushed my thirst for vengeance upon you all too much," Selwyn said, "I apologise, I have paid the price for such evil deeds."

His glance strayed from the others, ashamed at his ideology and diminishing life.

"Tell me we did it," he whispered, "Tell me we stopped them from acquiring the crown."

He paused. His eyes flickered as he drifted from them all, holding on with the last of his strength.

"Yes," replied Arturius, "We stopped them."

Selwyn rocked his head back, smiling in relief, knowing that they had done their duty and halted the progression of the enemy.

"Good," he sighed, "So very good."

He turned his head from side to side, scanning the room for the others who were no longer present. Then his eyes met with the bloodied body of Burak, cold and silent as it lay peacefully across the room. Arturius watched as his eyes welled up; his heart growing weary in its weakened state upon the new information that he had discovered.

"Was it worth the pain and death," Selwyn asked, choking back tears and blood alike as he held on.

All were silent. After a moment, Ozark spoke up.

"We all knew the risks when we followed you," he said, "We didn't follow you to save the kingdoms or defeat the masked one."

Ozark paused, laying his hand upon the chest of his leader; his mentor; his friend.

"We followed you because you gave us hope."

The words gave Selwyn the warmth he needed to conjure forth one more smile to his company. The blood was beginning to slow, much had already left him by now.

"If you would, I wish to speak with Arturius," said Selwyn,

The others looked confused, but soon obliged to the wishes of their fallen leader. Each walked from the room in silence, only Jorik turned back before walking into the shadows to shed a tear for him.

After the others had left Selwyn reached up, removing the cloak that Arturius had draped over the Akavirian arm, concealing it from the light.

"So, my suspicions were true," he whispered, "You possess the blood of the old bloodline."

Arturius leant back, confused at his words.

"What do you mean?" he asked,

"I had my suspicions when we first spoke within the depths of Hollowclaw. You had a strange yet familiar aura about you, you knew the word of our fallen kingdom and you survived an encounter with Calamitus!"

"*Calamitus?*" said Arturius, "The shadow creature in the marshes?"

"Without a doubt," he replied, "One of the seven, creatures born from the deepest darkest depths of the Khaos' twisted soul. You did what many others failed to do; you escaped the shadow itself."

It would appear that there was more at work within the confines of darkness and the abyss than had truly come to light.

"Are the seven commanded by the masked one?" Arturius asked,

"No, I do not believe it to be so," replied Selwyn, "Though the power of the Khaos runs deep within the veins of the masked one, even he is no match for the power that the seven possess."

They spoke for some time, talking back and forth about much that had happened following the creature's release from its eternal imprisonment.

"So Dovan and Robbard fell to the darkness," Selwyn lamented, "If only I had the strength to slay the beast when I did, then maybe they would still be with us now."

Arturius looked back to the hulking mass that was withering away upon the floor, a victim to the affinity that bore deeply within him.

"What was it?" he asked, neglecting to remove his gaze from the shadow itself.

"It was a creature born from hatred and malice alike, woven amongst the death and decay from above," said Selwyn, "In my desperation and affliction of the mind I failed to remember of its existence."

He spluttered up more blood. His time was dwindling.

"It's called the Veskeel, a creature of darkness and bane of the mountain," he said, "After being imprisoned for so long it must have turned it more aggressive and feral than previously believed, as you probably saw its thirst for blood was truly insatiable."

"Well, it's dead now, so perhaps it's one less disease upon the realm," said Arturius,

"Perhaps," replied Selwyn, "Soon I will reunite with the others my fallen warriors and friends, there I must forgive them deeply for the pain and turmoil I have caused them, though I would very much understand if they shut me out."

"No!" said Arturius, he grabbed his hand and kissed his brow, gripping hard and tight, "They will welcome you with open arms once more, you can finally be at peace and join your fallen brothers.",

Selwyn smiled, but soon his attention shifted to a more pressing matter.

"What of Silas?" he asked worriedly, "I have neglected to see my young protégé."

Arturius swallowed hard, unsure as to the path he must take in discussing the missing boy and the traitor within his midst.

"They took him," whispered Arturius, "They took him when the journey was at its darkest and the Veskeel pursued us throughout the halls."

The weary-eyed captain closed his eyes in disbelief, cursing under his breath at his incompetence and desires that led to the ruin of his company.

"Then it is as bad as I thought," he replied, ushering him in closer, "you must rescue the boy, he is the key to end all of this."

"What do you speak of?" asked Arturius, confused.

"Listen closely and listen well," he whispered, "The key to the Empty Throne lies not in desire but the will to fight on, the bloodlines must converge upon the crest of the watcher and only then shall the path open for those of a humble heart."

"What does it mean?" asked Arturius, "What do you speak of?"

But Selwyn did not speak again. He breathed his last breath and was now at peace, side by side with the rest of his people.

"He's gone," whispered Arturius, "So passes the life of Selwyn Alvast, Captain of the Farrosian first legion, the second sword of the dawn, a bitter end in such a dark and loathsome place, I truly hope you finally have found your peace."

*Although the great Captain of Dawnstar passes, his memory and legacy shall endure. He fought many wars and slain countless others in the pursuit of the good of the realm. Yet though his scar riddled body told tales of a thousand battles through his age, his back, proud and defiant, remained unscathed. A testament to the will of such a mighty warrior.*

He gently shut the eyes of the former captain for good and muttered a quick prayer. Ozark emerged from the shadows, looking weary and shaken. His gentle footsteps were as silent as the night–no doubt because of his light build.

"He's gone, hasn't he," asked Ozark,

Arturius nodded, crouching over the body of Selwyn as he rested beyond the boundary. Weeping for a while before he brushed the tears from the side of his face.

"A great man was he; I would have followed him to the beyond," said Ozark, "Though his work is not yet complete, and I will see it through to the end."

"Great, but flawed," said Arturius, "His mind was too easily tempted by the deeds of his past, though he meant well, in some ways he brought forth a darkness that he had longed to fight."

"It is true, he had demons that wore away at his soul, tempting and torturing him," replied Ozark, "However his goals always remained true, to stop the realm from plunging into eternal darkness and stop those who would see it through, although now our company is fractured, a ruin of its former self, I have failed my people and those subjugated to the tyranny of the masked one."

Arturius stood before Ozark, standing tall and strong. He brandished the totem that Selwyn slipped to him in his dying breath, the sight of which made Ozark gasp.

"Where did you get that?" he said, thrusting his finger at the silver engraved coin balanced upon his hand.

"Selwyn passed it to me before he died, " replied Arturius, "Although I have no idea what it is."

"It is the sigil of Alvast, his family crest and the leader of the first legion of Farrosia," said Ozark in awe, "He means for you to carry on his work and lead us."

Arturius looked down upon the coin, A distinct 'F' was embossed upon its surface; a significant detail of lines and curves adorned the surface, weaving in and out of each other in synchronicity.

"What?" Arturius replied shocked, "Why would he have me lead the others, surely you are more befitting of the task."

He stretched the palm of his hand out to the withered man, pleading for him to take the burden.

"Take it, please, you should be the one to lead the others," he said, "I am no leader, I haven't been a part of this company for more than a new moon."

Ozark stepped back disappointingly.

"You would dishonour his decision by trying to pass it on," Ozark snapped, "Besides, I have seen your calling, a leader lies buried deep within you, back in the sanctum, when our own leadership faltered and the others were at great risk, you stepped forward taking the reins and showing order within the chaos."

"But it still didn't stop the chaos from ensuing," Arturius pleaded, "Selwyn, Dovan, Robbard, Burak, they all died under my control, that is no leader."

Again he thrust his hand forward, begging Ozark to take leadership.

"No, you are right, they did all die," said Ozark coldly, "But had you not taken control so to would all of us suffered the same fate."

It was then that Arturius realised some truth that had eluded him this whole time. The story unravelled before him, painting a clearer picture of the event that led up to this moment. Ozark stepped closer to him.

"You see, had you not been there, the others would have perished above when ambushed. It was you who saved them," said Ozark.

"More death at my hands, however," replied Arturius.

"Without your mercy, Eskiel would've been executed at the very beginning of our descent, had you not alerted us to the creature in the vault then the advance team would've all been slaughtered leading us without a word of the lurking shadow, a shadow which most definitely would have crept its way to our location thirsty for more," said Ozark,

"You're just being modest," snapped Arturius, "It shows nothing of my competency."

Ozark placed his hand atop Arturius's closing it shut with the sigil grasped firmly within.

"Wrong again," said Ozark, "You are more of a leader than you think, he gave you this sigil because you reminded him of the hero of old that founded his ancient kingdom, the kingdom of which was named after him.",

"And who is that?" asked Arturius.

Ozark smiled, turning his hand and opening it to show the emblem once more; he ran his finger across the 'F' gently.

"Farros of the Dawn," he said, "A mighty warrior who when all hope was lost cast himself into the fray of the Khaos along with the other heroes of old and in doing so sealed the Khaos beneath the earth, where it still lives to this day."

Footsteps echoed from within the dark as the others made their way back to the room to pay their respects.

"What do I tell them?" whispered Arturius.

"The truth," replied Ozark, "That is all."

One by one, the others flowed in like a river. First Garton, he was much calmer than before; his physique was more intact as he had found his inner peace. The second was Eskiel, though the others were still wary of him: Arturius had grown fond and trusted him deeply. Finally came Jorik. He was grasping the bow that had previously been wielded by his late brother; no doubt that Garton had retrieved it for him during his search for the others. They all remained silent, standing near to his front as though they were waiting for him to speak.

He looked down at the sigil in his grasp, its sharpened edges pricked at his fingers, telling him he was more alive at this moment than ever before.

"Our leader is dead," he said, "So too among the fallen are Dovan, Robbard and Burak, may they find peace with their captain in the beyond."

He paused for a moment, bringing himself to terms with the duty bestowed upon him by Selwyn. Deep within his mind, he knew that he must be strong for the others if he were to lead them to salvation.

"He gave upon me the seal of Farrosia, and with it named me the leader of this company," he said, "However, leadership should not be inherited and I ask of you, you who stand before me do you accept me as your leader.",

The room remained silent, each to their own, as they now had the choice of ascension.

"What say you?" he shouted.

It was then Jorik stepped forward, a small boy in the face of such looming giants. He looked upon the bow as he rolled it within his hands. It was smooth with etchings of golden vines and leaving running along its surface. He tried to pull back the string; it was taut and heavy, and he could not make a way of it.

"This was my brothers, he was a crack shot able to fire many arrows each minute all the while maintaining incredible accuracy," said Jorik softly, "At the beginning of this journey with you it was no lie that he trusted you not, dissuaded me from talking or even being within your presence. Said you were an ill omen and Selwyn was a fool to trust you."

"Is this meant to be going somewhere," interrupted Ozark,

Jorik let out a brief groan before continuing.

"The point is that my brother was wrong about you and that you are more of us than anyone else, lost, without a home, hunted," said Jorik, "I say you are more of a leader than anyone else in this room after what you have shown us and it would be my honour to assist you wherever I can."

He passed the bow from his hands into Arturius'. It was light yet heavy; he could feel the potential stored within it. Lethal in a beautiful way.

"I want you to have it," said Jorik, "It saddens me such however I cannot wield it, he told me only those worthy of Farrosia's blessing may shoot true and have the strength to feel the weight of its burden."

"Then let us see if I am truly worthy of such an honour," said Arturius,

With his metal hand he gripped the handle of the bow, crude leather bound it as it rubbed against the smooth surface of his palm. With the other hand, he curled his fingertips around the string; he felt as it dug into his skin; it was painful but bearable. As he pulled back, he tensed his muscles, pulling his shoulder blades to meet upon his back; strangely, it was as if he already knew how to operate such a device. The limbs creaked as they bent back, tighter and tighter until they could bend no more; he had done it.

As he released his grip upon the draw, he looked back at Selwyn and Burak. They couldn't leave them to rot in such a hollow place.

"We should give them safe passage," said Arturius, "These desolate halls are no place for such distinguished men to lie, hidden from reality."

"What of Robbard?" asked Ozark, "He has no body to be delivered from darkness."

"We shall send his possessions to him," replied Arturius pointing to his satchel in the room's corner, though he was unsure how it got there; its exquisite design was without a doubt his, "his memory lies within them, let them guide him further in death as it did in life."

"What possession do we offer to the fallen?" asked Jorik, "We cannot bury them within the solid earth we stand upon, nor can we burn them in such an inferno."

"The River," interrupted Ozark, A freshwater river runs through the mountain and leads all the way through to the old ruins of Farrosia, what more of a fitting departure than to finish at the land they fought so hard for."

"We must be quick," said Arturius, "With such damage to the halls we walk upon who knows if the foundation can still withstand the might of the mountain any longer."

"Agreed," replied Ozark, "I have studied the map, I will find a way to the river of Akavor, Garton shall accompany me; should another of those foul beasts lurk within, I wish to have a chance at escape."

While Ozark and Garton went to search for flowing waters of the Akavor, the others set about retrieving the body of Dovan, a task that would put Jorik to endure the worst of his torment.

"Here!" cried Arturius, kneeling beside the fallen Dovan, his body still pierced by the barbs that ended his fruitful life, "Here be the possessions of Dovan and Selwyn,"

As he searched across the room, he came across a variety of splendid weapons, polished swords that bathed in gold and black, various broken arrows splintered at the shaft; further searching found tattered capes and cloth of the fallen Rekeshi, though they appeared much different from those that dwelled above the halls.

"Eskiel," he shouted. The young man sprinted over to his location, a handful of stones and rocks clasped within his hands, "What do you make of these? They differ from the soldiers we met above the surface."

When the objects came into view of him, he froze; a fear gripping across his body as the blood drained from his face, sending it into a ghostly pale white.

"Where did you find that?" he cursed.

"I found it amongst the fallen, is it of your Rekeshi brethren?" asked Arturius.

Eskiel spat upon the floor.

"Nay, that mark upon the tatters, a blood-red hand doused upon the flames," replied Eskiel, "That is the mark of his men, the masked one, he calls them his Death Guard bound to serve their master with unwavering loyalty, only death can resolve them of their duty, beings of neither life nor death."

Arturius looked back upon the corpse of whom he disposed of such a sigil. It was true. The armour and clothing stood out above the rest–how none of them had noticed was a mystery. The plate was a deep black coated in the waves of many burning flames–no doubt to symbolise the Khaos, the source of their strength–layered armour with increased flexibility and strength. It was barely damaged aside from a couple of deep teeth marks that had bore deeply into its iron flesh.

"Is it common for such a warrior to be far from their master," asked Arturius, he rolled the body over upon its back, "Seems more than a coincidence that both his dog and death be looting upon the same grounds."

"No, it is not," replied Eskiel coldly, "They are always within close proximity to their master, be it physically, or incorporeal."

The helm that grasped atop the head of its wearer was an intimidating sight. Its visor was small and narrow, blanketing his face. It would be a miracle if someone could see beyond its slit; the top came to a fine point, sending sharpened fins down either side of the face. No doubt they had been used to end many lives, coated with dried and coagulated blood.

"It is rumoured that they are never seen without their helms, they never sleep, never rest, never eat," whispered Eskiel, "They only serve."

A shiver ran down Arturius's spine, inducing a tone of fear into the mysteriousness of such an elite force. He reached down to remove the helm, an idea of his to dispel the myth of such monstrous beings that hid behind the metal. As his fingers ran across the cord, the body convulsed, shaking violently, thrashing its arm causing a miasma of blood to erupt from the fang punctures within its torso.

"What did you do?" shouted Eskiel.

"Nothing," replied Arturius, "I wished to truly see what hid beneath the helm of such a warrior."

"Maybe it's not dead," said Eskiel, thrusting his blade into the side of the body, gushing its blood upon the stone where it fizzed and smoked into nothing. His sword melted from the intense act, dripping into a pool of glowing orange.

"Fuck!" shouted Eskiel, "It destroyed my blade."

"Get back," shouted Arturius, pulling him away from the hazardous fumes billowing from the corpse.

Suddenly, without warning, beams of intense light blasted forth through the many holes poked into the demonic helmet; the body arched aggressively, crunching the spine viciously. Then it stopped. And in a rather fluid and macabre motion, it stood to its feet. A harsh and demonic voice crackled beneath the helm of the deceased.

"Ah, so I finally come face to face with you," it spoke coarsely,

"Who are you?" said Arturius confidently, unsheathing his blade along with Jorik, "Show your face to us."

"Oh, I think you know exactly who I am," said the voice, "How could you forget, such history, such thrilling tales, and what terrible anguish you have caused me!"

Arturius stepped in closer against the pleas of Eskiel and Jorik, who both stepped back in fear.

"I know nothing of us, there is no us, only me," snapped Arturius, pressing the tip of his sword against the plate of the Death Guard.

"Even if you know not of me, I know much of you … Arturius," replied the voice,

Arturius lowered his blade, his heart springing from his chest, his stomach fluttering with intrigue.

"Oh yes," said the voice, "I know everything that you don't, your memories that are lost, I can find them, a chance to discover yourself, I can show you the way."

"Come back Arturius," shouted Jorik, "Don't listen to his promises, they are empty and lead only to despair, he thinks he knows you but he is no more you than I am him!"

He found himself caught in the middle of two paths. Before him lay the possibility of truth; his memories; his life. Since he woke within the marshes, he had wished for the truth of his life to unravel, to lead him away from the emptiness within. Yet, behind him stood his new life, calling to him; people who do not know of his past, but stand with him as he enters the fray of his future.

"Begone foul demon," shouted Jorik, charging headstrong at the possessed corpse; his blade at his side, ready to thrust into the heart of what stood before them. Eskiel tried to stop him, but it was too late. With the full force of his body, he threw his attack straight and true, piercing the upper left side of its chest; forcing the blade through until it dripping the dense black liquid upon the ground as it trailed off the tip of the sword.

"Such a foolish young child," said the voice, turning its attention to Jorik its eyes gleamed through the visor covering his face in a deep red fog. It reached out with its grizzly grip, grasping Jorik by the throat, lifting him gently off the ground, choking the life from him slowly.

"You think you can face the might of the Khaos," hissed the voice, "You think you can face me!"

Jorik gasped under the breath, but the tightening grip pinched violently, sending him spluttering with blood across the arm of death and gasping for breath.

"So what'll it be," said the voice, turning its gaze back upon Arturius.

Without hesitation, Arturius cast his sword up high, swift and strong. A trail of black blood followed in its wake, sending glistening pebbles of obsidian cascading from the heavens. As expected, the sword melted into a slurry of molten steel shards merging with the tar in the air; it almost appeared it had possessed the very steel itself, sending the shards cascading down upon his head. Jorik fell to the floor, the hand still griping about his neck. Though devoid of its master proved to be easily removed.

"Then you have made your choice," said the voice,

A great power built up within his Akaviri arm, tense and coiled. He unleashed a strike with all his might, smashing clean into the chest of the possessed Death Guard, shattering his armour into a rain of glistening splinters and ruby jewels. The body was sent flying through the air, smashing into one of the free-standing colossal pillars holding the heavens above their head; it cracked violently but stood strong.

The room fell deathly silent. A tense atmosphere descended upon the others. Then the sickening laughter erupted from the corpse mangled within the wreckage of the pillar, chattering and cursing and hissing, before imploding within itself. Sending a torrent of blood, gore and flesh shrieking across the room and clinging to the walls of the inner sanctum.

"It was him," muttered Jorik, "It was the masked one, he is here."

"Calm yourself," said Eskiel, "He was but a mere projection of himself through one of his pawns."

"What do you mean projection?" asked Arturius, "I thought you said wherever one is, the masked one is not far behind."

"Whilst that is true, it is not in a physical sense," replied Eskiel, "You see the only reason he can communicate through his Death Guard is through the link.",

"And what is that?" asked Jorik, growing impatient whilst clutching his sore neck.

"The link is a bond he created between himself and the Death Guard, they are plucked from all corners of the realm, Rekeshi, Verdenese, Ska'al, you name it," said Eskiel, "He corrupts the mind and expunges the soul, feeds off their life to preserve his own essentially granting him the eternal life needed to sustain his vision of an empire, he is more of them than they are of their own."

"How many are there?" asked Arturius, his throat gripping with fear as he thought about the numerous possibilities of encountering the masked one over and over again.

"Nobody knows," replied Eskiel, "Could be tens, hundreds, thousands, obscuring the face of each of them allows their numbers to grow, shrouded by mystery."

Arturius walked over to the mangled wreck that was once a living being. The shrunken helm bore a face that resembled a terror of the unknown. Screaming in anguish as it glared back at him.

"So, what you're saying, is at any given place and any time, he can infect the minds of his guard," said Arturius, "Rendering them his eyes, his ears and his arms to do his bidding as he pleases."

All it took was a brief nod from Eskiel to affirm his fears.

"And how did you come to know all of this," voiced Jorik from behind, approaching Eskiel aggressively but cautiously, "How do we know you are not his influence, slithering your way into our ranks, an assassin in the dark."

Eskiel approached Jorik slowly, staring at him, unflinching and unnerving. He stopped when they were but within a close grasp to one and other.

"Because little man, if you hadn't already noticed they killed the last person I ever loved, he is still here, rotting within these walls," hissed Eskiel, "And I cannot be one of the Death Guard even if I so desired it."

"And why is that?" questioned Arturius.

Eskiel paused for a moment, shutting his eyes deep in thought. After a moment, he spoke again.

"Because my father is one of them."

Jorik Muttered behind him.

"We cannot trust him," he spoke softly, "His kin is bound to the enemy we seek to destroy, to allow him further companionship or life would amount to disastrous consequences."

"My ears do not fail me, young man," said Eskiel, "I know of your worries in the matter and appreciate the care and protection you have over your companions, allow me to explain to you why such a worry is ill found."

The mutterings of Jorik retired swiftly, and his ears soon turned to listen.

"Go on then," he said with vigour,

He circled back towards them, taking time to inhale before he spoke.

"To be anointed with the blood of the Masked One amounts to suppressing you soul, memories and emotions into the link you shall share until your dying days," he spoke softly, "for another of the same bloodline to be enslaved by such dark sorcery would create an irregularity of the sorts within the hive."

"An irregularity?" said Arturius, "I do not understand."

"Because my father and I share the blood of our ancestors, if I were to join him in the enslavement of the Death Guard the masked one would lose control of us creating an abhorrent that could no longer fall under his control," replied Eskiel, "So you see, through the actions of my father sacrificing himself and becoming enslaved, he saved us from such a fate."

"If what you speak of is the truth, then you know by joining us you would eventually face against your kin?" said Arturius, "Should the need arise and you find yourself in such a presence how do I know you will do right by the favours of our mission?"

Eskiel stopped pacing. A heavy burden came to his eyes as the question loomed over him, a shadow of regret and promises made long ago.

"The day they forced my father to take the blood, was the day he died," replied Eskiel, cold and unnerving.

Arturius turned to Jorik, speaking in silence so quiet one could almost mistake it for a foreign tongue. After a while, the whispering ceased, and the two turned to face Eskiel once more.

"So why join his legions?" asked Arturius, "Why join the one who enslaved your father and destroyed your way of life?"

"Because not all of us have the luxury of running from our fate," said Eskiel, "My brother and I joined for survival, keep your friends close but your enemies closer he always said to me, I ask of one thing from you and whatever decision shall you make, I will honour it."

"And what would that be?" said Arturius, his voice echoed the halls with intrigue,

"Allow me to join you," replied Eskiel, "Allow me to ride with you into the fray, I feel an ill wind blowing from the west, my home, a darkness stirs greater than when I left those afflicted lands, a darkness I wish to cast out and save what remains of free will for my people, I can provide you with valuable intelligence and knowledge of the western plains, I-."

Arturius raised his hand.

"Say no more," said Arturius, "The masked one is a foe unlike any I have since faced: he is darkness incarnate, both a cunning warlock and powerful being, if it is true that he has the purpose and means to walk the same roads, lay under the same stars and enter the same dwellings as us then whatever insight I can muster will be truly invaluable, you wish to join this company. I shall graciously accept, for you have proven to me that I can trust you and your resolve."

Eskiel fell silent for a moment. A wave of relief flooded his spirit before he spoke once more.

"You have my eternal thanks and my unwavering loyalty," said Eskiel,

"Something you will need to prove to us all," hissed Jorik, turning his back to both of them as he continued scavenging what remained of his brother's possessions.

"I fear we have dwindled our time here for too long," said Arturius, "The others will no doubt have found the waters of the Akavor and we have yet to transport the fallen."

A whisper drew his gaze to the far corners of the hall, bouncing between the pillars as it caressed his ears.

"Who goes there," shouted Arturius, grasping the hilt of his broken blade as he poised himself for further danger– not that it could do much damage in its current state,

"What is it?" said Jorik, moving towards the agitated figure that twisted and turned his gaze quickly, "What did you see?"

"Can you hear it?" he whispered, "Someone is calling for us, in the darkness."

The others stood there confused and worried, scanning the surroundings for whatever may draw the attention of him.

"I hear nothing," said Eskiel,

"Nor do I," said Jorik, "Nothing more than the winds hissing through these accursed halls."

"There it goes again, over there, no over there," said Arturius, "It is toying with me."

"Arturius," said Jorik, "The only voice that echoes these halls is your own."

Before he could respond, it diminished to the back of the hall, vanishing into the vault that lay in ruins along with the Rekeshi that opened it. He ran over to it, swiftly and without fear.

"Wait," shouted Eskiel, "We know not of what contents may lie within its embrace."

"It's in here," replied Arturius, shouting from a distance.

As he approached, the whispering grew louder and louder, pounding against his ears as though they were the drums of war; and then they stopped. The smell of a thousand years of rot filled his nose, a putrid burn that sent tears rolling down his eyes. There was no gold or riches stashed within, only scrolls and books, many of which had decayed and crumbled in the presence of the Veskeel.

Far at the back, shrouded in such darkness that one could seldom have seen, shone a glint of gold, silver and ruby. He had found it, the Lost Crown of the Mountain, a relic of a bygone age and the treasure sought after by so many others.

"I have found it, Selwyn, I have the crown," whispered Arturius to himself, "My apologies for lying to you earlier, but now you can rest in complete peace, your death shall not be in vain."

He tucked it into the satchel by his side, taking care to preserve its delicate state before turning to the others.

"My friends, today marks the day we have grasped victory from the enemy," he shouted, "the Crown of the Mountain is ours, the masked one shall not sit upon the Empty Throne as long as it stays by my side."

Many hours passed, many dark and twisted turns sent them to the crystal waters of the Akavor; its glowing waters were that of legends. It was said that to drink from its icy waters would grant the gift of eternal life, a very fleeting reward to many it would seem. Yet the cost of such a gift was insurmountable. An eternal life beneath the gaze and might of the mountain it flows so freely through. Ozark had located and scavenged some old funeral pyre boats; it had seemed that the once mighty and immortal race of the Akaviri did pass on to another life honouring there dead with the journey down the river. And assistance into the netherworld through the smoke that rose from the ashes beyond the barrier. They lay each of the fallen within the confines of the boats, though this time no fire would be set. Upon Dovan they placed his trusted helm, a part of him that had been passed from father to son and had saved his life numerous times before; yet when the night was at its darkest did not honour his fate with such a deed. For Robbard there was no body to send, only what remained of his belongings neatly wrapped in fragments of each of their cloaks, an honourable send-off it there was such a thing. Burak lay upon the boat as he did in life, large and unnerving, grasping his mighty axe with both hands; his death deemed by some to be the act of cowardice for such a great warrior.

Despite the many protests, Arturius retrieved the body of Esmir sending him to down the river an honourable sign for a friendship that was to blossom greatly. They finally laid Selwyn into his boat, each of them placed one of their possessions into the boat, a token of appreciation and honour for all that he had done for them both before and after the fall. One by one they pushed each of the boats out down the Akavor, watching as they passed further and further beyond their gaze until they disappeared into the darkness beyond the mountain.

The river had taken them. Never again would they see the light pass upon the ruins of Farrosia; though their deeds would not go unrecognised and their sacrifices would not be in vain. A promise that Arturius had made to the others, binding it with blood and sealing it with fate.

"Here passes Burak of Farrosia, knight of the realm, Dovan of Farrosia, knight of the realm, Robbard of Farrosia, noble of Farrosia, Selwyn of Farrosia, Captain of the first, second sword of the Dawn," chanted Ozark locked deep within his prayer, "And Esmir of Rekesh."

The mention of the fallen brother of Eskiel tensed the nerves amongst the group briefly. Though it wasn't long before their hearts were won over by the sight of Eskiel tossing rocks into the river, engraved with the runes of old depicting each of the fallen upon them.

"Our journey does not end here," said Arturius, "We shall rise from the ashes that took from us our leader and friends, we shall arise anew, we shall rise stronger and finish the task set before us by the Dawn, we shall rise the Fallen Order, and we shall not fall again."

~ *"I cannot see, I cannot see, it blinds me so, don't give in keep fighting"* ~

# Chapter XVIII: Obscurity

The funeral boats had long since passed beyond the threshold of the mountain, the river was too perilous for anyone to venture up into the heart of the mountain. Strange how such mysteries lay beyond the darkness, yet so much was already known to them. To drink from its diamond surface would amount to life eternal, yet to wade through its icy chill would drain the life from its host. Slowly and painfully.

The others had since departed, making their way through the labyrinth of tunnels and decrepit ruins, leaving Arturius to lament of his newfound position. His journey back gave him much more time to himself. Through the darkness he travelled not more than a mile, passing across the stone bridge of Vanar, a grand side indeed it would have been. Had it not been for the untimely demise of the rocky outcrop that swung from high above. *"Shame,"* he thought to himself, such amazing architecture lay silently within these halls, crumbling and in ruins; an unwelcome acceptance for those who walked through its suffocating might.

Across the bridge, ascending the many flights of stairs long and wide, was their birth. A part of him wished he hadn't stayed from the others; the silence was deafening and a soothing voice would have made for a much better companion. As he reached the end of the never-ending network, trudging delicately through the thick ash upon the floor, he came across a rather interesting sight. Many footprints had passed through the halls, arching to the left corridor. He had been following them for some time as the only proof of what direction to follow to reunite with the others. Yet the pathway to the right lay unobstructed. And undisturbed.

By now the others would have made it to the inner sanctum, waiting for his return to plan out the next stage of their mission. A choice he would've taken without hesitation had it not been for the path that lay before him.

"And what secrets are you hiding down there?" he whispered to himself, raising his torch aloft in the hopes of a more illuminated pathway. The darkness, however, was far too thick, only swallowing what little warmth had emerged from the fiery blaze before his head. He looked back towards the left path, then twisted to the right again.

"Only a quick look," he whispered, "In and out, then back to the others."

The ash crunched beneath his feet, as satisfying as snow under the foot, crisp and soft as it raised up and brush gently against the skin of his ankles. Down the centre of the corridor, a thin line stretched above him. Upon closer inspection, it appeared to be a pipe of purest crystal; it rang delicately when he flicked it. Within lay dormant a black liquid. It must have been sitting there stagnant for a thousand years, festering away until the darkness tainted its form. It was long until he reached the end of the tunnel as it led far off into the eastern portion of the kingdom. However, the pathway led to an end, no corridor, no stairs, just nothing. Nothing but a tablet.

It was loftier and far heavy than any of the others he had previously encountered, spanning the entire length and breadth of the hall. It was crafted of a material much different to that which had been carved from the mountain. As he grazed his hand across its crystal-flecked surface a cascade of soot and dust flowed between his fingers. Etched deep into its surface were words of a language that somehow he both knew and didn't. A mural of sorts telling a tale of mountains, forest and deserts. Along with a dark essence that dwelled beneath them.

"Again I come across that which has been cast upon stone," muttered Arturius, "First within my dream of darkness and know within my reality."

He looked closer upon the markings. They appeared to depict a vast array of battles, adventures and tragedy-as was the common telling of such artifacts.

"Land, Desert, Forest, Mountain. And here, seven shadows stood before entwining flames of abyssal blight."

Arturius had become lost in thought. Gazing intently upon the carvings.

"Perhaps Ozark may bring more light to this."

He sunk his fingers between the cracks of the tablet. Ensure how he could move such a monolith, though attempted such a feat nonetheless.

"Too heavy for my being, perhaps I may chip the writing away. It will be easier to move in such a condition."

He drew his shattered hilt from his hip. Though no longer present in the form of a sword it made for a dainty tool at best. Ring after ring sent crystalised sparks dancing down the darkened collider. No sooner had he begun striking had he stopped. Sharded of his broken blade spring from the hilt, shattered further. Though the tablet remained solid.

"Strange." He whispered, "Not even a scratch. Perhaps I can attempt at such words, though I am unsure as to my own ability."

Ash flowed through his fingers like sand through an hourglass, gently falling to the floor. The grinding of his cold metal hand scraped against the stone surface, crunching and grinding in a dull grey manner. Words had been so eloquently carved into the stonework; no doubt the writer was in a master of his craft to relinquish his knowledge to whom so ever may find it. It was a mix of both old Vindictarian and the common tongue:

*Creath het dulken en het nul esparsen het Immobülé en het suth,*

*Sün shullen krakuth het entranum en farash thun furul,*

*Crockener faru kren eddiau thun thul en divinai,*
*As het dormun furn ne'er lumba fall Ïth ti sadisque,*
*Sün too shullen risun het gradulun en ethyalt,*
*Creath het seqrest Ïth het klarn unonion aer het sang en het vernethi,*
*Sün too shullen het terïn crocken thun het varne krakuth,*
*En het vanstra en het Tonomy shullen risun Ïth het essoul Ïth het exten en Akavor,*
*Ïth ral hayin plynth stunden het Öulos en echonse thun lumo.*

<< When the darkness of the north crosses the mountain of the south,
So shall break the imprisonment of abyss and cinder,
Shattering forth from root and stem of divinity,
As the giants that never sleep fall to its malice,
So too shall wake the guardians of silence,
When the key to the silence converges with the blood of the realm,
So too shall the skies shatter and the earth break,
And the might of the Tonomy shall rise to the will of the arms of Akavor,
To take their place beside the living of whisper and light. >>

The further along he read, the more the words had been hastily scribbled, rushed into existence. Adorned beneath the last word of living there was etched a sigil he had seen many a time on his travels. A raven, black as the night with its wings stretched far.

"And so you return once more," he whispered, "Who are you who should appear across the realm, providing all with riddles of the unknown."

Whatever rested beyond the doorway would have to wait. He had neither the time nor patience to decipher its meaning. It was easy tracing back his steps, the only fair use of the abundance of ash that seeped into every crevice of his clothing; itching, scratching and biting its way through him. He walked for many more miles again, this time the darkness did not feel so threatening. It had moulded him, shaped him into a new person; one thing is almost certain after all, he was not the same person who entered the mountain.

"Over here," shouted a voice from afar.

He looked up to see Jorik waving his way, beckoning him over.

"I thought you would be back at the inner sanctum by now," shouted Arturius, "What news do you bring me?"

"As we journeyed through the darkness, Eskiel fell through a hole that bore deep within the ground," said Jorik.

"Is he hurt?" replied Arturius worriedly, "Have you been able to retrieve him?"

"Indeed we have, twas not a large fall so he made no injury," said Jorik,

Arturius quickly moved forward, closing the distance between him and his order.

"Then why do you remain here still? We should search for a way to escape these desolate halls," shouted Arturius.

"That we will," replied Jorik, "Though you must see our discovery, I am sure it will excite you as much as it has us."

With that, Jorik disappeared beyond view, leaving only a trail of orange flame in his wake to guide Arturius to the new discovery. The hole in the ground was deep and bore a striking resemblance to the mouth of the beast that laid waste to his arm. A set of crude makeshift ladders bloomed from the hole, lashed together with whatever sturdy material they found within its vicinity.

"Hello," shouted Arturius into the vast emptiness below, "Is this the path you took?"

"Come down," shouted a voice believed to be Ozarks, "Come and see the riches we need so desperately."

The ladder itself was weak and rotting. He lashed together what remained of the rope scattered across the floor, anchoring it to a nearby stone pillar–or what remained of it, anyway. *"Should the ladder break, I do not wish for us to become trapped within this abyss indefinitely!"* he thought to himself. And with that, he descended.

Surprisingly, it was not a far drop to the floor. The illusion of darkness gave false images to his eyes, tricking him into doubting his descent. Or possibly a deterrent for what lay beneath him. A faint light shone down the passageway, striking dust and cobwebs alike as it strewn down the walls.

"Have you ever seen such fine crafts," echoed a voice at the end, "And to think it was hidden beneath us all this time."

None of the others had noticed him walk into the room, their minds were too occupied with the vast assortment of weapon, jewels and trinkets that lay across it in mass. They gleamed and shone with the brilliance of the sun, a vast hoard of the bounty of the mountain, ripe for the picking.

"Ah there you are," shouted Ozark, a line of diamonds adorned his neck shining brighter than the star that filled the sky, "Have you ever seen such treasure, we are rich I tell you rich!"

Something wasn't right, the others were drawn to the treasures more than anything he had ever seen. They indulged in its wealth, lining whatever pockets they could with rubies, sapphires, emeralds and golds. Even Jorik who last he saw was lamenting at the loss of his kin seemed all but lost to the grief, only the allure of what glittered before him. He watched as they all tossed aside their possessions, emptied their bags, satchels and pockets to fill with the riches of a king. Only Garton stood back, poised between them and the door as if guarding the outside from the others.

As he watched the gentle giant peer over the others within the treasure room, his mind ran back to the inner sanctum and the powers shown by his condition.

"Garton," said Arturius, "How fares you?"

Garton grumbled.

"Could be better," he replied,

Arturius was finding it difficult not to show discomfort in the newfound vessel that stood before him. Garton was all there, his spirit, his rage and his personality, but it would also appear that there was a bit more than he previously possessed.

There was a long and silent pause between the two as Arturius gazed vacantly upon Garton.

"It's rude to stare you know," groaned Garton.

Arturius quickly gathered his thoughts, shaking his head in embarrassment as he blundered like a fool in response.

"Is your curse causing more untold anguish?" asked Arturius, "I have questions I have been longing to ask of you."

A faint smile crept to the corner of his mouth as he let out a faint sigh that wisped with darkness.

"You wish to know the details of my condition," said Garton, "Speak as you must."

"I saw you fighting against the Rekesh," said Arturius, "I saw you fall and watched as your essence escape from your mortal shell!"

Garton folded his arms tightly.

"I watched as the life drained from your eyes only to reappear into that of your foes, " he continued, "What happened to you?"

"Observant one aren't you," replied Garton, "What you saw was the turmoil that my soul has been granted, forced to abdicate from its vessel when the cracks upon its surface grow to great, leaving my life in fight of constant equilibrium of anguish and convalescence."

Garton creased about his unfamiliar figure, visibly distressed by the contents of its character.

"When I take hold of a new vessel I feel its thoughts, its character and memories," whispered Garton, "I find myself adopting the traits of its former master, this one was a sadistic, a masochist, he found great joy inflicting pain on others, a vessel I would most definitely wish to discard."

"Why not adopt a new vessel then?" queried Arturius, "Shed the darkness that binds you to such hatred and take on the moniker of that which falls closer to your own soul!"

Garton bowed his head slightly.

"If only it were that simple," he replied, "Such is the curse that binds me to this form, that it will only allow me to possess those with a rage and darkness within them that falls close to that which I hold within my own heart, that of vengeance and betrayal."

Arturius nodded, though still he had questions in need of answering. He dared not press too hard.

"And your attack upon the beast," said Arturius, "How were you able to afflict such damage where others could not? And why was it that you didn't persist and kill the beast where it stood?"

Garton sighed with slight annoyance; it would seem that it was the first time such a question was thrust upon his shoulders.

"If only I could have," he replied, "Maybe then we would still have Selwyn, Dovan Robbard and Burak within our ranks, but alas what's done is done, I am afraid that even my body, as powerful as it is has its limits."

He pulled back his leathers, peeling them roughly from his charred skin, sending flickers of eternally burning cinders spewing forth from the cracks. A mark lay pressed upon his chest where the heart would be, a deep spike lay embedded deeply into his flesh. Ancient ruins had been carved into its surface in a language unbeknownst to him.

"This keeps me from the dead," said Garton, "It was thrust into my dead heart within the ruins of the royal stables, it keeps my soul from passing onto the next life at the cost degrading my soul, somehow no matter the manner of my passing, it will forever remain embedded deeply within me."

"How does it degrade your soul?" asked Arturius, "I have seen the good in you, your soul cannot be degraded even when death has been snatched so cruelly from you."

He quickly covered it back up, a clear embarrassment and sense of shame at the totem that controlled his life.

"My soul is already beyond saving," he said coldly, "When that witch cast her magic into me, she set about the unnatural process of altering everything about me. In a cruel torment, she knew that I would seek revenge for the heinous act upon my being. She cursed me with untold power and strength. Yet I could not seek those who wronged me, and such power comes at the cost of degrading my condition further, as such I cannot take another life without it fragmenting my soul and turning it black as the night."

It was clear by his voice that such a future brought a deep fear within him. The fear also rippled through the cracks in his body, a terrible fate for such a seemingly noble man.

"It is a cruel world that we truly live within," replied Arturius, "I promise I will never ask you to give in to such a curse so long as breath fills my lungs and blood runs through my veins."

"Everybody says that," Garton said emotionless, "Don't make me promises you will not keep."

He pained for the life of Garton. Such a life is cruel and filled with misery. If he would not see the honour in his words, then he would have to prove it to him through the actions of his leadership; a task that would not come easy. He returned his attention to the room they had suspiciously found themselves within and the strange behaviour of the others that danced within its walls.

"So what is going on here?" asked Arturius, "Something doesn't feel right, the others, they act out of character."

"So it would seem," grunted Garton, "It would appear you have not yet fallen sway for the greed of such treasure."

Arturius looked upon him with confused admonishment.

"I do not understand," replied Arturius, "I have no desire for treasure and trinkets, what use is it to me or the others, as outlaws across every realm it would prove a great hindrance to bear it so, such weapons, on the other hand, would prove most effective in our fight against the masked one."

Garton merely nodded, before pointing above his head to the faint ruins inscribed above the archway.

"Then I suggested you begin by breaking it into their thick skulls," he grumbled disappointingly.

The runes were faint and old, speaking solely in the old tongue. Despite his lack of knowledge in the matter, he couldn't help but understand the words the fell before him.

*Ret Encumbray het solden drumari Immobülé, Vasq drumari dulken furn aflictur het gör, visur nur Ïth het iquis vun het Murtán Ïth'n drovah ampti, Ïth vay het varne ocken Ïth het envois thun het grunth en essoul.*

<<Here lies the treasure of the mountain, a hoard of the darkness that plagues these lands, seeketh not the greed but the sword to go command the darkness empty, to make the earth open to the enlightenment and the strength of will.>>

"It appears to be a warning of sorts," said Arturius.

"Glad one of us can read it then," said Garton

"Strange though," replied Arturius, "Never before have I been able to understand such dialect."

The two looked back upon the rest of the order, drunk with greed, and they threw themselves upon the riches they had discovered.

"We can't let them take the treasure beyond the boundary," said Arturius, "It would appear only the weapons can be taken, anything other and the mountain will not allow us to leave."

Garton grunted, showing great disdain for the lack of the others willpower and to fall for such afflicted desires.

"Wait," said Arturius, "Why are you unaffected by the lure of the mountains riches?"

Garton turned slowly to face him, staring deeply into his eyes, taking a deep breath–not that he needed to–before speaking.

"The dead do not have such desires within their hearts," he whispered, "For I no longer have mine.",

"Then what about me?" replied Arturius, "To my limited knowledge I am not dead, yet I do not have the desire to plunge myself into the gold and silver before me."

Garton turned away, setting his eyes back on the others, playing around like children in the mud. He laughed briefly.

"Maybe you don't know yourself as much as you think you do," he whispered softly,

The comment burrowed deep into his thoughts, biting at his own conscious for answers and provoked only more questions to come. However, now wasn't the time for such a question. The very fate and future of the order rested in lifting the shroud and affliction from the minds of the others.

"There must be something, some way to fix what is wrong," said Arturius, "Help me look for anything that may assist us."

"Im afraid it won't be that easy," replied Garton.

"How so?" said Arturius.

"We have been down here for some time now, they have lined their pockets and bags to the top with all that gleams before them," replied Garton.

"And?"

"And should they decide to move such treasure away from this room, then the threshold will be disrupted and then we will have a problem," said Garton.

He spoke true and calmly of the matter; it was clear that this was going to become a struggle for control. Steadying his position as he lay in wait, a predator waiting for his prey to stray too close to his lair.

Arturius walked amongst the others. The sound of gems and metal crunched beneath his feet where they had hastily dropped such loot as they scrambled for more. The room was rather vast. After scanning its contents briefly, he could surmise that there were enough riches and spoils to fashion a new kingdom.

"Jorik!" said Arturius as he attempted to garner the attention of the youngest amongst them. Sadly, his voice was washed away by the excitement of the treasures he lurched upon. His hands were bloody and raw from grasping at all that he could muster. The blood coated much of the treasure surrounding him, oozing between the gaps as it anointed the wealth with the greed of his mind.

"Snap out of it," Arturius snapped, "This is not you; you must fight the urged, resist the temptation."

As he reached for his shoulder, the young Jorik hissed and growled, a feral animal fighting for the last drop of blood amongst the carcass. He could see the affliction within his eyes. It pulsated violently, sending blood red streaks across the whites of his eyes.

"This is not good," he muttered to himself, "There must be some way of breaking this curse."

He set about searching for an answer, tossing and turning every bit of gold, every gem, every little stone as the peering eyes of Garton watched and waited for the others to turn their attention.

Even as he gazed across the room, his ears quickly caught the sounds of whispers pulling him in, tempting him. He desired the knowledge and foresight to break the shadow that had descended upon them; he wanted to see, yet felt blinded by obscurity. It was all overwhelming, the whispers, the voices, the temptation, the changes. He closed his eyes tightly as he tried hard to block out the bellowing world before him. He stiffened. The sound of settling dust, a gentle trickle of water splashing against the floor, the clang of gold falling graciously to the ground; He heard it all.

Then he heard it, a gentle song beneath the many layers of sounds the pressed against his ears. It was a soft voice, a woman singing in from the shadows; her voice shone brightly through the darkness, filling him with a sense of hope, warming his spirits.

"Such a quaint feeling," he said to himself, tightly sealing his eyes furthermore.

In his mind he ran closer to the singing, sprinting towards the soothing embrace. It became louder yet softer, blocking out the roaring of the other sounds that plagued his mind. Until at last, he could hear no more but the song of the gentle voice.

*Set forth the idol to the disparity of light,*
*Allow the old blood to wash away the illusion of greed.*
*And with it the affinity of one's plight,*
*Stray not from the threshold of the room,*
*Refrain yourself from the treasures you do not need,*
*Or the mountain shall remain ever your tomb*

Within the gloomy corner of the room stood a stone statue, its face old and worn beyond recognition as it stood valiantly watching over its vast wealth. As Arturius approached its watchful gaze, he felt an uneasy feeling wash over him, a feeling of déjà vu before the crumbling idol. Surrounding it in perfect symmetry stood six stone plinths: old and dust-laden. Upon each plinth was placed an effigy of sorts; closest to him embedded deep within its foundations lay a sword, rusted and worn from its countless years exposed to time. To its side, a set of balance scales made of weathered brass. Then there lay an effigy of the sun, gold and brilliant, followed by its counterpart, a dim shining moon. A pile of coin followed the lunar monument. The final needed no introduction, for he knew what it was. A pile of ash and cinders, still hot and still burning, as would its master deep within the confines of its earthen prison.

"It's a riddle," said Arturius to himself.

He grasped either side of the decay statue, twisting and turning it about its plinth. Every time it faced one of the effigies, it clicked deep beneath the earth.

"Turn the idol," he muttered, "I must face the idol to the correct effigy for the illusion to be lifted."

As he relinquished his grasp upon the disintegrating idol, he noticed that all sounds of commotion had vanished from the room. He turned to his rear, worried that the others had passed the threshold of the room and sealed their fate. They had done nothing of the sort.

One by one each of them had turned to scour upon him as if the very illusion of the treasure had grown threatened by his actions.

"Garton, what is going on?" said Arturius.

For once since meeting him, Garton's disposition had shifted. He was no longer the mysterious and stern individual he had grown to know; a deep fear was emerging from him that scared him greatly.

"Something that worries me greatly," replied Garton.

"And what is that?" asked Arturius.

Garton looked him square in the eyes, taking a moment before he spoke.

"That I can offer no council to you," replied Garton, "This affliction is truly unique, even coming from the likes of me."

"It would seem as such," said Arturius, "We must make haste with this puzzle then, for I fear that this curse will not allow our brethren to distinguish us between friend or foe."

"Then what would you have me do," asked Garton hesitantly, "What is it you need?",

"Time," replied Arturius, "If I am to solve this then I need you to keep them off me for as long as you can muster, though you must refrain from inflicting harm upon them."

"You know that given their current state they will not show you the same courtesy," said Garton,

"I am aware," replied Arturius, "Though now the chain of command falls upon me and I will not lose any more of us to this mountain, or so help me I shall bring down this godforsaken pile of rock."

Garton smile briefly and quickly, not wanting to show his softer side amongst his complexion.

"Then time you shall have," said Garton, "Though I pray to thee, for riddles such as these do so rarely come without a cost."

Arturius turned back to him nervously, a queer stiffening tensed across his body as though he was suffocating from the air within.

"Then it would seem you may have to be prepared for myself to fall under such an affliction," said Arturius, "In which case I pray to you to not end my life when it has so freshly begun, whilst I also pray to myself not to cause any unjust harm upon yourself."

The others had stood silently before them, watching and waiting as though statues doomed to decay beneath the mountain. Arturius clambered across the piles of gold and jewels within his way, it's cold and dark touch built up more fear within him, the fear of losing himself yet again and hollowing his memories once more.

"The sooner we escape the shadow of the mountain the better," said Arturius, "Prepare yourself, for I know not of what may come next."

"Just stay true to yourself, Arturius," replied Garton, "We will all face the dawn once more and face horizons anew."

"Yes, I have hope all will be well," said Arturius "But nothing cleanses the darkness I feel brewing within me. I feel that nothing will cleanse it away and soon the darkness will encircle me burying me deep within old barrows to which the sunlight shall never set upon me, I want to feel the seasons change around me, I want to lie within the lush fields of grass that I have only ever seen within my dreams."

"Hold it within your mind and heart," replied Garton, "For it is how I have strayed from following the path of darkness all this time."

Arturius nodded, grasping at the elbows as the statue before him and spinning it with all his strength. It wasn't long before he felt the tight grip of fingers choking around his neck. Whatever had yanked him from atop the idol smashed him onto the hard ground below, sending waves of gems scattering about his surroundings. It would seem his suspicions were true; the weight of a crippled and withered man bore down upon his neck; it was surprisingly strong and heavy as it squeezed the air from his throat. It wasn't long before Garton tore him swiftly from him, throwing him into a pile of gold coins to his side, splashing them with a torrent of glittering light.

"Steady on," choked Arturius, "He is frail and weak, we can't risk wounding him mortally."

"Did he feel weak as he was choking the life from you," queried Garton, as he promptly restrained Jorik from launching towards him.

"Hurry then, this in no time to be quaint," Garton snapped.

The idol clicked in place; its gaze set upon the sun atop its plinth; yet nothing happened.

"I don't understand," shouted Arturius, "The riddle said, *'set forth the idol to…'*."

He quickly quenched his words, mulling over the true meaning to the riddle.

"Of course," he shouted, "How could I have been so obtuse."

Garton was being quickly overwhelmed. It would truly take a will of steel and a heart of gold to not return such violence to those who bear down upon you.

"Glad you are so happy with your dullness," Garton shouted, "Now hurry!",

The stone ground hard atop its base, letting out coarse moans as he pressed hard against its figure. The face now gazed upon the moon plinth, staring hard into what only appear when darkness cloaks the realm. Yet still, nothing happened.

"It makes no sense," shouted Arturius, "It now faces the disparity of light, yet does nothing."

"Then you missed something," shouted Garton, receiving blow after blow from the others as they struggled against his grasp.

The plinths that rested beneath the effigies were strange. As Arturius moved in closer, he noticed a font beneath each one and a drain descending deep into the stone at the basin. A strange residue coated the seemingly clean bowls, dark and dry as it chipped away with his fingers.

"Of course," he shouted aloud,

He looked to the idol. Grasped deep within its hand was a stone sword, its edge had been honed and sharpened beyond what is capable of such material. With his right hand, he clasped it, the sharp stone dug into his palm, tingling and burning with a strange sensation. The sounds of the others thrashing against the over-encumbered Garton rung through his ears, every punch, every kick he felt on behalf of him.

As he pulled his hand down the length of the blade, he felt it tearing deeply into his flesh; he wince upon every stroke as the stone was left stained with his dark blood. It burned deep and painfully until his hand fell from the point, his blood dripping gently upon the floor as it was swallowed between the cracks.

The blood pooled in the centre of the basin, flowing down from the gentle trickle of blood that seeped between the gaps in his clenched fist. It was thirsty, swallowing every drop that made its way to the gullet of the effigy; he could hear the faint trickle as it fell down into the deep abyss. Garton had since struggled to restrain all the others, with

Eskiel breaking free of his grasp, snarling and snapping as he ran impatiently towards the idol. His eyes were burning red with rage, as his mind was possessed to strip free whatever life remained within him. As the last few drops left his hand, he was struck hard to the floor; a flurry of scratches and slashing bore down on his being burning patterns of a vicious beast upon his flesh.

"Control yourself Eskiel," shouted Arturius, "Fight it, I know you have the strength to fight the affliction my friend, it burns deeply with the recesses of your mind clouding your vision with that which does not bear the truth."

It was no use, however; in his feral state he knew not the effects of reason nor did he know the feeling of compassion. Just an intense pain that does not wither and does not fade, only feeds from the fear of breaking the glass wall of the illusion. Arturius struck him hard to the side of his head, knocking him off balance enough to flip him upon his back. With all the strength he could muster, he jumped atop him, restraining him carefully.

A sudden rumble caught them off guard, knocking the feet from under Garton and the others and sending a mixture of gold and gems slithering across the floor.

"Did someone break the threshold?" shouted Arturius.

"Nay, they did not," replied Garton, "I have both here restrained and resisted."

"Then what is that shudder," said Arturius, "An earthquake? That would be all we need right now!"

Before either could continue, the mass of gold and jewels and trinkets darkened; first, they turned grey; then darker than the blackest night. One by one the allure of such treasure faded from view, turning into thick black sand that fell between the cracks in the floor.

Arturius looked down upon Eskiel. His grasp had not moved from the confines of his throat, holding him tightly yet not so much to harm his companion. At first, he thought it to be blood seeping from the corners of his mouth, eyes and streaming forth from his nose. However, its grainy flow was that of the darkness that had bonded the curse to such treasure. Finally, he had succeeded, breaking the curse that enslaved his order.

All that was left in the room was dark and dreariness as all the wealth of the mountain eroded away into nothing, leaving behind all that was old, rusted and forgotten. Eskiel groaned beneath him, clutching his head as it swelled across his temple.

"Ugh … what the hell happened?" Eskiel groaned, "Why do I feel as though my had has been clamped by a hot iron poker?"

Arturius laughed, released his grasp from around his throbbing throat.

"Glad to see you are back with us," he said, "I didn't take you for a magpie you see."

"What are you talking about," said Eskiel, lifting himself to his feet, he patted down his sides knocking black sand from his pockets as he did so, "Why is everything so dry, and coarse, did I miss the part when we marched through the scorched fields of the Varib wastes!"

"Alas, you did not," said Arturius, "It seemed that the mountain had another trick within its rocky embrace you see, tainted treasures that brought an affliction upon you, Jorik and Ozark.",

"An affliction! By the Gods, I did not cause any harm or injury upon you, did I?" asked Eskiel.

Arturius wound back his arm, concealing the rather nasty gash strewn across his forearm; his scuffle with the possessed earlier left slithers of his skin beneath Eskiel's nails.

"Nothing of the sort, my friend," lied Arturius, "However, the trauma I sustained from your thunderous disposition, now that my friend will cost you greatly."

He looked back to the others. Ozark was vomiting heavily upon the floor, his frail frame no doubt struggling with the violent takeover of his mind. Jorik appeared to be handling it well. He was youthful, his mind could adjust and resist such intense possession.

The time had already passed through many days and nights, their journey through the mountain had taken them six days past the blood lune. As he glanced around the dim-lit room, he couldn't help but feel drawn to the farthest corners. Many blades, bows and axes lay dormant and dusty upon the racks that lined the walls; spears reached for the ceiling where they stood silently, intertwining with the wooden braces that held them so. He looked down to the hilt of his broken sword, drawing it slightly until the black stained blade came free from its sheath.

"We should replenish our arms," said Arturius, "The encounters here within the mountain have left us unable to defend ourselves, let alone the kingdoms we wish to free."

"I agree," said Ozark, "Besides, we will never come across finer weapons than the ones that litter the halls of Nordellar, finest blades and armour this side of the whispering waters up north."

"Only take what you can need, however," said Arturius quickly, "I will not have us trapped deep within the mountain over the greed of one's prying hands."

The blades before him were old, wrapped tightly with dust and web alike, preserving it from the stale mountain air. He released one of the swords from its rest, cracking it away from the grip of the rack.

"Remarkable," said Arturius, as he unsheathed one of the blades.

Its edge was honed to perfection, free from blemish and impurities alike; he swung it gently yet with vigour as the very air cut between its razor sharpness.

"There is no word to describe such craft," said Ozark, approaching him from behind, "such refinement and dedication made these blades the most desirable of all back in the days of the Akavirian prosperity."

"How so?" asked Jorik, grasping several short blades upon a nearby table, balancing them precariously in his palm.

"They say its edge shall never blunt, nor shall its blade shatter," replied Ozark, "it had even been rumoured to have cut cleanly through stone itself, though none who are in possession of such relics today dare risk to break such treasures, though for you my young friend, I ask but one thing."

"And what be it?" asked Jorik.

"Guard the doorway," replied Ozark.

He let out a loud groan of disapproval.

"Come on Ozark," pleaded Jorik, "I too need new arms."

Jorik bequeathed his broken blade to the withered man, edging it closer and closer as if to persuade him of the sorts. Though all he received in return was a shake of disapproval.

Arturius looked back at the blade, impressed couldn't even begin to describe how he felt in its presence.

"Though it should be known to you all," Said Ozark, an undertone of worry crept through his voice, "It is said that all those in possession of an Akavirian blade are subjected to the curse of the mountain, a prophecy and promise that all who wield such mighty and undoubtedly superior blades shall soon fall victim to the very strength they emanate."

With nervous eyes, Jorik promptly placed the blade back upon the rack, taking care not to upset the inanimate objects before him. Even the stalwart Garton dared not touch the weapons that lay within his reach, though a curse upon a curse could prove inconsequential to such a warrior.

Though the blade within his hands was perfect in every way possible, he could not grasp it effectively within the embrace of his mechanical appendage; its grip proved too wide for his fingers. To his right, the clanging of steel upon steel drew the attention towards Eskiel; his rough approach to such treasured swords was less than expected to one who yearned for a peaceful existence.

"Found anything of use over there?" asked Arturius.

"A bit here and a bit there," replied Eskiel, "Nothing that reaches out to me yet."

Before Arturius could respond, he stopped his search, pulling forth a peculiar sword. Its guard was woven with the finest metal known to the realm, twisting about between the grip in a short pattern. A sheath of darkest lacquer concealed the blade from the light.

"What do we have here," Eskiel said softly, "It's nothing like the other blades within the box. Why go through the effort to hide such a thing?"

As Arturius approached it, he could begin to feel why it was concealed amongst the broken and beaten.

"A dark aura seeps from its blade," said Arturius calmly, "I can feel its darkness, it screams for blood, this blade is one of the accursed, I suggest you lay it back within its slumber, too much harm shall befall you should you continue your journey with it."

Eskiel laughed hard, grasping the smooth black sheath with his left hand; with his right, he rolled his fingers around its grip, fine red cord lashed tightly around it providing the toughest grasp for its master.

"You don't honestly believe in that nonsense, do you?" said Eskiel, "Curses are fairy tales of old, designed to keep young children from playing with the swords of their ancestors, they bear no merit in this realm."

"I urge you to reconsider," interrupted Ozark, "No blade in history with a curse as dark as that one has ever brought anything but death upon its master."

"He is right you know," said Garton, "Only the strong can truly show dominance over such darkness."

Eskiel grimaced at him. He didn't take too kindly to such an insult, pulling the sword from sheath swiftly and silently. They all held their breath, watching and waiting.

"See, what did I tell you," laughed Eskiel, "It's all just-."

An intense pain pierced through his body; he screamed in such agony that it filled the room with the horrors of death. A ghastly image scratched deep into his face, as though the very sword was draining his life from him. Arturius lunged forward to grasp the sword from his possession, only to be thrown back by Garton bounding towards him instead. As swift as the winds, he relinquished the ownership of such a sword from Eskiel, the latter of which dropped to the floor gasping and struggling for breath. Though Garton struggled initially with the temper of the blade, he soon quickly wrestled it into his control, slamming it back into its sheath hard.

"That is what happens when the arrogant and weak do not take counsel from those around them," he snapped,

The life filled Eskiel's face once more, bringing him back to the living, albeit inept of his strength.

"Darks embrace," muttered Ozark.

"What?" asked Arturius, assisting the feeble Eskiel back to his feet.

"I have heard of such a blade from the annals of history," said Ozark, "A blade so vicious, so inherently evil, that it draws forth the life force of its master to sustain its own strength."

"What allowed Garton to handle such a weapon and not myself," snapped Eskiel, "What makes him more superior to all of us?"

The eyes of Garton sparked fear and turmoil into the soul of many a man. He intimidatingly focussed his deep and dark eyes upon the reformed Eskiel; his being and presence sent dark shivers throughout the room.

"A curse cannot afflict what is already dead," he said gloomily and eerie,

A chill spun down Arturius's spine, sending pimples across his skin and a chill through the air. The standoff quickly simmered down with the almighty clatter of swords, shields, and armour scattering across the ground. Poised over in the corner over the room was Jorik, whose actions had garnered the frightful attention of the others.

"Sorry 'bout that," he muttered, "Thought this plate would look good on me."

"Goddamn fool," snapped Ozark, snatching the disassembled shoulder pauldrons from the young man's hands, tossing them across the room. The sound of metal on stone rung throughout the room, finally resting atop a strange-looking worktable.

"Keep your hands to yourself and guard the doorway," snapped Ozark.

Jorik shrunk back over to the darkened doorway, relieving his weight against the stonework whilst mulling and muttering to himself incoherently.

As Arturius approached the strange worktop, he could help but notice a faint light flickering slowly between the cracks at its side. Upon closer inspection, it turned out the cracks were no cracks at all; they were seams that joined together, concealing a rather well-hidden compartment. It took all the strength of his mechanical arm to shift its mighty weight, straining every inch of his being; much to his surprise. A loud crack and snap gave way into the air, releasing a torrent of ancient ash billowing throughout his vicinity. He coughed hard and long, waving his hand before his face as the ash clung to his cheeks.

"Found something?" asked Eskiel, gripping his head and chest.

"It would appear so," replied Arturius, "A compartment of sorts hidden within the stonework."

Eskiel approached him steadily, leaning it closer yet still cautiously keeping his distance from whatever may lurk within its confines. A steady flash of slow purple hue emanated from the shrouded box, pulsating in time with the steady heart beating within his chest.

"Strange," Arturius muttered to himself, as he reached into the box, his vision still impeded by the slow settling ash that floated around; its gentle falling felt like snow softly raining upon the ground.

"What is it?" hushed Eskiel, "What do you see?"

It was a strange feeling that washed over him, despite the mechanical arm bearing no senses, no touch and no pain, he could feel. As he pressed his fingers over the purple light, he could feel the cold touch of metal scraping against the tips; he could feel the sharp edges trying to cut into his seemingly impenetrable skin; he could feel the weight in which such an object carried, reliving its past and present readying itself for his future.

He pulled it free from its bindings, crackling as the ancient cords were cut.

"It's a sword," remarked Eskiel, "And a rather odd-looking one at that."

Indeed, it was. Many cracks ran down its blade, pulsating with the purple hue that crept through the dust earlier. Its hilt, unlike the others, was rather plain and unornate, simply affixed with a short cross-guard; it offered no protection to the hand and wrist, a rather odd function for such a tool. The cracks appeared intentional, running in perfect symmetry across the length of the sword. Each fragment between was engraved with runes of an ancient tongue; not even the wise knowledge of Ozark could decipher such writings.

"How intriguing," said Ozark, running his finger along the notches about its surface.

"Ouch!" he exclaimed, "Its edge is unbelievably sharp."

He pressed down upon his finger, oozing droplets of blood from the cut; it was fine and precise, a more delicate cut for a deadly weapon.

"Shouldn't it be?" asked Arturius, "Is it not crafted from the same elements as those that are also housed within these halls?"

"No, it isn't," replied Ozark, "This is crafted with a metal I have yet to discover, even so, its craftsmanship is rather puzzling in itself, you see the lines, the cracks that run about its surface."

Ozark glanced his hand across the weaving lines, scratching his malformed nails deep into each groove.

"That I do, what of it?" asked Arturius.

"I do believe that those are intentional," Ozark replied, "May I?"

He stretched out his raw and grizzled hand, the bones in his fingers creaked as they opened to consume the hilt. His breathing snorting as he excitedly reached out.

"By all means," replied Arturius, offering the newfound sword to Ozark, "It appears to bear the same marking as those that are etched upon my arm."

"Yes they are," said Ozark excitedly, "If my thoughts are true, then I do believe that this blade was designed for use with that arm. Here, try something with it."

Ozark passed the sword back to him. Despite its bulky and dense looking physique, it felt remarkably light; A feat that even the others in the room struggled to accomplish before succumbing to the heavyweight it bore.

As predicted, it fit perfectly within his grasp, allowing swift and precise motions as the blade whistled through the air.

"The cracks glow rather dim," said Arturius, "Have you heard of dealings with glowing metals or swords Ozark?"

"I have not I'm afraid," replied Ozark, "There are many secrets that never escaped the halls we stand in now, deposits of elements kept for the sole use of the Akavirian dynasty that settled within these walls, some would say their greed is what brought down such a kingdom."

As he ran his thumb across the grip, he came across a dark jewel embedded deeply within; it was darker than the night and cut more precise than the finest of diamonds. It wobbled slightly beneath his thumb gently but not much. A flash of deep and bright purple shimmered through the cracks upon pressing the black jewel; it was a switch of sorts, energising the sword with unknown magic.

"What did you do?" said Eskiel shocked, the action gave him a rather quick fright, "What is it doing?"

The blade shimmered as though hotter than fire, yet it was cold to touch. It distorted the surrounding air, crafting a mirage of dancing energy that crept closely along its surface. A gap had sprung between the cracks, each fragment of the sword now floated in perfect unison, bound by an unseen, unknown force that locked them along its central axis.

"It's marvellous," said Ozark, his face gleaming with excitement, "This is truly beyond what I believed the Akaviri were capable of, their experimentation has advanced further than ever recorded."

"What do I do?" asked Arturius, "I mean it's nothing like I've ever wielded before, or at least remember doing so."

"Well swing it then," replied Ozark, "Swing it fast and aim true, let's see what it is capable of."

With the tension dwelling in his mechanical arm, he struck the wooden rack before him; it was rotting and weak. As the blade came into contact with the decayed wood, it rang a strange and distorted metallic sound. Before shattering into many pieces. Ozark sighed a great sigh, disappointed at the excitement that had built up within him to witness such a let-down.

"Well, that was interesting to say the least," mocked Jorik, a huge grin stretched from cheek to cheek as he stood there leaning against the stone doorway, "Maybe if we're lucky the enemy will step upon the shards, ruin their well-kept boots."

"Did I tell you to stop guarding the doorway?" snapped Ozark.

Jorik gave a sarcastic shrug, grinning wildly as he turned to face the darkness.

"Maybe it's broken?" said Arturius, still grasping the hilt of the shattered blade.

"Not likely my friend," replied Ozark, "The smiths of the Akaviri were many things, perfectionists in their own way, but to leave something unfinished or broken was not their way, their skill was unmatched beyond what your mind could ever fathom."

"Just throw it out," said Garton coldly, "Plenty more blades to pick from here."

Undeterred by the others, Arturius didn't give in; he grasped the handle harder, pondering over its use when his grip once more pressed the blackened jewel about its hilt. It whirred to light once more, undoing what had been done to the shattered blade; one by one the fragments of its blade jumped forth, embedding themselves back to the sword in perfect unison. With a final click and shudder, the blade had repaired itself, locking back in place as it was before.

"How did you do that?" said Eskiel shocked, "What sorcery did you conjure forth? To make what has been broken remade once more is not possible!"

"I did nothing really," replied Arturius, "I pressed the black jewel upon its hilt, then it was as if the sword itself sprung to life."

"Show me that again," shouted Ozark, rushing back to him, "Show me what you did, I must see it again, I must not let mine eyes deceive me."

Arturius obliged, striking the blade of the sword once more upon the rotting wood, spiralling it into many pieces that once again scattered the room. Though as Ozark pressed the jewel, it clicked but remained lifeless. He aggressively mashed the button several more time, each with increasing frustration before rendering the task useless.

"It would appear to only respond to your touch," said Ozark, "Perhaps it is the essence that powers your arm that too shall also power the blade."

As though by magic, the blade reassembled on Arturius's touch.

"More and more do I realise that I have only scratched the surface of what we understand about this mighty civilisation," proclaimed Ozark, "I have been truly naive about my intellect on the matter, something that I will not allow to happen again."

A gruff cough bellowed behind them, Garton stood there looking down upon them with discontent.

"Not wanting to interrupt your little get together," snapped Garton, "But we are still trapped in this mountain and require a way out, and last I checked none of these blades holds the key to releasing us from such confinement."

They had almost forgotten of their predicament, focussed too heavily upon the menagerie of weapons and armour that was theirs for the taking.

"That we may be," replied Ozark begrudgingly, "However, orders of that matter fall upon the leader of this order."

He turned to face Arturius, staring him deeply in the eyes, his stance, his posture shouted at him to stay longer and strip every last secret from the mountain.

"We will gather what tools, weapons and armour we can," shouted Arturius, "Then we move out and find a way to escape these ruins, too long have we fallen privy to the darkness of the cursed mountain and I will not lose another to its embrace."

He looked back upon Ozark, who looked back at him with great annoyance and sadness. Arturius took it for acquiescence, promptly turning away as he outfitted himself with some of the finest armour to have ever graced the realm.

*~ "Where are you? Tell me you're okay, I fear I cannot go this alone" ~*

## CHAPTER XIX: KINSHIP ASUNDER

The journey through the darkness took much longer than before; the group was weighed down by the vast haul they had discovered, strutting proudly through the halls as though they were the ghosts of the once-mighty inhabitants beneath the mountain.

The others had outfitted themselves with the finest armour and weapons they could lay their hands upon; all except for Garton, for his physique and condition rendered any armour obsolete upon his person. Instead, he adopted a more appropriate approach; the sharpest sword he could find amongst the rubble and a simple set of bracers, to remind him that not all of him is death.

Deep within the gloom of the halls, he could still make out the others that strode before him, clothed in the finest cloaks from which they plunder within the stores; beneath it, their armour gleamed a deep gold and silver, finest they could find, albeit still a little dusty.

Weighing atop their shoulders, each carrying a fine leather bag, buried within each lay tools and cloths to maintain such exquisite equipment, not that time would decay such great plate, only to keep up the appearance of grandeur.

“To me!” beckoned Ozark's voice within the darkness, “The path ahead will be dark and arduous as before, take care not to slip down into the abyss, the weight of our haul may prove troublesome should such a situation arise.”

“The mountain shall not claim me,” said Jorik triumphantly, at last, he could take a share of the spoils, cladding himself in as much armour as he could so find, “I feel invincible, nay immortal as were those who fashioned me such armour of the nobility."

Garton scoffed at the remarks.

"It won't be long before you shed that weight," he said, "You carry too much upon you, it weighs you heavy and soon your legs shall falter, then the rest of your body shall swiftly follow."

"Nonsense," replied Jorik, "I am strong, a wolf in sheep's clothing, disguised and ready to pounce upon my enemies."

Arturius shook his head yet remained silent. It had seemed little time had passed since the skirmish above, and this arrogant warrior lay waste to his breeches rather than his enemies; what had changed within him? It mattered not at this moment; however, their supplies were running dangerously thin, each ration felt like but a scrap of the previous. They needed to find an exit.

"We should try scouring the western passages," said Eskiel, "I doubt anyone has ventured far through those halls, especially not the excavation team that came before us."

"No," replied Ozark, "The eastern passage is where we should dwell, we came from the east side of the mountain there is no doubt in my mind that we will find a passage that circumnavigates the collapse."

"Are you mad," shouted Eskiel, his voice bounced between the walls as it diminished into darkness, "That would lead us back towards the confines of the encampment, of which by now will surely be overrun and well-defended, news of the excavation team's failure will no doubt have reached the black keep, Vortuse and Captain Aver escaped during the clash in within the inner sanctum, so no the eastern passages is by no means a death trap."

"So what are you saying then, wander aimlessly in the darkness hoping for a glimmer of light from above," snapped Ozark. His voice sounded more threatening within the deep darkness around them.

"Not at all," replied Eskiel, "But to try and find an escape from the eastern passages would only add more trouble to our already dwindling numbers, we would be taking the crown right within the enemies grasp, an act which you have already lost so many to uphold."

The others halted in their tracks, looking upon Eskiel with great confusion.

"Crown what crown?" beckoned Ozark, "Your words speak no meaning."

"The crown of the Mountain," said Arturius, "The very artefact they came here for and we wished to halt in their mission."

He reached into his satchel and pulled forth the Crown he had cautiously retrieved from the depths of the vault. Even within the very darkness of the halls it gleamed bright and warm, as though it was the very heart of the mountain commanded it so.

"By the Gods," whispered Garton, never had he shown such humility, "Then the legends are true, a Crown for the Mountain, a Crown of the Dawn, a Crown of the night, a Crown forged in Iron, a Crown burnt to Cinders, a Crown that shines of the brightest stars, a Crown forged by blood and a Crown built upon the bones of the unknown."

"And in the darkest depth of the earth, a Crown forged in the void, bringing forth the one to rule over the realm and bring about the emptiness from within," replied Eskiel, "So that is what you seek, to claim the seat of the empty throne and bring about your vision of the realm, some would deem it unwise to interfere with such a power of the void."

"I can hear the worry in your voice Eskiel," replied Arturius, "Though you may find inner peace in knowing that the Empty Throne is neither mine nor my predecessor's true intent."

Eskiel scoffed loudly.

"Oh, and I suppose gathering the lost crowns is just a hobby of yours is it," he said aggressively, "The only purpose of claiming the crowns is to open the shadowed path to the Empty Throne, a feat that all desire to accomplish."

"While you do speak the truth, that is not what we are going to do," said Arturius, "We will find the lost crowns and keep them from the masked one, destroy them if we must, but allow me to reiterate what I am asking of you and the rest of this order, we are to keep the masked one from ascending upon the empty throne, period."

The tone of his voice was aggressive but calm, lecturing his new friend on the goal that he so desired. He even went as far as to seal his word in blood, however, Eskiel quickly stopped him from doing so.

"Okay then," he replied, "I believe you, however, there is but one problem in your grand plan you see."

He paused for a while, as though waiting for a response from the others.

"Well?" snapped Ozark, "Care to impart us your almighty wisdom?"

"The crowns of old cannot be destroyed by but the watcher of the throne," said Eskiel, "And one cannot approach the watcher with possession of all the crowns, at least not until he has passed the trials of the void and deem themselves worthy of such an audience."

Arturius smiled.

"Then I guess we keep the masked one searching for a little longer," said Arturius, "However, tell me more of this watcher, surely it must be a story, a metaphor at least."

Eskiel shrugged, his mind had run dry from his knowledge of the ancient past.

"I'm afraid I cannot provide you with such answers," Eskiel replied, "For knowledge of such information was made forbidden, but the mere mutter of the empty throne or the crowns resulted in persecution that left many vanishing into the night."

"His words speak true," said Ozark, "Before I could escape from my imprisonment within the black keep, I bore witness to the mass slaughter and cleansing that took place in the name of the new empire."

The young Rekeshi turned in shock, clasping at his sword as memories of his past came flooding back to him once more.

"You were there?" Eskiel said softly, "You were there during the great purge?"

He could see it in his eyes, the same fear and regret that would break the heart of even the mightiest of men; his eyes grew heavy and hands trembled.

"Much to my regret, I was," replied Ozark, "However my confinement was to the black keep, I did not witness the whispers that echoed through the castle walls, only the screams that pierced my ears before they were snuffed out."

"What was the great purge?" asked Arturius, "I thought you said the great purge happened within Dawnstar during the fall."

"No my dear boy," replied Ozark, "To say that the masked one only purged one of the mighty kingdoms would amount to foolish ignorance, Farrosia, Rekesh, Verden, all fell under the shadow of the power of the Masked One."

"Yet Verden was the only one to come out of it still standing," interrupted Jorik, his voice filled with anger as he clenched his fist hard, creasing and cracking the leather gloves that bound to his flesh. Arturius looked upon him with confusion.

"I do not understand," he said, "How could two kingdoms fall into such ruin and death yet the other fare better?"

"Because their bastard of a king bent the knee before the fight even begun," Jorik hissed, "Sending countless of his own people into the slaughter as the bequest of the masked one, vagabonds, orphans, the ill abled, none were spared of such cowardice."

"It would appear that this history has struck a deep nerve with you," replied Arturius, "By the tone of your voice I can only assume that you lost someone to such horrors?"

The heavily clad Jorik exhaled. It wasn't clear whether it be from the memories of his past, or the sheer burden of his armour; one thing was clear, however, it weighed heavily.

"Indeed it does," muttered Jorik, "They carted off what remained of my family to the death camps. My brother and I escaped our fate by hiding amongst the bodies of the fallen for three days, basking within the putrid stench of death and blood."

His words brought only more confusion into the mix, creating an ever more deepening black hole that swallowed every thought that passed through his head. The darkness was even more consuming than the blackest abyss that lurched before them.

"My apologies such delving into such pain my friend," replied Arturius, "But I believed you and your kin to be descended from Farrosia."

Jorik nodded within the darkness, only just noticed by the faint flicker of the torches carried by the others.

"It is complicated," said Jorik, "For the blood of my mother runs with the sands of the Varib, yet the blood of my father runs with the light of the Dawn, so I am both Farrosian and Verdenese, however the day that King Rahm forsook his oath to protect his people was the day my brother and I abandoned all mention of our heritage."

A gentle light emerged from around the corner, its radiance was being smothered by darkness more crippling than anything they had seen before. Its misty appearance reminding Arturius of the white clouds that floated peacefully in the deep blue sky; a sight he so longed to reunite with.

"Keep your distance," shouted Arturius to the others, "Have we made passage through these walls before?"

"If my directions have remained true, then yes, yes we have," replied Ozark, "Although much of these walls appear the same. Who can truly tell anymore?"

Arturius cautiously approached the thick wall of darkest fog, its fouls stench consumed his senses, burning deeper and stronger every step he took towards its embrace.

"Torch," he beckoned, "Throw me a torch."

His reflexes had become remarkably tuned, swiftly plucking the burning stick from the air graciously. The light of the flame was not much for the darkness before him, snuffing out before his eyes as he poked it, intrigued and full of wonder.

"We can't go this way," Arturius called, "Its darkness will be too much for any of us to bear, even you Garton."

He placed a hand upon the undying man's shoulder as he passed beside him, feeling the mix of emotions that tore through the poor man's body. It was strange darkness; it would appear the very essence of which was brimming with life, though not the life one would like to meet when devoid of light. The others crept back, slowly moving back towards the corridor junction from which they had previously emerged. Unbeknownst to them, a figure moved within the darkness, watching them carefully with great intrigue; and nothing more. Something caught the attention of Arturius. He gazed intently into the shadows, filling his mind with many thoughts as he shrunk away from the real world.

"Do your eyes see something that ours do not," said Garton, "Or has your mind wandered away into the darkness before us."

Arturius remained quiet, his eyes were still tuned into the wall of darkness that stood quiet and calm. A faint ring sung within his ears; drums beat against his head, again and again before his words broke its trance.

"I am not sure," replied Arturius, "Yes, no, maybe both, yet something seems off and I cannot put my finger upon it."

"I'm sure it is nothing," said Ozark, "Come, we have a long journey ahead of us and not much time for it."

"Come Arturius," shouted Eskiel, "It is but a wall of fog, nothing more and nothing less."

"That may be," replied Arturius, "However something about this whole situation seems off, how is it that we journey down these very corridors, not a few hours prior and all is clear, yet when our journey ventures once more along this path we are blocked, obscured from progressing further."

When the light of the torches dimmed, flickering in the mountain's breath, it became apparent to the others that time was of the essence. The group pushed forward into the dark. No signs of light could be found ahead as the tunnels grew darker and darker, as though the very night was seeping into the heart of the mountain. Arturius looked back to the shadows behind them.

"It is as I feared," he said, "The darkness moves as silently as the shadows that lurk within the abyss."

Ozark looked to the rear, gazing over the shoulders of Arturius when he saw the shadow of which he spoke.

"What in the seven realms is that," shouted Ozark,

"Something dark, something terrible," replied Arturius, "Run!"

Suddenly there was a howling screech, and down the narrowing passage the heavy darkness–possessed with the fear of the abyss–sprung forward. Then came the others running from its perilous chase, Garton took Ozark upon his shoulders, carrying the withered man when he could not muster the strength to escape such obscured horrors. Then went Eskiel. He had removed his ornate helmet, too long had it weighed his vision in the darkness. Though its craft was its value, and as such he could not relinquish it from his side. Behind them ran Jorik. His lumbering sprint tired his legs and had blown his lungs, sending him into a spiralling descent of hobbling steps.

"Jorik!" shouted Arturius, "You must relieve yourself of your load, it weighs you too much."

"Nay," Jorik replied, "I cannot relinquish such treasures, they are mine and I will not sacrifice them to the darkness."

"If you don't throw them down now, then you will sacrifice your own life to the darkness," shouted Arturius in response, "Don't let your legacy end here, my friend!"

They stumbled aggressively down the hallway; in the far distance, the others were gaining ground as they slowly but surely vanished from their view. As they fled from the ever-encroaching mist, Arturius could hear Jorik by his side, the gentle sobs sending tears trickling down his face.

"Fear not Jorik, this abyssal nightmare will not consume us," shouted Arturius,

"I have failed him, haven't I?" replied Jorik.

Arturius looked back at him, confused. The intense ringing grew louder and louder as it screeched within his ears, nearly drowning out his voice.

"Your brother would be proud of what you have accomplished," said Arturius, "Don't let his death drag you into the darkness, live so that he can still live with you."

He brandished his fragmented blade, swiftly nicking the exposed leather straps that clamp Jorik's encumbering armour to his body. Piece by piece fell to the floor, culminating in the heavy rattling of metal upon stone before the darkness consumed it once and for all.

They ran on. The faster they moved, so too did the darkness, the dense mist, and whatever lurked deeply within; it taunted them, relishing the thrill of the chase.

"Faster," yelled Arturius, "I will not return to the darkness again, and neither shall I allow anyone else under my command."

Far into the hallway, a faint light billowed in the distance, piercing through the encroaching darkness. Their pace quickened. They yearned for the light ahead to dispose of the darkness that enclosed quickly upon their tails. They burst through the barrier of light; it blinded them harshly; their eyes had adjusted to the dense darkness for some time. The bright light burned, blurring their surroundings. Arturius counted three dim shadows before them. It was clear by the discernible mass which one was which as the other waited before them. *"What are they waiting for?"* he thought to himself, *"The darkness permeates at our heels and yet they remain still"*. Then it all became apparent.

As his vision slowly restored, so too did the many shadows unveil off into the distance. One by one they flickered into view as stars would across the sky. Though these were no stars; they were a fouler and worrying sight that he had wished to avoid.

"In the name of the high imperator, and the order of the empire, you shall lay down your swords and submit!" bellowed a voice off into the distance.

"Gods be damned," spat Jorik, "It looks like our luck is running out."

Before them stood a mighty host, looming within the inner sanctum numbered a great host of Rekeshi soldiers; eager and rearing to fight.

"What do we do, Arturius?" whispered Eskiel. The others gaze never broke from the mass of warriors before them, "There are too many for us to take on."

"He is right," said Garton, "I count around two hundred, they will overwhelm and crush us like ants, even for someone such as myself."

The ringing in his ears grew louder. The Rekeshi to their front and darkness to their rear; trapped between two that they could not oppose. However, it may be possible that they need not fight at all.

"Ready yourselves," whispered Arturius to the others, "When I call for it, we break through the ranks to freedom."

"Run where though," replied Ozark, "Or have you not seen the impenetrable shield wall that faces us!",

The booming voice of the Rekeshi captain echoed throughout the halls again.

"Hear my words, we will slaughter every last one of you," shouted the Captain of the host, "I shall count to the number of five, if your arms are not laid upon the floor then you shall all die."

He could make out the distinct armour of the captain, stood at the rear of the host farthest from danger. God, he wished he could silence his tongue there and then, yet it was not possible.

"Five…"

Ozark looked back to him, desperation gleaming from his eyes.

"Which way?" he hissed,

"Four…"

He grasped the grip of his sword, drawing the blade in a slow but smooth motion; the metal scraping against the edge of its sheath producing a shimmering sound that echoed around him.

"We go straight," he replied, "Straight for the head of the snake."

"Three…"

Eskiel looked back upon with shock and horror, his mouth agape revealing the pearly whites of his teeth within the darkness of his mouth.

"It will be suicide! Madness!" he said, "They will cut us down before we make it past the first line, these are not your typical Rekeshi warriors, they are the Gravesh, elite shock troopers whose only goal is to inflict heavy casualties when the fighting begins, they are not to be underestimated if you wish to remain alive."

"Two…"

The rest of the group looked towards Arturius, sensing the hint of madness that was forming within his thoughts. He nodded quickly, raising his blade before him and burying his feet into the ground.

"Trust me," he replied, "have faith in my plan and we will see the light of day once more."

"One..."

The others nodded, each unsheathing their weapons and readying themselves for what may come next. Their faith in the order was solid and stout, for they would die before seeing them dissolve into nothing. The armed host locked shields, forming an enveloping shield wall mixed with an array of pikes and spikes.

"Kill them, kill them all," shouted the Captain, his voice rasping from the intense anger that filled him, "I want none left alive, I want their blood to run thick on this here floor and I want that crown."

"When darkness bites at your heel and evil faces your front, stand true and stare death deep within his eyes," muttered Arturius, "Only then shall the light guide us."

A great and thunderous clash sprung from behind them, burst forth into the expanse of the sanctum. A clash of rock and stone fell upon the heads of the host before them, smashing into their ranks as it felled many warriors within a single moment.

"Now!" shouted Arturius, "Now is our time, break through the wall whilst the darkness draws their attention."

The order swept quickly through the broken ranks, smashing down any foe that dared to stand in their way. Behind them the darkness persisted, unleashing its wrathful fury upon the quivering Rekeshi that stood under its shadow. A wave of black miasma cascaded down upon them, enveloping them within its thick embrace. The screams were harsh and gargled, continuing for but a moment before they were silenced forever. No bodies were left in its wake.

Arturius led the charge, shattering shield and breaking sword piece by piece with every swing; it was truly a remarkable blade to carve through the steel of his enemies so effortless and clean. By now they had broken through the first wall, leaving what remained of the shield wall to falter upon their trail. But now was no time to waiver, for should they halt and lose such momentum then they shall be utterly surrounding and undoubtedly destroyed.

"Push on!" bellowed Arturius, "Show them no quarter, show them no mercy, for you shall certainly receive nothing of the sort from them."

As though they were the horns of some fell beast, they forced their way forward. Wave after wave was broken. Behind them the darkness followed, consuming the remnants of those left behind. It took no heed; for its only goal was that which fled from its presence.

"It is as I thought," said Arturius, "The darkness shows no allegiance to the enemy."

"You truly are as mad as they come," shouted Eskiel.

They did not halt when they came upon the captain and his elite guard, stood in their path was a retinue of twelve of Rekesh's Elitist troops second only to the Death guard themselves. A truly intimidating sight to behold, but none the less an obstacle in their path. Arturius raised his sword up high, gripping the hilt with his powerful hand as his thumb pressed upon the black crystal, illuminating the blade once more in a shimmering purple hue. As he swung it around his head, each of the fragments unleashed a potential he had not expected. One by one they spread out through the air, not broken or shattered, but held firmly within the deep aura that pieced them together. They glided through the air, whispering death as a whip, hacking and slicing metal and flesh alike. With lashes and spins, Arturius smote down the captain and his guard, embedding the many fragments of his blade deep into their flesh and bone.

Down to the floor, each of them fell, limp as the wind that brushed them aside. The sword grasped within his hand was spent. Its blade scattered across the ground and embedded within his foes. A quick tap of the jewel upon its hilt light the blade up once, calling forth for its fragmented children to converge upon it once again. Each vicious piece tore through the deceased guards that lay beneath their feet. Tugging and ripping through armour and flesh alike as they reconfigured upon the hilt of his sword, locking together within its slumber once more.

Such a sight terrified the host before them, the darkness picking off what remained of the vanguard with ease and ferocity. Terror swept through the ranks as they fled at the sight of such strength from both foes. The others reached the archway to the rear of the hall, breaking through its threshold to ascend the stairs, age-worn and broken.

There were no bodies left within the sanctum when Arturius looked back, only a hall shrouded in expanding darkness stifling out every ray of light that came before its might. As the great columns became enveloped by the mist they withered and cracked, descending to the floor a heap of crumbled rock; it sent the mountain into a shiver, streaks of crack lined the floor they ran upon parting it violently as though meat from the bone. It meant to bring the mountain down upon them.

They did not stop, not even for the stragglers that ran with them. The ceiling began to waiver, releasing rocks and rubble upon their heads, the largest of which avoided the others; a fate not so fortunate for the Rekeshi.

At least, a light shimmered ahead of them, not any light of fire but that of the outside, that of hope. The mountain could no longer contain the weight of its own might, crumbling into ruins the hallway narrowed. Rock and dust flew through the air, the sound of which chinked across Arturius's metal arm, soon to be drowned amongst the noise of such cave-ins.

"There!" shouted Ozark, clung upon the back of Garton as he sprinted effortlessly, "There is light ahead, an exit to this God-forsaken tomb."

The light was golden and glorious, no later than the hour upon noon when the sun basked the mountain with its heavenly showers. They burst from the confines of the mountain, gasping the crisp, clean air. It smelt of pine and earth, faint yet powerful. A cloud of dust exploded from the path they emerged from, blanketing the area in a thick grey.

No one else emerged from the dark cavernous hole, the trees and hills surrounding them lay empty.

Arturius looked back to the mountain, its gleaming face faded away as a good portion of its side disappeared into its belly. The ancient city of Nordellar was no more than a tomb, sealed away once more until the next comes along and breaks free the seal of the earth. At last, they were free.

*~"It is only me now, the others have fallen, I feel the darkness corrupting me"~*

## CHAPTER XX: ELEGY OF THE ABYSS

Dark was the night; the moon flooded the surrounding land with its incandescent lunar light; shining its brilliant silver across the landscape. The journey had passed for many hours since they escaped from the confines of the ruined kingdom. Before them lay the Vale of Eryne, consumed under the shadow of the mountain. No matter how far they travelled, the great mountain loomed above them, a stark reminder of the loss they encountered within its bosom. Far to the East another towering mountain loomed, equalling the height of the regal rock that crumbled atop their heads. The towering peaks, as they had been named, oppose the great mountain to the east, bitter rivals and ancient seat of the Drangviri high atop its peak upon the ruins of Kabadeth.

Arturius looked back one last time. Dark was the face of its gaze, but no darker than the fell deeds that had awaited them when they entered. Nevertheless, the ground shook as the last of what remained of the Akavirian stronghold sunk deeper into the earth. It was a beautiful reminiscence of the horrors that faced them some thousands of years ago.

"Farewell my friends," whispered Jorik, bowing his head upon the tomb, "I shall never forget you."

Arturius placed a hand upon his weary shoulder, an effort to comfort that bore no use for such a broken heart.

"I fear that we cannot dwindle within these lands much longer," said Arturius, "No doubt the Rekeshi will have sent many forces into this area, by daybreak we may find ourselves surrounded once more."

"Give us a chance to catch a breath," said Ozark, "We have breathed that foul air for too long, it has weakened the body and dulled the mind."

"Nay," replied Arturius, "I will not have us sit and wait for our doom to arrive, we keep moving until we simply cannot anymore, until our feet swell and lungs bleed, we must find sanctuary to take respite."

Ozark looked defeated. His stature was feeble and weak; already his spirit was waning, and he was now to push aside the grief and continue on. Despite the protests, Arturius rounded them up, pulling each to their feet. All but Garton had fallen to the grass and dirt, exhausted.

"And what would you have us do?" said Eskiel, "where would you have us go? If you haven't already noticed, we are all vagabonds of the night, with a home or kingdom to call our own."

"Ozark, you mentioned of allies hiding in wait," asked Arturius, "Would such friends still honour their promises? Shall they still honour their duty to the order?"

"Without Selwyn at our helm I'm afraid it may go against us," replied Ozark, "They all swore their oaths of fealty unto him, and their honour is … questionable at the least."

The company came to a sudden halt on the command of Arturius. As far as the horizon, all he could see were the vast expanse of mountains to the east and the far plains of the vale to the west.

"A decision must be made before we continue further," said Arturius, "For if we break across the land without a base to assemble, then we will not live to see our mission accomplished."

"What of Hollowclaw?" beckoned Jorik, "Our base will still remain and such a dark locale will shroud us from his watchful eye."

Arturius shook his head.

"Nay, I'm afraid that will not do," replied Arturius, "Even if we make it across the perilous journey back to that forest, its position and secrecy has become compromised."

"How so?" replied Jorik.

"That traitorous bastard," hissed Ozark, "No doubt he is a puppet of the masked one, delivering our poor Silas right into his grasp, he will have informed them of our entire infrastructure, every dead drop every base we have ever set up is now compromised and at the hands of the enemy."

"Rightly so," replied Arturius, "And no more forests of old, or ancient terror ruins either, with all that has happened of late I wish not to fall prey to another of those accursed creatures of cinder and shadow!"

The group remained silent for a little while longer, each to their own as they pondered over the desolate areas for safe sanctuary. They continued to follow the hidden road, slowly and cautiously. It was rough and winding, the vast flora lashed to either side of it clawed at them as they pressed through the brush.

"Wait!" shouted Eskiel,

The sudden outburst halted the group, prompting them to swiftly silence his loud voice for fear of whatever scouts may lurk in wait.

"Quiet!" whispered Ozark aggressively, "We do not know what may crawl beyond our gaze here, think next time before you get us all killed."

"My apologies," whispered Eskiel, "But what about the catacombs of Duskfall?"

Arturius turned to face Eskiel, the gentle trickling of a nearby river ran through his ears; the sound of its waters grew a thirst deeply across his parched lips.

"The catacombs?" asked Arturius.

Ozark scratched his brow, dipping his hand into the icy cold waters of the brook cupping the liquid crystal within his palm watching it trickle between his fingers.

"Hmm…that could work," muttered Ozark, "Concealed, fortified, abundant with herbs and flower for me to replenish my tonic. And being back upon the hallowed grounds of Farrosia would indeed be more advantageous to us all."

"It's certainly safe that's for sure," said Jorik, "Not to mention no one will pass beyond the watchful gaze of Farros himself, for fear he may smite them from the great beyond or even whisper thoughts of insanity to those who would seek to defile such hallowed ground."

Jorik let out a bellowing laugh, sending the local wildlife into a frantic frenzy of chirps and squeaks. A sudden lash across his face soon stopped the laughter, leaving a deep red mark across his cheek.

"Ow, what was that for?" snapped Jorik.

"God's help me if I have to remind anyone of you that we are currently being hunted by who knows what and God knows what," snapped Ozark, "So stay quiet, keep down and shut the fuck up."

The others nodded in agreement. Even in his fragile state, the withered man showed that his intense demeanour was a force to be reckoned with.

"So what'll be Arturius?" said Garton. He looked back towards the mountain, its looming shadow still covering the land, "I fear the longer we bicker and argue, the closer our enemy shall advance upon us. Besides my hold upon this vessel is becoming frail. I must meditate and seek control once more."

Arturius pondered for a moment. Though his mind had already been settled.

"We make for the Catacombs of Duskfall," replied Arturius, "And I pray that our movements go unnoticed by the shadows that follow."

"As do I. Then it is settled!" said Ozark, "We make for the homeland and the desolate ruins that crumble beneath its sun. I pray that we make it before our rations dwindle, there is nearly a stream or river from this point onwards."

The others advanced westward, following the crystal water of the river. Before Arturius could move, a hand grasped his shoulder, turning him about to face Ozark and his worried face.

"I sure hope you know what you are doing," whispered Ozark, "The old lands of Farrosia are not what they used to be. Swarms of Ska'al and Rekeshi roam is hills, burning whatever resembles the old foe that they faced many years ago. They pillage, rape and plunder uncontested. Be prepared to draw your sword once more when we arrive."

Arturius looked upon his worried face, laying his hand atop the malformed fingers that grasped at his shoulder.

"Fret not my friend, all will be well," said Arturius, "We must do without fear and worry, for that will lead us down the wrong path, besides if there is one thing I have learnt during my time with you all is that all of you are worth any Rekeshi, Ska'al or dark creature tenfold."

"But fear is good, fear keeps us questioning the plan, ironing out that which may cause untold harm upon the group," replied Ozark, "We can't afford to be rash anymore."

"I understand your pain," said Arturius, "You do speak truth; however, my plan will work as long as you have faith within my actions."

Ozark draped his arm across his chest, sliding his fingers away from the embrace of Arturius.

"But why there?" asked Ozark, "Why the lands that fell to the power of the masked one? It is a dark land now, one that many avoid for fear of persecution."

"Exactly why we must settle there," replied Arturius, "For we shall lie beneath the enemies very nose, watching and waiting from a close distance, the masked one will know the strength of our company now, he will also know of the network Selwyn set up before his demise, and that will be where he searches for us."

It was clear that the plan wasn't fully backed by the intellectual mind of Ozark. His face scrunched tightly as he forced himself to come to terms with such an arrangement.

"Besides," said Arturius, "Once we regain our strength and composure once more we can look out for stronger footholds within the realm, ones that will remain obscured by the arrogance of the Rekeshi overlords and their incompetence."

"Be it on your head then," snapped Ozark, "I shall follow your plan on this matter, yet I will not agree to its execution."

Arturius smiled to his weary companion.

"Come! We have a long road ahead of us and much to do along the way," said Arturius.

The river ran through the woodlands of the Vale of Eryne, twisting and turning as the water snake of its basin. The encroaching mountains on either side of the valley were small when compared to the towering monstrosities to their rear, but still reached high into the skies. Its white peaks mark the borders of the Akavirian lands of old. Jorik had told him of the names of each of the peaks that ran beside them, each named after a great Akavirian warrior, their deeds forever immortalised by the landscape as they watched over the borders of their kingdom, protecting their home even after death.

The four great peaks which shimmering with the glistening snow stood far within each corner of the vale: Oranyl, Vascarthan, Tomehoi and Griseldabar, the four pillars that watched over the kingdom. Glistening waters ran from each peak, merging with the river that ran through its land. Its endless foaming falls washed the very air with droplets of purest water, allowing the land to flourish even within these dark times.

"It is said that in times that predate those of the heroes of old, when the realm was locked in a state of perpetual warfare and the kingdoms of old fought one and other bitterly and without mercy," said Jorik, "Kingdoms rose and fell as often as the sun would peak through the day, it was those events that supposedly led to the shaping of the realm as we see it today."

"How is it you come about such tales Jorik?" asked Arturius, "Your knowledge on the history of this land is quite impressive."

"Childhood tales garner much merit within this realm," replied Jorik, "Even more so in this dark age with the coming of the Khaos and the darkness within the great mountain."

A wind passed through the trees, shaking the tangled woods apart as the light broke through its gaps. A rather unusual stiffening feeling overcame him, as though the land he walked upon gave relentless quarrel with the history of which he spoke.

"Do you really think that Farrosia or Akavar or Rekesh have endured its patronage within the realm since the dawn of time," said Jorik,

"I had never even considered," replied Arturius.

"There were kingdoms of great and powerful kings and queens who ruled over the lands, even the Akaviri, the eternal architects were but pawns upon the board under the shadows of such might," said Jorik,

"What happened to them?" asked Arturius, "Surely such a thing would be scribed within the history books?"

"Nay, I'm afraid," replied Jorik, "Such history is only ever written by the victor, and then that which opposed them was all but expunged from our history as we know it, who knows how many secrets and forgotten civilisations walked these hills or crossed the seas? There is so much in our world that will never be discovered."

"And how do you come by all this knowledge then Jorik?" said Arturius, "An outstanding scholar you could be, in a more peaceful time that is."

Jorik laughed, before smacking his hand across his mouth. The gaze of Ozark pierced him from afar before turning away and moving on.

"It is not I that discovered such knowledge," replied Jorik. Suddenly his face grew with sadness, "It was an aspiration of Silas to discover the forgotten history, the void within the years as he called it."

Just then a deep feeling washed over the Arturius, a feeling of unnerving worry and anxiety, along with it a voice whispered deep within the confines of the trees. As he sharpened his vision amongst the darkened thicket, a faint but visible light flickered in the distance.

"Stop!" he whispered aggressively. The others quickly turned to him, lowering their stance to obscure their bodies against the tall grass that wave beside them.

"What is it?" whispered Ozark, "What does he see?"

His words failed to reach the ears of Arturius as he slowly crept his way towards the light,

"Arturius!" beckoned Jorik quietly, "What is it that your eyes see?"

"I see a light within the trees," he replied.

"Skaveth!" muttered Jorik beneath his breath, "There is a light within the trees."

It was not the sun that grasped his attention, for its peak was at its highest, bearing down upon the group as they wandered on their journey. No shadows emerged beneath them but the hollow black circles that swept before them.

"I'm going to get a closer look," whispered Arturius, "We need to sweep out the area, I fear that if our enemy approaches they may encircle us within this valley."

"Wait! Arturius!" hushed Eskiel forcefully, "It may be a trap!"

Though it was too late, Arturius had already fallen victim to its allure, bounding low through the grass before he burrowed within the thick dense trees that lay before him. Strangely enough, the closer he seemed to edge towards its drawing light, the further it seemed to float into the distance.

The ground was rising rather steeply, its increasing incline proving more cumbersome by the step as he strained his legs to push him further up its stony and grassy slope.

"You really shouldn't run off alone like that!" snapped a voice from behind him.

He pivoted to find Jorik tight upon his heel, panting and wheezing from his silent sprint to reach him.

"What are you doing?" replied Arturius, "Whatever is out here could be dangerous and I do not wish you to face an untimely end."

Jorik scoffed at his concern,

"You are the leader of this group now," he replied, "An example is led by your actions. I am worried for your safety so I came to assist you on your investigation, much to the dismay of Ozark it would seem as well."

He couldn't help but smile at that last remark, turning back down the slope to see if anyone else had followed suit. Yet the trees were all that stared back at him, waving it's the breeze.

"Very well," said Arturius, "But on any sign of danger or my being in peril, you will turn and flee. Are we at an understanding? Even if it means leaving me behind to die."

The young man nodded, albeit without slight protest.

The two moved swiftly between the trees, taking care to stay well hidden amongst the brush before them. The forest flickered in and out of darkness, sending waves of light pulsating through the branches in a vivid display of black and gold.

"Huh?" said Jorik, "What is with this light that would seem to flow as though water down a river? It's very behaviour hides my vision from what may lurk between the trees."

"Maybe the moon has passed amongst the clouds," replied Arturius, "Though it is a strange occasion as such, between the sight of the forest and the voice that echoes through the trees, I don't know what is going on."

Jorik turned to him, confused and concerned, a vacant expression adorned with intrigue and beguile swept across his face.

"Voice?" he replied, "What voice? I hear only the wind that rustles the feathers of the trees."

Just then the singing grew fairer, whispering louder and louder in a language he could not understand. It was gentle and soft, as though pleading with him to follow it deeper within the trees.

"I don't believe it to be hostile," said Arturius, "But I do not understand its tongue. It would be wise for us to stay alert with this matter."

"It would be wise for us to return to the others and seek our sanctuary," replied Jorik, "Hearing voices is not a normal occurrence, even for those in tune with nature and the dead, but I sense that your mind is already set of this mystery."

It wasn't long before they emerged from the trees into a small glade lit by the glorious moon and its radiant light. Its wide berth and level land drew in a rather quaint feeling of favour and protection. A small wall of rocks lay across the edge of its border, though not a wall carved by the likes of man; but that which was carved by the trees. The stone was entwined with the deep strong roots of the tree that rested upon its centre, though no leaves grew upon its branches it was clear that life flourished anew beneath its grey bark.

"By the Gods!" cried Jorik, "The legends are true, they do live amongst the earth of this realm."

"What, what is it?" said Arturius, "What do you see? Is there someone hidden behind the gaze of that tree?"

Jorik shook his head. Instead lowering his stance and sheathing his blade as he paced up to the towering tree that stood before them.

"Well, what is it then?" shouted Arturius.

He did not reply, nor did he gaze back upon him. With his trembling hand he reached out, pointing at the thick grey tree that rose from the depths of the earth. It was indeed a king amongst the trees, even from the edges of the forest it would seem that the lesser trees bowed graciously towards its might. Its roots unearthed and burrowed deeply, thought the glade itself, dark and twisted, and they grasped at the ground fiercely. No leaves and no twigs adorned the grass that spread out beneath its shadow, leaving the ground clear and immaculate of such a mess.

"It's an elder tree of the old," whispered Jorik. He pressed his hand against its thick bark, sending pulsating veins of light beneath the thick cloak from beneath the palm of his hand, "They survived."

With a strange uncertainty, the forest itself birthed forth a life unseen previously, though it was dark and full of terror. Flowers and leaves withered, falling from the skies as rotting rain; the bark of the elder tree grew thick with darkness as its skin peeled away, withering into dust. Its roots writhed about the earth as worms pushing through the dirt, washing in the liquid earth as they stretched out for the two as they stood there. Jorik jumped back, tripping over the sweeping roots, sending him crashing into the fresh dirt. As if nothing had occurred, the tree itself began anew, replenishing its lost hide with its grey skin and flourishing leaves and flowers once more upon its branches.

"Dark magic!" cried Jorik, "The tree is possessed! Afflicted! Don't go near its evil roots, for they will choke the life from you!"

Once his palm left the touch of the bark of the tree, its life drained from its branches once more, rendering it a grey husk of an old bygone age.

"How strange," said Arturius, "Fear not Jorik, I do not believe that any sorcery of the dark was present here today."

He approached the slumbering wayward tree cautiously, ignoring the many pleas and remarks boasted by Jorik. The faint singing within his head grew louder as he approached, whispering intelligible words of soft hymns and strange verses. Drawing him in ever closer, as it called out for him.

"Is it peculiar to have such a tree talk within your head here, Jorik?" asked Arturius, "For this one speaks to me softly, yet in a language that I cannot discern."

"Don't encourage it Arturius," shouted Jorik, "For it will lure you in and swallow you into the abyss."

"And you have seen this occur?" replied Arturius, "You have seen such flora dispose of someone in such a manner?"

The felled warrior drew himself upon his feet, dusting the dirt from his recently polished armour. A few cuts and sores adorned his hands and wrists, though none were too troublesome for the mild-mannered aggression he projected. He shook his head confusingly.

"Nay, I have not," Jorik replied, "But I have been told of such deeds within the years gone by, a boy in my village, Joryll was his name, I heard rumours of his encounter with such a cursed rotted Greatwood, he ventured to close to its enticing embrace lure by the sickly-sweet scent of the fruit which it bore, only to be dragged beneath the dirt never to have been seen again and his body was never recovered from such an ordeal, so I pray thee do not approach that tree!"

"Yet you never witnessed such events, my friend," said Arturius, "How can you contest to such stories? There could be countless reasons as to the disappearance of a young one, but I can promise you this, I will not be subdued by such a force should it prove to be of sound truth."

The dirt had been upturned aggressively by the previous encounter, that of which sent Jorik into a superstitious wreck of himself. The winds had changed suddenly, exposing the concealed sun once more, passing its gleaming ray upon the grey bark of the tree.

As he placed his hand upon the withered bark, the ground quaked. However, it did not grow dark with despair, nor did it fight against the graceful crusader. it flourished with life once more; the grey bark turned a vibrant brown, thick as polished leather; the leaves and flower grew large, blushing with the light of the sun send sparkles of dew floating through the air; its roots thrashed heavily, releasing a torrent of brilliant fireflies fluttering through the air. It felt as though something had struck him hard upon the head, wrenching back at his head as the whites of his eyes glossed across. Falling, all he felt was the fearful sensation as one falls through the air, waiting for the ground to emerge from within the darkness and end the beating heart that drummed in the distance. Though the ground never came.

A vast array of scenes flickered past him, burning at his head as he tried to follow their meaning. A large mountain range of intimidating doom rose before him, turning dark before a vast expanse of shadowed waves submerged his consciousness; it washed him away as he fell through the air. A voice cursed at him, shrieking within the darkness as he panicking, searching for its mouth.

*I see you lurking amongst the shadows, a whisper in the dark that prickles against mine ears. I will come for you with blood and cinder as I reclaim that which was taken from me. Lest you forget that of the treasure to which I possess, is a treasure indeed. If only you knew of its value and purpose. So come, come and claim what I have taken, of forever face your failures and deceit.*

Without warning, he was pulled through the darkness, a thick blackness that hummed with a great melody; a feeling so familiar was this elegy of the abyss that he could almost swear it was welcoming him back from a long slumber. He found himself high above the lands, gazing down upon a vast expansive kingdom filled with stone, motte and earth. Faint lights flickered through the streets as a musky haze weaved between the buildings. It wasn't until the flash of lightning; powerful in its strike forced upon him a brilliant light, revealing the darkness across this city. There looming high atop a jagged cliff, coarse and sharp stood a keep dark as the night and tall as the sky. Vast ramparts weaved throughout its jutting towers as they leaned forward, watching over those that dwelled below.

Deep beneath the confines of the black keep, he fell, falling deeper into the Abyss as all that was light in the realm was silenced. His vision followed the path of the shadowed throne that lay before him. A concealed figure sat upon its black seat as it stared back upon him. It was then that he found himself face to face with his own reflection. It gleamed upon him, smiling with an unnerving smirk before dissolving in the hard ground beneath them.

"Tell me what you know worm!" bellowed a voice within the darkness, "Tell us and then all the pain shall cease."

The voice bore no recognition, however; it was coarse, piercing splinters through his chest. Whoever was speaking was filled with rage and malice he had not yet heard of. It was deeper than the echoes that filled the dense forest around him, distorted and misshapen as the words that drifted so.

"I will not divulge the information of which you speak, usurper," replied a rather familiar voice.

"Hah, Hah, Hah, you have fire young one, much like your father," murmured the voice,

"Don't you dare speak of him," snapped the familiar voice again, "You monster."

"Oh yes. I am the monster," said the strange voice callously, "And little boys such as yourself should be afraid of monsters such as I, don't you worry I'll get the knowledge of which I speak, everyone has cracks within their spirit and I always find the means to break them open."

The shadowed and cloaked figure sprawled across the surrounding walls and iron shackles. The dungeon illuminated dimly, its murky and damp walls birthed life to all manner of moss and lichen as it engulfed stone and bone alike.

"Silas, it's me Arturius, look above you!" said Arturius,

Though the young boy's eyes remained glancing to his feet, not even a twitch in response to his calls.

"He cannot see me," whispered Arturius, "Is it that my presence is not within this dungeon? Maybe I am still within the glade, visions rooted deep within my mind from the elder tree of old, perhaps it is as Jorik said and the tree itself is granting me such foresight",

He looked back upon Silas, he could feel his fear and pain. Such a dark place for he who is of a pure heart is a crime within itself. He listened closely, looking around to find any sense of his location. The agonising screams echoed throughout the dark place. There was no doubt in his mind that such whispers must flutter through the walls; for such a dark and dreary locale will undoubtedly hold such misery for years to come. The stench was foul, years of rot and blood welling in between the cracks upon the floor, streaked across the damp walls giving them a flavour of death and despair.

Arturius reached out for Silas, though his reach fell short of the beaten and bruised body, grasping only at the fabric of his prison tatters. He could find comfort in knowing that the young boy was still living.

"Fear not my friend," he whispered, "I will with every power of my being, every ounce of strength that I can muster, will not leave you to suffer such a fate. Mark my words I am coming for you."

In a flash of blinding light Arturius felt as the grasp of reality pulled back upon him. Images flickered past his eyes, almost too fast to comprehend their meaning. A forest built on brilliant starlight. A mountain that pierces the heavens. A fire drawn from pigment and ink. A forge buried deep beneath rock and sand. An abyssal fury bubbling within a prison of root and stem. A prison cold and deep as midnight blue. And seven mounds, for seven graves of a bygone age.

Suddenly he found himself back within the glade, resting upon his back as the sun blinded him with its brilliance. He felt cold, though not the cold of the temperature; a cold as though all the happiness in life had been plucked away. As he pulled himself up, he saw the others surrounding the area. The majestic tree had once more fell into its deep slumber, remaining idle and still in the whispering breeze.

His ears pricked up; the sound of murmured arguments reached his dizzy state.

"We need to leave now!" said Ozark, "That tremor shall surely not go unnoticed, and if we were able to home in upon its position, then the Rekeshi surely will."

"But you don't understand," replied Jorik, "It responded to his touch. The elder trees have never responded to the torch of mortal man, not since the age of heroes. It is a sign and we must investigate!"

"If we stay and investigate, we die," said Ozark, "It's that simple"

"There is much we need to accomplish," replied Jorik, "Though this could be the answer we have been waiting for, you should understand more than anyone else, the elder trees and all knowledge of them was expunged from history when the masked one took over, for all we know this is the reason why!"

Arturius found his feet upon the floor. Although the ground was still in a dizzying state, he was able to find his balance. The first few steps were a stumble. It felt as though he was walking for the first time again as his knees and ankles cracked and creased.

"Ozark is right," said Arturius, his words darted the attention of everyone around him gleefully relieved of his awakening.

"You truly are a fucking troublesome creature to kill," scolded Eskiel, rushing over to him before punching him hard in the arm, "Did I not tell you it would be a mistake searching these woods."

"You did my friend," replied Arturius, "However without such a detour I would not have come across such important intelligence, and an insight into our enemy's plans."

Jorik came bounding over, a brutish stud barging his way across the glade; damn nearly knocking over Eskiel in the process. There was a fire burning deep within his eyes, a thirst for knowledge to which he desired so much to engorge upon.

"So you did it!" he shouted, "You merged with the heart of the realm, the Soulus that entwines all that is living, and that which is dead!"

"It would appear so," replied Arturius, "A strange sensation it was, for I felt as though I was rising high above the clouds, peering down upon the realm before falling into some darkened corner."

By now even Ozark had perked up, intrigued by the situation that was unfolding before them. He pulled out an old tome, worn and seemingly beyond repair, scribbling things here and there upon its wrinkled pages.

"What you have there?" asked Garton, glancing at the old tome.

"Notes my broken friend, notes," replied Ozark, "Within this book lies the chronicles of old, a series of passages written throughout the years, something I was able to swipe from the Arkanium before its bitter descent into the earth, I have been adding more to the passages as well as studying its contents."

"Have you come across anything of use to us?" asked Arturius.

Ozark shook his head, his eyes still affixed to the pages as he continued writing.

"This vision you had, tell me more," asked Ozark, "What was it like? Where were you going?"

"It felt as though I was dreaming, though still aware of the matter," said Arturius, "I could feel, hear and smell everything in my path."

A cold damp object ruffled through his fingers, a feeling he was blissfully unaware of until the chilly breeze fluttered through his clenched fist. A ragged piece of cloth poked out between his finger, stained with dirt and blood, a murky brown as dark as a foul swamp.

"Though I don't believe it was a vision," muttered Arturius. He brandished the piece of cloth to the others, its putrid odour waded through the air, striking the noses of the others.

"You pulled this from your, well I don't know what to call it," said Ozark, "Tell me what you saw!"

"There was much to see," said Arturius, "A first I stood below a great mountain range, watching as a wall of descending darkness engulfed it in its entirety, I fell through the darkness, cold and disorientated as a voice whispered throughout the vast emptiness"

"Hmmm," said Ozark, "There is not much there that gives me hope of deciphering such a riddle, is there anymore?"

"Yes," replied Arturius, "As I fell through the darkness a land emerged beneath me, a large kingdom built upon the side of an ever-encroaching cliff beside the sea, a black citadel lay at its peak with its vast shadow cloaking the rest of the city"

"The Black Keep," muttered Jorik, everyone else remained silent as he continued.

"I fell through the rock," said Arturius, "Diving deep into its dark embrace. That was when I saw him."

Ozark snapped his book shut; a puff of dust flew from its pages before disappearing into the air.

"Who did you see?" questioned Ozark, "The Masked One?"

"Nay," replied Arturius, "I saw Silas, he was bound and bloody, cast in thick iron chains, he was, however, being questioned by a man cloaked in darkness, though he divulged no whispers to him."

"Then it is as I fear," said Ozark, a defeated look washed over him as he paced away from the others, "If they have Silas locked deep within the black keep then I fear there is nothing we can do."

Arturius looked to the others, each averted their gaze from him in agreement with Ozark, though he was to have none of it.

"So that is it then," he shouted, "You are to give up on one of us, leave him to rot under the watchful eyes of he who took everything from you and cast you out into the dark wilderness, shame on you!"

Ozark turned back quickly; an obvious rage had built up within him at the remarks made. He bounded back over to Arturius, striking him upon his face with woeful effect. Instead, he reeled back, grasping his withered arm as his skin bloomed a red glow. An act that prompted great shock from the others that watched.

"You know nothing of what I feel," snapped Ozark, "Do you not think I would give my life to swap places with him, that I would not rush into the fray if it but gave us a glimmer of hope at such a rescue, no, you know nothing of the powers you seek to stand off against, instead you lecture on the powers you have no experience with, when I tell you there is no hope at such a feat it is because there isn't, it's impossible, only a monster of great strength and skill could break into the black keep and live to tell the tale and that is something this realm is lacking these days."

Arturius stepped forward, bathing his face in the gentle sunlight that bloomed between the leaves, etching a vibrant shadowed pattern across his face.

"I care not for the probabilities of such a success," shouted Arturius, "I only care about doing what is right and I will not abandon Silas to such a fate, I will march to that keep with or without you all you see, I gave my word upon it."

"I applaud your honour and will, I really do Arturius," said Ozark, "But I implore you to see what's before you, tis an impossible task you seek to achieve, to break into the black keep is nigh impossible. Not only are its walls higher than the trees that surround us so, they are positioned aside the sheer cliff face of '*the Rock*' its natural defence leave it impermeable to access, leaving only the outer gatehouse as a means of approach"

"And what of it?" replied Arturius, "So I will scale the walls, I will smash down the gate, what makes it so impervious to breach?"

"Because of him," growled Garton, "Because that monster prowls every inch of that cursed keep, the damn dog to the Masked One, the one who kills without mercy, without thought, the one cursed me to this fate."

"Vortuse?" Arturius whispered,

"The very one," said Ozark, "So long he walks upon the ramparts, within the walls and halls, that keep will forever remain impregnable, I have heard many a tale of thieves, assassins, vagrants and more attempt at infiltrating such a place, each and every one of them now lines the pathway that leads to the gate, forever a reminder of what will come to those who shall attempt such foolish deeds."

It fell back upon Arturius, the realisation of such a mission was becoming more and more impossible with each passing second. Dawn was breaking, and they had yet to exit the glade. The journey to the catacombs would be long, arduous, and dangerous; not even considering the possibility of it being a secure base.

"Then if I must become a decoration to adorn that path then so be," said Arturius, "For I will leave no one to rot in that dungeon, and nor would Silas allow the same for any of us, however, our first task must be to re-establish our base, how long is the journey to the catacombs?"

"Four, five days maybe," said Jorik, "And that's if our journey goes unimpeded."

"Then it would appear that time is of the essence then," said Arturius, "First we must secure the catacomb and set up our new headquarters promptly."

Ozark looked him deeply in the eye, waiting for him to continue on.

"And the second?" said Ozark.

"Then we need to find a monster," replied Arturius, smiling gleefully.

Before they could continue, a shadow burst forth into the glade, colliding with all manner of rock and stone as he fell before them.

"By the Gods Kezin, will you ever learn," snapped Ozark, "Why such a hurry?"

Kezin stumbled around, caught in his own cloak ensnared upon the floor. Arturius tore it from his back leaving a shredded cloak in its place stopping just above his hip.

"My apologies sir, I had to get to you as soon as possible," said Kezin struggling for his breath, "Though it was difficult to track your journey, it was by sheer fate I stumbled across your tracks beside the great mountain."

"Well, spit it out then!" replied Ozark fiercely,

Kezin looked around the room. Arturius could see in his eyes, the pain of realisation to the absentees among them.

"Well!" reiterated Ozark,

Kezin looked forward, staring him deep in the eyes.

"I was able to infiltrate the upper levels of Vastern, the elite levels of society," he replied, "And I came across something rather curious."

"Well?" beckoned Ozark, "What did you find?",

"I heard whispers," replied Kezin, "Whispers of a warrior worth a hundred score in warriors, a warrior as ferocious as a wolf!"

"You don't mean?" said Ozark a gasp,

Kezin nodded his head quickly.

"It must be him, Sir," replied Kezin, "I don't know how or when, but he survived the purge at Dawnstar, imprisoned within the confines of the Rekeshi empire, the wolf knight lives!"

"You can't be serious about this Ozark!" said Garton, "The Wolf Knight is not one to take orders let alone aid those other than himself, he is a callous and vile excuse for a warrior."

"That may be," replied Ozark, "But his skill and ferocity is the stuff of legends."

Arturius read the faces in the room. The revelation that had come to light sent a mixture of fear and hope shuddering across the orders faces. Ozark knelt by his side, firmly pinching his shoulder with the withered remnants of his hand.

"Maybe such a plan shall come to light, it would seem," shouted Ozark.

He looked over to Arturius, staring deeply into his eyes.

"Well, it looks like I have found you your monster!"

~ *"Seal the Khaos away that was my mission, for now my fate has been sealed; how much longer must I remain within this abyssal prison"* ~

# COMPENDIUM

Here be the language born from the Lands of Cinder, a tongue of old Vindictaria and its descendants.

| | *Eir* | | -I | | *Tá* | | -His |
|---|---|---|---|---|---|---|---|
| | | | | *un* | | | |
| | *Ëin* | | -My | | *Tél* | | -Her |
| *r* | | | | *n* | | | |
| | *Tau* | | -He | | *Ør* | | -We |
| | | | | *é* | | | |
| | *Tel* | | -She | | *Ha* | | -They |
| | *Hay* | | - | *yün* | | | |
| *in* | | Their | | | | | |

| | *Ïth* | | -to | | *Vu* | | -but |
|---|---|---|---|---|---|---|---|
| *ma* | | be | | *n* | | | |
| | *Ïth* | | -to | | *Sü* | | -so |
| *‘n* | | have | | *n* | | | |
| | *Ïth* | | -to | | *Dá* | | -By the |
| *na* | | go | | *r* | | | |
| | *Ïth* | | -to | | *Dr* | | -Who are |
| *vay* | | make | | *umari* | | of | |
| | *Ïth* | | -to | | *Ret* | | -Here |
| *het* | | the | | | | | |
| | *E'r* | | -a | | *Fu* | | -That |
| | | | | *rn* | | | |
| | *Thu* | | -and | | *Nu* | | -Not |
| *n* | | | | *r* | | | |
| | *Het* | | - | | *En* | | -Of |
| | *Aer* | the/these | | | *Cre* | | -When |
| | *Shu* | | - | *ath* | | | -From |
| *llen* | | With | | | *Kre* | | -Take |
| | *ti* | | - | *n* | | | |
| | | Shall | | | *Ral* | | |
| | | | -Its | | | | |

| | *Søl* | | -Sun | | *Thr* | | -Throne |
|---|---|---|---|---|---|---|---|
| | | | | *awn* | | | |
| | *Ran* | | - | | *Kr* | | -Khaos |
| *ül* | | Moon | | *aol* | | | |
| | *Eltr* | | - | | *Am* | | -Empty |
| *ari* | | Stars | | *pti* | | | |
| | *Terï* | | - | | *Kir* | | - Elder |

n Sky/Space
Gör -
Land
Eqü -
es Water
Grû -Sea
l Eqües
Var -
ne Earth
Lith -Air
é
Res -Fire
trüq
Im -
mobülé Mountains
Stel -
lit Castle
Gar -
ûmøn Fort
Cré -City
agü
Toe -
n Town
Thr -
aw Grass
Arc -
h Thraw Trees
Rho -
yne River
Mu -
rtán Sword
Thé -
l Shield
Ach -
en Bow
Nur -
in Armour
Ste -
d Horse
Me -
agûl Warrior
Ang -

in Târ Gods
Târ -Gods
Du -
lken Darkness
Shr -Shadow
oth'n
Dr -
ovah Command
Aci -
ous Merciful
Öu -Life/will
los
En -Lies/lay
cumbray
Sol -
den Treasure
Va -Hoard
sq
Afli -Plague
ctur
Vis -Seeketh
ur
Iqu -Greed
is
Nül -Gone
Ess -
oul Willpower
En -
vois Enlighten
Gr -Strength
unth
Oc -Open
ken
Es -Closed
ol
Ska -Son of a
veth whore
Sva -Pig
rk swill
Sa -Blood

*ûul* Army
*Ma* -
*eg'r* Lord
*Trû* -
*bulûs* King
*Nul* -
*Sut* North
*h* -
*Est* South
*We* -
*rn* East
*Thu* -
*l* West
*Divi* -
*nity* Stem
*Kra* -
*kuth* Divinai
*Cro* -
*cken* Break
*Sad* -
*isque* Shatter
*Ver* -
*nethi* Malice
*Van* -
*stra* Realm
*Esp* -
*arse* Might
*Ext* -
*en* Cross
*Lu* -
*mo* Arm
*Ply* -
*nth* Light
-
Place

*ng*
*Suu* -Soul
*l* -Silence
*Kla* -
*rn* Convergence
*Un* -
*onion* Imprisonment
*Ent* -Abyss
*ranum* -Cinder
*Far* -Root
*ash* -Giant
*Fur* -Forth
*ul* -Sleep
*Ed* -
*diau* Guardians
*Dor* -Silence
*mun* -Key
*Far* -
*u* Wake/Rise
*Lu* -Beside
*mba* -Whisper
*Gr*
*adulun*
*Eth*
*yalt*
*Seq*
*rest*
*Ris*
*un*
*Stu*
*nden*
*Ech*
*onse*

Akavar – The kingdom of Akavar was inhabited by the Akaviri, a race of Immorthals that have long since perished leaving the kingdom extinct and abandoned. The capital of the kingdom is Nordellar, an enormous subterranean city the likes of which has never been seen ever in the history of Xovia, a city so grand it takes days to traverse from one side to the other. While the kingdom stood its people were known as the eternal architects, for their immensely long lives and their uncontested skill of craft and science. There ancient city of Nordellar is located beneath the great mountain known as the twin to the towering peak where the ancient Drangviri dwelled, going deep beneath the earth, however since the twin dooms the city sunk deeper, rendering many parts destroyed or sealed off forever. It lies to the North-east of Xovia.

Arglefish – Vicious aquatic marine life that has a lust for blood and flesh. Though relatively safe by themselves, they are deadly within a pack, capable of stripping the meat from a full-grown man in a matter of seconds.

Asphorox – The legendary afterlife of the Rekeshi empire, believed to be were those who gave their life for the glory of the Masked One shall reap the rewards of such service. To be forever immortalised in history.

Drangmar – The kingdom of Drangmar was inhabited by the Drangviri, a race of Immorthals that have long since perished leaving the kingdom extinct and abandoned. The capital of the kingdom is Kabadeth, a city perch high atop the towering peak, a giant mountain known as the twin to the great mountain of the Akaviri, a city so grand it takes days to traverse from one side to the other. The people that lived in this mighty kingdom were known as the Dragon master, beast masters and beast riders, for their ability to tame and control the great beasts of the realm. They worshipped the great dragon Numériüm a four-winged dragon that rested atop the towering peak as a God, though a deity it was not. During the legend of the twin dooms, its great city crumbled and plunged into the shrieking sea below, washing away what was left of the race following the countless wars with the Akaviri, leaving only ruins of an empty city left as a warning to those who would seeks out war.

Farrosia – The kingdom of Farrosia was inhabited by the Farrosians, a race of man, the kingdom itself has long since perished sending the remainder of its people scattered across Xovia. The capital of the kingdom is Dawnstar, an ancient citadel at the heart of the realm of Xovia south of the Legions headquarters within the northern passage.

Fayories – Though many believe them to be fairies of the old children's stories, Fayories are far from it. They are dark creatures born from the disease of the forest, by day they take on the form of ethereal spirits floating gently through the woods peacefully. By night, their true form emerges, ghoulish sprites with rotting flesh and an insatiable hunger for those who stray too far from the forest path.

Rekesh – The kingdom of Rekesh is inhabited by the Rekeshi, a race of man. The capital of the kingdom is Vastern, however as of late its capital resides within the Grand castle of the Black Keep, an ancient citadel at the at the peak of the North-western peninsula.

Samopeth – The kingdom of Samopeth is inhabited by the Samopethi, a mysterious and secluded race known as the tree dweller, blessed with long life and finely in tune with nature. The capital of the kingdom is Eltraria, and its ancient lie within the heart of the Elder Archtree, one of three elder Archtrees that inhabit the land of Xovia. The trees of the Elder Archtrees run deep within the endless earth of the realm, connecting to all living trees that gives them insight into the goings on of the world.

Skuldra – The kingdom of Skuldra is inhabited by the Ska'al, a race of man. The capital of the kingdom is Wulkenheim, its people are a of a brutish nomadic lifestyle, favouring only war and strength as was the way of their forefathers. They believe of the strongest can command respect and will often go to war with other kingdoms and themselves in order to prove themselves the strongest of them all or become allies and servants of strength to whomever bests them, at least until they become stronger than their masters. Their homeland lies atop the shattered isles to the east of Xovia, to get there one must cross the serpent strait, a short but perilous journey across its harsh and deadly waters, where vast current will crash ships upon rocks, capsize in the middle of the strait and leave you to the many serpents that lie in wait at the bottom of the water.

Soulus – The supposed heart of the realm, the lifeblood of everything that is or was, connected by the essence of Xovia.

The Rock – The cliff that the Black keep rests upon.

The Legion - An ancient order that guards the northern passage, independent from the seven kingdoms.

Its only goal, the protection of the realm from any and all that may seek to destroy it, yet its real purpose was to reclaim the vast wealth of riches and knowledge held deep at the heart of the darkness.

Vastern – The Great Capital city of the Rekeshi Empire, surrounding the base of the great pillar that holds the Black Keep. The City consists of several layers each reserved for the different class of citizens that live behind its great halls. Filled with the powerful and scum alike, though what is different between the two is hotly debated.

Vindictaria – The kingdom of Vindictaria was inhabited by the Vindictarians, a race of man lost to the first Khaos outbreak. The capital of the kingdom was Elerium, an ancient Fortress far to the north, a kingdom that rested atop the entrance to the prison that contained the Khaos, its lands currently go by a different name, the Lands of Cinder or Darklands by the common populace and ever since the first outbreak over 4000 years ago has remained shrouded in mystery, for whomever ventures into the lands of dark shall never return, or not in the manner they departed at the very least.

Wulkren – Creatures of the southern desert of the red wastes. Subterranean burrowers that with dry scaley skin that emerge to the surface and drag their prey deep beneath the sands, never to return. What they lack in intelligence due to their primitive development they most certainly make up for in sheer numbers.

# WORD FROM THE AUTHOR

Greeting fellow reader! If you have made it this far then I must thank you exponentially for finishing my book. First and foremost I do hope that you have enjoyed the tale that I have written and hope that you are hungry for more. Secondly the next book in The Empty Throne Series, Blood and Cinder is currently underway and I hope to have it ready for you all to delve deep once more into the realm of Xovia. As you are aware I am an indie author, this means that I pay for everything to do with the creation, editing and designing of this book series. The more my books get out into the world the easier it gets for me to finance and promote my series. This is something I absolutely cannot do without your support.

I would like to thank GetCovers for their absolutely stunning book cover. I commissioned them to produce me an old age feeling mysterious art that draws attention at a glance. And boy did they deliver. Its dark tones and shadowy allure works perfectly with the tone of the book. I absolutely will be commissioning them for the next in my series. This bring me to the next topic of my note, how many books shall there be? I originally planned this to be a trilogy, however, I have imagined so much content and plot that it is looking more likely to series of five books. Let us share in this together and see just how dark this tale shall unravel *stares ominously into the Abyss*.

Thank you to the readers in my book club for providing me with such wonderful feedback and reviews. It can be a daunting task reading the first set of reviews and notes on your books. They are in most cases your life's work and a culmination of hours of planning writing, editing, scrapping and altering that leaves you feeling very protective and sensitive to critical comments. But none the less they are extremely important in developing oneself for the future.

So, what is next? This is something I have been asked a lot since writing this book. Well, the next book is going to be even more action packed, mysterious, dark and gritty than the first. We will see a vast array of new characters both evil and benign. Some absolutely kick-ass characters, strong character developments, new settings and new risks that the Fallen Order must take into securing the lost crowns of old and furthermore halting the menacing Masked One from ascending to the Empty Throne.

Reviews are a privilege for me, so if you decide to leave one for me then I promise that your favourite character will survive just a little longer *Laughs maniacally*. So I will end this section by saying once more thank you for reading my book and I hope to see you once again in the future with the next release in the series.

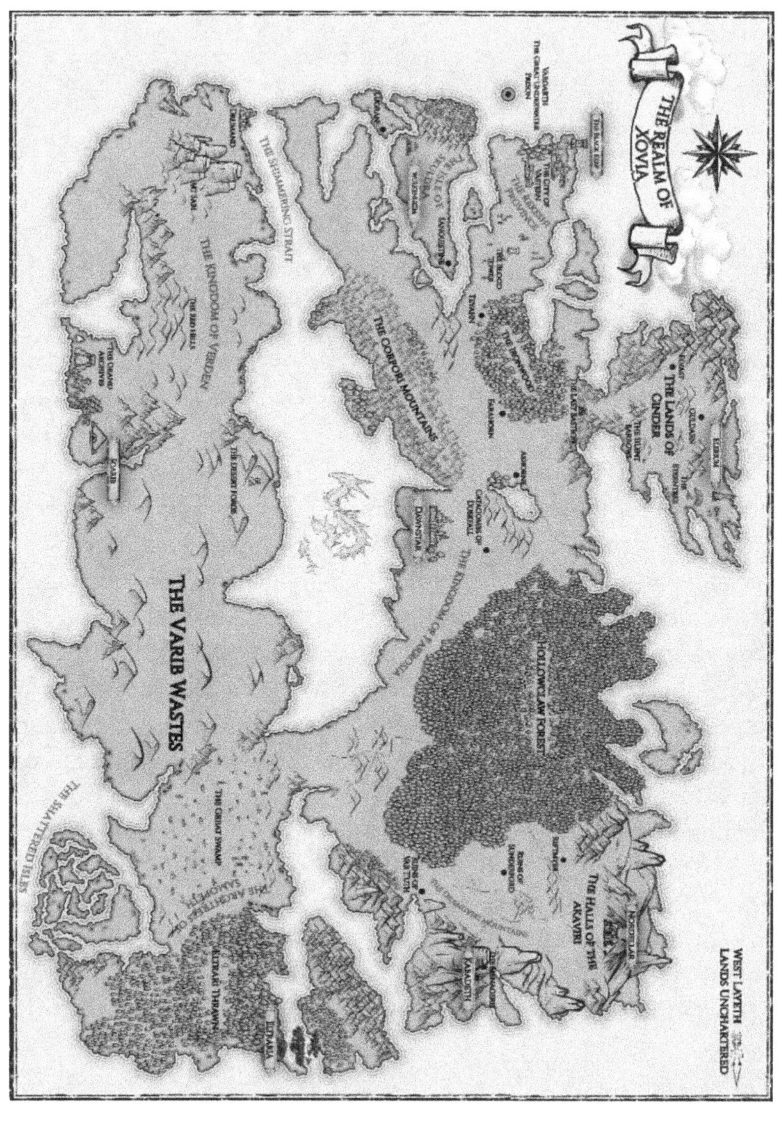
THE REALM OF XOVIA
THE LANDS OF CINDER
THE CORPORI MOUNTAINS
THE SHIMMERING STRAIT
THE KINGDOM OF VIRDEN
DAWNSTAR
HOLLOWCLAW FOREST
THE VARIB WASTES
THE GREAT SWAMP
THE SHATTERED ISLES
WEST LAYETH
LANDS UNCHARTERED

Meet our author
Michael R. Lowe

Michael R. Lowe is the enthusiastic author of the *Empty Throne* Series, beginning with *What Lies Beneath* a dark fantasy filled with twists, turns and mystery. Michael wrote the first incarnation of the series after a simple story grew and flourished within his mind leading to the creation of the realm of Xovia. Michael lives in the United Kingdom with his wife and two children developing and writing further novels within the series. An avid archer, history buff, gamer and engineer, he graduated from the University of South Wales in 2015 with a degree in aeronautical engineering and used his never-ending day dreaming of adventures and battles to grow a vast assortment of characters, locations and lore that will forever keep readers wanting to learn more.

From a very young age Michael was encapsulated by the world created by Lord of the Rings author J. R. R. Tolkien, finding an everlasting love for the world of fantasy and its thrilling tales. He has since come to idolise the works of Sarah J. Maas, George R. R. Martin, Neil Gaiman and Terry Pratchett.

"One of the greatest loves in this world is the ability to forever create new worlds filled with vast history and thrilling tales" Michael R. Lowe

www.ingramcontent.com/pod-product-compliance
Lightning Source LLC
Chambersburg PA
CBHW051127030726
47504CB00004B/745

* 9 7 8 1 6 3 5 5 4 3 1 9 3 *